SANCTUARY

KAREN EAST

SANCTUARY

*To my friends and teachers who live on the Lac Courte
Oreilles Reservation in northern Wisconsin.*

ACKNOWLEDGMENTS

I wish to thank the folks at Archway Publishing for their guidance and support. I am also grateful to my mother and grandparents for the values they gave me.

PROLOGUE
OCTOBER 30, 1998

When Rachel Anderson planned her move to northern Wisconsin, she knew she was cutting it close. The weather at the end of October was iffy. Snow and wind could come without warning, but she didn't anticipate the fog. It wasn't that wispy fog that blew away with a light breeze that happened often along the river. This time, the river was producing fog that billowed up from its banks and spread out, encompassing the entire state.

This wasn't a trip that she could put off. This was the trip that Rachel knew would change her life. There was urgency in this flight away from everything that had become familiar to her.

Rachel was fifty-seven years old. She had left northern Wisconsin when she was thirty-four, lured by a belief that there was world outside of the one she knew.

She had found her way out of a violent marriage. In trying to make sense out of what happened to her, Rachel began reading, researching the issues that fed into the permission given to men to beat their wives. She learned that this was an issue about values and the worth of women.

When Rachel was a child, her grandmother told her that if she didn't like what was happening in a given situation, she should try to change it rather than simply complain. In response to her grandmother's message and her experience, Rachel had become an activist.

She had many feminist beliefs prior to her marriage. Rachel hadn't heard about feminism until the feminist movement began attracting the attention of the media. She had grown up in a family where women were valued. Her beliefs about women and equality were similar to the messages espoused by women she saw on national news programs and talk shows, those who were tired of oppression.

Rachel began searching for a place where she might become part of something bigger. She found a community where there was a women's center. Without any job prospects or any education beyond high school, she took the money she got from the divorce settlement and moved herself and her children to the community from which she was now fleeing.

Rachel had become a spokesperson. She demonstrated against violence toward women. She pushed for changes in laws so that women would have some protection through domestic abuse restraining orders. She went to trials for women who had killed violent spouses.

In the meantime, she managed to get two degrees and became a social worker specializing in community development. She raised her children.

Somewhere along the line, the FBI developed a file on her. She was questioned as a suspect every time there was an incident, a bombing, or a threat and whenever Rachel made a statement to the media about the rights of women and the lack of law enforcement response to violence toward women.

Rachel and a group of newly found friends started a domestic violence shelter, seen as a place of suspicion by neighbors, who often called the police with complaints of the odd comings and goings at the shelter.

The latest interrogation had happened about three months prior, after a barge was sunk in the river. The barge belonged to a man who was tried and found innocent in the murder of his wife.

Rachel had nothing to do with the barge. She had often stated publicly that she didn't believe in violence. Yet every time something happened that involved domestic violence, Rachel was called in for questioning.

The last time she was questioned about the barge, Rachel decided it was time to move and start another chapter in her life. The interrogation made her realize that few had paid attention to what she said and did.

She didn't think she would ever forget it.

"What is your name?" asked the FBI agent, John Murphy, a man who had interrogated her many times.

"Rachel Anderson," she replied.

"Where were you on the night of July 31?" he asked.

"Do you mean last week or the year before?" she responded.

The man sighed. "Last week, Ms. Anderson. You know what I'm talking about," he said.

"No, I don't know what you're talking about," she replied. "I was on vacation last week. I went to northern Wisconsin to visit friends. I thought you would know where I was because I saw someone who looked like he was following me, and I figured it must be one of your colleagues."

"You must be imagining things," Agent Murphy responded. "Why would we waste manpower following you around?"

"Well, you seem to be wasting manpower right now, questioning me about something that happened when I wasn't here," Rachel said.

"On July 31, a barge belonging to a company owned by a man who was acquitted of murdering his wife was sunk just outside of town. It was carrying goods from New Orleans to St. Paul. Because it was interstate traffic, that makes it a federal crime," the agent said.

"I don't know why you think I would do something like that. I preach nonviolence. That means I don't destroy property. I think there was a demonstration outside the courthouse when that man was acquitted. Even though I wasn't here at the time, demonstrations are what I do, among other things. I don't sink barges. I hope no one was injured," she said.

"No, no one was injured. The barge was anchored just outside of town, and all the men on board managed to get off safely," said Agent Murphy.

"I'm glad innocent people weren't hurt. I don't think that sinking a barge belonging to a company that man owned will make him change his ways. He must have a lot of money, and I'm sure the ship was insured," said Rachel.

"One of these days, we are going to catch you, and you will go to prison. Just about every time there is a demonstration or a protest about domestic violence in any part of the country and you are there, something out of the ordinary seems to happen," said Agent Murphy.

"I have not broken any laws," said Rachel. "I am simply trying to help women be safe. Can I go now?"

Agent Murphy stood and opened the door, gesturing to Rachel that she could leave. As she left, Rachel realized that too much had happened, and John Murphy wasn't going to leave her alone.

Rachel spent the next week trying to figure out what to do. She expressed her concerns to her friend Martha.

"I'm scared. That agent threatened me. He said he was going to catch me and I would spend time in prison," said Rachel.

"Well, he can't catch you if you aren't doing anything wrong," said Martha.

"I think he can build a case against me," said Rachel. "He can take a given situation, accuse me of organizing and collaborating, list my history of activism, and make me sound like I'm involved in activities when they can't find the culprit."

"Rachel, you're sounding paranoid. Who are *they*? I think if you just lie low for a while, all this will blow over," said Martha.

"*They* are the FBI and the police. What do you mean by this will blow over? What is there to blow over? I wasn't even here, and I was called in as a suspect. I have never committed a violent act," said Rachel.

"What are you going to do? Your life is here. You are who you are. We need you," said Martha.

"I don't want to become a martyr for any cause. I don't want to go to prison. I have credentials I didn't have when I came here. I think it's time to move. I can find work up north as a social worker," said Rachel.

"What makes you think that the FBI is going to arrest you for demonstrations and words?" Martha asked.

"Don't you remember? I helped John Murphy's ex-wife find a divorce attorney when no one in the area wanted to represent her because her husband intimidated everyone. She got a divorce, and we found a way for her to leave the area, go into hiding, and find a new life. He hasn't forgotten, and he isn't going to. He said he would catch me, find a way to accuse me of something, and make the accusations stick," said Rachel.

"I forgot about that," said Martha. "I guess I just figured that after she was gone, he would quit bothering you, especially after he didn't find anything that could trace you or any of the rest of us to her."

"Well, I haven't forgotten. I think of it every time something happens that can be vaguely connected to me. I've been scared ever since John Murphy's wife came asking for my help. Now I realize that John Murphy isn't going to leave me alone, and I have to do something to protect myself," said Rachel.

Martha began to cry. "I'll miss you. I'll miss your humor, your energy, and your courage."

"You'll just have to come visit me in the woods," said Rachel.

The two women embraced. Having made the decision, Rachel made the rounds of friends and colleagues, saying goodbye and inviting all to visit her.

Next, Rachel spent time looking for work and finding a place to live. It happened quickly, and she found herself going back up north, her efforts hampered now by the thick fog.

Rachel had found work on an Indian reservation. She had grown up around Indian people, and her family had many Indian friends. The Indian people she knew were kind and gentle and seemed to have a sense of acceptance about life. She decided to take the job on the reservation when it was offered because she wanted to learn from people who seemed to have something to offer that she hadn't found in her life.

The fog was making it impossible to see anything. She hoped that the impenetrable white wall in front of her would dissipate the farther she drove from the river.

Even though she couldn't see, Rachel wasn't going to stop; the fog couldn't get any worse, and she wanted to believe that it would lift. As she peered through the windshield, looking for any little break, she had a sinking feeling that it wasn't going to improve. Her driving was hampered not only by the lack of visibility but also by the mesmerizing quality of the fog. It was difficult to concentrate, and the light from the headlights was reflected back to her.

She wasn't sure where the road was, and she didn't think she would be able to see any oncoming traffic if there was someone else desperate or foolish enough to be out in this mess.

Rachel glanced at the odometer often to see what progress she was making, afraid that any time spent not staring through the windshield would cause her to veer off the road. The car seemed to know its way, as she had made the trip frequently. Even though she left northern Wisconsin looking for something better, she often went back to visit.

She had changed during the time she was gone from home. She had defined her sense of self and her purpose. She tried to live by the message given by her grandmother about doing rather than complaining.

At the same time, she often found herself complaining without finding solutions. She sounded like her grandfather, who would pound his fist on the table and say, "By God, that's unconstitutional," about a wide variety of issues. "Don't ever trust politicians," he would say. "They say a lot when they're campaigning and then don't follow through on anything." She often criticized the values espoused by politicians and the media— values pulled out of the dusty trunk of history and used during election campaigns, then stored away after the voting took place.

The old values seemed to have turned corners and become invisible, leaving people to make up new rules that would fill in the gaps. She noticed that people fought over points of view, demanding conformity rather than diversity, and she agonized over the term "politically correct," believing that the concept suggested there was only one way to think. Rachel saw something sinister in all of this. She couldn't say what exactly what was sinister, but she thought the acceptance of diversity had to do with freedom. The last interrogation and the threat to take away her freedom convinced her that she needed to leave if she was going to find safety. She wondered if she could ever move far enough away to be safe. The fog seemed to be stopping her from leaving.

Droplets of water clustered on the windshield, and Rachel turned on the wipers while she wiped the inside of the windshield with her sleeve, trying to clear away the white blanket in front of her. *At least the fog is probably keeping them from following me. I must be the only fool out in weather like this*, she thought

Her fear as to what might happen to her competed with her concentration on driving, and Rachel gripped the steering wheel, believing that white knuckles would prevent an accident.

After four hours of traveling through the fog, the car turned into the driveway of her new home in the woods. She looked forward to the isolation brought by the trees that surrounded the house just outside of Hayward, a little town like many towns in northern Wisconsin. It was a clearing in the woods, surrounded by forests of mixed hardwoods and pines. The trees shut out the rest of the world.

Rachel found her way inside the house, relieved. She wasn't quite sure how she got there. As she fell into bed, she thought, *Tomorrow I'll start a new chapter. I don't know where it will take me, but I hope it's better than what I left.*

CHAPTER
August 20, 2039

Minneapolis, Minnesota

Janet Ryan changed busses three times to reach the neighborhood where her parents lived, each time swiping her ID through the monitor, depositing tokens, and using her family privilege card to pass out of one sector and into another. With each swipe of her ID, a camera took a picture of her that and filed it in the Homeland Security computer that kept track of who traveled out of their neighborhoods and why.

Janet got off the bus a couple of blocks from the park where she was to meet her parents. As she walked, she noticed that the air quality was better than usual. She had checked with the Weather Channel and found that they recommended a number 3 EZ Breathe scarf to filter out the ever-present chemicals that permeated the air. Janet was surrounded by the daily messages on the news channels, the Weather Channel, and billboards proclaiming that the chemicals that were sent out into the atmosphere by the factories in the greatest country on the planet were a necessary part of doing business.

Janet walked slowly, not wanting to breathe too deeply. Doing so might allow too many of the chemicals in the air to tax the scarf's filtration system, in which case she could inhale a dangerous level of the noxious air and get sick.

As she approached the edge of the neighborhood park, Janet spotted her parents sitting on a bench. She waved in recognition, and they waved back.

"Hi, Jannie," said her father, Jim, as he hugged her. After their embrace, Janet turned and hugged her mother, Emily, who started to cry.

"Mom, what's wrong?" asked Janet.

Janet's mother didn't answer, and her crying became more intense. Janet positioned herself between her parents as her father said, "Let's walk. We need to talk."

The Ryan family walked slowly into the park and down a path that took them away from the areas where people usually gathered.

"I don't think the listening devices extend this far into the park. We've asked you to come here for your monthly visit instead of coming to the house because we want to make sure nobody overhears us," said Jim.

"Why do you think anyone would hear us?" asked Janet.

"Oh, this isn't newsworthy to anyone except us and Homeland Security. I turned fifty-five two weeks ago. I got notice that I have to sell the business and move to an elderly home. Your mother can come with me, or she can move to a small apartment near the home," said Jim.

"Oh my God. I thought you were exempted from the elderly expectations. What happened?" asked Janet.

"As you know, we were promised that we would be exempted when we participated in the Rebirth of the Cities Plan. I designed the new neighborhoods that put people in specific sectors as a way to prevent terrorism.

"Just in case the promises made to us weren't kept, we managed to work out a deal with Josh Connor, my partner, to put the architecture company in his name and to pay us in cash over time. We didn't dare put the money in the bank. We hid it in the house and started looking for the group that was rumored to get people out of the country. We couldn't seek asylum until we reached the ages where Homeland Security could move us. We're now considered political refugees.

"I never knew that all those houses and apartments in all those neighborhoods would be used to restrict people the way they have. Families with a member who has been accused of committing a crime can't move out of the neighborhood. They can't send their children to college. People in working-class neighborhoods can't ever get out. Their children can't go to college and are only eligible for blue-collar jobs. It's almost like slavery. I wonder sometimes if I would have cooperated had I known the outcome. Then I think about the fact that I really didn't have a choice, even though certain privileges were dangled in front of my nose," said Jim.

"Where will you go?" asked Janet.

"We can't tell you that. You'll be under suspicion the minute they figure out that we're gone. Right now, we have people driving by the house all hours of the day and night checking on us."

"If you're being watched so closely, how can you get away?" asked Janet.

"Jannie, in spite of the fact that we have few freedoms anymore and we are all under surveillance most of the time, there are some clever people who figured out how to work around all of this," said Jim.

"So how will I know that you're safe?" asked Janet.

"Well, we haven't figured out how we'll be able to contact you. The person who is helping us has told us just to focus on getting out. He says that the rest of it will get taken care of as we go," said Emily, wiping away her tears.

Janet turned to Emily. "What am I going to do without you—without both of you? When I was a kid, you used to tell me stories and give me the history of this country. I thought that when I became a newspaper reporter, I would be able to write about the truth. All I get to do is rewrite stories that have been altered and even made up to keep the illusions going.

"Our voting process has been contaminated by money, and Congress is owned by big business. The president is a figurehead, and everything is controlled by Homeland Security. We have toxic air because all of the restrictions regarding harmful emissions have been lifted so that major corporations and their executives can make more money. It's like those books you told me about—*Fahrenheit 451* and *1984*. I want to come with you," said Janet.

"You can't," said Jim. "You aren't considered a political refugee because you're too young."

"Why do you have to go to an elderly home?" asked Janet.

"We've talked about that," said Emily. "We have to go because youth is more important than age. We think the government conducts experiments on elderly and nursing home residents to find out how to slow the aging process. Certainly those experiments on the elderly may benefit youth, but they aren't going to benefit the subjects of the experiments."

"Is all of this really controlled by Homeland Security?" asked Janet, turning to her father.

"You know it is. Everything is controlled, and we're all under some kind of surveillance through credit cards and cell phones. We can't travel anymore. Do you remember the vacations we used to take? That was a way of life for many people," said Jim.

"We're told that we can't travel because there isn't enough fuel and oil for family cars," said Janet.

"I know what we're told. Hybrid cars are so expensive that most people can't afford to buy them. Fossil fuels are primarily for use only by the military, Homeland Security, and public transportation. The amount of gas sold to gas stations is rationed, as is the amount the stations sell to individuals. Security keeps track of people using old cars by making sure that gas stations take only credit cards. If someone buys too much gas, they're put on a security level and monitored by Homeland Security. The number of vehicles manufactured for private use is limited to people in government and CEOs of big corporations. The old cars that were dependent on fossil fuels are still around. I hear there's a black market devoted to buying and selling old cars.

"Because we can barely travel outside our sectors and certain public places, we have these virtual reality museums sponsored by the Smithsonian to keep us happy. The museums tell us a variety of things, all of which are probably false. Visits to the virtual reality museums and places like the Mall of America are supposed to satisfy any desire to travel, said Jim.

"Homeland Security says they need to keep track of us because there are so many terrorists. Foreigners keep sneaking into the country, and there are American citizens who want to overthrow the government. At least that's what I hear at work," said Janet.

"I have trouble believing that I'm hearing you say this," said Jim. "I thought I taught you better than this."

"When I lived at home, I got all of these history lessons from you and Mom every day. I don't get them so often anymore. When we talk on the phone, our conversations are monitored, so we can't talk about anything that might get us into trouble. When I come to the house on my monthly visits, we have to be careful because someone might be listening.

"I want to ask you something. When all those terrorist attacks happened all over the world in 2020, do you think they ever caught any of the terrorists?" asked Janet.

"I wonder if those attacks ever happened. We can't travel to Mount Rushmore to see if it's still there or if it was blown up like we were told. We can't go to France to see if the Eiffel Tower is still there. We can't go to Brazil to see if the statue of Christ overlooking Rio de Janeiro is still there," said Jim, listing the sites that were said to have been bombed out of existence by unnamed terrorists.

"Homeland Security controls the information. When they control the information, they control what we think and do. The air quality interferes with the amount of oxygen we take in, making it hard to think clearly and make good decisions. We are at the mercy of Homeland Security and the major corporations that control the government.

"The alleged events were said to be responsible for changing our way of life. We aren't supposed to question anything the government does because it's considered unpatriotic to do so," said Jim.

Janet sighed. "I remember our trips together. We went to stay at some resorts in Wisconsin. I saw a couple of black bears and some deer. We went to Disneyland. I think almost everybody my age went to Disneyland. We saw the Grand Canyon."

Jim interrupted Janet's memories. "We were lucky. We had the money to go to all those places. There were lots of poor people who couldn't afford to go. There still are lots of poor people, and they can't afford the admission price for the virtual reality museums."

"I wonder what it's like in the country," mused Janet.

"I've heard that folks who live in the country don't have the same kind of restrictions and surveillance that we have. Homeland Security has enough to do in all the urban areas. There are no jobs out there because there are no factories, so most people live off the land," said Jim.

"How can they live off the land?" asked Janet.

"I've heard that the air out there is cleaner. It stands to reason. There are no factories, so there's no chemical smoke belching out of chimneys.

"There's also a belief that people who live in the country are dumb and are satisfied with what they have. They have no desire to make a lot of money. They don't pose a threat. They have no interest in trying to overthrow the government," said Jim.

"If that's so, then why all the surveillance and control over our lives?" asked Janet.

"Power and control keeps those in charge in charge. And those in charge don't want to give up what they have," said Emily. "So you two can talk about this all you want. There aren't any solutions. The only answer is to figure out a way to leave and do it without getting caught. Those who get caught disappear, and we rarely find out what happened to them. It's time for us to head back. We don't want to get caught before we've left.

"We think it would be a good idea for you to come for your visit next month. If you skip it, then Homeland Security might think you know something about where we've gone, and they'll pick you up to question you. So, if your visitation bus card hasn't been canceled, come to the house as usual.

"We've given you all we know how to give you, Janet. If we could take you with us, we would. We can't, so we pray that you will be okay and will find your own way in this mess," said Emily.

"When are you leaving? Can we talk on the phone before you go?" asked Janet.

"No, Jannie. We don't know who might be listening. We think Homeland Security will come to question you. The less you know about our escape, the better," said Jim.

"Will I ever see you again?" asked Janet as she cried and hugged her parents, who had no answer for her question.

The family members composed themselves and walked back to the park bench where they had met. They hugged for a long time. Janet's parents went back to their house and waited to be rescued, while Janet rode the bus back to her apartment.

Jim Ryan was the architect, and Emily was the interior designer chosen by Homeland Security to develop the plans for the neighborhoods in the Minneapolis area, which ran south to Rochester, west to St. Cloud, north to Taylor's Falls, and east to the Wisconsin border. The neighborhoods were designed in the early 2020s. The project was countrywide and took about ten years to complete. It was designed to contain people and prevent them from moving around. Factory workers lived near the factories, professional people lived near their places of employment, aging families lived in specific areas, and families having a member who committed crimes lived in certain neighborhoods. The neighborhoods also had populations of certain ages. These gated areas kept people where they were supposed to be. The Ryans had been promised certain privileges for their forced cooperation in this project. Not all of those were kept.

The disappearance of Emily and Jim Ryan was discovered a week after their meeting with Janet. Because there was no information as to when they might have left, searches were conducted, and agents in regional field offices were contacted to expand the searches. The most intense searches were to the north along the Canadian border.

The Ryans were taken to the Blackfeet Reservation in Montana, where indigenous people from Montana and Canada aided their passage to Canada, where they would be treated as political refugees. A refugee center staffed by other refugees from the US helped them with housing and employment.

After a month passed, Janet rode the bus to her parents' house. She knocked several times and then used her key to gain entrance. The house didn't look any different than usual. Her parents had traveled light. The reality that they were gone hit Janet, and she sat on the couch, crying. She didn't see the camera recording her visit. When she left, she anticipated a visit by Homeland Security agents. No one came. She didn't know what that meant. She went to work, came home, shopped, and went to the virtual reality museums. She didn't try to make any long-term plans. She didn't try to make any new friendships. She just existed.

Homeland Security placed her on level-one surveillance, a designation that meant an agent would be assigned, and security cameras equipped with microphones would be placed in her apartment. Her innocent-appearing behavior meant she must be planning something.

CHAPTER 2
November 12, 2039

Janet added physical activity to her routine. She spent weekends walking in the parks that surrounded the neighborhood where she lived, even though there were times when the air quality presented challenges and there were televised warnings to stay inside. At one time, the parks included the clean water of the lakes and rivers and the trees and other plants that were part of the Minneapolis landscape. Ducks and geese had lived in the waters during the warm months, flying south when they anticipated the coming of winter. For several years, the waterfowl could no longer breathe the noxious air, and the lakes and rivers held a thick, gooey, silvery substance that killed anything that ventured into it. The dead trees had been replaced with plastic substitutes. During the changes of the season, buttons were pushed in park offices, and the appropriate color of leaves came out of slots in the branches and trunks. There was still playground equipment in the parks, but it wasn't used often.

Janet's neighborhood was made up of young professionals, and some of the parks that bordered her sector also bordered the neighborhoods of young professionals who worked at the University of Minnesota. People living in these neighborhoods worked nearby and took public transportation to work.

On an unusually warm Saturday in November, Janet rode a bus to one of the parks even though the air quality was poor. A stiff wind, coupled with the thick, soupy air, made any movement difficult. Janet was equipped with her EZ Breathe mask, a plastic device with nylon mesh that filtered contaminants.

When she got off the bus, Janet hunched her shoulders, bowed her head, and pushed through the resistant sludge that passed for air.

It had snowed earlier that week, but the fifty-degree temperature melted the snow and left a black residue that was melting, the runoff draining into the thick silver-colored mixture in the stream beds.

Janet wandered away from the areas where people congregated, preferring to be alone. Head down, she noticed little about her surroundings. She caught movement out of the corner of her eye and looked up, spotting a familiar figure she hadn't seen in years.

The gray-green air and the use of facial scarves and masks to filter out the particles made it difficult for anyone to recognize familiar faces, so most people looked for those they knew through body recognition.

It was easy for Janet to recognize her childhood friend Sally Marshall. They were opposites in body shape, size, and personality. Janet was tall and slender and wore her black hair long and straight. She considered privacy important and didn't reveal much about her emotions.

Sally was short and blonde and had a figure that stopped just short of ample. She was outgoing and made friends easily. Her facial expressions gave her emotions away.

The two women recognized each other at the same time and came together, their arms outstretched. They hugged and laughed and then adjusted their facial masks, which had slipped out of place while they hugged.

Janet noticed the man standing behind Sally. "Who's that, Sally?" she asked.

"Oh, that's Jeff Morgan, my boyfriend," said Sally, turning to acknowledge him.

"How long has it been since we've seen each other?" asked Janet, eyeing Jeff with suspicion.

"A long time. My folks said you were working for the *Herald*," said Sally.

"Yes, I am. I got the job right after I graduated," said Janet.

"Well, you know I went to school in Michigan. I just got a job back here at the U. I work in student affairs," said Sally.

"I'm so glad to see you. We can get together and make up for lost time," said Janet, dropping her voice to a whisper. "Who is he?"

"Like I said, that's my boyfriend," said Sally. "Jeff, meet Janet, my oldest friend."

Jeff nodded at Janet, hesitant to get involved. He didn't always trust Sally's openness. There were times when she identified people she had met a couple of days earlier as friends.

Janet and Sally walked together, arm in arm, while Jeff hung back, allowing the two young women their reunion.

"I've been at the U for about a year. It was easy to make the decision to come back here. I grew up here. My parents were here. Oh, Janet. My parents are gone. I don't know where they are. I went on my monthly visit. and the apartment was unlocked, and all their stuff was still there, and they were just—gone. I looked for a note or something. I haven't been able to sleep since then. I don't know where they are. I don't know if they got picked up by Homeland Security. I don't know if they're dead," said Sally, starting to cry.

"Wait a minute. How long ago did your parents leave?" asked Janet.

"They left about three months ago," said Sally.

"I think they probably went with my parents. I don't know where my parents went, but they left about the same time. At our last visit, they told me they were leaving. They wouldn't tell me where they were going. I think your parents probably didn't tell you because you have trouble keeping secrets," said Janet.

"I guess I just have to hope that they're all together." Sally sniffed, her tears streaming down the inside of her EZ Breathe mask. "I'm glad we met today. We've joined this group," said Sally, looking at Jeff.

Jeff looked at Sally and shook his head.

"What's wrong?" Sally asked.

"You don't know if we can trust you," said Jeff, nodding in Janet's direction.

"I've known Janet since we were five years old. We were always together until we graduated from high school. I know her better than I know you," said Sally.

"So what's this group? I thought groups were frowned upon by Homeland Security," said Janet.

"Well, we don't know yet. We've organized. We don't have meetings all together. Security is really tight at the U. We have little groups within the big group—work groups. Each work group has specific tasks to perform. Right now, we're trying to find out the real history of our country."

"So you're willing to take risks to find out about history?" asked Janet.

"Well, we want to make change. We want the government to take responsibility and clean up the air and the water. We want to get some of our freedoms back. You know, the freedoms we had when we were little and the freedoms our parents talked about. We don't think constant surveillance is a solution to fear of terrorist attacks. We don't even know if there are terrorist attacks anymore. We don't know who writes the news and if it's real or made up," said Sally.

"So how do you think you're going to do that?" asked Janet.

"We don't know yet. We think if we start with history, we'll get some idea as to what we can do to get the government to respond to us," said Sally.

"Oh, they'll respond all right. They'll put surveillance on you and round you up, and no one will ever see you or the members of your group again," said Janet.

"We don't know if we'll be able to do all of this. We can be the first generation to start this movement," said Sally. Maybe we can do enough to set an example for those who follow. Why do you look so skeptical?"

"Because I am skeptical. I think that what you're doing is dangerous," said Janet.

"Somebody has to do something. We can't just sit around waiting for someone else to make the moves," said Sally.

"Speaking of trusting anyone, how can you trust Jeff and the people who are in your group? What if there's a spy in the group?" asked Janet.

"If there was a spy in the group, we'd know it by now," said Jeff. "Group affiliation is illegal and we'd have been arrested."

"You have a point, Janet. At the same time, I can't live like this anymore. I'm tired of wearing scarves on my face. I'm tired of looking over my should to see if someone is following me. I'm tired of being so restricted I don't know how to live anymore, and I miss my parents," said Sally.

"I think you already have her answer. She doesn't want to have anything to do with this," said Jeff, looking pointedly at Janet. "For all you know, Sally, she's going to report us."

"How dare you, Jeff. I'm not going to argue about my best friend. She is and always will be. She's always been skeptical. That doesn't mean she won't get involved," said Sally.

"It's okay, Sally. I don't know if I want to get involved in your group. It sounds dangerous. What is it you want me to do?" said Janet.

"Well, we know that there's no written history we can trust. It's all been altered by Homeland Security. Before that, much of the history written about the United States was written in a way that portrayed European immigrants and settlers in a positive light and didn't report on the slaughter of indigenous people. Same with the government. So we're questioning if written US history was ever an accurate portrayal of anything," said Sally.

"So how do you think you're going to find a different portrayal and how do you know you can find any portrayal that's accurate?" asked Janet.

"That's where you come in, Janet. We found out that there's an old woman living on an Indian reservation in Wisconsin who dropped out just before 9/11. She's a feminist and an activist. We need someone with good interviewing skills to go there and talk to her and bring back information," said Sally.

"How would I get there? How would I get past all the security gates in the city?" asked Janet.

"The group would find you a car and would develop a plan for you to travel, so you would be going at times when security isn't as tight. You would get directions to the woman's home. I know it's a risk. Just standing here, the three of us talking, can raise suspicion and put us all on level-one surveillance," said Sally.

"I'm not sure if it's worth the risk," said Janet.

"We can set you up with a contact and a meeting place. We can meet here next week, and I can give you more information then," said Sally.

"And I can decide if I want to do this," said Janet.

"You can back out at any time," said Sally.

As they parted company, Janet and Sally were watched by their respective level-one surveillance agents. Jeff, seen in the company of two women on level one, was also placed on surveillance. An agent would be assigned to him when the agents met for their weekly briefings.

Janet and Sally returned to the park the following week. The weather was colder and the air clearer. Both women wore winter coats and number 3 EZ Breathe scarves.

"Where's Jeff?" asked Janet.

"I left him home. I wanted to be able to visit with you without having him question whether or not you are trustworthy. What do you think about joining us and taking on the task I described for you?" asked Sally.

"Well, I guess I'm willing to think about this. I haven't made up my mind for sure. I think I need some more information," said Janet.

"We have a contact set up for you. He says he thinks it would be best to wait until after Christmas to meet. He's going to check with his family to see how they want to manage all of this, because the old woman I talked about lives with his family on a reservation in Wisconsin."

CHAPTER 3
February 18, 2040

Janet walked into the café in Dinky Town, near the University of Minnesota, Minneapolis campus, looking furtively around for the man she was supposed to meet. She wore a dove-gray wool coat that came to her knees and spike-heeled dove-gray leather boots that stopped just below her knees. Her press card, identifying her as a reporter with the *Minneapolis Herald*, was pinned to her coat, visible to anyone who looked. The card gave her a right to travel to all of the gated areas of the city for work. She stripped off her gloves and her EZ Breathe scarf, then removed her coat and hung it over her arm. She was surprised there was no security equipment in the café's entrance, as she was used to passing through metal detectors.

Janet looked around the café. The large room had a row of stools along a counter that was covered in worn red Formica. The seats on the stools were covered in thick red plastic, the rips and tears mended with plaid duct tape. The tables in the middle of the room had worn red Formica tops, edged in stainless steel, and the chairs were covered in the same worn red plastic as the stools and the same patterned duct tape. The booths along the outer walls had the same Formica tops and battered red plastic seats. The floor was covered in old black-and-white tiles, the colors worn to dark gray and dirty white.

There were a few people in the café, some sitting at the counter drinking the variety of beverages offered on the menu. A man dressed in a tweed sports coat and jeans sat in a booth reading a newspaper. Janet saw him look up from his newspaper when she entered. He glanced her way and went back to reading his paper.

Janet wondered who he was. *Has he been sent here to find out what I'm doing? If he catches me, what will happen?* She started to panic, almost forgetting her reason for being there, when she spotted a young man who fit the description of the man she was to meet. Antoine LaRiviere was over six feet tall and dark skinned, and his long, black, curly hair was pulled together and held in a single braid that fell down his back. His shoulders and muscular upper arms filled out the plaid flannel shirt he wore. His worn navy-blue wool jacket was spread across the seat next to him

He watched Janet's approach. He liked her looks, but she appeared to be stiff, tense, and unsure of herself. *I'm going to have some fun with her,* he thought.

"Antoine LaRiviere?" she asked.

He nodded.

Janet waited for him to say something. After a few seconds of silence, she said, "I'm Janet Ryan."

"Who?" he asked.

"I-I'm Janet Ryan. I was told to meet you here. Don't you know who I am?"

Antoine grinned. "Yes, I know who you are. You look so serious. So you're the reporter who's going to my reservation to interview the woman we know as Old Woman. I guess you were chosen because you're supposed to have interviewing skills, and because of your job, you'll probably be able to travel outside the city without getting caught."

Antoine nodded, looking at her knees. "Don't your knees get cold? Everything else about you is covered to guard against the cold, and then you have bare knees. How can you walk in those boots? What happens if you hit a hole in the sidewalk?"

"I'm dressed like I dress for work. I'm supposed to look like I'm working. That's how I can pass through the gates."

"You dress like that for work. Why?" asked Antoine.

"Because that's how professional women dress," said Janet.

"Why?" asked Antoine.

"I don't know why. We just do. If we dressed differently, we would probably be under suspicion," said Janet.

"So, if you dress comfortably, you would be under suspicion," said Antoine. "You would be suspected of what?"

Janet decided that she couldn't follow this. "I don't know. You act so calm about all of this. Aren't you afraid we're going to get caught?"

"I think we've got a pretty good chance of getting caught because you act like you're doing something wrong. Why don't you at least try to pretend as if this is a normal part of your routine?" asked Antoine.

"I don't understand why this place was chosen for us to meet. I think most restaurants have listening devices. You're sitting here talking openly about what we're doing as if there's no threat of any kind," said Janet.

"I come here a lot and meet with others who helped plan this visit. Nothing has happened so far, and the noise from the street would make it hard for listening devices to pick up conversations," he said.

"Who is *we*?" Janet asked.

"So you don't know anything about the group? Do you even know why you're doing this?" asked Antoine.

"I'm not sure as to what I'm supposed to be doing. I met my friend Sally in the park. I hadn't seen her for several years because we were split up when we went away to college. That's what happens now. Friendships and alliances are discouraged. So are long meetings with acquaintances. We spent our time talking about the group Sally and her boyfriend, Jeff, had joined. They said they joined the group because they were looking for truth. They said they didn't know exactly what that would lead to.

"I've been dissatisfied with my life for a while. I thought I would find out more about the group and see if it's something that can take me out of the rut I've been in. So I agreed to get involved. I'm not sure what I'm going to do because I think this is risky.

"After the time I spent with Sally and Jeff, someone I didn't know contacted me on the bus when I was going to work. He sat down behind me and started whispering. I thought he was an in-person obscene phone call at first. Then I heard him talking about the group and what my assignment would be.

"He told me that the group was made up of people here at the U who were uncomfortable with the way things are. He said that we had been robbed of our history and that there was at least one person who could teach us who we used to be before the terrorist attacks of 2020. He told me that my role in the group would be to go to this Indian reservation and interview this elderly woman who escaped the purges that came with the

Post-Millennium Adjustments and the War on Terrorism and bring back the information to the group.

"Apparently the group doesn't really know what it's going to do with the information, but the group believes they need to do something to change the way things are," said Janet, looking around the restaurant. "Who is that man over there, pretending to read the newspaper?"

Antoine lifted his eyes to look at the person to whom Janet was referring. "Oh, he's a professor at the U. He comes in here a lot," he said.

"He could be a Homeland Security agent or an informant," Janet said. "What are you doing here?" she asked Antoine. The anxiety welled up, and her thoughts began to race. She was about to enter the realm of incoherence.

"What am I supposed to call you?" she asked.

"Most people call me Antoine," he said, finding her confusion amusing.

"That's not what I mean. My dad told me the word Indian was not accurate because Columbus made a mistake and thought he was in India. Nobody corrected the mistake. Then I heard the term *indigenous people*, and then I heard Native American," said Janet.

"Well, according to the feds, we are American Indians. They couldn't use the term Native Americans because the Alaskan indigenous people and the Hawaiian indigenous people are native Americans also.

"So we call ourselves by our name that we have used for many thousands of years. We are Anishinaabe. I am from Lac Courte Oreilles Reservation in Wisconsin," he said. "Our culture is different from yours, and we have different values and a different way of life.

"When I was twelve years old, my uncle Joe prepared me to have a vision. I went into the woods and fasted for four days. I was surrounded by trees, plants, water, birds, and animals, who are our relatives. I had a vision that told me I was to go to school in the white man's school in town, graduate, and come here to go to the university. In my vision, I was surrounded by white people, and I saw the big buildings of this city. I got the message that I was to get involved and be a part of this group. I'm supposed to watch out for the people in the group. I am following my vision," said Antoine.

"So you just blindly follow this dream you had?" asked Janet.

"That's right. When we have visions, we are to follow them. The vision leads me on a path where I will learn and profit.

"I don't like it here. Your values are different than ours. The air is so poisonous from the factory smoke that we all have to wear masks. Some days it's so dark that all I can see are shadows. I don't like waking up in the morning and having to check the air quality on TV to find out what kind of mask I have to wear today, and I don't like the tasteless processed food. I don't like having to watch my back because Homeland Security is constantly watching to find out who the terrorists are. I think they suspect everyone, even themselves. When I finish this, I'll go back home," said Antoine.

"How will you know when it's finished?" asked Janet.

"I will know," said Antoine enigmatically.

Janet didn't know if he was playing with her, so she decided to follow up on something he had said. "How are your values different from ours?" she asked.

"We believe in sharing. We protect the environment. We watch out for each other. We live off the land, and when we kill an animal for food, we use all of the animal. We make clothes, tools, and most other things that we need from the animal, and we have ceremonies for the animals that give their lives so that we may live. We believe in showing honor, dignity, and respect to Mother Earth, the sun, the moon, and everything the Creator has given us. We keep the water clean. Living a good life means more than making money and gaining power. Everything we need is provided for us by the Creator, and it is important to show Him honor, dignity, and respect by living our lives in harmony with nature," said Antoine.

Janet thought Antoine was a little weird. "Our culture believes the same things as yours does," she answered.

"You have a strange way of showing that," said Antoine. He decided he had said enough for now.

Silence settled over the booth. Janet didn't know what to say. She was not used to being challenged, and Antoine's brief description of his lifestyle was foreign to her. She knew he lived in the country. She hadn't thought much about the people who lived outside the city or what life might be like out there.

Janet prided herself on seeing things differently than her peers because of the things her parents had taught her. She thought she knew a lot about the history of the greatest country in the world, as the US was referred to in news stories. Janet thought she saw the world through eyes that were different from those of most people, and now she was in a situation where everything about her was being challenged.

I am thirty years old, she thought. My parents gave me oral history lessons because they said that history had been changed to suit the points of view of the people in control. I know that the chemicals in the air aren't good for us, and I know that we aren't told the truth about the wars that always seem to be happening somewhere in the world. I have to adapt to all of this. I am here. I can't escape, and I have to figure out what to do. I don't like this guy. He seems to think he knows all there is to know about life. I don't even know if I want to complete this assignment.

"I thought if I joined this group, I would get to see my friend Sally. So far, I have seen her twice in the park. We had to cut our visit short because we thought the Plasti-Dogs we saw running around might be carrying listening devices," she said.

"What are those things anyway? Have you ever seen a live animal?" asked Antoine.

"I had a dog when I was about ten years old. She was a cocker spaniel, and her name was Lucy. My parents had gone to the grocery store, and they left me home with the dog. I took her outside to play and forgot to put the breathing mask on her. We were running around the yard. She started gasping for breath, fell over, and died. We buried her in the backyard. Soon after that, Plasti-Dogs came on the market, and pets, like cats and dogs, were no longer available. They had trouble surviving in the bad air. There were a lot of stories on TV and the internet that said that pets carried diseases that humans could get. My dad said that's how they got us to accept the Plasti-Pets. My parents asked me if I wanted a Plasti-Pet, and I said no. I didn't think a piece of plastic could take the place of Lucy." Janet paused, tears in her eyes, her voice shaky.

Antoine took advantage of the pause to wave at the waitress, a young woman clad in a sweatshirt and jeans. She came over carrying menus.

Antoine asked Janet, "Do you like omelets?" She nodded. Antoine ordered for her and asked for two cups of hot water.

When the waitress left, Janet asked, "What's the hot water for?"

"I bring my own tea. I have peppermint leaves, and I mix them in the water. Unless you don't like peppermint, I think you'll like the taste," he said.

Their food came shortly after. The omelets didn't look like they were made from the powdered eggs found in the grocery stores.

Janet cautiously tasted her omelet. The flavor burst in her mouth like fireworks at Fourth of July celebrations. "What's in this?" she asked.

"I bring my food from home. There is venison—deer meat—wild rice and green peppers and fresh eggs. The café keeps it and cooks it for me. I usually run out before my next trip home.

Just then Hal Emerson walked into the café. As supervisor of the Homeland Security agents, he assigned the people who followed suspected terrorists. Once in a while, he assigned himself a subject to stay sharp. He had been following Janet since her parents' absence was discovered. She hadn't done anything out of the ordinary until today.

Hal paused briefly, his eyes scanning the room to find Janet. She was sitting with a dark-skinned man whom Hall thought was probably Native American.

Well, Hal thought, *if he's outside the reservation, he's fair game for surveillance and anything that might come after that.* He smelled their food and called the waitress to his booth. "Whatever it is that those two are having," he said, nodding in the direction of Janet and Antoine, "I'll take the same."

The waitress nodded and backed away, not knowing what to do. She walked over to Antoine and whispered, "That guy wants to have what you're having."

"Okay," said Antoine.

"Are you sure?" asked the waitress.

"My people share, and I'm expected to share anything that anyone might ask for. What's a little food?" asked Antoine.

When they finished eating, Janet and Antoine resumed their conversation.

"I have some questions," said Antoine. "How did Homeland Security get so much power?"

"Well, we had a lot of chaos in the government. But there are many different aspects to all of it. I think the first thing that happened that allowed the rest of it to happen involved the press. For a few years, there was a campaign to denigrate the news media. It got so bad that many people were convinced that they couldn't believe anything they heard on television news or read in the newspapers. The news broadcasts became programs in which reporters from other news agencies, both newspapers and television and radio news, came on the air to back each other up. It was hard to know what was being reported.

"Then, a new television news channel came on. There were questions as to who started it and who supported it financially. There was a rumor that the new channel bought product ads at a cheaper rate than the older networks.

"The new channel was called Western Hemisphere News. It promised to air all of the news in the Western Hemisphere and news from overseas that affected citizens and countries in the Western Hemisphere. They also had a website, and citizens were invited to report news. No one appeared to check on the validity of any of the news. The established television news channels were driven out of business because the public no longer paid any attention, and advertisers quit buying air time from them. PBS hung on the longest, even though the government had cut funding for public broadcasting.

"Some of those old journalists were my heroes. They were why I decided to go into journalism," said Janet as her eyes teared.

She regained her composure, giving information as if she was reporting the news. "By this time, the Western Hemisphere News was reporting on terrorist attacks, even though ISIS had been just about abolished. No one knew if the reports were valid. When the press was left in tatters, there was a series of executive orders, including one that gave sweeping powers to Homeland Security. At that time, the government was blocking immigration from nations that were suspected of harboring terrorists who were said to be planning and executing attacks throughout the world. This had been tried before and was shot down by the courts, but because of the increase in terrorist attacks, the safety and sanctity of the US was said to be of paramount importance.

"Because of the crossovers between federal departments, like the military and the intelligence agencies, Homeland Security was put in charge of all of them. Homeland Security controls most things. The department even has a division that censors books, movies, and music," said Janet.

"What are these Post-Millennial Adjustments I keep hearing about?" asked Antoine.

"They're a series of executive orders designed to provide jobs and create opportunities for young people. People were working past the social security retirement age. Older people had jobs that could have been given to younger people. Also, social security was costing a lot. My parents said that the government had been taking money out of social security and using it for other things for years. So, anyway, people were expected to retire when they reached age fifty-five. They had to move out of their homes and apartments and into elderly-living facilities, where their social security money would be used to pay for their stay. If they refused, they would have to move in with family, as their houses were claimed by the government and resold; the money was used to supplement the cost of keeping people in elderly-living facilities. If the elderly lived with family, they received no social security, and all of their expenses had to be borne by the family.

"Next came the development of the gated neighborhoods. We are assigned to neighborhoods that put us closer to work, saving money on transportation. It also allows Homeland Security to keep better track of people. We don't travel outside the city anymore. We have all we need here, and we have virtual reality museums that create experiences for us without having to travel long distances on vacations.

"They started putting limits on vehicles about the same time as the terrorist attacks of 2020. The military needed fossil fuels for their vehicles, and wealthy people needed fuel for recreational vehicles. There wasn't enough oil to go around, and car manufacturers were making more and more electric cars, which were very expensive. Free travel to any place people wanted to go made it hard to keep track of everyone. Public transportation was encouraged, and travel out of the city was discouraged. That's why the virtual reality sites were developed," said Janet.

"It's hard to travel outside the city. If people are driving old cars, they are put on level-one security. This means they are watched by Homeland Security to see if they engage in other suspicious activity.

"I have access to a vehicle through work. When I go out on local stories, I can take the vehicle. We just got some new electric cars that can be tracked to make sure we aren't engaging in unauthorized behavior. With the old cars, I would get gas at a gas station and pay for it with a credit card. The credit cards could be traced, so the newspaper could keep track of my movements."

"I haven't been here that long. It sounds like you can't do anything on your own. You can't even live where you want to," said Antoine.

"All of the changes are supposed to keep us safe," said Janet. "I don't think that's true, but I don't have other opinions and observations to guide me anymore."

"It sounds like the terrorists are the government," said Antoine.

"Shhh. Someone will hear you. Let's not put judgments on all of this. So I'll just continue where I left off.

"Homeland Security began censoring all forms of communication. Anyone using the internet needs a password, and that password restricts the sites that any individual can use. The sites are determined by one's profession, college major, and the section in which someone lives. The only website that can be used by all is Western Hemisphere News. Homeland Security says that all of the precautions allow them to keep track of people and that this is how they keep us safe. Our cell phones are also restricted based on work, school, employment, and family."

"I thought you were a newspaper reporter," said Antoine.

"Well, I thought that's what I would be when I majored in journalism. What I do is simply rewrite stories that come from Homeland Security. Once in a while, I go out on local stories, but those have to be edited by Homeland Security before they are printed. The local newspapers and television news are the only systems that still exist outside of Western Hemisphere News. Most of what the local news media reports on is local and regional. WHN reports on national and international news," said Janet.

"You make it sound like all of this is normal," said Antoine.

"I don't think it's the way things should be, but it's the way things are," said Janet. I don't understand how you can live in this country and not know all of this."

"Tribes are sovereign nations. We live in rural and frontier areas. We used to be controlled by the federal government and had more laws to follow than any other population group.

"We started getting stronger. When we were allowed to build casinos, we used the money to build alliances with other tribes and with environmental groups. When our rights were violated by government agencies, we had protests, and we fought in court.

"For some of us, there was a series of protests against the feds and against big corporations. Native people from all over the country would come to protests. We were joined by activists from foreign countries. The feds didn't like that attention. The protests damaged the myth of the US being a leader in the protection of human rights. When we quit being dependent on the feds and quit using technology, we found that we could survive. We didn't need the feds for anything, except to leave us alone. They did that because they had so much to do in the cities. We worked out an agreement with the feds. They granted us full sovereignty, which included a nonaggression pact. We can still use educational resources, and we can be employed in nontribal entities. We can travel to other countries on tribal business, if we can figure out how to get there. Other than that, we are separate nations. So we choose to live as we did before your ancestors came here," said Antoine.

"We rely on hunting, fishing, and gathering for our food as we did in the past. We have gardens now to supplement the food that grows naturally. We trade with some of the nonnative people who live in the area. That's how we get the eggs.

"We harvest wild rice every fall, and we can hunt and fish on our land all year round. When I come back here after a visit home, I usually bring back some fresh venison. We also preserve some food by drying, canning, and freezing.

"We don't use electricity. Some of us use solar power for heating. In order to freeze food, we cut big hunks of ice from the lakes and rivers and store it in small huts. We cover the ice with sawdust, the leavings from the wood we harvest for heating and cooking. The ice usually lasts from one winter to the next. We store our canned goods underground so they don't get too hot during the summer," said Antoine.

"I don't understand most of what you said. You don't have electricity? How do you live? How can you grow food when the air is so polluted?" asked Janet.

"You'll see when you go to visit," said Antoine.

"How do you communicate if you don't use technology?" asked Janet.

"Before colonization, we communicated by sending runners to spread information. We do that now. It's called the Moccasin Grapevine. We get up with the sun and go to bed when it's dark. You'll understand that better if you decide to go to my rez," said Antoine.

"How do you get messages overseas or long distances?" asked Janet.

"We have contacts in Canada. There are Canadian Anishinaabe, and there is a reservation that straddles the border between Minnesota and Canada where we can pass freely into Canada," said Antoine. "I've been at the U for about a year. I can't get used to all of this checking surveillance."

"This all started around 2020," said Janet.

"Well, we sure heard about it when it was happening. But because we don't have electricity, we didn't get the coverage that you did. I can see what things are like outside our reservation, but I don't know what happened to create the changes. For me, coming here is like coming to a foreign country. I guess some of it has to do with the terrorist attacks. I've heard about them most of my life, and I remember that the grown-ups were pretty shook up, wondering what was going to happen to us. How old were you when the terrorist attacks started happening again?" asked Antoine.

"I was ten. We had our TV turned to the news constantly after we first heard about the attacks. There wasn't anything else on TV, other than the jewelry channels. My dad would turn those on just to get a break. After a few minutes, he would turn back to the news," said Janet.

"What happened?" asked Antoine. "I was three or four when all that went down."

"Okay. Well, there had been that war in the Middle East that, I guess, never stopped. We would be at war with one country, and when we would sign a peace agreement, there would be another country with whom we would go to war. My dad said that most of the wars were citizen uprisings against governments and civil wars and we had no business sticking our noses in them. He said that the US was interested in some of those countries because of their oil. He said we didn't understand other cultures and tried to convert the whole world to our definition of democracy. There had been terrorist attacks for years, and my dad said that the government decided to make changes that would keep us all safe, but in order to do that, we had to give up our freedoms, even though we were still a democracy," said Janet.

When Antoine heard the word *democracy*, he quit listening and interrupted Janet. "I don't think your country knows what the word democracy means. Many generations of our people have suffered at the hands of what you call your country. There was a time when we believed that we were all going to die because of white men."

"I know that. My dad and mom told me about the history of Native American relations with Europeans and Americans," said Janet, hoping to placate Antoine. It didn't work.

"Americans? Your country was named after a European man. So you honor someone who killed native people," he said.

"I'm sorry. I have never talked to anyone who is Anishinaabe. I guess I don't know what words I can and can't use. Do you want me to talk about the terrorist attacks of 2020 or not?"

"Yes, I do. I won't interrupt again," said Antoine.

"Okay. Well, my dad said there had been a period of time when there were no terrorist attacks. ISIS was thought to have been wiped out. And then there were several attacks on the same day, September 11, 2020. All over the world, famous landmarks were destroyed, and many people were killed, according to Western Hemisphere News.

"The next outbreak happened on Columbus Day the same year. The Vatican was bombed in Italy, and Madrid, Spain, and Rio de Janeiro, Brazil, experienced planes crashing into their government buildings.

"After the first attacks, there was a lot of speculation as to who had done all of this. No one claimed responsibility for it.

"Then came the second set of attacks. Wall Street closed for about a month. Some people started withdrawing money from banks until the president crafted an executive order that said that account holders could only draw out $1,000 a month. We were told that this would save the economy.

"My mom said that some people questioned whether all those attacks were really taking place. Mom said that people who questioned whether or not the attacks really happened disappeared. After a while, nobody questioned the attacks. WHN reported that we were under siege.

"My dad said that's when the government started promoting spending money on stuff as a way to be patriotic. He said it was a distraction from the real issues," Janet said.

"What did he think the real issues were?" asked Antoine.

"My dad and my mom said the real issues were saving the earth from the pollution created by the factories, racism, sexism, ageism, and the elitism of the politicians and the CEOs of companies who made outrageous sums of money, driving up the prices of manufactured goods and creating a culture in which there were homeless, starving people.

"Anyway, Congress started passing legislation to offer more power to Homeland Security, promoting the loss of individual freedoms as patriotism. It's when cities got the funds to put in security in all public buildings and places of business. That's when we got the metal detector gates everywhere.

"When the cities were reorganized and people were moved to new neighborhoods, there was less diversity in the neighborhoods. This was supposed to cut down on the opportunities for unrest among people. Streets were changed so that there were two main streets in a neighborhood—one going north and south and one going east and west.

"There were community centers built in each neighborhood for community gatherings that were planned by the neighborhood associations. Some say that the associations are arms of Homeland Security. When there are neighborhood gatherings, attendance is taken. People who are consistently absent are put on level-one security and are watched by Homeland Security agents. I've heard that people on level-one security are tracked by entry-level agents, giving them an opportunity to learn how to follow people."

"So what else do people have to do to get on level-one security?" asked Antoine.

"Level-one security is for people who still drive their own cars, go into neighborhoods where they don't belong, and spend below the minimum amount they are supposed to spend. It's also for people who are just seen as suspicious. This would be people who don't dress the way they are supposed to. Professionals, like me, are supposed to wear clothing similar to what I'm wearing for work. I can dress casually when I'm off work, but the clothing has to respect my status. I've heard that there's a group of people—families—who have lost loved ones in industrial accidents, and they are watched closely to see how they're spending their settlements."

"Level-two security is for people who continue with level-one behavior and go outside their neighborhoods more than four times a month. People are placed on level-three security when they appear to be gathering with people outside their designated neighborhoods.

"We can't go outside of our neighborhoods except for family visits or work assignments. We can take the busses that go to the Mall of America and the virtual reality museums," said Janet.

"Why did people just go along with all of this?" asked Antoine.

"After the 2020 bombings, people were more willing to give up freedoms to keep our borders safe and to stop insurgents from creating more threats to our citizens. There had been an increase in the number of mass random shootings, and the government had to do something to stop this.

"I think that by this time the air quality was so bad that people were breathing in less oxygen, and they didn't think clearly. That, plus the reports of attacks all over the world and the constant broadcasting about those attacks scared people enough that they were willing to go along with just about anything. Besides, what were they going to do?" asked Janet.

"I have trouble understanding how millions of people would just give up their rights," said Antoine.

"I don't think you get it. You weren't living here," said Janet.

"You're right. I probably don't get it. I come here after all this has taken place and wonder how things got to be this bad. I understand why my mom didn't want me to come here. She never told me exactly what she was afraid of, but she sure is afraid for me being here," said Antoine.

"There's something I don't get. Why can't you just bring the information from that old lady to the group?" asked Janet.

"I suggested that," said Antoine. "I was told that having an outsider go to my community would give everyone in the group a good look at how we live. I take many things for granted. At least that's what they said," said Antoine.

"So when am I expected to go to your reservation?" asked Janet.

"Well, not yet. First, we need to meet, probably one more time, so I can orient you to how things are there. I have some more questions about your world. I haven't been able to ask a lot of questions. I just go to class, and I meet with members of the group and help to plan assignments.

"I also need to make sure you get out of the city safely and get back safely. Right now, it's too cold for you to travel there. You can't use your company car. I guess there are tracking devices on those cars. The group will find a car and make sure it's drivable," said Antoine.

"That will put me on level-one security or maybe level two," said Janet.

"I've heard that security is lax at certain times of the day, and you can pass through the gates, and no one will check you out," said Antoine.

"Where do you find a car?" asked Janet.

"There's a black market for cars. I don't understand this. We don't have a lot of vehicles where I come from. But we take good care of them. We have a lot of scrapped vehicles that we use for spare parts. I just thought most people in the city had their own cars until I came here," he said.

"We used to get lots of people from the cities. At first, it was just in the summer. Then some developers decided to figure out ways to bring people in during all four seasons. That's dried up because people can't go outside the city. Then the CEOs from the big corporations started buying up property near the reservation. I guess they can run their businesses from their home computers. So they take advantage of our clean air and water.

"We used to have copper mines, and there was a push to develop iron mines. My people and some other folks who lived in the area demonstrated and strongly objected, going so far as to sit on the railroad tracks to stop the trains that brought in the sulfuric acid to process the copper. We also set up camps on land that was to be mined to discourage the mining companies," said Antoine.

Janet was getting more comfortable with Antoine, almost forgetting her concerns about getting found out by Homeland Security. Their three-hour visit seemed shorter.

A man in the restaurant nodded at Antoine and pointed with his head to the stranger who had been sitting in the restaurant for the time that Janet and Antoine had been there.

Antoine acknowledged the man, Bill, who was a security guard at the university. Bill, who had his own escape plans, supplied Antoine with information about security sweeps and other activities of university security. When he caught Antoine's eye, Bill looked at the clock on the wall above the counter.

Picking up the cue, Antoine said, "I think that's all for this visit. We'll meet again soon."

"Where?" asked Janet.

"Here. It's the safest place around," said Antoine. "I think you'd better leave first. I'll wait a few minutes before I go. We don't want to be seen together outside. Can't tell who's watching us."

As he left the restaurant, Antoine looked around to see if anyone was following. *I used to think people here were paranoid*, he thought. *Now, I just think they're cautious.*

Janet picked up the bus, changed twice, and got off a couple of blocks from her apartment. She noticed that the air quality had declined appreciably. She walked slowly so as not to have to breathe deeply, as her filtered scarf would not keep out all of the chemicals in the air.

She noticed a shadowy figure across the street that she couldn't quite make out. She thought it might be shadows from the streetlight that barely shone through the thick, dark air. She decided the best thing to do was to ignore it and just get back to the filtered air in her apartment.

Once inside her apartment, Janet locked the door and took off her scarf, coat, and boots, wiggling her toes as they cramped coming out of the confinement of her boots.

She was tired, as she had not spent that much time talking to anyone since she had last seen her parents. She lay down on her couch, thinking she was at least safe within the confines of her apartment.

What am I doing? she thought. I don't know if I want to meet with that guy again. I don't know if I want to take a chance driving out of the city. I don't know that there's a point in getting to know people I won't see again when this is over. I don't know what this is and what it will be like when it's over. I don't know that I want to risk getting caught. I don't have a safe place to hide out. I don't know if I want to continue living half a life. I don't get to do any real writing on the newspaper. I just get to reword stories that have been censored by Homeland Security. This isn't what I thought a career in journalism would be. I just don't know.

After a while, Janet got up and started pacing. She went to the window and tried to peer through the gray-green chemicals that pressed up against the glass. She saw the blurred outline on the sidewalk again. *Why would anyone be standing out there when the air quality is so bad?*

Maybe I'm imagining things, she thought. Maybe the shadow was the guy in the café. Maybe he was a Homeland Security agent and was following her. Did they pick up on unusual behavior that quickly? Maybe she was just too tired.

Janet left the window, turned on television, and watched a nature program focusing on the lifestyles of a wide variety of animals found in North America. She watched without seeing until it was time for her to go to bed.

CHAPTER
February 18, 2040

When he saw the lights in Janet's apartment go off, Hal Emerson left and went back to his own apartment in the Minneapolis Homeland Security building. He felt satisfied with his surveillance. *I'm glad I decided to take this assignment*, he thought. *I'll pay a visit to the* Minneapolis Herald *on Monday morning.*

Hal Emerson had been with Homeland Security since he was a teenager. He and his brother, Will, had enrolled in the Homeland Security Youth Training Corps. Their parents had been hesitant about their enrollment; however, any parent who didn't enroll their children was subject to Homeland Security surveillance.

As members of the HSYTC, all children were encouraged to report any suspicious behavior by anyone, including their parents. Will turned his parents in because they kept books that had been written before Homeland Security took over censorship of all written material.

Homeland Security agents raided the home, confiscated the books, and arrested Hal's parents. Hal never saw his brother or his parents again. Because he was essentially an orphan with information damaging to the sanctity of Homeland Security, he was placed in a Homeland Security living facility, where he was indoctrinated further into the goals and objectives of the agency and trained as an agent.

Because he didn't want to disappear like the other members of his family had, he went along. Hal was an apt student and rose in the ranks to be a supervisor. The personal goal that he didn't share was escape. Every time he traveled someplace, he watched and waited for the opportunity to activate his plan.

Hal's supervisor at Homeland Security, Jim Remington, became his mentor and his hero. Hal's escape plan gained some urgency when he was assigned to pick up his mentor and his mentor's wife and bring them in to be placed in elderly housing.

Hal went to the Remington house and found it empty. Jim and his wife had apparently realized that they would be taken into custody and disappeared. Hal didn't know that Jim had been planning for this for several years and had joined relatives in the mountains in Montana who had established a community for people who didn't accept the new way of life established by the federal government.

This was Hal's moment of truth. When he reached fifty-five, someone would come to get him and take him to an elderly facility. He began planning and decided that his best chance of escape would be to contact a Canadian operative when he attended negotiations between Homeland Security and Canadian intelligence, designed to find common ground on matters involving US citizens seeking asylum in Canada.

Hal knew he would be given political refugee status in Canada if and when he escaped. He also knew that the border between the US and Canada would not stop Homeland Security agents, some of whom he had trained, from crossing into Canada to look for him. At one of the meetings with Canadian officials, Hal had made contact with Rene Le Blanc, a man who worked in Canadian intelligence.

Rene expressed surprise when Hal asked him how US citizens got to Canada. "You expect me to tell you how people escape your country? Do you think I'm that stupid? I don't want to help you capture them. I help them find safety in my country."

After he first brought up the subject, Hal decided to simply try to establish a friendship with Rene. After a couple of years, Hal asked again about escaping to Canada. "I want the information for myself, and I have money to purchase property," said Hal.

"So you want to come here to Canada?" said Rene, surprised.

"Here's what I know," said Hal. "We spy on our own people and end up manufacturing charges against them. We arrest them, they are tried and found guilty, and we never know what happens to them. When any

US citizen reaches age fifty-five, we are shipped off to elder facilities where experiments are conducted to help scientists figure out how to slow the aging process.

"I was expected to round up my supervisor and mentor when he turned fifty-five. When I went to his house, he was gone. There was a nationwide search for him, but they never found him."

"We have stories about the restrictions your government places on citizens. Can you not expose the truth as to what has happened to the freedoms in your country?" asked Rene.

"No. Everything is monitored and censored. I'd be tried as a traitor and would probably get the death penalty. There would be a public execution. I need to have a place where I can come when the time is right."

"Why do you want to come to Canada?" asked Rene.

"I've heard that Canada is self-sufficient and truly practices the freedoms that our country claims to have. Besides, there are remote places where no one will be able to find me," said Hal.

"There are remote places where you won't be able to survive. I don't know how many people will be willing to help you when they find out who you are and what you've done. I'll see what I can do. Northern Ontario is probably the best place for you," said Rene.

The following night, Rene took Hal on a sightseeing tour. Rene had managed to arrange for a special tour of one of Toronto's museums that told the story of the French in Canada and the attempts at freedom from British rule. Most of the signs and other written displays in the museum were in French, so Rene translated. The stories were new to Hal. Canadian history had never been taught much in American schools, and certainly a history filled with protest and revolution would not be taught.

During the tour, Rene informed Hal of the arrangements he had made. "You are to give me the money. Tomorrow during one of our breaks, I'll show you the title to the land and give you directions to get there. As you wish, a house will be built there. A caretaker will live in the house and will be paid out of the money you give me now. When you decide to come, you can come to any of the refugee centers along the border and contact me. I will send someone who will take you to your house. If, for any reason, I am not available, any of the staff in the refugee centers can assist you."

"What if arrest orders have already been sent? We sometimes send out orders with charges that make escapees look like dangerous criminals."

"You talk about escapees. We use the word refugee. We receive lots of those arrest orders. We assume that many people coming from the United States are political refugees. Our government has allotted money to operate refugee centers for US citizens. Your government has allotted money to hunt them down. I hope you can see the difference."

Hal paid Rene $600,000 to ensure his future, and he continued to save money without using banks. Now all he had to do was find the right time to leave.

Hal spent his Sunday writing notes about his surveillance of Janet Ryan and checking on her journey to Dinky Town. He went into the computer program that gave information as to the schedules and assignments for newspaper reporters in the Minneapolis area and found that she had no business in Dinky Town.

This is exciting, he thought. Maybe I'll be able to close in on a potential terrorist cell. Maybe this will be the one that helps me get out of here.

CHAPTER 5
February 19, 2040

After a restless Sunday, Janet welcomed the opportunity to go back to work on Monday. She checked the air quality on the Weather Channel, got ready for work, and boarded the bus half-full of people on their way to work.

There was no visiting on the bus; people did not mingle, except at the community gatherings designed to encourage young women and men to develop relationships.

It was hard for passengers to recognize one another because of the filtered scarves and masks. Janet noticed that she had become adept at recognizing people by body shape, the way they sat, where they sat, and the kind of clothing they wore. She had taken the same bus to work for the eight years she had been employed at the newspaper.

Some passengers came and went within short periods. She never knew where they went after she noticed their absences, and she didn't want to think about it. Janet would nod at the passengers who, like her, seemed to stay. She met some of them at the community gatherings. Over the last year, her attendance at such gatherings had dwindled. She didn't like the idea of contrived meetings to look for a mate, and her lack of trust in others made it difficult for her to strike up a conversation with anyone she didn't know. Her absences were noted by attendance clerks and recorded.

The air quality had improved today, putting Janet in an optimistic mood. It looked almost like daylight. The filtered scarf Janet wore around her face was lightweight. The weather was mild for February, and the wind was light. She got off the bus at her stop and walked into the building housing the newspaper offices. She acknowledged coworkers and looked forward to work.

When she got to the newsroom, Janet noticed that Lloyd Holmgren, her editor and supervisor, had his door closed. She could see a man through the window and thought he looked familiar.

Hal had been waiting for Lloyd in Lloyd's office for some time before Lloyd walked in. When he saw Hal, Lloyd jumped. He hadn't seen Hal for three years. The last time was when his best reporter was suspected of being a member of a terrorist cell. Hal had directed Lloyd, giving him orders as to what big news item to assign to the reporter. The stories in that news item were carefully scrutinized to find evidence of the reporter's thoughts and feelings that were consistent with terrorist activities. The reporter was arrested, along with members of his group. Lloyd was not informed as to the disposition of the case, but the reporter never returned to work.

"Sit down, Lloyd," said Hal. "I need to let you know that we have one of your reporters under surveillance."

"Who is it?" asked Lloyd.

"Janet Ryan—unless you can give some explanation why she was in Dinky Town on Saturday wearing her press ID and talking with a U student for almost three hours," said Hal.

Lloyd tried to come up with an excuse for Janet. "I don't know why she was there. Maybe we should call her in and see what she has to say," he said.

"You know we don't operate like that. She's under surveillance. We'll come up with an assignment that will help us to analyze her thinking. We'll also be following her. She knows better than to go outside her neighborhood and other approved sites. She misrepresented herself by wearing her ID, pretending to be on the job," said Hal. He stood. "I'll be in touch. Oh, by the way, the same rules apply as they did in our last collaboration," he said as he walked out of the office.

Lloyd had been promoted to editor of the *Minneapolis Herald* after the previous editor had been brought in for questioning by Homeland Security and had not returned to work. Lloyd had spent the last five years waiting to see if Homeland Security would come and take him away even though he didn't think he had done anything wrong. As a result, he had developed a tic—one eye twitched when he was nervous.

Lloyd pulled the blinds in his office and waited for the tic to go away. *Collaboration*, he thought. *That was no collaboration. I lost a good reporter.* No one figured out what the reporter's group was going to do. They just knew that the group was meeting illegally. *Who knows what Janet is doing? I can't warn her. I hope that things work out for her. I doubt that they will.*

CHAPTER
February 19, 2040

Hal took some deep breaths, squared his shoulders, and put a smile on his face as he walked into the briefing room. "Good morning."

He was greeted with enthusiasm from agents who believed they were keeping America safe by catching people who looked suspicious.

The agents were expected to repeat the forbidden behaviors they used as guidelines before every meeting. They did so now.

"People whose families have disappeared. People who travel into areas where they don't belong. People who don't attend community gatherings. People who drive cars. People who have jobs that give them access to sensitive material."

The chanting filled the briefing room. When it stopped, Hal chatted with the agents, sounding as if he had a personal interest in each of them. It built enthusiasm and morale among them.

Hal was highly regarded by the people he mentored and taught them everything they knew about surveillance. They had learned all about double-negative suspicion, a term used to describe the actions of those under surveillance who looked too good to be true. They were under surveillance for a reason, so none of their activities should be seen as innocent.

Hal had singlehandedly rounded up several people who were thought to be members of terrorist rings that were plotting to attack federal and state government buildings. People came under suspicion because of their behavior, and surveillance revealed that they fit at least three of the five criteria.

When the leaders of the groups had been arrested and questioned, other members were found and brought in for questioning. As was common, the suspicion was high but without any concrete proof of terrorism or plots against the government. Agents were told that they didn't need to provide concrete proof. They were to follow the guidelines they chanted every Monday morning, identify those who fit the profile, bring them in, and let the justice system do its work.

Hal knew that many innocent people had been tried and convicted of terrorism. The process of trying and convicting was thought to keep the country safe. The public trials were preventive measures that would make people think twice before they questioned the government, especially Homeland Security.

It was easier to be an agent today than it was in the beginning, because the restrictive laws that protected the civil rights of citizens had been abolished for the safety of the American people.

"Okay. Let's see what we've got today," said Hal, walking over to a writing board that covered one wall in the room. "We have John, whose subject is Jeff; Alex, whose subject is Antoine; and Marie, whose subject is Sally. And we have Hal, whose subject is Janet.

"I decided to do a little surveillance. It sharpens my skills. I'll start," said Hal.

"Janet Ryan is a newspaper reporter with the *Minneapolis Herald*. She was in the Dinkytown Café on Saturday with your guy, Alex. They were together for over three hours. Antoine takes food that he brings from home to the café, and they fix it for him," said Hal.

"Antoine's schedule has stayed the same, except for his meeting with Janet on Saturday," said Alex. "I didn't know that he brought his own food with him. Is it important?"

"Yes, it is. It goes to your powers of observation," said Hal.

"Back to Janet Ryan. Let's see what criteria places her under suspicion," said Hal as he wrote:

1. Parents disappeared, probably in Canada.
2. Recent contact with childhood friend whose parents also disappeared.

3. New friendship with Indian man who has also been seen in the company of subject's childhood friend, Sally.
4. Fewer shopping trips to neighborhood stores.
5. Travel outside her neighborhood.
6. Misrepresentation of her purpose by wearing newspaper ID badge when she isn't working.
7. Lack of attendance at neighborhood gatherings.

John spoke up. "Jeff doesn't do much that's out of the ordinary. But every time Jeff leaves one of his classes, another student, a female, comes and sits in the chair Jeff vacated. She talks to a student sitting next to her for a few minutes, and then they leave. She's not very neat in her appearance. She spends time smoothing her clothes around her body, her hands brushing the edges of the seat. When she and the other student leave, she messes with her purse, pulls out a tissue, and blows her nose."

"Good observations," Hal said. "What do you think all those hand movements mean?"

Marie spoke up. "Well, she could be palming something small in her hands and passing it on to the other student, or maybe she's just nervous."

"Okay," said Hal. "We don't know for sure what she's doing, just that it doesn't look right. Should we assign someone to her?"

"I don't think so," said Marie. "Jeff already has an agent. Too many people assigned in the same area might raise suspicion and cause the group members to rein themselves in."

"Any other thoughts on this?" asked Hall.

"I think we should check her out sooner rather than later," said John. "If we don't find anything, we can eliminate her. If we continue to see the behavior that has attracted attention, we can add her to the group we're investigating," said John.

"I think you're right," said Hal. "Susan, she's yours."

"Okay. Should I attend the class she's in with Jeff?" asked Susan.

"No, find out who she is and where she lives and begin watching where she goes and what she does," said Hal.

"Okay, let's switch to another suspect. What do we know about Sally?" asked Hal.

"She works in student affairs, and she's really scattered. I don't think she's organized enough to be part of any kind of subversive organization."

Alex answered. "Double negative. She's under surveillance, and her parents disappeared. Her lack of organization may be a ploy to direct suspicion away from her.

"What else do you have on her?" Hal asked.

"I think that's the problem. I have a lot of random pieces," said Marie.

"So being disorganized does serve a purpose," Hal said. "Let's review."

"Okay. I got this assignment after she was seen with Jeff and then with Janet. At first, it looked like she had simply stumbled into a relationship with Jeff. Her meeting with Janet appeared to be random. Then it was discovered that both her parents and Janet's parents disappeared about the same time.

"Since the first couple of meetings, Janet and Sally haven't seen each other. This is unusual because they're old friends. As scattered as she appears, Sally makes it to work on time. Her position in a subversive group would be key. She's involved with students, and we believe that Sally, Janet, Jeff, and Antoine are involved with students who are in a group that advocates insurrection," said Marie, Sally's agent.

"Okay. Do we have enough for pick up and detention?" Hal asked.

"No. We don't know what they're planning to do that would pose a threat to our country. If we brought them in for questioning, their absences would be noticed, allowing the others to get away. If we wait, further connections will turn up, and we can pick up more people at the same time, interrogate, and get more names," said John.

Hal nodded. "I think we may be able to wrap this up before fall. There's tension and stress involved in subversive activities. Someone will slip up, and the group will start unraveling. Then we'll make our moves. Be sure to let me know if you see someone else who needs surveillance. Call me when you spot anything unusual. Now, let's get back out there. We are protecting this great country of ours. We are making America safe for the American people."

CHAPTER
February 19, 2040

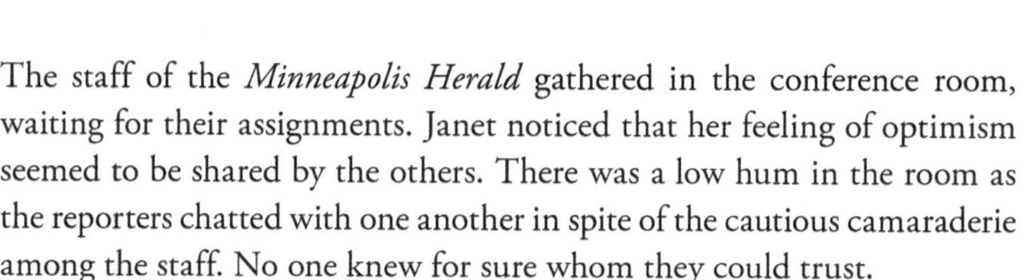

The staff of the *Minneapolis Herald* gathered in the conference room, waiting for their assignments. Janet noticed that her feeling of optimism seemed to be shared by the others. There was a low hum in the room as the reporters chatted with one another in spite of the cautious camaraderie among the staff. No one knew for sure whom they could trust.

Janet teased Tom Jenkins, the photographer with whom she was often teamed. "Don't you know that stuff will kill you?" she said, nodding at his coffee.

"Well, they won't let me drink anything stronger, so I'm stuck with caffeine. Besides, it gets me going in the morning," he said. "I notice that you don't drink anything except water. Your grocery bill must be pretty high. All that bottled water."

"Well, coffee has water in it, so you must pay for caffeine and water," Janet responded. "I rely on me for energy. I eat a good breakfast and walk up and down the stairs in my building a couple of times before I go out and get on the bus. Besides, the quality of water is bound to improve soon so we can all drink tap water."

"So you exercise at home and have a membership at a gym too. I guess that makes you the queen of fitness. Maybe you can make extra money as a trainer—get your own TV show," Tom said.

The conversations faded, and silence took over the room as the reporters and photographers waited for Lloyd's greeting. Janet liked Lloyd. She thought he was a good editor and appreciated the direction he gave her—letting her know when her writing lost objectivity and took on too much attitude.

Lloyd walked in at ten o'clock. Janet noticed that his tic was back and wondered what was going on.

Lloyd greeted the staff with his traditional greeting. "It's a good morning in Minneapolis."

"Yes it is," the staff chorused.

"Time to get to work and let the citizens know what the news is," Lloyd said. "Let's start with assignments."

Lloyd went through the list efficiently, spending time praising each staff member. The meeting finished by eleven o'clock.

Janet spent her day rewriting the stories that came over the internet from Homeland Security censors. She left the office and went home to find an announcement from the utility company in her mail.

Do Your Part!

Water rationing will begin Monday 2-21. Water
pressure will be cut back. Bottled water will be
available in the schools and day care programs. Two
gallons of bottled water will be available for singles
at the neighborhood community center.

Plan Ahead!

The Post-Millennium Survival Catalog for Singles, "Millie," had also arrived in the mail. It advertised new plastic dishware in bright colors—two to a set. The ad said the dishware would accommodate the water rationing—better cleansing with less water. There was a picture of brightly colored tumblers and plates adorning a kitchen table.

I haven't spent any money on myself for quite a while. Maybe I can go down to the kitchenware store before it closes and pick up some new dishes. I think I have enough water to last me for a while, thought Janet.

She left her apartment and headed for the Millie outlet kitchenware store just down the street. When she reached the store, Janet passed through the metal detector and entered into the small shop filled with brightly colored plastic dishes and microwave-safe containers. The displays were designed to catch the eyes of the shoppers. The store and the products sold in the store were designed for singles—people who didn't need a lot of tableware and who used microwaves exclusively to cook meals—meals that were processed, preserved, and packaged and needed only to be reheated.

Janet strolled through the tableware section. The items described in Millie were arranged in a display, featuring tableware in red, white, and blue, advertising the patriotism involved in saving water.

Janet picked up two packages of two each that contained bowls, plates, beverage containers, and flatware.

When Janet got to the checkout, the clerk praised her for her choice. "Aren't these nice. These dishes came out at just the right time. Just in time for water rationing. And when the rationing is over, we can still save water using these because they clean up with less water. Just use the water-saver cycle on the dishwasher. We are so lucky to live in a country where companies anticipate our needs," she gushed.

Janet feigned a smile. I wonder where they get these people. Do they just come this way or do they have to be trained? She paid, took her package, and walked back home.

Even though she didn't think much about her previous meeting with Antoine and what she was going to do about it, she stopped before entering her building and looked around, searching for something or someone who was not part of the neighborhood. She saw nothing unusual. She entered the building and settled in for the night.

CHAPTER 8
March 1, 2040

Spring is coming, thought Janet as she walked home from the bus stop. The weather was warmer, and there was less wind. She walked slowly, enjoying the change from the darkness and biting cold. She reached her building, walked into the lobby, took off her filtered scarf, and opened her mailbox to find a slip of folded paper. She shoved it in her coat pocket and walked up the stairs to her apartment. Once in, she hung up her coat, took off her boots, and unfolded the paper. The message on the paper read, "March 18, 10:00 a.m. at the café."

Janet's heart beat faster, her breathing uneven. I haven't made up my mind yet, she thought. I almost forgot about this. What do I want to do? March 18 is two weeks away. At least I'll have some time to think about whether or not I'm going to break all the rules and go to Antoine's community to gather information when I don't know what the group is going to do with the information and I don't know if it's worth the trip. Maybe I don't have to decide right now. I'll go on with my life and wait until the eighteenth.

The two weeks passed quickly. On the eighteenth, Janet got up and decided to go to café. She dressed as if she was going to work, pinned on her press ID, got on the bus, and headed for the restaurant. Her bus changes from one neighborhood to another were recorded on the Homeland Security computers and the cameras that captured her image.

When Janet got to the restaurant, she looked around for Antoine and didn't find him. She walked tentatively to a booth and sat down. A waitress came, and Janet ordered a bottle of water, telling the waitress she would wait until her companion arrived to order food. She noticed the man that

Antoine had acknowledged at their last meeting and nodded. He shook his head. She looked around to see if there was a suspicious person there. She didn't know what a suspicious person would look like in that setting because no one else looked familiar to her.

Antoine walked into the café about ten minutes later. He spotted Janet, smiled, and came to join her. "How are you?" he said.

"I'm okay. I was worried. You weren't here when I got here."

"I suppose there's a lot to worry about if I don't show up," he said. "What did you think?"

"I didn't think anything. I just thought you'd be here when I came in," Janet said.

"Well, I guess that means everything is okay now. But then again, I don't know that anything is okay. You have a messed-up world here," Antoine said.

"What do you mean? This is your messed-up world too," said Janet.

"I'm only here temporarily. One of these days, something will tell me it's time to go home, and then I can go back to the woods where things make sense to me," said Antoine.

"Who's that guy at the counter? He was here last time, and you nodded at him," said Janet.

"That's Bill Scott," Antoine whispered. "He's a university security agent."

"Doesn't that mean he works for Homeland Security?" asked Janet.

"Keep your voice down," said Antoine. "Yeah, he does. But he's got some family issues. I don't know the details. His sister wants to leave. She's a widow with two kids, and Bill fills in for their dad. He says his sister has wanted to leave for a long time, and he's come to believe that she's right and that the best thing they can do is leave. He has some contacts with a group in Montana. He's not sure when he can leave, but when he thinks the time is right, they'll pack up and go to Montana.

"I met Bill when they were updating security devices in the student apartments. He started asking me questions about my home. He seemed to know that he could trust me. We decided to meet at the Wednesday-night card games at the student union.

"When Bill and I were at the card games on the same night, we acted like we didn't know each other. Bill's job is to let us know if we're about to be arrested. He might not have time to wait for the card game, but he will let us know," said Antoine.

The waitress came to take their order. "Well, I guess we'll have omelets with green peppers and some real cheese. And we'll have hot water for our peppermint tea," said Antoine.

Antoine turned to Janet after the waitress left. "Today, I'm going to give you a lesson in culture to prepare you for your visit to the woods," Antoine said.

"I don't know if I'm going," said Janet.

Antoine raised his eyebrows. "Well, you need to make up your mind. Otherwise, there's not much sense in having this conversation."

"I'm afraid I'll get caught," said Janet.

"Yeah, you could. I can't give you odds on that. Have you thought about what your life will be like if you don't do this?" asked Antoine.

"My life will be the same as it is. I'll just keep putting one foot in front of the other. Then maybe I'll find a way to leave, like my parents did," said Janet.

"So you'll just keep on in the same way," said Antoine.

"Yes," said Janet.

"So you'll keep writing the phony stories and pretend that your job is worthwhile. You'll go to the Mall of America in your free time and visit the phony museums and watch movies that have the same plots and pretend to be entertained," said Antoine.

"What is there about your life that's so much different?" asked Janet.

"Let's see. When I get up in the morning, the air is clear. I don't have to wear masks and filters. I hunt and fish to provide for myself and family. I don't have to worry about people following me around to see if I'm a threat. How's that for starters?" asked Antoine.

Janet was silent, trying to decide if the risk of getting involved was worth it. She didn't know what to think. When the food came, all the flavors made her wonder if all the food in Antoine's community tasted that good.

"Okay. What if I get caught?" she asked.

"We think getting caught means Homeland Security would rack up a lot of assumptions based on your behavior. We'll have an escape plan in place, and I'll help you get out before they arrest you," said Antoine.

"Where will I go?" she asked.

"The quickest place to go would be to my community," Antoine said.

"Won't someone come there to look for me?" Janet asked.

"No. Shortly after your government set up gated cities, we quit taking grant money from the government, and they made a deal with tribal communities to stay out. We became self-sufficient. We have full tribal sovereignty."

"So do I need a passport?" asked Janet.

"No. You need the permission of the elders. They've given permission for you to come for a visit. You can be there for a week. In that time, you can learn more about us," said Antoine.

"I thought I was supposed to get some history from that old woman who lives there," said Janet.

"The elders think it's important for you to gather some information about our customs and values. You can bring that back to the group. The elders think that if the group is going to eventually do something to change things in your country, you need to know what can be different, or you'll probably just recreate what already exists," said Antoine.

"I don't understand how your people can just change our plans," said Janet.

"Well, you're going to be visiting our community. You can visit with the old woman, and you can visit with my family. Now I'm going to give you a lesson in Ojibwe manners. First, keep your head bowed when you talk to elders. It's a sign of respect. When someone seems to be nodding upward with their chin or pursing their lips, they're pointing at something." Antoine demonstrated the behavior. "If someone offers you something or offers to help you in some way, accept it. When you have a conversation with someone, speak slowly and listen. If the person who's speaking pauses, don't assume they're finished. Don't ask a lot of questions. Our people are storytellers. They tell stories that will give you your answers.

"Remember that you're a guest. When you ask questions, don't challenge. It is disrespectful. Respect is important to us. My people have a long history with whites, and many don't trust and will question your motives. If you don't know something that is asked of you, just say you don't know.

"I think you have enough information to make the trip. The car will be parked in the garage a block down from your house. Your permit to travel outside the city will be in the glove box of the car. The keys will be in your mailbox the morning you will be leaving. There will also be a suitcase with clothes and other things you'll need when you're up there. When you leave the city, cross over into Wisconsin, take Highway 35 north to Highway 8 and go east. You'll see a gas station in a couple of miles. That's where you change clothes. Then go until you come to Highway 40 and turn north until you come to a small store. You can stop there and ask for directions to my grandmother's house. The path up to the house is about a quarter of a mile, and it isn't paved," said Antoine as he stood and put on his jacket. "The plan is for you to leave on April 1 and return on April 8. The weather should be decent by then. If it does snow, it will melt quickly because the sun is high in the sky," said Antoine.

"But I still don't know if I want to do this," said Janet.

"I suggest you make up your mind pretty soon. The plans for your travel and stay are in place," said Antoine.

Janet sat for a few more minutes watching Antoine walk out the door. She shook her head, stood, and left the cafe. As she walked down the street to the bus stop, she shifted her eyes from side to side to see if anyone was following her. The sidewalks were empty.

CHAPTER
March 18, 2040

Hal Emerson had sent an agent in his place to follow Janet Ryan. He didn't want to call attention to himself at the café because he wasn't a regular customer. The agent sat at a booth a few feet down from Janet and Antoine and heard bits and pieces of their conversation. It sounded like Antoine wanted Janet to take a trip, and Janet didn't want to go. Even though she had broken the law with unauthorized travel outside her neighborhood, she appeared to be a reluctant player in an unidentified drama. The agent didn't think there was enough evidence to bring her in. If Homeland Security gave her free rein, she might make a better witness later on, depending on whether or not she went along with whatever it was that Antoine wanted her to do. The agent waited a few minutes before he left the café. He didn't see a need to follow Janet, as she would probably return to her apartment.

In spite of the loss of civil rights of citizens, Hal followed the rigid protocol Homeland Security maintained to ensure the loyalty of its agents. The agency believed that if it was obvious that they were arresting people on spiderwebs of suspicion, the agents would lose their zeal and would quit the agency, although the latter would be hard to do because of the top-secret nature of the agency.

While people were arrested on circumstantial evidence and manufactured charges, senior agents worked hard to create images that suggested the American people and those suspected of terrorism still had rights.

Hal believed it was his responsibility to maintain the illusion that when people were under surveillance, the evidence against them had to be airtight. This was the best way to maintain order among the Homeland Security agents. They had to believe that they were doing their patriotic duty to keep the country safe from terrorists, many of whom appeared to be average people. It was getting harder for Hal to believe in the illusion. Until he could leave, he had to be a good agent and teacher.

Hal resumed his surveillance of Janet after the Monday-morning staffing when he and his agents decided to continue the surveillance and wait for the drama to unfold. He also decided to use another person to engage Antoine. Hal wasn't sure how this would work out, but he would start the process and make decisions along the way. He sat at his desk, thinking, and decided to call Bill Scott and put him to work.

"Bill, can you come to my office right away? I need you to do something for me."

A few minutes later, Bill walked into Hal's office.

"Bill," Hal said. "You've worked for Homeland Security for fifteen years. That's a long time."

"Yeah, it is. I like my job, and I like the students. I believe it's an honor and privilege to serve my country and the American people," said Bill.

Well, he's got all the right words, thought Hal.

"I'm glad to hear that, Bill. We need trustworthy people like you working in key positions. I'm going to ask you to give a little more for your country and the American people. I want to give you a special assignment.

"We're looking for the members of a subversive group that may be eating away at the very fiber of this country. We think you might be able to help us because we believe some of the members are here on this campus," said Hal.

Bill tried to put on the appropriate facial expression, even though he wasn't sure what that would be. He leaned forward, opened his eyes wide, and gave what he thought was a look that said he was eager to serve his country. "How can I help?" he asked.

"Well, I understand there is a Wednesday-night card game you attend," said Hal.

"Yeah, I do. I decided it would be a good way to look for suspicious activity," said Bill.

"I like your spirit. We appreciate your willingness to take suggestions. We want you to send some messages to one of the guys who comes to the card games," said Hal.

Bill waited for Hal to continue.

"We are concerned about the loyalties and connections of Antoine La Riviere," said Hal.

"You think he's a terrorist?" asked Bill.

"We don't know for sure, but we think he might be. We would like to pick him up for interrogation, but we don't have enough evidence," said Hal.

"What do you want me to do? I've never been really involved in all of this before. I put in surveillance equipment and look for suspicious activity," said Bill.

"We want you to be obvious about this. We want you to strike up a conversation with him, ask him questions about how his people live, what kind of money they get from the government, things like that. Go out for coffee with him after the card games. After you do all of that and you have his trust, we'll let you know what we want you to do next," said Hal.

"It might take a while. He doesn't come to all of the card games," said Bill.

"We don't want you to try to rush anything. Just take advantage of any of the opportunities that come up," said Hal.

"I'm honored that you picked me for this job," said Bill.

Hal stood, indicating that the meeting was over.

Bill walked out of the Homeland Security Building at a leisurely, unconcerned pace. His first impulse was to get a hold of Antoine right away, but he knew that any ill-timed action on his part would betray him.

Bill went back to work and finished out the day. When he got home, he sat in the kitchen trying to decide what to do next. He resumed his evening activities, ate supper, and cleared the dishes. He picked up a deck of cards and started playing solitaire while he was trying to think up a way to contact Antoine without looking suspicious.

Bill continued to do his job, and when Wednesday night came, he went to the card game, anxious to see Antoine, who was absent that night. Bill sent a message through one of the other group members that Antoine should go to the student union and find the deck of cards on the table closest to the checkout.

His first task completed, Bill spent his time being as routine as he knew how to be. He wondered if he was a suspect. If he was a suspect, it wouldn't matter what he did.

Bill had been a loyal, even zealous if low-level Homeland Security employee until his brother-in-law, Phil, was killed in a chemical explosion at his place of employment. The explosion evaporated his body. There was a memorial service but no casket. Bill believed it was his responsibility to take care of his sister, Shirley, and her two children, Jimmy and Cindy, who had been eight and four at the time of their father's death. He listened to Shirley's complaints about the restrictions placed on her by Homeland Security.

"I'm expected to spend my settlement from Phil's company on a regular basis. I have a debit card. I go to the mall and buy stuff, mostly for the kids. Then I take it back and get cash. I buy most of the stuff they need at yard sales. I've got the money stored away. Maybe I can use it to buy our way out of here. Phil's dead, and I'm looked on with suspicion. That's not right. I'm going to get out of here. I don't know how yet, but I'll figure a way," she said.

Shirley continued with her daily plans that she knew she would need in order to come up with the plan to leave. She and Bill would plan after the children were in bed.

In spite of her complaints, Shirley considered herself lucky. She had two healthy kids. She worried about them growing up without a dad. The children didn't get into any trouble, and they had friends. The dads in the neighborhood included them in family activities. Shirley spent her time with the other moms in the neighborhood. She figured she was under surveillance and wanted everything to look as normal as it could be. She knew she could play this game for a while because she would be leaving.

Bill decided that this task given him by Hal Emerson might lead to a way out. He told Shirley.

"So they give you a job to spy on someone. How is this going to lead to a way out?" she asked.

"I'm not sure yet," said Bill. "You just need to be ready to go when the time comes."

"Oh, I'll be ready. Did you know that your nephew, Jimmy, is in the Homeland Security Youth Corps?" she asked.

"No. When did that happen?" asked Bill.

"He turned twelve last year, and they recruit twelve-year-olds. I could have said no, but I figured that would lead to another level of security risk. Besides, every boy in his class is in the youth corps. Have you heard those stories about kids spying on their parents and turning them in to DHS? My own son, and I don't know if I can trust him," said Shirley, wiping tears from her eyes.

"Well, with you for a mom, I don't think he's easily swayed," said Bill.

"I don't know. I don't want to lose him. I want to get out of here," Shirley said.

"Just keep doing what you're doing, and I'll figure it out," said Bill.

CHAPTER
March 22, 2040

Bill met Antoine at the coffee shop he designated in the note passed at the card game. They sat in a booth away from other customers.

"As a security officer here at the U, I'm an employee of Homeland Security. I've been given the assignment of befriending you to find out if you're a member of a terrorist group," said Bill.

"A terrorist group!" exclaimed Antoine. "Where would anybody get that idea?"

"Well, Homeland Security keeps close tabs on everybody, especially college students. I guess they believe that students are idealistic and don't have enough experience to understand that terrorism jeopardizes lives and our way of life," said Bill.

"I come from the rez," said Antoine. "We have clean air and water. We live off the land. I don't understand what way of life you're trying to preserve."

"I'm not supporting these beliefs, just giving them to you," said Bill. "Anyway, DHS has gotten wind of an alleged group that's started up here. I don't know why they think you're part of it. I just know that they do, and I'm supposed to befriend you so I can get information. I give the information to DHS, and when the time comes, they arrest all of you."

"So I'm supposed to trust and tell you if I'm in this group or not. Just for right now, let's play cards, have coffee, and see what happens," said Antoine.

Bill and Antoine walked out of the coffee shop and separated.

April 1, 2040

Janet continued her routine—going to work, coming home, and taking occasional trips to the Mall of America. She didn't make up her mind about the trip until the night before she left. On April 1, 2040, she watched the weather forecaster standing next to a weather map with a big red seven, explaining that the air inversion trapped the factory emissions that would normally travel into the upper atmosphere and out into space. He said that the cold front that passed through had not only produced unseasonably cold temperatures but had also brought snow. He talked about how lucky they all were because the ozone layer had dissolved into patchy pieces of gas that mixed with the chemicals and dirt in the air. As the mixture floated upward, it bonded to the pieces of the ozone layer, creating platelike objects. This loss of the ozone layer allowed the necessary factory emissions to go up and out, reducing the amount of noxious gasses people had to inhale for the good of the greatest country in the world.

I don't know why those big globs of gas are referred to as plates, thought Janet. I guess I do know. It's something else they can tell us to make us believe everything is okay in spite of the state of things; we have no air quality, the water is sludgy at best, and the trees and plants are dead. If we call those undulating shapes held together by the particles that rise up out of the industrial chimneys plates, we can have a celebration each time one of them floats by and pretend that everything is okay.

Janet dressed, donning her blue paisley number 7 EZ Breathe scarf. The scarf matched her blue coat, her miniskirt, and the faux leather gloves she had ordered from *faux!*, the catalog especially for young, single women. The dove-gray, faux-suede, spiked-heel boots she wore added to the ensemble, as did the medically prescribed paisley wrist splints that she took along just in case the position of her hands on the steering wheel caused some discomfort. The splints were paid for by her medical plan as a preventive measure against the carpal tunnel syndrome that came with too much time on a keyboard. Her outfit suggested that she was working, and traveling outside her neighborhood would not cause suspicion as she passed through the neighborhood checkpoints.

Janet left her apartment, went to her mailbox, and found the car key with a tab showing the license plate and her forged travel papers to present to the Homeland Security checkpoint attendants if she was stopped.

As she left the building, Janet was met with large gray blobs of snow. She remembered when snow used to fall in delicate flakes. Now, the flakes collected the sludge in the air. She walked to the garage and found the car. When she opened the door, she saw a can of motor oil and a note. "You might need to put more oil in, as this is a burner." She cautiously pulled out onto the recently plowed street.

Janet remembered Antoine's words when he gave her April 1 as the day to travel to the reservation: "If it snows, it will melt quickly because the sun is higher in the sky." She hoped he was right.

She was stopped at the last checkpoint. The attendant, a Homeland Security worker, asked to see her travel permit. Janet had trouble getting it out of the glove box. Her hands were shaking, even though Antoine had prepared her for this possibility, giving her a script if she was questioned.

The attendant looked at the photo on the document and stared at Janet. "Why are you traveling?" he asked.

"I'm going to visit a relative in Wisconsin," she said.

"Who is the relative?" he asked.

"Well, it's my grandmother," she said.

"Where does your grandmother live?" he asked.

"She lives on the reservation near Hayward," Janet replied.

"Why does she live on a reservation?" he asked.

"Um, she's enrolled there," Janet said.

"Your travel permit says you're Caucasian," the attendant challenged.

"Yes," said Janet. "I don't have enough Indian blood to qualify as Indian." She tried to hide her trembling from the attendant, who reluctantly stamped the travel permit, indicating that Janet had been checked and approved for travel.

The attendant would record this incident on computer files and send it to the Minneapolis Homeland Security office, while the computers in the eastbound checkpoints would provide a photographic record of her passage through each spot.

After Janet left the last checkpoint, she spent much of her driving time checking the rearview mirror to see if she was being followed. The trembling in her hands subsided. In the weeks before she left, she had practiced in front of a mirror to display a look of calm self-confidence so she would not arouse the suspicion of Homeland Security personnel when she stopped at the checkpoints. She figured she must have passed the scrutiny of the attendant or she would have been arrested when she was being questioned.

Janet maneuvered the snow-covered roads that slowed her progress. The car was producing a black cloud that became a shroud enveloping the car.

The farther she drove, the lighter the air became, gaining translucency and losing its yellow-green-gray tinge. In direct proportion to this change in the air, the emaciated silver light from the sun was getting stronger and brighter, heating the car's interior and creating an illusion of warm weather in spite of the below-freezing temperatures. Even though the air was lighter, the cloud of burning oil interfered with her view of the countryside.

Janet continued to feel ambivalent about the trip she was taking. She believed she was putting herself in danger and that she had probably been under surveillance since she met Antoine at the restaurant in Dinky Town. Even though she pretended she was on an assignment by wearing her press badge, that information could easily be checked. She had traveled outside the areas she was allowed on her personal time. At the same time, the farther away from the city she drove, the less she worried about surveillance while still questioning why she was putting herself in danger.

What am I doing? she thought. This is the craziest thing I've ever done. I don't know why I joined that group. Was it just because I thought I would be able to see Sally? I'm supposed to go Wisconsin, to an Indian reservation, to meet with someone who's apparently going to give me information that will be helpful to the group. I don't know what the group thinks it's going to do with the information I bring them. They think they can overthrow the government. I doubt that, but then again, I wish we could. Maybe we can.

Janet opened the car window a crack, wanting to breathe fresh air. Some of the oil spewed out of her tailpipe, while the rest of it seeped into the car, soaking the car's interior and permeating the fibers in her clothing.

Janet would have to get her coat cleaned when she got back. She wondered if the cleaner would report the oil smell. Everyone had a responsibility to make sure that others followed the laws and the Post-Millennium Adjustments, reporting anything suspicious because of the potential of endangering the way of life enjoyed by all Americans.

The forged documents provided by the group proved ownership of the vehicle. The Homeland Security attendant who had questioned her had not asked her to prove ownership of the car.

While most of the American people living in urban areas believed that their safety was at risk because of terrorist threats from other countries, they didn't realize that their restricted existence was a product of a government that fostered and encouraged paranoia. This, along with the lack of oxygen in the air, gave government more power and control over a compliant and complacent populace.

Those who saw through the subterfuge were isolated and dared not speak of their misgivings to friends and neighbors. It was unusual but not unheard of that small groups of people gathered for the purpose of overcoming the collusion between government and big business. The groups most often consisted of people who remembered, if only vaguely, a time when freedom meant unrestricted travel, some choice as to where to live, and the ability to criticize the government without repercussion. The groups disbanded after they realized there was little they could do to influence or overthrow powerful entities. If they were found out before they disbanded, group members were rounded up for questioning and charged with illegal assembly, plotting to overthrow the government, and affiliation with terrorist organizations. There were public trials, imprisonments, and disappearances.

By the time suspects were charged, arraigned, and tried, they had been questioned for long periods. There were rumors that torture was used to get confessions. Suspects who confessed and named cohorts as coconspirators were led to believe that their cooperation would buy their freedom. This didn't happen. Once taken into custody, no one was released. They might talk about their experience, and the government didn't want the general public to know what went on.

Those who could afford lawyers sought representation. They were given a list with names and phone numbers and called when they were allowed to do so. Those who didn't have the funds were referred to public defenders. By the time suspects had legal representation, there was little attorneys could do to provide adequate defenses.

Janet passed into Wisconsin and saw a Welcome to Wisconsin sign. It had taken her about an hour to get this far. Soon, she found the exit off Highway 94 to 35. She turned north and after a couple of miles saw the gas station where she was to change her clothes and the license plates on her car.

She turned into the parking area. When the owner of the station came out, looked her over, and made note of the car, Janet said, "Hi. I guess I'm in the right place."

The man said, "I don't talk to people who come in here to change clothes and license plates. It's dangerous. Just do what you came to do and leave. We're all better off being anonymous."

"Where is the restroom?" asked Janet.

The man nodded toward the side of the building. Janet walked over to a door that said, "Women," opened the door, found the light switch, and walked in, locking the door behind her. The room had a toilet, sink, and no heat. She shivered and changed quickly from her fashionable city uniform to the utilitarian sweater, pants, boots, and down jacket that had been provided by the group. The clothes seemed masculine to her.

Janet remembered her mother saying that men designed clothing for women that served no useful purpose. She said women's clothing made women helpless and unable to fend for themselves, at which point her father would add, "She means rape."

Janet had paid little attention to the evolution in women's clothing spurred by the Post-Millennium Adjustments, until today. Women's clothing was designed to make a fashion statement as opposed to providing comfort.

Janet came out of the restroom and asked, "Where do I change the license plates?"

"Back behind the trees," the man said, nodding in the direction Janet was to go. She started the car and followed a path behind a copse of trees, then took pliers out of the glove box and changed the plates. She pulled out onto the roadway and continued her trip.

She passed open fields covered with new snow. There were occasional houses with wood smoke wandering out of chimneys. Mailboxes stood at the end of driveways.

Janet had been on the road for about two hours when she noticed that the open fields were giving way to tall pine trees growing close to the narrowing road. Although the air was devoid of the chemicals that hovered over the city, the sky was overcast, and the snow continued to fall.

The roadway looked as if someone had plowed earlier, as the snow on the road was not as deep as it was on the shoulders. The road was slippery in places, and Janet slowed down, remembering the instructions and admonitions about driving on ice and snow in her high school driver's education course. Janet wondered if driver's education was taught in high school anymore.

The scenery captured her attention, making it hard to keep her eyes on the road. New snow weighed down the branches of tall pines. *They look like wealthy women wrapped in ermine coats*, she thought.

When Janet reached an even narrower road, she turned and slowed down to thirty-five miles an hour. She wondered how long it was going to take her to get to her destination. In good weather, the trip was about four hours.

Janet was nearing the reservation. Some of her fear about getting caught had dissipated. If she was stopped, she would give the same story about visiting a grandmother.

Janet drove for a couple of hours and was beginning to think she had missed the store that Antoine had given as a landmark when she saw a small building with a sign that said Hanson's. She pulled into the parking space at the front of the store, got out, and went inside. A gray-haired woman was putting packages wrapped in white paper in a chest freezer. The freezer was covered with signs that said, "Fresh game and fish."

"Hi," said Janet.

The woman stood up and turned to look at Janet.

"I'm looking for Antoine LaRiviere's house," said Janet.

"Oh, well, you go down about a mile and turn left. Then you'll see a big sign by the side of the road that tells you you're entering the reservation. You'll be on a gravel road, but I don't think you can tell that today. Then you drive five more miles and cross the bridge and find the first house on the right. You can't see the house from the road, but you'll see the path that goes up to the house."

"Thanks," said Janet.

"Sure," said the woman. "Drive slow. There's a lot of snow out there for this time of year."

Janet left the store, got in the car, and drove, keeping track of her progress on the odometer. *I'm almost there*, she thought. *So far, so good.*

CHAPTER 12
April 1, 2040

Antoine went to the Dinky Town Café for his breakfast and for a meeting with Tiffany, one of the group members. Shortly after, Tiffany came into the café and slid into the opposite seat in the booth.

"Jake stopped by the garage. The car's gone, so Janet must have left," she said.

"I hope she makes it okay," said Antoine. "The weather isn't the best."

"How long is the snow going to last this time of year?" asked Tiffany.

"I don't think it's going to be a problem on her way home," said Antoine. "It'll probably stop by tomorrow, and it'll all melt by the time she leaves."

"I heard that Janet's not too enthusiastic about her assignment," said Tiffany.

"I think she's scared she'll get caught," said Antoine.

"Well, all she's supposed to do is gather some information about history. The way things were before 2020," said Tiffany. "I suppose Homeland Security could put her on a higher security level. Then, when she doesn't do anything else that's suspicious, they'll probably forget about her."

"Is that the way it usually works?" asked Antoine.

"I'm not sure. We haven't heard about any prosecutions of traitors lately. So who knows what they do?"

"You have to live with a lot of restrictions. Doesn't it bother you?" asked Antoine.

"Sure, that's why I joined the group—the no-name group that isn't sure what it's going to do," said Tiffany. "But, then again, I don't know any different. It's been this way most of my life."

"I'm just glad I don't have to live here. I hope my job is about over so I can go home," said Antoine.

"What's your job?" asked Tiffany.

"I'm the coordinator for Janet, and I'm supposed to make sure everyone in the group is safe," said Antoine.

"Oh. So what do you do if we're not safe?" asked Tiffany.

"I help you escape," said Antoine.

"That sounds like it could be a big job. Do you have a plan?" asked Tiffany.

"Sort of. It's too early to tell what's going to happen next. I have a contact who brings me information about the comings and goings of Homeland Security," said Antoine.

"So, right now, you're not very specific. Well, I've done what I was supposed to do today, so I'm going home," said Tiffany, sliding out of the booth. "See you later."

Antoine thought about his vision and knew he was to remain loyal to it. He knew that he would know when he had completed what he was supposed to complete. He realized that his vision was one in which he would learn patience. He was impatient at the moment. After eating his meal, he left the café and went back to his dorm room. He spent the weekend studying for his classes, unaware of the cameras that had been installed in the room during his absence.

CHAPTER 13
April 1, 2040

The trees closed behind her as Janet passed the sign announcing entrance to the reservation. Animals stood just barely in the trees, watching her. She could see the light reflecting in their eyes but wasn't sure what kind they were.

Janet saw a space cut into the edge of the road and pulled in. Her 150-mile trip had taken five hours. She got out of the car and pulled the suitcase out of the trunk.

Janet followed a path that led away from the road. The cold air wrapped around her body like a suit of armor, making it hard for her to move. She walked under the canopy created by the snow-covered tree branches and soon saw a two-story log house with smoke rising out of a stone chimney. Janet liked the smoke smell but had never smelled burning wood. It was colder here than it was in the city, and the cold took precedence over the fear as to what she would find when she entered the house. Janet hurried, anticipating the warmth promised by the chimney smoke.

A barking dog crawled out from under a porch banked with snow. The space underneath the porch provided shelter, and the snow provided the dog and her family with insulation from the cold. The dog was large with long, coarse, black, brown, white, and tan fur. She looked like the pictures of wolves Janet had seen on the televised nature shows that told viewers that nature was alive and well outside of the polluted cities. The dog stood alongside the porch barking, announcing Janet's arrival while not interfering with her approach.

Janet walked up onto the porch and extended her hand to knock on the door, which opened before she could knock. A small nut-brown woman with deep creases that traveled in unbroken circles around her face held the door for Janet to enter. He long white hair was pulled into one braid down the middle of her back. The woman looked older than anyone Janet knew. Her lined face suggested she was way past the mandatory age for nursing home admission. She had a hooked nose, wide mouth, and black eyes.

"Hello, I'm Sonia Black Bear. You must be Janet. I'm Antoine's grandmother. Just leave your suitcase, your boots, and your jacket out here," said Sonia, pointing to the entryway with her chin and lips.

As she went into the large kitchen, Janet saw a dark-skinned man, not much bigger than Sonia, with traces of gray in his long black hair, which was pulled back and held with a narrow piece of cloth. He was sitting at a rough wooden table, ignoring Janet's presence, his hands wrapped around a cup with steam rising from it.

Janet looked around the room. There was a large, black, rectangular object that seemed to be generating the heat in the room. Next to it was a pile of chopped wood. There was no other stove and no refrigerator. Janet looked up and saw cupboards. There were no light fixtures on the ceiling or anyplace else. The table where the man sat was surrounded by unmatched wooden chairs. The room's décor spoke to practicality rather than design.

Sonia pointed with her chin and lips at the man sitting at the table. "This is my son, Joe La Pointe. He's Antoine's uncle."

Joe nodded without looking at Janet. His eyes were focused on the tabletop. He and Sonia had been arguing shortly before Janet arrived. "That old woman could get us all into trouble," Joe had said to Sonia, lifting his head and pointing with his chin and his lips toward the sleeping figure who sat wrapped in an afghan and shawl in a rocking chair in the next room.

"I don't see why, after all these years, any white person would come here to listen to that old woman's stories," said Joe.

"We have been lucky to have Old Woman among us since you were a small child. You have listened to her stories. I don't know why she wouldn't share them with someone else. Your nephew sent this young woman," said

Sonia. "He is in the city because of his vision. This young woman must be part of his vision."

Joe saw the look on Sonia's face and had decided to quit the argument. He was used to losing arguments with her, and he had been taught to respect his elders. He often wondered if anyone would respect him when he was an elder.

Joe saw Janet's presence as an intrusion, and he knew enough about the past intrusion of whites into his community to be resentful and frightened. He didn't know about much of anything good coming from white people.

Joe couldn't remember a time when Old Woman hadn't been in his life. She joined the family when he was a child, had helped his mother raise him, and was a member of his family and, therefore, not white.

Joe knew that Old Woman's time was short, and he did not want to share her with an outsider. He had trouble imagining what the rest of his life would be like without her. Joe liked the sameness of the days that had been without surprise for a long time. Then his nephew left, and now a stranger had entered their house.

He watched as Janet removed her outer clothing. Cold air tumbled out from the layers and settled on the kitchen floor, displacing the air warmed by the woodstove. As Sonia nodded in Old Woman's direction, Janet's eyes followed. Joe was helpless to stop the intrusion, but he didn't have to make her feel welcome. He would leave that task to the women.

Old Woman stirred, aroused not so much by the sound of voices or the opening and closing of the door as she was by the cold air that had come in and followed a route along the floor to her, coiling around her ankles like a snake. The cold air had traveled a long route south from Canada, across the expanse of water known as Lake Superior, and settled into the community where Old Woman lived, lurking outside until an opened door allowed its entrance.

Old Woman slowly opened her eyes and began to accustom herself to her surroundings. The little black dog sleeping in Old Woman's lap was disturbed by Old Woman's movements. The dog moved around to find a comfortable spot. She yawned, snorted, and buried her nose in the afghan again, showing no interest in the visitor.

Old Woman took her time coming around, as she had been dreaming about spirits, who were coming to her frequently, preparing her for her journey to the Spirit World. With each dream, she was reluctant to come back and had trouble remembering where she was when she left the dreams.

Old Woman knew that she was experiencing something often defined as senility. From all her years in this community, she had learned that there was another way to define this change in one's faculties. The spirits were coming to help her move beyond this world and into the next. Old Woman was starting to see her passing as a gradual, adventurous transition.

She was ready to go. She missed all of the friends she had left behind when she came here to live. She knew they were in the Spirit World because no one who stayed in the community she left so long ago was allowed to get old. They perished with the birth of the Post-Millennium Adjustments that ordered people fifty five and older into nursing homes.

Old Woman had heard stories about the things that happened in elder-living centers. She knew that many of those who refused to go were taken forcibly or they committed suicide. Once in a while, she would hear bits and pieces from the reservations in northern Minnesota about people who crossed over the border into Canada by way of the Boundary Waters, swimming, hiking, camping, and boating their way through the maze of islands and the connected bodies of water.

The only people who contacted her from across the border were her children and grandchildren who had been given political asylum because they were her relatives. Because she was not a native person and was old, she would have been arrested had she left this community. Her family was viewed with suspicion because they were her family. They came to visit from time to time, guided by people who knew how to avoid border patrols.

Sometimes Old Woman saw old friends in her dreams, and she was comforted knowing they were in the Spirit World and away from the terror that seemed to permeate the lives of all who lived in the greatest country in the world. She welcomed her dreams, anxious to see those who would greet her when she passed on.

Today had been a good day to dream, and she was reluctant to join the present. Old Woman stretched, straightening out the kinks in her back, thinking back on her life and the sum total of mistakes and adventures. It had gotten harder to separate adventures from mistakes; she was here because of her life, and she had resolved most of her regrets over time.

Today Old Woman knew that she was very old and that her time here was short. Time kept passing, sometimes seeming to move at different paces, depending on the day.

Old Woman believed that youth held promise, and promise was never a sure thing. Promise glided along a path, creating choices that wove together into a tapestry holding opportunity and adventure, both of which were games of chance with unknown outcomes.

Lately, the spirits in her dreams did not fade as she awakened. Even though she couldn't see them as she saw them in her dreams, she sensed their presence. Once in a while, she heard one of them giggling. The others seemed to be more serious, sending her messages that told her she had something important to do before she passed. Whatever she was to do, it would represent everything she had experienced in her life.

When Old Woman first faced the realization that the spirits were here to accompany her to the end of this life, she was frightened and used denial to deal with her discomfort, pretending that the visits from the spirits were the delusions of senility. She would rather be senile than face the prospect of her death. She thought she had slipped, fallen, and entered into a world occupied by crazy people. Shortly after, she started to realize that people who probably denied the existence of spirits defined the presence of spirits as craziness and senility.

As she settled into the acceptance of a new reality, each dream had been clearer than the one before. The dream from which she was awakening showed her friends and family members who had passed before. Those she had known during her lifetime looked as they had in earlier years when they were together, young, self-assured in the knowledge that they held the answers for a better world.

They were in a room the Old Woman recognized. Ah! That's the parlor in that old house—the women's shelter! We worked so hard fixing that place up! Let's see, I think that opened toward the end of the 1970s. Yes, that's when the women's movement started pushing the Equal Rights Amendment. There sure was a lot of conflict over that. That's about the time I was asked if I wanted my daughter to die in a war. I said I didn't want either of my children to die in one, she thought.

Old Woman looked around the room. Even though the room was familiar, she didn't recognize everyone. Nothing stayed the same for very long—the figures flowing, changing color, shape, and clothing, becoming other people, replacing the originals in the vision, floating from one scene to the next, a foglike curtain shifting with each scene.

As the scenes changed, she realized that the people in them changed as well, going back further into history. She thought that they must be ancestors that lived long before her, replacing the friends and relatives she had seen when the dream opened.

She thought that some of the gray figures in her dream were Quakers who had been part of the Underground Railroad prior to the Civil War. Old Woman had old family papers that told their stories.

She saw her grandparents. Her grandmother was talking to some people who spoke in a lilting, musical language that Old Woman recognized as Norwegian, the language of her great-grandparents who came to America because of the promise of land and education. Old Woman realized that some of these must be the ancestors whose families stayed in Norway and fought in the Norwegian Resistance during World War II.

She saw her grandfather, looking peaceful. She didn't remember him that way. He always seemed to be in turmoil over something—the wasting of natural resources, violations of human rights. Old Woman admired his decision to starve himself when his life no longer had dignity. She missed him.

Old Woman saw her mother and heard her mother's laughter in response to something said by another woman who was wearing clothing from the 1600s. The Old Woman saw people who had been strong, principled, and outspoken. Even though she couldn't identify most of them, she could tell by their clothing that their lives had covered many centuries, and she knew that many had suffered because of their beliefs.

The room in the dream got bigger as it continued to fill with people. She saw women from her life sitting together on an old battered couch that represented all of the furniture found in the women's programs of the 1970s and 1980s. The women were backlit by a sun-filled window, the light setting them apart from the rest of the spirits in the room.

Beyond the window were mountains, and the scene changed, moving as if it was filmed from a train traveling through. When the scene shifted, the camera entered a small compartment in the train where Old Woman could see her friend enjoying the view out of the train's window. She died because doctors had refused to listen to her complaints. She was just a woman.

The camera returned to the scene in front of the window, where Old Woman saw Mary, a woman she had known for thirty years. When the changes came about, Old Woman had not heard from Mary anymore and assumed the worst. Mary was a sister with whom she had shared pain, happiness, and whimsy. Even though Mary was in the room, she was sitting in a canoe in a river, laughing and giggling with Eleanor, who wore long, dangling earrings and fluffy, gypsylike clothing, her white-blond hair piled on top of her head like whipped cream on top of an ice-cream sundae. She talked in that breathy voice about the needs of rural women— her favorite subject.

Old Woman saw another friend, Pat, talking to someone she didn't recognize—a woman with tattoos and a Harley T-shirt holding two babies in her lap. Andrea, the grant writer, was talking with Ruth, who was dressed in business clothes. Ruth was always trying to let everyone around her know that she was a professional.

Jean and Joanne were talking to someone about lesbian women. They needed to let everyone know that lesbians were women too.

Old Woman missed them all. As she separated herself from the dream, Old Woman realized that they had all gathered on her behalf. That was when she realized this room full of radicals was preparing to greet her when she died. She wondered if this was called a postmortem party.

"I just hope it's not like a Tupperware party." She sighed.

Having lived half her life in a culture where dreams were a prediction of things to come, Old Woman didn't try to find a psychological meaning to the dream. She accepted the fact that she would die soon and pass on to the Spirit World. When she found herself wanting to join the spirits in her dream, they began to fade, leaving their message clearly in her mind. She was to do something important before she died. When she did whatever it was she was supposed to do, she would gain wisdom and acceptance about the meaning of her life.

As she left the dream, Old Woman began to hear and feel what was going on around her. She tried to concentrate on the messages in the dream. She hoped that the wisdom and acceptance she was about to gain didn't come on the heels of pain, as it often had. She was of the opinion that while pain had once been a teacher, she preferred to learn in other ways now. She had been waiting for several months to find out what was left in her life besides the repetition of each day. Even though she knew she was still contributing to the household, she felt as if her contributions diminished in importance with each day as the frailty in her body increased.

Old Woman had learned that it would do no good to go looking for signs that would predict her short future and impending death. Those things would come to her, she would complete the tasks given to her, and when her life was complete, she would join all of the people she had known and loved in her life who had passed before her. The visit from the spirits made her aware of the fact that she would also meet people she had never known in her life, spirits of her ancestors whose experiences existed in the blood that flowed through her veins.

While waiting for the tasks to come to her, the Old Woman continued to think and to learn. She became aware that her beliefs about the path on which she had traveled had been narrow and unimaginative. While sitting and sleeping in that rocking chair, she came to know that her path was a small part of a longer road that started with the beginning of time, similar to a James Michener novel. Not only was she merely a bit player in the longest-running morality play in history, she was also just one runner in the ultimate relay race. The awareness had been easy for Old Woman because living here had helped her cleanse most of the self-importance she had learned in her culture. Humbling experiences took nothing away; they just added to her sense of irony and gave her a broader view of her life and her connections with others.

Her tangential thoughts began rounding themselves up, wrapping Old Woman in a cloth of consciousness in which she realized that her last task was to pass down the history she had taught to her adopted family to a woman from the outside world. As her awareness of the presence increased, she felt the cold around her ankles and the presence of a stranger in the house. The cold was familiar, but the stranger frightened her, as there had been few strangers here over the years. When they did come, she was afraid that they were government agents who had come to arrest her because she wasn't supposed to be here. She was old, and she was no longer useful according to the standards established by the Post-Millennium Adjustments.

Sonia and Janet turned as they heard Old Woman stirring in her chair. She was mumbling, half in and half out of sleep. She paused from time to time, as if she was carrying on a conversation with someone. Old Woman lifted her head and blinked in the sunlight.

Even though she felt safe here with her adopted family, Old Woman had struggled with her aging for a long time. She tried to pretend that the infirmities that often went along with aging had skipped over her. She had little ways of faking things when she couldn't remember, and Sonia, Joe, and the children went along with her to respect her dignity. They understood her fear, as there were many family stories about Native interactions with white men's culture, and everyone in the community lived with the historical and present consequences of those interactions.

As she shifted in her chair, trying to find ways of warming her feet and ankles, Old Woman began putting together the events that had awakened her. The stranger who was in the house brought in the cold air when she opened the door, and the shifting of the dog in her lap was also a response to the cold air. Old Woman turned her head and watched as the stranger removed her heavy clothing. The dog, disturbed again by Old Woman's movements, turned, glared at her, jumped down, went into the kitchen, and asked to go outside.

Another blast of cold air came in when the dog was let out. This was confusing to Old Woman because the day before, the temperature was in the sixties, and all the snow had melted. The position of the sun above the trees in the southwest told her it was early afternoon, while the frosty edges on the windows told her the temperature was down around freezing.

Old Woman's attention turned back to the kitchen, where Sonia was speaking to the stranger in a whisper. "I won't wake her. She isn't very cooperative when someone wakes her up. You will be here for a week, so there is time for you to talk to her. There are many things you can learn here, and the Elders Council has decided that you are to learn about our culture. I am to facilitate your experiences here."

While Old Woman's disorientation was the result of aging, Janet's disorientation came from entering a world about which she knew nothing. Everything about this trip—the drive, the unfamiliar surroundings, and the people—disoriented her. "I thought you said she had agreed to the interview. I drove a long way and at considerable risk to meet with her. I expected her to be ready."

"I also told you she probably wouldn't remember that she had agreed to the interview," said Sonia. "What she decides to share with you and when is up to her."

Old Woman interrupted. "Sonia, why are you whispering? Who is that in the kitchen?"

Sonia approached Old Woman. "This is Janet Ryan, the reporter you agreed to meet with."

Awake now, Old Woman said, "What did I agree to meet with her about?"

Sonia stepped aside, allowing Janet to come into the room and stand next to Old Woman. Janet decided she would stand until she was asked to sit, thinking that standing would show respect. She had been taught that youth, not age, was to be celebrated, and she was impatient with the people around her. They were all old, and she didn't know what she was supposed to do around old people.

Janet had never seen people over the age of sixty, and her curiosity made it difficult to keep from staring at Old Woman, taking in all of the unfamiliar details.

The skin on Old Woman's face hung loosely over her bones, and the skin on her hands was the thickness of onionskin and covered joints misshapen by age and arthritis. Finger bones jutted at odd positions. She had a full head of white, curly hair and was dressed in a loose-fitting leather dress with beaded flowers on the shoulders and neckline. Fringes on the bottom of the dress brushed against beaded moccasins. When Old Woman had arisen that morning, she knew that someone was coming to visit her and wore her best clothes.

Janet thought Old Woman stopped just short of pictures she had seen of Egyptian mummies at the virtual reality museum. Just as she was beginning to think that her trip had been a waste of time, something told her to wait and pay attention to the manners and rituals of the people in this house. She didn't understand much of what she had seen here so far, but she did know that she should wait to be invited before she made any moves. Janet silently thanked her parents for teaching her about manners.

When Sonia stepped aside, Janet saw this as an invitation to address Old Woman directly. As Janet approached, Old Woman began to look her over, obvious in her curiosity. Her status as the oldest person in this household gave her permission to do as she pleased, regardless of the discomfort of others.

Old Woman thought Janet could pass. She tensed, waiting for Janet to announce that her great-great-ever-so-great-grandmother had been an Indian princess. *Anything short of that*, thought Old Woman, *and she can stay.*

Old Woman looked over Janet's clothing, pleased that this stranger had dressed sensibly.

Janet approached Old Woman and addressed her in a tone usually reserved for small children. "Rachel, I am a reporter for the *Minneapolis Herald*. I have been asked to interview you for an underground newspaper published by a group of people who want to learn about our history and find out how our country has evolved. We don't believe that our country is a democracy anymore. We want to figure out how to get back there. I am told you know a lot about history. You are one of the very few people left who remember the years before the millennium. You are said to be a feminist."

Old Woman grabbed the arms of the rocker and struggled to stand. The dog, who had come back in and resumed her place in Old Woman's lap, fell to the floor. Regaining her balance, the dog snorted and glared at Old Woman.

Old Woman turned to Sonia. "Why did you let this woman come here? She could get us all in trouble!"

Joe looked in from the kitchen, nodding his head.

As Janet tried to explain herself, Sonia interrupted. "Old Woman, this young woman is from an underground newspaper that is circulated to students at the University of Minnesota. She is here because the group she belongs to is trying to create a movement. Their history books are censored. They have no one to ask except you."

Old Woman grinned. The smile bunched up her wrinkles, making her look younger. She giggled, relaxed, and responded to her audience. "I agreed to talk to her? You must have waited a long time to catch me in a good mood so I would say yes to this."

Sonia smiled. "I asked you last week after I spoke to the Elders Council about it. The council said that she needs to learn some things about our culture. The council says that anyone who wants to make changes in the white man's culture needs to learn about our culture so they can understand that there are other ways to live. She's here for a week," said Sonia as she turned and looked at Joe, reminding him that the decision to allow entrance onto the reservation hadn't been one made only by the women in the house.

"Well, I suppose she can come in," Old Woman said. She turned to Janet. "I have some rules for this meeting. You may address me as Old Woman. It'is my name now and it's a sign of respect. You will not talk to me as if I have trouble understanding what you are saying. You will talk to me in a normal tone and at normal volume. My hearing is good. I don't remember the present as well as I do the past, but my changes in memory do not mean I lack the ability to understand.

"I think for this first meeting, we should get to know each other. Please sit over there," Old Woman said, nodding toward a couch that was positioned to separate the living room from the dining area.

Janet looked over the large room, taking in details. The dining area had a large wooden table and chairs that did not match. Old gouges marred the bare, unfinished wood of the table. The chairs looked newer than the table but wobbled and creaked when anyone sat on them, telling the sitter to move little and get up carefully.

Janet did not see a television, a computer, or any electric appliances. She didn't hear the hum of the electricity she took for granted.

Janet had no familiarity with this kind of quiet. *I wonder what they do at night. They must be very poor*, she thought. She was quickly losing any of the sense of self she had when she arrived and didn't know what to think when Old Woman scolded her.

Janet lowered herself onto the couch indicated by Old Woman. It sagged, bringing her close to the floor, her knees higher than her waist. She looked expectantly at the couch in front of the window, wishing she could change places.

"I don't want you to sit there," said Old Woman, responding to Janet's look. "It will block my view of the lake. If that couch is uncomfortable, it may help you realize that the people in this house have been living with discomfort created by white men for over five hundred years. Who are you? Why are you here?"

Janet shifted forward, trying to find a position a little more comfortable than her current one. "My name is Janet Ryan. I would like to get some information from you regarding recent history."

"You just got here. How long will you be staying?" asked Old Woman.

"I'll be going home next Saturday," said Janet.

"Have all the history books been rewritten?" asked Old Woman.

"We're not sure," said Janet. "All written material is reviewed and edited by Homeland Security."

"Who is the we you're talking about?" asked Old Woman.

"Well, I belong to this group that's looking for the truth about how we got to where we are," said Janet.

"And where is that?" asked Old Woman.

"We live in a world where everything is controlled. We can't travel. The air is toxic. And we have to live in assigned neighborhoods. Anyone fifty-five and over has to retire and live in senior housing. From there, people are sent to nursing homes when they need more medical care. We've heard that people in nursing homes have to participate in experiments to find cures for aging. We don't have any fresh food anymore. Everything is processed and packaged," said Janet.

"Is this the group in which Antoine is involved?" asked Old Woman.

"Yes. He's my contact, and he made the arrangements for me to come here," said Janet.

"When I give you the information you want and you go back to your home, what happens to the information?" asked Old Woman.

"Well, I'm supposed to leave it with the car in the garage," said Janet.

"What happens next?" asked Old Woman.

"Someone will come and pick up the recording, which will be written and distributed among group members, I think," said Janet.

"Your plan doesn't sound like much of a plan to me," said Old Woman. "It sounds like Homeland Security runs things and people are always under suspicion of something. So what can you do to create change?" The question was more of a challenge than a question.

"I don't know," said Janet.

"I wonder if all of this is too much for your group. Maybe you should just leave and go someplace safe," said Old Woman.

"But you were an activist. You demonstrated, and you managed to get legislation passed," said Janet.

"Yes, and I left when I didn't like where things were headed. I had enemies. If I had stayed where I was, I would have died, either because of my enemies or because of the way things are now in your world. I am too old to live in your world. When the elders are killed off, wisdom is lost," said Old Woman.

Just then, the kitchen door opened, and two children entered. The children stopped in the kitchen when they saw Janet.

"Sierra, Cody, I want you to meet our guest," said Sonia, leading the children toward Janet.

She stood and said, "My name is Janet Ryan."

"Janet will be staying with us for the week. She'll be sleeping in your room, Sierra," said Sonia.

"Oh, I don't want to inconvenience anyone," said Janet.

"It isn't an inconvenience," said Sonia. "We share what we have. You are our guest. You can pick up your suitcase from the entryway, and Sierra will take you up to her room. You can continue your meeting with Old Woman tomorrow," said Sonia.

Janet followed Sierra up a stairway and into a room that sat directly under a peaked roof with exposed roughhewn beams. A quilt decorated with needlework designs of multicolored flowers connected by green vines covered a bed that sat in the middle of the room. A chair and table covered with beads, needles, and thread sat near the bed. A cluster of beads that took the shape of flowers sat in the middle of the table. Braided rugs covered a floor of wide wooden planks. The walls were the wooden logs that made up the outside of the house.

"Oh, that quilt is beautiful," said Janet.

"Thanks," said Sierra. "I made the quilt with my grandmother's help. Do you want it?"

"Oh, no. It looks like you put a lot of work into it," said Janet.

"Yes, I did. The Old Ways tell us that when someone compliments us on something we have, we are supposed to give it to the person paying the compliment," said Sierra.

"I didn't know that. I really can't take that beautiful quilt, but I think it will keep me nice and warm tonight. Where will you sleep tonight?" asked Janet.

"I'm going to go my auntie Corrine's house after supper. I'll be back for breakfast," said Sierra.

"Thanks for giving me your room," said Janet.

"Okay. I'm going downstairs now," said Sierra.

I wonder where the bathroom is, thought Janet after Sierra left. *I guess I'll have to find out.* She went downstairs and into the kitchen, where she found Sonia adding wood to the fire in the stove.

"Where is your bathroom?" asked Janet.

Sonia pointed with her chin to an area on the far side of the kitchen. "It's over there."

Janet followed Sonia's directions and saw another room with the door slightly ajar. Janet walked into the bathroom and found a scarred wood vanity holding a porcelain sink. A bar of rough-looking soap sat in a small dish. There was a bathtub and shower. On the other side of a short wall was a toilet.

It started to sink in. This was a house with no electricity and no central heating, but somehow they had a sewer system and running water.

When she returned to the kitchen, Janet asked, "How do you manage to have running water and a sewer system?"

"This area has many artesian springs, and we have windmills that pump the water into towers," said Sonia. The water is cold, so we heat pots of water on the stove to pour into the tub and to heat water for washing dishes on the stove. The drainage system is left over from the days that we were implementing what were thought to be modern conveniences."

"I thought the power from windmills could be used for electricity," said Janet.

"For a long time, our elders have believed that electricity is evil. We haven't seen that electricity provides anything that we absolutely need," said Sonia.

Just as Janet was about to ask why electricity wasn't vital to the community, Sonia said, "We're going to start fixing supper. You can help." She led Janet to a table in the middle of the kitchen and picked up a roundish brown object out of a small pile of similar-looking objects. "These are potatoes. I don't suppose that you've seen them raw like this. This is a peeler. You peel the skins off the potatoes. Then you rinse them off in that pan of water in the sink. Cut them in fours and put them in the pot of water that's warming up on the stove. When you finish with the potatoes, you can help with something else."

As Janet was peeling the potatoes, Old Woman walked into the room and over to the cupboards in the kitchen. She gathered plates, glasses, and flatware, arranging them on the two dining tables.

Janet didn't know Old Woman could walk. She stared at Old Woman as if a miracle had taken place.

Old Woman looked at Janet. "Who are you?" she asked.

Confused, Janet looked around and shook her head.

Sonia addressed Old Woman. "Janet came earlier today. She is staying with us for a few days. She's Antoine's friend from the city."

Janet began peeling and cutting the potatoes. She nicked her fingers several times, drawing blood, thinking that packaged food was easier. When she finished with the potatoes, Sonia took them and placed them in a pot of water and put them on the stove. Janet found a corner in the kitchen where she could stay out of the way of Sonia and Old Woman, who was mixing and kneading dough and placing it in a pan of cooking oil on the stove. After a few minutes of cooking, she would turn the flat, round piece of dough over to cook on the other side. Old Woman saw Janet watching her and said, "This is probably the unhealthiest food we eat here. It's part of the history of this and many other native communities. Native people were having trouble feeding themselves when they were refused their treaty rights to hunt and fish when and where they pleased. They started getting government commodities, and flour and lard were among those. They made bread dough and cooked it in lard. It's called fry bread. Because fry bread helped out during those hard times, it became traditional. So we have it with most meals."

Sonia was browning meat. Glass jars with vegetables sat on a counter near the stove. "This is venison—deer meat. I'll be heating vegetables that we canned last summer," said Sonia.

The rich aroma of the food whetted Janet's appetite. She hadn't eaten a meal since she left the city, and the prepackaged food she ate had little aroma.

When the meal was ready, Sonia said, "Janet, you can sit over here," motioning with her chin toward the large, round oak table. "When we have extra people for meals, adults sit in the dining area, and our children eat in the kitchen."

Everyone gathered around the table and passed serving bowls and plates. Old Woman pointed out a bowl filled with something Janet hadn't seen before. "That's wild rice in that bowl over there. It tastes really good when you put gravy over it."

When everyone finished eating, each took their plates and tableware to the counter beside the sink. Sonia put a kettle on the stove to heat water to wash the dishes, while Old Woman scraped food scraps into some bowls. One she kept in the kitchen for her little dog. The other she put out on the steps for the outside dog and her pups.

When the water was hot, it was poured into the sink, where cold water from the tap was added. Old Woman assumed her position as dishwasher and looked at Janet. "You can dry the dishes, and Sierra will put them away. Did you just come or have you been here all day?"

Janet opened her mouth to respond but couldn't think of what to say. She turned to Sonia, who said, "Old Woman, this is the woman that Antoine sent here to talk to you."

Old Woman looked at Sonia and nodded in Janet's direction. "Did I talk to her?"

Sonia smiled and said, "You met after your nap today. She'll be here for a week and will be talking to you some more. She is going to learn about some of our ways."

The sun was still above the horizon while the corners of the house were getting dark when the women finished washing the dishes. A lamp fueled with bear grease sat on the oak dining table, lighting the table's surface. Sierra was doing beadwork with Sonia. Cody sat near Old Woman, listening as she read aloud from one of her books. Old Woman leaned sideways to catch the light from the lamp on the table, looking over the rims of her reading glasses at Janet, pointing with her chin at another book sitting nearby. Its paper cover was faded, making the title unreadable. Janet reached for the book and opened it. The title page said *Night Flying Woman*. The book was a series of stories about Indian life. Janet settled in, reading, unaware of her surroundings until the others in the house interrupted her concentration. She looked up and saw that the sun had set, and darkness covered the house.

Sierra put away her bead work, put on her coat, and bid the others good night as she left to go to her aunt's house.

"We go to bed when it gets dark," said Sonia.

"This early?" asked Janet.

"It's dark. We don't need to stay up later. If we keep the lamps going too long, it wastes the fuel in them," said Sonia.

Janet climbed the stairs, undressed, and lay down on the bed. The mattress was thin, and the springs sagged. She wondered if Sierra hadn't gotten the better end of the deal.

Janet lay in the strange bed in the strange house without electricity. She was here, and she would spend her time breathing fresh air and meeting people who were different from her. She went to sleep and was awakened by a dream in which she saw Sally and Jeff in a canoe filled with backpacks and duffels. They were paddling quickly as they headed out into a big lake, so big that Janet couldn't see land on the other side. Throughout the night, the dream came and faded, leaving only the horizon where the lake met the sky. Each time the dream began, Janet saw Sally and Jeff farther out into the lake, until they became small dots and then vanished.

CHAPTER 14
Sunday, April 2

Janet was awakened by the aroma of food cooking and voices coming from below. She dressed and went down to the kitchen to find out what she could do to help.

Sierra was helping Old Woman, who was standing in front of a cast-iron griddle with a spatula in her hand, cooking pancakes. "Sierra, did you get an extra plate? Don't forget we have a guest."

Sierra nodded. The plates were sitting on the two tables, waiting to be filled with food. Sierra was prodding bacon frying in a large cast-iron pan.

"When you check that bacon, make sure you don't get too close. It might spatter and burn you. I think that bacon is done. Take it out, one strip at a time, and put two strips on each plate. When you get to your grandfather's plate, put on two extra strips." Old Woman leaned over toward Sierra. "If you don't give him extra, he will start complaining that he works harder than anyone else in this house. Then your great-grandmother will start arguing with him. Sometimes all it takes to prevent an argument is two strips of bacon. Remember that, and you can have a peaceful life." Old Woman winked at Sierra, who grinned.

Just then, Old Woman noticed Janet standing in the doorway. "Are you looking for something to do? Come on in. You can pour tea and milk. Don't worry where you set it; everyone can help themselves. You can also get the butter and the syrup off the porch. I'll bet you haven't tasted homemade maple syrup, have you? It's out there in a jar."

As she headed for the porch, Joe and Cody came in carrying armloads of wood. Janet nodded and said hello to Joe, who didn't respond.

"Old Woman," he said. "Have you got our breakfast ready? I hope you remembered that I need extra bacon."

"It's easy to remember that," Old Woman said. "I know that if I forget, I will have to listen to you complain and argue with your mother. I like a peaceful breakfast."

"You mean all I have to do to get you to remember extra bacon is to complain about something?" Joe teased back.

"No, that probably won't work. I won't be able to remember everything you complain about. I just remember those things I can do something about." Old Woman put a plate stacked high with pancakes on the table. She turned and said to Sierra, "Go tell everyone that breakfast is ready. If they aren't out here in five minutes, I'll feed it to the dogs."

The family came into the kitchen, sat down, and ate without talking, passing syrups, jams, and the platter of pancakes around.

After the breakfast cleanup, Sonia sat down with Janet in the kitchen.

"When will I be able to talk to Old Woman?" asked Janet.

"Later," said Sonia. "She has her time for herself in the morning. She says that she wants you to see her library."

"Does she have old books?" asked Janet.

"Old Woman loves to read. She has saved books from before the millennium," said Sonia. "Come, I'll show you."

Janet followed Sonia through the hall into a small room filled to capacity with a narrow bed, a small bureau, and a rocking chair. Behind it hung a rectangular, faded piece of striped cloth, edged with fringes. The bare wood of the floor was covered with a variety of hand-braided rugs. On the wall opposite the rocking chair were shelves filled with books.

Janet gasped when she saw the worn, faded covers on the books. "Those must have been written before the PMAs!"

Well, thought Sonia. *At least she knows the books are important.* "You're welcome to look over and read any of these books. You are not to take them with you when you leave."

"Oh, I wouldn't dare take any books with me. I might get caught. Then I would be in trouble," said Janet.

I wonder what she would do if she wasn't worried about getting caught, thought Sonia as she left the room.

Janet lost her sense of time and place as she read. She was transported outside and found herself sitting under a tree near a river. The cold water rushed impatiently to a confluence where it would merge with a larger river. The journey continued down to another river, where it would join with the waters that came together from many other rivers, all of which poured their contents into the Mississippi, following along the ancient riverbed to the Gulf of Mexico, where it all would recycle and join all of the streams and the currents of the world's oceans.

The water, seeming to anticipate its fate, bubbled and gurgled, dancing beneath the sun's rays, sounding like the steel drums of the Caribbean. The noise and the reflection of the sun's rays against the water brought the animals to the banks of the river to dance, celebrating the new season that followed the long winter.

Everything is connected, thought Janet.

She started a book titled *I Heard the Owl Call My Name*. As she began reading, Janet heard someone giggling over her shoulder. She turned to look and saw no one. A puff of warm air surrounded her for an instant. She stopped reading. The sensations she experienced seemed to be part of the book. She had read about half the book when the voices she heard from the kitchen brought her back from the riverbank.

Janet put the book down on a table, marking her place with the faded book jacket.

Janet walked into the kitchen to find Sonia sitting at the table with Joe. He nodded in her direction, stood, and said, "C'mon, Cody. Let's see what's going on outside."

"He acts like he doesn't want me here," said Janet.

"He doesn't," said Sonia.

"I didn't come here because I wanted to. The group sent me," said Janet.

"You didn't have to come," said Sonia. "We are cooperating because my grandson had a dream. We don't have to like this, but we have to respect his dream."

"I don't understand why you place such importance on dreams. I have dreams all the time. They are just leftover thoughts from what I do during the day," said Janet.

"We have been living by our dreams ever since we can remember. In spite of all that white people tried to do to destroy us, we're still here. We believe that we are here because we respect our dreams."

The two women sat in silence until Sonia said to Janet, "My boy Joe has had many losses because of white people. He lost his wife, Emily. She had driven into town and was hit head-on by a car that crossed the center line. The sheriff said the man was in a hurry.

"The day that Emily died, Joe brought his children here. On the reservation, they were sheltered from the chaos in the rest of the world. Joe saw no reason to send them to school in town. He wanted to keep the children close to him and out of harm's way. The children learned how to survive by living off the land. Old Woman taught them how to read and write. My daughter, Corrine, and I taught them beadwork. We gave them our values and the Old Ways of our ancestors.

"The children grew quickly, as children do. Joe's son, Greg, married Alicia, a young woman from a nearby reservation. They had two children, Sierra and Cody. They moved into the house where Joe and Emily had lived."

Sonia paused, her voice low and heavy with the grief that welled up when she told of her family's loss.

Janet leaned forward, her mouth open as if to speak. She took a breath, and Sonia held up her hand and shook her head. This wasn't a conversation or an interview in which Sonia would answer questions.

"Greg was hunting with friends when some hunters from the white community came onto the reservation and approached them, accusing them of hunting illegally. When Greg argued, the six white men overpowered him and his friends, beat them with their rifles, and left them lying in the woods. One of the injured men, unable to stand, crawled to Greg's house, leaving a trail of blood.

"When Alicia saw him, she dragged him into the house, ran over here to get Joe, who, along with his son-in-law, Mike, ran into the woods, following the blood trail. They found the other two men. Mike carried one of the men out of the woods and took him to a healer. Joe carried Greg's body here, and I took care of him, got him ready for ceremonies, and made a pair of moccasins.

"We brought Alicia and the children here to live. Alicia just sat and stared out the window. One day she got up, said she was going into town, and never came back.

"Old Woman and I helped Joe raise Greg's children. Joe taught Cody to hunt and fish. Sierra learned her role from her auntie Corrine and from Old Woman and me. We shared the pain and the good times of the children. Time moves faster when we're busy, and one day, the Old Woman and I looked at each other and said, 'We're getting old.' We laughed and kept on living.

"Others in the community took notice of the Old Woman's contributions. She told historical stories as well as tending to any children who happened to be here. She became a respected elder and became known as Old Woman.

"She is my good friend and a member of our family. She says that the spirits tell her that she will be passing on soon. When that happens, I will get her ready for her journey and make her a pair of moccasins," said Sonia.

"I don't understand why you make moccasins when someone dies," said Janet.

"We do more than that," said Sonia. "Even though the body dies, their spirits live. We get them ready to go on their journey to the Spirit World. We give them a change of clothing, other items they may find useful, and dress them in their finest clothes. The moccasins are new so they don't wear out on the journey.

"Joe is afraid you will bring trouble here. He also wants to spend more time with the Old Woman before she passes on. The time you spend with her takes time away from him," said Sonia.

"Why doesn't he just tell me to leave?" asked Janet.

"Because Joe prepared Antoine for his dream, and Antoine believes you are part of that dream," said Sonia. "Our ways tell us to respect our guests."

The two women sat in silence for a while. Janet didn't know what she was supposed to do next. In the city, her life was mapped out for her, and the physical boundaries set by the walled neighborhoods set limits and dictated her lifestyle.

Sonia spoke. "Why don't you take a walk down by the lake? Follow the path that goes around the lake. You'll see another path that joins the first one. It's a deer run, and you may be able to see some deer."

"Do you eat deer meat?" asked Janet.

Sonia nodded. "We eat the meat of many animals."

"I don't understand how you can kill deer. They're so pretty," said Janet.

"When the Creator made all of this," said Sonia, sweeping her arms around her surroundings, "He made us after Mother Earth, all that is in the skies, the plants, and the animals. We are dependent on all that came before us. When we kill an animal, we have a ritual to honor the animal and to remind us not to squander. We take only what we need, and we use all of the animal, not just the meat." Sonia paused, waiting to see if Janet would respond.

When she didn't, Sonia said, "It is warmer today than it was yesterday. You won't need a heavy jacket. Most of the snow has melted, so it will be muddy. Step carefully. C'mon. I'll show you the way."

The two women picked their way through the mud. Sonia showed Janet the path and then left, headed back toward the house.

Janet followed the trail. The clearing disappeared, overcome with tall trees and brush. The mixture of oak, maple birch, aspen, sumac, and bushes and plants, hardy enough to survive the short summers and long winters, rose up from the leftover snow blanket that had protected them from the cold. As their leaves budded out from underneath the blankets, they yawned, stretched, and quenched their thirst by sucking up groundwater enriched by soil and the fallen leaves from the previous autumn.

The smells of spring and the warming air served as an alarm clock for the hibernating animals and reptiles who were roused from their beds when the earth turned itself to the sun and the warm winds brought the smells of spring. The turtles came up out of the muck and burrowed into the sand and mud to lay their eggs.

The smells of spring were joined by the smell of wood smoke coming from the chimney.

Janet stopped. She saw three doe drinking in the lake. They looked at her, not moving. She had never seen any wild animal this close. When she was a child, she went to the zoo with her parents, where fences kept the animals away from the humans who paid to see them.

She didn't know how long she and the deer had stood looking at each other when one of the deer began snorting and stamping her feet.

Janet didn't know what that meant but thought, *This can't be good*. She decided to go back to the house.

Janet opened the door to the smell of food. She took off her vest and boots and went to help.

After lunch, Janet approached Sonia. "When can I talk to Old Woman?"

"You can talk to her now before her nap. Sierra and I will be going to Corrine's for a while."

Old Woman came into the living room and sat in her rocker. The sunlight coming through one of the windows was at her back.

Janet believed that Old Woman could give her information that would be helpful to the group, as Old Woman had lived the history that had been erased from Janet's life. At the same time, Janet had trouble understanding how history affected the present. She wasn't happy with this Post-Millennium Age. Any changes she wanted were changes that would benefit her and those like her. She had no sense that change most often created some discomfort, no matter how welcome. The information Sonia gave Janet was foreign to her. So much of what she heard was quickly forgotten. She went into the living room and greeted Old Woman briefly, in a hurry to begin the interview.

"Sonia just finished telling me her story. She said that you have been here for many years. I wonder what made you decide to come here," said Janet.

Old Woman was having trouble remembering who Janet was. She was frightened, fearing that someone was coming to take her away She shrank in her chair, becoming almost invisible. "Why are you asking me that? Are you going to turn me in?"

"Why, no. I came on Saturday, and today is Monday. I'm a friend of Antoine's. I came here to talk to you, to learn about the history you have," said Janet.

Hearing Antoine's name, Old Woman relaxed, her body filling the chair. "I came here three years before the millennium. I came because I was afraid of the things I saw happening in my culture. To me, things were spinning out of control. Every time something became a problem in the culture, new laws were passed to control it, and no one seemed to see that the problems were with the culture, not the laws.

"I started looking for work up north—this area—because I thought things would be simpler. I didn't think anyone would coming looking for me.

"I was able to find a job here as a tribal social worker and to make friends. I have learned something every day that I have been here. I was told once that I earned my way here. I don't know if I ever saw things that way, but maybe it doesn't matter how I saw it as long as others did.

"When I quit working, the Post-Millennium Adjustments were in high gear,, and the Homeland Security Office was gaining power every day. If I leave here I could be arrested because I'm considered dangerous, or I would have to go to a nursing home and be part of the experiments about which I've heard rumors. I asked for permission to stay. I was told I could do so if I had a family with whom I could live. I was also told that the permission was for me and not for my children and grandchildren.

"I talked with my children. They and their families were granted asylum in Canada because I am a political activist. I am considered a radical because I worked in the women's movement and because I worked here." Old Woman giggled. "I guess it's all in the perception."

"I chose to stay here because it was dangerous to try to cross the border into Canada. I can stay here because Indian reservations are sovereign states and can make their own decisions about who lives here and who doesn't. I suppose the government could find some way to circumvent all of that and come in and drag me off, but I don't think it would serve much of a purpose. Besides, they have enough trouble trying to maintain control in their own world. They really don't have the time or the resources to try to control what happens up here in the woods."

As she listened, Janet watched Old Woman, studied her. Old Woman's eyes had a sunken look, surrounded by folds of skin that made it look like her eyes had almost disappeared into her skull. As she told her story, tears fell, traveling down the wrinkles to drip onto the yoke of her deerskin dress. The strong voice was incongruent with her shriveled body and quavered when she spoke of her life and losses.

"I haven't seen my children for a long time. I know they are still alive and they and their families have all become Canadian citizens. I would like to see them, but it's more important for me to know they are safe and well. Every once in a while, someone travels across the border from Canada and brings me information and family pictures. We don't keep the pictures out in the open because we just don't know what might happen. We don't know that the government will keep its promise to stay away. It's more important that I have my children in my heart."

Janet was uncomfortable witnessing the open emotions of Old Woman and thought this might be the time to divert the conversation to something less painful; at least she hoped it was less painful. "So this family you live with has adopted you," said Janet.

"I suppose you could say that. We didn't ever have a formal adoption ceremony, but I'm a member of this household.

"It was several years after I moved here, after I retired, that I heard the reports that came from the outside world about the loss of the free press and the power gained by Homeland Security. I tried to ignore all of that. It was hard to believe that the country was no longer a democracy. I suppose I have ignored what's happening out there. It's easy to do that here. Our lives are busy. I feel safe here most of the time. Then you came and brought reality with you," said Old Woman. "We'll talk some more later. Right now, it's time for my nap."

Janet went upstairs and lay down on the bed. Morning had come early. Her walk provided more exercise than she usually had, and the fresh air seemed to tire her out. She closed her eyes and rested, half in and half out of sleep. The deer she had seen by the lake came to her in a dream. The doe stood in front of her two fawns, staring at Janet. Then it faded. When she woke up from her nap, she smelled food and went down to the kitchen to help.

After supper, the family settled down. Cody, whom Janet judged to be about eight years old, told a story with the use of a puppet.

"This is Miranda Moose," said Cody, holding up a puppet. "This is a story about how Miranda got to be so mean. Many years ago, Anishinaabe were the only humans here. We shared the land and everything here with all of the animals. We were all happy, and we respected the animals, and they respected us.

"Then one day, some men who were different came to trade in furs. They introduced alcohol to the people who didn't know what alcohol would do to them.

"There were so many animals killed for their furs that the Anishinaabe couldn't use all of the meat, bones, and the rest of what the animals had to offer. The dead animals lay all over in the forest.

"Miranda didn't like what she saw. She was sad and mad because so many of her friends and relatives were killed. She didn't want to be the next to be killed, so she moved her family far into the woods, away from the humans and the other animals. When she thought she was safe, Miranda cried for many days.

"One day, Miranda heard some noises in the woods. There were voices, and she heard sticks cracking as people stepped on them. She watched as she saw men like the fur traders take their axes and cut down the huge trees. They loaded up the trees on skids and used horses to take the trees away. Miranda followed and saw that the men were dumping the trees in the river. The whole river was covered with trees, and Miranda knew that the fish would die because there wasn't enough oxygen in the water.

"Miranda got mad and charged the men, who scattered and ran. They came back the next day and took more trees. Miranda decided to find the Anishinaabe and see what they were going to do about the trees.

"She traveled through the woods and came to a village that she knew. She saw the men and women who had been her friends lying on the ground, some stumbling around, smelling of the alcohol the white men had given them.

"Miranda ran into the middle of this scene, yelling and stamping her feet. 'Look at what's happened to you! You have to save us.'

"The people ignored Miranda. She hung her head, her tears flowed, and she moved her family deeper into the woods, to a place where there were no humans at all.

"She soon heard noises again. She crept toward the noises and saw the white men with axes building houses from logs. People came to live in the houses. They shot the deer and elk, Miranda's cousins, and they dug up the land. It looked to her like they were planting something.

"Miranda decided not to move again. She carried on raids into the new communities, roaring, stamping her feet, and shaking her rack of horns.

"Soon the people began building roads and poured a stinky black liquid on them. Miranda charged the road builders, who scattered when they saw her, but they kept on building roads.

"Some had rifles and began shooting at Miranda. She ran back to her home. Soon cars were traveling on the roads. They were often confronted by Miranda, who would stand in the middle of the road, waving her head back and forth. The cars would stop, and Miranda would charge them, ripping into them with her horns.

"Miranda saw that nothing was changing because of her efforts, and she settled into a deep depression. She quit eating and even quit charging cars. Then, one of her grandchildren came to her and told her to come out of the woods.

"Miranda followed and came to the old village. She saw that the Anishinaabe people had quit drinking alcohol and had gone back to their old ways. No one came to repair the roads, and very few of those other humans came around. The animals returned, and Miranda came out of hiding.

"The end," said Cody.

"I like that story, Cody," said Sonia. She turned to Janet. "Cody made up this story."

Janet nodded. She was uncomfortable, as it was obvious to her that the story was about white people and how they had changed things when they came here.

Darkness had settled into the corners of the house, and everyone went off to bed.

Janet lay her head on the pillow. She quickly fell asleep. The dreams came again.

She saw herself flying, arms outstretched, catching the wind currents. She was above a snow-covered landscape. There were pine trees whose branches were sagging to the ground under the weight of the snow. Then the surroundings changed, and she was in a room with her parents, sitting at a kitchen table, in front of a window framing the snow-covered scenery. The room was sparsely furnished. She watched the scene, viewing herself and her parents, who were happy, laughing, and talking, sharing stories.

When she awakened in the morning, Janet felt as if the dream had assured her that her parents were safe some place.

CHAPTER
April 3, 2040

It was five in the morning, Monday, the second full day of Janet's visit. Sonia had been up for about twenty minutes. She had started a fire in the cookstove. A second woodburning stove was left cold because it would be warm enough to keep just one fire heating the house. She sat at the table with her cup of peppermint tea, listening to the soft creaks and groans of the house that permeated the silence. To Sonia, those noises were the house breathing. She believed that the house carried all of the memories and the energy of her ancestors, all of those who had lived here and those who currently lived in the house.

Sonia liked this time of day. She shut her eyes and let thoughts and memories come. She was grateful for her life, and she welcomed the spirits of her ancestors and her grandmothers. Sonia believed that Janet's presence here was part of the process that would take Old Woman to the spirit world.

As she sat listening to the house and the birds singing outside, Sonia wished that this quiet time would last longer. Soon, the soft noises would be covered by the stirrings of her family getting ready for the day.

Sonia sighed and stood up. It was time to start breakfast.

She was joined in the kitchen by Old Woman, who cooked wild rice that had been soaking in water all night. Sierra came into the house from next door and poured raspberry juice in glasses.

Janet awakened to the sounds coming from the kitchen and got up. She had slept well, and she remembered the dream about her parents. She went into the kitchen just as the family was sitting down to eat.

"Good morning," Janet mumbled, feeling guilty because she hadn't gotten up in time to help. She drank the sour juice and hesitated before tasting the wild rice.

"We call wild rice *mahnomen*. Wild rice brought us here from the east. It's an all-purpose food. We eat it with almost every meal, and it is good for us," said Sierra, finishing her endorsement of the product.

When they had finished eating, Sonia said, "Janet, you can help clean up. After that, you and I can talk."

"I thought I'd be meeting with Old Woman," said Janet.

"You can meet with her soon," said Sonia. "Old Woman's stories are only part of what you'll learn here."

When Janet finished the dishes, she joined Sonia at the kitchen table. The sun was shining through the east windows, warming the house.

"Come and sit," said Sonia. "The elders have given me a task. I am to talk to you about the way things were here and what happened to change things. You can turn that thing on if you want," said Sonia, nodding at the recorder in Janet's hand.

"I am going to tell you part of the story of this family. I know that you came here to interview the Old Woman, and you will. Your experience here is about our community, so first I'll tell you about our history.

"Before we came here, we lived on the East Coast. We were told by our prophets that men with pale skin and hair on their faces would come, and we should get out of their way. We started a long journey that lasted about five hundred years. We were told to come where food grows on water. That's wild rice, and we found it in the many lakes and streams that surround us.

"We were self-sufficient and were respectful of the resources the Creator gave us. We lived to be very old, and we respected the Creator by taking care of Mother Earth and Her resources.

"Then Europeans came. Cody's story about the moose tells us what happened in the fur trade and the time when this land was stripped of all the trees so white people could build houses.

"After the United States came into being, they brought us treaties to sign that they didn't keep. Their broken promises resulted in many deaths among our people, and we were ready to go to war. The government was afraid of us because there were a lot of us and we were good at protecting against our enemies. We had been weakened, and some of us thought that we would soon die off. So we ceded territory in a treaty and kept large parcels of land called reservations."

"Why didn't you just move someplace else?" asked Janet.

"Because we are supposed to be here," said Sonia.

"How do you know you are supposed to be here?" asked Janet.

"Because our stories tell us that. You white people let others write your stories for you. You assume that they tell the truth and that the information is factual. But because you let others tell your stories, you don't know if they are true. We tell our stories in our families and pass them down through the generations," said Sonia.

"When you're talking about the past, you make it sound like it's the present and you are part of it," said Janet.

"The past decides the present. What happens to my ancestors affects me. We are at this place today because of all that has gone before," said Sonia. "We believe that it's best for us to live according to our Old Ways, ways that were given to us by the Creator. I had to learn much when I came here because my mom and grandmothers had lost those ways.

"When I came here, there was a mix of beliefs and values. Most of the disagreements between our people were the result of the loss of our Old Ways and the assimilation of some people to white men's ways. They forgot who they were."

"What do you mean—they forgot who they were?" asked Janet.

"We were forced to live with your ways and your values," said Sonia. "After the federal government took our land, they forced us to give up hunting, fishing, and gathering even though the treaties guaranteed our rights to live off the land. We were expected to learn how to farm. It's hard to farm with the short growing season and sandy soil. The government insisted that each family live on plots of land assigned by the government. Then the federal government came along with surplus foods. People who are starving will eat just about anything, and that's what surplus commodities were—just about anything. When people quit eating the foods that were good for them, they started getting sick.

"Things kept changing, and when we had money and could buy groceries, we bought the same junk white people bought. People, all people, kept getting sicker and sicker, and medical science kept coming up with new medications to fight the new illnesses.

"Many people here continued to live off the land, but the animals and the fish had been poisoned from all the poisons in the plants and the water. After we unplugged and the cleansing plants came, we all began eating only the foods given by the Creator. Stay awhile and you will see people who worship food. Food is part of our ceremonies and for good reason. We all get sustenance from food. We need to take care of the environment if we are to live. I think it's too late for those people who live away from here.

"Before the surplus commodities, when people were still living off the land, the government decided to send our children to boarding schools. My great-grandmother was kidnapped and sent to a boarding school in Chicago," said Sonia.

"Who kidnapped her?" asked Janet.

"The government," said Sonia. "They cut her hair and didn't let her speak Ojibwa. She had to dress like white women. She ran away many times. When the boarding school people found her, they would bring her back and punish her. When she graduated, she was ashamed of what had happened to her. She stayed in Chicago and found work as a maid in the home of a wealthy family. When the man in that family attempted to have sex with her, she smashed him in the face with her fist. She left and found another job as a maid, and another wealthy white man tried to have sex with her. This happened many times, with the same outcome, and she couldn't find work anymore.

"Grandmother walked and walked, sleeping in alleys, finding food in garbage cans. One day, she walked into a bar and sat on a stool. A white man came up to her and offered her a meal and a drink. Grandmother had never tasted alcohol before. When she took a drink, not knowing how to sip, she was overwhelmed by the taste. She coughed and coughed. The man laughed and said that he thought he could teach her some things. He took her to his house, forced himself on her, and told her she would do what he wanted or her would kill her. He sold her to other men for sex, telling her she had to earn her keep. Drinking became part of her daily life. It helped her forget the shame she thought she brought on herself.

"Grandmother had one child, my mother's mother, Harriet. Grandmother kept Harriet with her. She was afraid that someone would come and take her away. Men began preying on Harriet when she was about four. Harriet thought this was to be her life. She had my mother, Clarice, who was forced into the same way of life. My mother was raised in a bar. Men began taking advantage of her when she was a small child. My mom had my three sisters and me. Men gave her money for sex, and that's how we survived. I was about two years old when some people who said they were our relatives found us in a bar in Chicago. They brought us home, to this house. We had many relatives here who helped take care of us.

"My mom and my grandmothers worked hard to sober up. My great-grandmother never did. She died from cirrhosis when I was about sixteen. I went to the elders, and they told me how to prepare her for her funeral. I did that and made her a pair of moccasins with the help of one of my cousins."

Sonia paused. Her eyes were full of tears, and her voice was shaky. She continued. "The elders told me stories about my family and how they lived before the kidnapping. The stories helped me to discover who I am. They told me I was like my great-great-grandmother, a medicine woman with great powers. Even though I had known for some time that my family had existed since the beginning, I began to understand that my life was meant to be lived in honor of all those who came before me and all who would come after.

"When my grandmother Harriet got sick, I took care of her. As she was dying, she looked at me and said, 'Ogitchedakwe!' I hadn't learned to speak the language yet, so I went to the elders. They told me my grandmother had named me Warrior Woman. They told me it was up to me to figure out how to live the life of a warrior woman. I prepared her for her funeral and made pair of moccasins."

"So your great-grandmother, grandmother, and your mother were all prostitutes," said Janet.

"No, they were slaves. They had no other choice but to do what they did. They survived. That's why I am here. That's why my sisters are here," said Sonia.

"We grew up in this house with my mother. There was no electricity or plumbing available to the houses on the reservation. Those things were installed later," said Sonia.

"But you don't have electricity now," said Janet.

"No, we don't," said Sonia. "When we didn't have electricity or plumbing, we thought that if we had modern conveniences, we would be better off.

"The government offered us the opportunity to get grants. So we wrote grants and got programs. We had youth programs to prevent youth from getting into trouble, women and infants programs that focused on health and nutrition, and a variety of other programs meant to improve our living situation. We continued to receive surplus commodities, a program that offered us free food, but it wasn't healthy food.

"In the 1980s, we got substance-abuse programs, and by that time, we had a health clinic. In the 1980s, laws were passed that would allow us to develop casinos. The casinos would provide jobs and revenue so we could develop infrastructure. We got casinos in the 1990s. The profits from the casinos and the grants created a growth explosion. More of our people found jobs in our community, and we had money to spend. We were encouraged to acquire technology to meet the demands of the growing services. Some folks thought all these changes were dangerous, like the changes that had happened during the fur trade. Others just thought that all of the changes would save lives and make life a little easier."

"So the casinos encouraged your people to gamble?" asked Janet.

"No. The casinos were built to employ tribal members. Most of the people who gambled there were nonnatives.

"With the advent of casinos, we began relying on technology more and more. We had computers to do the grant reporting. We had computers to send emails. We had computer programs for the health clinic. We could buy computers with the grants. After the grants were done, we kept the computers and used them for something else. When we wrote new grants with the old computers that went with the old grants, we got new computers," said Sonia.

"Today you don't have computers. I don't understand how you can get along without them," said Janet.

"It's easy. We just use old ways of communicating, and we take care of ourselves the way we used to. If we want to talk to someone, we go to see them. We rely on the gifts and strengths of all of the community," said Sonia.

"The elders were telling us that we didn't need the computers. They said that technology was evil and that it was evil to waste resources and spend money just to spend money. The elders began writing a newsletter. They used pens made of feathers and ink made from berry juice. They walked throughout the reservation to deliver the newsletters to each family. The elders quit going to council meetings, using the elder newsletter to spread their messages. They said that the tribal government was a product of the Bureau of Indian Affairs. After a while, we started listening to the elders. No matter how many services and how much money we had, we still had substance use and the illnesses that go along with it.

"The community was divided into two groups—those who thought technology would keep the reservation going and those who thought all technology should be abandoned. Some believed that once the technology was gone, we could only survive by going back to the Old Ways.

"There were many community meetings where we would talk about what to do. We kept talking and talking, and the computers kept running, and the casinos kept making money, and people continued to drink alcohol. More and more people were going to work and putting their children in our day care centers.

"At the last council meeting about computers and technology, an old woman spoke up and said, 'Why doesn't somebody just go unplug everything?' Someone else said, 'No one knows where it's all plugged in.' No one agreed that this should happen, and no one disagreed, and no one at the meeting seemed to know the location where everything plugged in.

"Two days later, someone snuck up to that place where the power originated and started unplugging and cutting cords. Whoever it was must have been watching for a long time to figure out where all those cords went.

"Things started to slow down. The whirring noise that had become part of the community slowed down, and, finally, everything stopped. It was quiet. No one knew what had happened. We all just sat very still for about an hour. Then someone called out, 'What happened?' Someone else called, 'We're unplugged.'

"It was quiet again. After another hour, one of the women hollered, 'We need to fix supper.' I think women in every village on our reservation reached the same conclusion at the same time. All of the older women got out their old iron cook pots and started fires to cook meals. The men went out to shoot deer and catch fish. The children went with their parents to find wild plants they could eat.

"This went on for about three days. People were getting up with the sun and going to sleep soon after it set. We were hunter-gatherers again.

"Then everyone went to the community center that casino money had built. The people who worked in the youth program in that building were paid by grants. They continued to come to work, but none of the children came to play basketball because they were with their parents gathering food. The workers wondered what would happen if none of the children came to play basketball. If they had no numbers to report, they might lose their grants. When the youth program workers saw everyone coming to the community center, they got out their paper and pens and had everyone sign in. They had something to report for their grants, but they had no computers to report on.

"As everyone settled into a circle at the community center, the old women talked about how things used to be. They talked about cooking over fires and gathering food. They talked about living without money, sharing, and trading instead.

"Everyone decided that since they had been okay for three days, they could try it a little longer. They said that they didn't like those tourists who came to the casino anyway. Someone asked what they should do about the grant reporting. There was some discussion about that, and then someone said, 'Forget about it. We don't need grants. Just write a letter to those grant people and tell them that we are all done counting Indians. We are going to live the way we are supposed to live. We are going to live like Anishinaabe.'

"When the children went with their parents to look for food, they found scraps of electrical cords scattered throughout the reservation. It looked as if the person who pulled the plug made sure that we couldn't plug in again without some work. The children were told to collect all of the pieces they could find. They brought them to the community center, put them in bags, and stored them in the closet. We didn't want to bury them because plastic doesn't decompose, and we didn't know what those plastic cords might do in the soil over time.

"Those three days we gave ourselves to see if we could make it have turned into twenty-five years. We don't have grants, and we don't have electricity. Our children don't have to sign in and be counted in

Washington when they want to play basketball. If we need something that comes from a store, we take things we have made or fresh fish or venison or wild rice into town and trade.

"We were doing well with our decision to go back to the old ways. Some of us had this nagging thought that we probably couldn't always live off the land because our land and water were still being poisoned by the white man's technology. We were thinking about it, but we didn't know what we could do about it.

"Then, a couple of years after we unplugged, a woman walked into our community center. We all knew she was there, and we went to see what she wanted. We knew she had something important to tell us. We knew she didn't happen upon us by accident. She wore long robes made out of bearskin. Her hair was white and reached down past the middle of her back. Her face was wrinkled, and she looked like she was two hundred years old.

"She sat in the middle of our circle and passed around tobacco, tobacco that didn't come from a package. She told us that tobacco came from a plant whose ancestors went back hundreds of years.

"The woman brought out some plants from a leather bandolier bag decorated with seeds and porcupine quills. She told us that if we planted those in all of our lakes and rivers, the water would be clean. All of the plants that used to grow here would grow again. She said those plants would cleanse Mother Earth and the air that surrounds our community. The animals would be healthier, and we would not have to worry about which animals we killed for eating. She said the mercury would leave our rivers and lakes, and the fish would be safe to eat again.

"That woman said she was giving us those plants because we had unplugged. She said that it wouldn't do any good to use those plants if we were using technology because everything would get dirty again. She told us to use our ceremonies and rituals to respect Mother Earth and all that the Creator had given us. She said that we should respect ourselves and remember the stories that had been given to us by our ancestors and our elders.

"We believed her because she knew about us and came to us dressed like our ancestors. We knew she had power because of the ancient bandolier bag she carried. Some were hesitant to plant the plants. Others said that we had little to lose. If we continued to depend on technology and the white man's money, we would die out.

"One of our medicine men had predicted that everything on Mother Earth would die because of the poisons in the water and the air, poisons that came from taking the chemicals out of the earth. He said that the minerals and other resources in the earth were in balance as long as they remained where the Creator put them. When mining and oil drilling became accepted practices, Mother Earth was out of balance, and the resources that came from Mother Earth became poisons. He said that the poisons would kill all that was living on Mother Earth. He said that when this happened, Mother Earth could be rejuvenated. We had heard what he had to say, but we didn't know what to do with it until that person pulled the plug and pulled us away from technology.

"First, we had to decide to keep the plants. There was little talking and lots of head nodding. Plants have a way of traveling where they want to go, so if we planted them, they would decide where and how they would travel. Then we decided where to plant them and who would plant them. When we passed out the plants and started for home, we noticed that the woman was gone. No one saw her leave. We knew we were doing the right thing because she left the plants with us.

"Our children went with the elders and planted the plants along the banks of the rivers and in the middle of our wild rice beds. As they planted, the elders told the children stories about the Old Ways. Our children came home, changed from their visits with the elders. They didn't complain because they didn't have new shoes. They started playing the old games. They kept basketball. When the hoops rusted out, they figured out ways of making new ones out of deer antlers.

"Since we got those plants, everything is better here. People don't drink alcohol anymore. They don't use other drugs anymore. We use natural medicines to treat illnesses. People live off the land and take only what they need. We practice our rituals and ceremonies. Everyone works, and everyone shares. We show honor, dignity, and respect to ourselves and to all that the Creator has given to us. The plants the children put in the soil and the water have taken root and have spread throughout our community. There is balance here.

"Some of our people wanted to let the white people know about the cleansing plants. They thought it was what we were supposed to do because we believe in sharing with others. We talked about it for a long time. Then someone remembered what that woman had said about using technology. We agreed that we couldn't get whites to stop using technology. We don't have any experience that tells us that white people listen to what we have to say. We decided that we would keep the plants for ourselves.

"We believe that most people who live outside of our reservation will die because they continue to misuse the resources the Creator put on Mother Earth. Everything outside of our reservation is dirty except for some other communities like ours.

"People try to correct the problems by making more things to protect them from the poison that surrounds them. As they make more things, they create more poison. Animals know better than to soil their homes, but many humans don't.

"When most of the people in the cities are dead, we will start to move outside of our communities to clean everything. We teach these things to our children. We teach them how to live with the Old Ways. We respect Mother Earth. In showing our respect, we honor the Creator. Our children learn to read and write, but the most important thing we can teach them is how to live with honor, dignity, and respect," said Sonia.

"Don't you miss having modern conveniences?" asked Janet.

"I think your term 'modern conveniences' says a lot," said Sonia. "Technology is a convenience. As such, it isn't something we have to have to survive."

"But don't your children have to compete in the world?" asked Janet.

"Only if they want to. If any child wants to grow up and leave here, they have a chance to go to the school in town, the way Antoine did. They can go to college if they want to. Those who go to college usually come back here. They don't seem to like cement, bad air, and packaged food," said Sonia.

"Not everyone from this community lives like we do. Some people have moved into the white man's town because they like having electricity. There is another group of people here who don't live in houses. They live in wigwams made of birch bark. We believe they are responsible for keeping the birch trees alive. The wigwam dwellers peeled the bark off the birch trees to make their houses. The trees know that they serve an important purpose.

"Many years ago, when the drinking was so bad here, we had many house fires. People would get drunk, smoke cigarettes, and pass out. Hot coals from the cigarettes would start fires. Houses would burn to the ground, and the bodies of the people in them would be found among the ashes and cinders.

"Some house fires started because the HUD houses the white man's government built for us were poorly built and had faulty furnaces and bad wiring. Those houses had no flame-retardant materials. Some people thought that the HUD housing was built that way to deliberately to kill us off.

"We lost many children in those fires. Children lost parents and grandparents. The people who live in wigwams are survivors of house fires. They think houses like ours are dangerous. We don't have furnaces or electricity. We all use wood for fires. Those wigwam people remind us of those hard times we had.

"It was predicted a long time ago that we would return to the old ways. Before we did, we tried to do little things here and there that would start the process of returning to the Old Ways. I don't think anyone ever thought we could just do it, but we did. Whoever it was who unplugged us knew it had to be done that way," said Sonia, pausing, taking a breath.

"What about nonnative people who want to come here, like Old Woman?" asked Janet.

"We are cautious as to who comes here. Your ways are different from ours," said Sonia.

"Doesn't Homeland Security come here? Don't they control what goes on here?" asked Janet.

"No and no," said Sonia. "When we unplugged, we became self-sufficient again. We contacted your government and told them we would no longer be taking anything from them. We entered into an agreement with the government. We would be completely sovereign, and they would leave us alone. We did ask that any of our children who wished to attend your universities could do so free of charge. This agreement also says that when one of our members attends a university, they are subject to your laws and consequences of those laws.

"There are many more communities like this in this country and in Canada. Even though the border between the US and Canada is closed, we can still travel there because many of our people live there. We are one nation. We don't recognize boundaries that are drawn on pieces of paper.

"As we unplugged and went back to our ways, we gave up parts of your culture that had been put upon us. We don't want your culture. We have done well with our own.

"We prefer to live in our own communities and on our land. It is rare for white people to come here. We usually get two kinds—the do-gooders who come thinking they are going to teach us how to live, without realizing that the white culture is falling apart, and those who come thinking they will learn how to be Indians. Very few come like that Old Woman came. She came here honestly. She came here to get away from the white man's culture and to learn how to live and get along with us. She is the oldest of four generations who live in this house. She teaches history to my great-grandchildren. We all learn from one another in this house. Elders teach us tolerance simply because of their presence. They have wisdom because they have lived so long.

"Old Woman knows many things. When she was younger, she had some control over how she shared her knowledge. She hasn't lost her knowledge. Her ways of remembering have changed. The spirits are preparing her for her journey to the Spirit World. This means that she tells stories, wanders off, visits with the spirits that come to visit her, and forgets that you are here and why you are here. She is very busy, even though she spends a lot of time sitting in that chair with that old dog.

"We respect and honor her not only because she is an elder but also because she has honored us by learning and living our ways. I'm sure that your interviews with her will teach you a lot. I think that you will have trouble understanding her. She has learned to teach the way we teach—through stories. When you hear a story, you learn what you are supposed to learn. The only test is to gather the wisdom that's in the story and put it to use.

"Most of what you learn from her will be about yourself. She doesn't apologize for her memory or her age. She knows that she knows many things and that it is her responsibility to share what she knows.

"She will not say that she has become Anishinaabe. She knows that this is an insult because we are who we are when we are born. Sometimes she says, 'I am a white woman.' She used to do that to let people know she knew she was different. I think it was her way of apologizing. Now, I think she says it so she won't forget who she is. All I know is that she is my friend, and I will take care of her and protect her for as long as I can. When she walks on, I will make her a pair of moccasins."

"So you don't believe in senility," said Janet.

"No. We go through stages of life, and each stage brings with it new beginnings," said Sonia. "When we are fortunate to live long lives, we begin our journey to the Spirit World before we pass on. This means the spirits come to visit us and prepare us to enter the Spirit World." We're in an in-between place.

"I don't understand what your purpose is. Don't you want to get ahead?" asked Janet.

"Our purpose is to protect Mother Earth and to use her resources wisely. It is our purpose to raise our children with our values and to help them discover who they are," said Sonia.

"When Old Woman came here, I was raising my children alone. I met her at a baby shower, and we became good friends. She moved in here to help me raise my children, as my mom had trouble with daily living. My mom had nightmares, and she was always afraid that someone was going to hurt her.

"My older sisters were drinking, and the social workers in town came and took their children away from them. Old Woman and I decided to take the children in. We went to all of the foster homes, gathered the ten children together, and brought them here. Social workers came to our house and demanded to know what I was doing. They left when I told them that I was saving them money because they wouldn't have to pay for foster care.

"The years Old Woman was working and we were raising my children were busy years. There have not been many years when there were not young children in this house.

"We have always been busy. We lived in the moment, took care of children, sent them on their ways when they reached adulthood.

"Time has caught up with us. Everyone in this house knows that Old Woman will die soon—not simply because she is old; she could probably live another ten years.

"I feel the presence of spirits in the house. At first, I felt them only when Old Woman napped, but lately they are here most of the time. I am understanding more about the spirits and passing to another life. When they are here, the house feels full.

"I don't want Old Woman to leave, as she has been part of my life and the life of our family for most of my life. I'm getting used to the spirits, and I take comfort in their visits, knowing that they are preparing Old Woman for her journey. It's something I can't do for her. I get comfort knowing that Old Woman isn't dying; she is passing on to another life," said Sonia.

Sonia poured Janet a cup of peppermint tea, talking as she moved about the kitchen. "I'm sure it's hard for you to understand Old Woman. I know that you probably haven't seen any elderly people since you were a small child. Old Woman says that in your culture elders are not valued; that's why there aren't any. She says that even before the millennium, your culture didn't have much use for elders. It's always seemed funny to me that the white man had medicines that prolonged life, but when people lived to be so old that they couldn't take care of themselves, they were put in nursing homes. When your elders wanted to die, they weren't allowed to, and if someone else killed an elder who wanted to die, the killer was put on trial for murder."

Janet was silent as Sonia talked. She took issue with the way in which Sonia included her in this condemnation of white culture. She thought that now was not the time to argue.

Just then, Old Woman walked into the kitchen. She looked at Janet and said, "Do you want to talk to me?"

Janet nodded.

"Then let's go into the living room." Old Woman turned, walked into the room, and sat in her rocker.

"You want to talk to me about history. Well, what kind of history should we talk about? There's detail history. That's when we list dates and things that happened on those dates. Then there's reasons. That kind of history talks about why things happened the way they did. Then there's attitudes, culture, and beliefs. And after that, history is recorded based on the point of view of the teller," said Old Woman.

"Well, I'm not sure. I learned about some things from my parents. I guess they taught based on reasons, and they gave me dates but not really specific dates. They gave me eras," said Janet.

"I think I'll start with a foundation," said Old Woman. "When Europeans came here to settle, some came to escape religious persecution. They had a hard time at first. They had trouble raising crops, and they stole food from indigenous people. The indigenous people weren't happy with this, and King Phillip's War happened. The Europeans had an attitude of superiority and thought that indigenous people were savages, even though indigenous people lived in harmony with nature.

"More and more Europeans came and brought more and more conflict with them. After the Revolutionary War, the colonies formed a government. Some say that the democracy they formed came from the Iroquois. The new country, America, welcomed more and more immigrants who needed more and more land. They pushed the indigenous people farther west, killing many with weapons, disease, and heartbreak.

"The history that was written by settlers was not the history of indigenous people. The white man's history interpreted the slaughter of indigenous people to be accomplishments by brave pioneers. Indigenous people were forced into positions where they signed treaties, ceded territory, and kept small plots of land for themselves. They expected whites to honor the treaties. That didn't happen," said Old Woman.

"But didn't they lose wars?" asked Janet.

"Not all tribes fought wars with Americans. This is a place where we have to look at reasons. Indigenous people were trying to protect themselves against whites who were slaughtering them. That's self-defense, not war.

"Imagine this. Let's say you had a house that served you well, and you lived among your relatives, all of whom had houses. Someone comes along and says, 'You'll have to move, and we'll decide where you move and what and how to pay you. When it's time for us to pay you, we'll tell you where to go to collect the money, and you'll have to bring your family with you in order to get full payment. When we distribute the money, if anyone shows up and says you owe them money, we'll give them some of your money,'" said Old Woman.

"That's the way it is now for us," said Janet. "We all have to live in a specific neighborhood, and most of us can't own property. I'd have to be very wealthy in order to own a house," said Janet.

"I heard something about that. We hear rumors from time to time. I never know which to believe," said Old Woman.

"My parents said that we treated indigenous people badly," said Janet.

"When the government first came into being, there were laws written that said they would make native people dependent. They accomplished that by killing the buffalo. The rights of indigenous people to hunt and fish were taken from them.

"Whites believe that their society is superior to native culture because of technology. They don't understand that their lack of respect for the environment kills many people," said Old Woman.

"I don't like it when it sounds like all of you who live here blame any problems on white people," said Janet.

"Sometimes it's hard to hear the truth," said Old Woman.

There was a long silence. Janet could hear the birds. There were no birds in the city.

"I hear Sonia making lunch. Let's help her," said Old Woman.

After lunch, Janet walked outside and took the path down to the lake, where she saw several deer standing along the shore, their tan coats blending into the sand beach. She came around a curve in the path and saw a small stream that emptied into the lake. It was midafternoon, and the sun was beginning to fall slowly toward the tree line. The temperature fell in accordance with the loss of light.

Janet's eyes followed the stream away from the lake and into the woods. She took a few steps, found a log, and sat until she began to shiver with the cool breeze. She walked back to the house, where supper was being prepared.

The aroma of the food caused Janet's mouth to water. She saw that food preparation was taken care of, so she set the two tables. She saw the bowl of wild rice and a platter with dark meat.

Sonia said, "That's duck. Joe and Cody went duck hunting today."

"I sure am hungry," said Janet.

"That's the fresh air, and this food has taste and no preservatives," said Sonia.

After supper, the family gathered around the firepit. No one spoke.

Joe sat with his arms wrapped around Cody and thought about the past. He thought he would never be happy again when his wife died. He followed the traditions he had been taught, and for the first year after Emily's death, Joe didn't speak her name or visit the grave. He was so lonesome! He didn't want to impede her journey to the Spirit World, so he did everything he was supposed to do to let her go, except he couldn't help thinking about her.

Old Woman told him he would be happy again. He asked her if she meant he would find another woman. She said, "No. We don't know whom you will have in your life. You'll find things that will make you happy. You will love your children and your grandchildren. Giving to others is the greatest gift we get from the Creator. You will give to many people in your life. Maybe there will be another woman, but it's not a good idea to fill your days thinking that another woman will bring you happiness."

Thoughts of those times and Old Woman's words came to him as he sat by the fire with his mother, this woman he called Grandmother, and his children. The wood fire was reduced to cinders, ashes, and smoke. It was dark, and the family went to bed.

Janet fell asleep quickly and began dreaming. She saw herself on a path; it didn't look like the paths near the house where she now slept. She was jogging, and there were eagles overhead. One of them grabbed some kind of object flying through the air, landed a few feet from Janet, and used its claws to rip apart its catch. The eagle lifted off the ground, circled above Janet's head, and continued its flight a few feet ahead of her, as if leading her toward a destination.

CHAPTER

April 4, 2040

While Janet's stay on the reservation continued, her absence didn't go unnoticed in the city.

Hal Emerson paid an early morning visit to Lloyd, who jumped when he walked into his office and saw Hal sitting in his chair.

Hal said, "So you weren't expecting me."

"No, why would I be?" asked Lloyd.

"Well, your star reporter is off for a few days. Do you know where she is?" asked Hal.

"No, I don't. I figure you'll check up on my staff," said Lloyd.

"If you did check on her, you would find that she isn't at home," said Hal.

Lloyd paused. He didn't want to ask where Janet was, and he didn't want to know.

"We know that she left the city last Saturday about eight o'clock in the morning. One of our drones followed her to an Indian reservation. Do you know why she would go there?" asked Hal.

"No, I don't. Like I told you, I don't keep track of my staff when they're off work," said Lloyd.

"We think she's fallen in with a group at the U that's trying to develop a plot to overthrow the government," said Hal.

"How could a group of people at the U overthrow the government?" asked Lloyd.

"Well, we don't know yet. We do know that the longer the group meets, the bigger the plan. They might hook up with some other folks, and who knows what could happen next?" asked Hal.

"Where would Janet Ryan get the idea to go to an Indian reservation?" asked Lloyd, forgetting that his plan to handle visits with Hal was to avoid getting hooked.

"I know what the laws are regarding travel. I guess I don't know enough about how you people operate. This just doesn't sound like a big deal to me," said Lloyd.

"We believe it is a big deal. She meets with an Indian man and then travels to an Indian reservation. I don't think that's a coincidence. I have a plan, and I expect you to carry it out. When Ms. Ryan gets back from her little vacation, I want you to put her on the local news. This means she is to travel to breaking news sites and write the stories. I've already made arrangements to have her computer hooked up to our offices. We'll read her stories and evaluate them for anything she says that might sound as if she is discontented.

"Next, the Eleanor Roosevelt Ozone Plate is headed this way. I don't know how long it takes to get here, but when it gets closer, you will put her on that story. She will be expected to create stories about the EROP and all the accompanying festivities. She is to go to the various agencies that are involved with the EROP and interview staff. This way, we can have several agents placed in those agencies, and they can evaluate what she says and does.

"I will place an agent in your offices. She will pose as an intern who will work with Janet. With all of this surveillance, we'll be able to figure out what Janet Ryan is doing," said Hal.

"Has there ever been a time when you had suspicions about someone and found out you were wrong?" asked Lloyd.

"No. We work very hard to keep our country safe. After all, it's the greatest country in the world," said Hal as he rose, moved around Lloyd's desk, and left.

Lloyd's tic came back. It was another one of those days that he was late for a staff meeting. He sat at his desk thinking about his fears of Homeland Security. He wondered what they might do to him if he took an assertive stance. What purpose would such a stance serve? Well, maybe my tic wouldn't come back every time Hal pays me a visit. Maybe I'll be arrested. Maybe I won't. Homeland Security will want to keep me in place. Maybe I could have done something about the last two reporters who disappeared when they followed the approaches of ozone plates and the celebrations accompanying the ozone plates. Maybe nothing would change.

Lloyd went into the conference room and took note of his staff in ways he hadn't done before. He thought they were all patriots, doing jobs that fell short of their early expectations. They didn't complain. They were good people, most of whom were supporting families. It was time for him to stand up for all of them.

CHAPTER 17

April 4, 2040

Janet awakened early, unsure of where she was. Her dream told her she was on a path with an eagle overhead. She felt the quilt over her and realized she was in bed.

She lay quiet for a long time, listening to the creaking the house made. When she heard people talking and moving below, she got up and dressed. She was unsure as to the time. "What day is this? How long have I been here? Let's see. I came on Saturday, so Sunday was the first full day I spent. Yesterday was Monday, so today is Tuesday. I go home on Saturday," she said aloud as she dressed. She joined the others at breakfast. As usual, Joe and Cody left while the women cleaned up.

"It's a nice day. Why don't you spend some time outside?" suggested Sonia.

"I thought I would be able to continue with my interview," said Janet.

"You can talk to Old Woman this afternoon. She's conducting a history class with the children later this morning.

"Old Woman tells the children stories about history, and Joe tells them the stories that only one of our people can tell them. When Old Woman passes on, Antoine will tell them our history, and Old Woman will be included in his stories," said Sonia.

"I don't understand the way things are here. I don't want to believe that Old Woman will die simply because I am done with my interviews," said Janet.

Sonia paused, hearing the Old Woman's voice telling her about white people. "We are taught that we know more than others do and that we are in control. We believe that we can cause things we can't cause and can control things over which there is no control, like the weather."

Sonia shook her head. "You and your interviews will not cause Old Woman to walk on. She is old. She has this time with you because it is something she is supposed to do. We honor that."

Janet was silent. She felt as if all her time here was spent getting lectured.

Sonia interrupted her thoughts. "You can walk along the lake and take the path off to the right. Old Woman wants you to see the waterfall."

Janet headed for the lake and found the path that Sonia had suggested. It followed alongside a stream that emptied into the lake. The path was rocky, and she stumbled and fell a few times. She was about to give up and go back to the house when the path became flat stone, almost like a sidewalk. Janet heard rushing water ahead and came to a curve in the path.

Just around the curve, she saw a two-tiered waterfall pouring down between two stone cliffs. The water poured over the flat stones and brought out the red, orange, and yellow of the stones. Adding to the ambience, the early-morning sun shone through the light mist surrounding the falls. The green from the trees and bushes reflected in the mist, tinting the air. Janet gasped. The scene surrounding the waterfall included large wooden frames made out of sticks bent over like semicircular hoops, their ends poked into the ground. She thought they must be frames for some kind of buildings. There were bare strips on the birch trees where someone had cut into the bark and pulled it off. There was nothing like this in the virtual reality museum. This place seemed magical, and Janet wanted to explore.

She climbed up the path to the top of the cliff and sat, her feet dangling over the edge. Janet leaned back against a tree trunk that grew out of the rocks and shut her eyes. She didn't ever want to leave.

As she sat, Janet heard tinkling like a triangle. She opened her eyes and saw a small figure hovering in the mist above the waterfall. *I am seeing things!* A spirit had materialized, looked at her, bowed, and floated away on a breeze.

A patch of warm air came on the breeze, surrounding her like a blanket. She heard the giggling she had heard when she was reading in Old Woman's room.

Janet soon fell into a light sleep. She was awakened by some rustling sounds downstream and opened her eyes. She saw a black bear with two cubs splashing in the stream. The bear looked at her, opened its mouth, and yelled, then gathered up the cubs and disappeared into the trees.

Janet got up and followed the path over the top of the bluff and met up with five doe and twice as many fawns, their backs sprinkled with white spots. They had gathered to drink. Squirrels ran through the tree branches, chasing one another. Birds were singing. The sounds were like music.

Janet sat on the ground, wet from the mist of the waterfall. A large rabbit hopped slowly over to her, stopped, twitched its nose, and stared. She sat and watched, not wanting to scare it off. The mist, plants, trees, and animals surrounded Janet as she inhaled the sweet-smelling air.

Plant shoots were pushing their way out of the ground and through the debris left last fall when the trees lost their leaves. She heard small, light voices coming from the trees. She looked but didn't see anyone, although the spaces between the leaves and the trees seemed to be filled with something she couldn't see or define.

Janet sat until the sun was overhead. She got up and walked back along the trail, stopping to look at the plants along the way. Her route took her back to the lake, where she saw fish jumping out of the water, catching the bugs that hovered just above the surface. There was a canoe with two boys fishing.

The sights, the sounds, and the smells were overwhelming. All of the messages about the importance of success, money, and power in her world meant nothing. This world was filled with clean air, the drama of nature, and the colors of the forest. Janet felt filled with wisdom through her discovery. She wanted to tell someone but didn't know if her newfound wisdom would be welcomed. She decided not to say anything. She lingered alongside the lake and then continued toward the house.

As she walked along the path, Janet noticed a large, round, grayish object on the ground. She slowed as she approached it and was reaching for the object when a large, dark hand clamped her wrist from behind and pulled her away.

Janet stiffened and gasped. She turned her head to look at the man who was holding on to her. He was over six feet tall. Mike White Eagle was dark, and his facial features included high, flat cheekbones and a prominent, hooked nose. His hair was black and long, pulled back and held with a slender strip of cloth. He let go of Janet. "That's a snapping turtle. All they know is to protect and feed themselves. You almost lost a hand."

Janet stared at him.

The man introduced himself. "I'm Joe's son-in-law. I believe you're the woman who is staying at his house."

Janet continued to stare. Mike shook his head. "You look like you're afraid of me." He raised a hand to stop her from speaking. "This isn't about me coming up behind you. Am I too dark for you? What do you think I am going to do to you? Whatever it is, I'm not interested."

Mike found a thick stick and held it near the turtle's mouth. The creature lunged and grabbed the stick. Mike pulled back his attitude, knowing he was to show respect to the visitor.

"Here," said Mike. "Help me carry this back to the house. The women can make turtle soup. This is your contribution to the food supply."

Janet grabbed the stick, and she and Mike walked back to the house. When they arrived at the house, the family was eating lunch outside at a picnic table.

Sonia, seeing the turtle, said, "Oh, good. I'll get that ready to cook after we eat lunch, and we can have that for supper tomorrow night." Joe rose from the table and got an ax. Mike hoisted the turtle onto a chopping block made from a tree stump, held the turtle's shell steady, and pulled on the stick, causing the turtle to extend his neck. A swift stroke of the ax decapitated the turtle, and a spray of blood surrounded the chopping block.

Janet decided she wasn't hungry.

After lunch, Janet decided to take another walk. As she walked around the corner of the house, she stopped, staring at the scene in front of her. Janet let her breath out quickly, swallowing to keep from vomiting.

Joe had the bloody carcass of a large animal with short tan hair on the picnic table where the family had eaten lunch. His arms were covered in blood. On the ground beside the table were what Janet thought must be the innards of the animal. Judging by its short coat, she thought it must be a deer. Cody was standing off to one side with two other boys.

How anyone could kill a deer? thought Janet as she gagged at the sight and the smell of the dead carcass.

Just then, Mike came out of one of the outbuildings carrying a big black cook pot. He looked at Janet and then at Joe, who looked at him. Joe turned his head to keep from laughing.

Mike set the cook pot on the ground and grasped the antlers, pulling each to create a gap in the skull where Joe had cut into the bone. The skull cracked, and Joe reached in to scoop out the brains. He looked up at Janet as he put the brains in the pot. "We're having venison stew tonight."

Janet said, "Where is Sonia?"

"She's on the other side of the house by the firepit," said Joe.

Janet hurried away and found Sonia standing over a metal frame with a hook in the middle. The hook was holding a black cast-iron pot. Sonia was pouring water into the cook pot. Just beyond the cook pot was a large, rectangular frame holding a grill.

Sonia looked at Janet. "I'm getting ready to cut up the venison for stew. You can help."

Sonia said, "Sierra, go in the kitchen and get a knife."

Sierra came running over and went into one of the outbuildings. She came out with a sharp knife.

Sonia pointed with her chin and her lips. "That frame over there is for cooking meat. The soups and stews are cooked over this pit. That stand over there is for cutting meat and vegetables. During the warm months, we cook outside. We don't often use the cook stove in the kitchen. That building over there is our summer kitchen, and that big hunk of wood is a cutting board," she said.

Janet stood waiting for the venison to appear. The smells of burning wood and fresh air blocked the smell of the freshly killed deer. Some of the packaged food she bought had flavoring that suggested it had been cooked over a wood fire. A couple of years before, there had been a cancer scare because the additives that created the wood smoke flavor had been found to cause cancer in rats. It had been taken off the shelves, and a new sprinkle-on wood smoke flavoring had appeared in stores.

At first, cooking from scratch seemed a bother to Janet. Now, the preparation and eating were parts of the meal ceremony. She just didn't like to see dead animals.

Joe came around the corner, holding large pieces of meat in his hands. He nodded at Janet. "Are you ready for some fresh venison?" he asked.

"I guess so," said Janet. "I haven't eaten any kind of fresh meat since I was a kid. I had forgotten that in order to get meat, someone has to kill the animal. My food is processed, and I just do what I have to do to eat a meal. I don't think about how we do things or why."

"We are taught why we do things the way we do them. In the winter, we tell stories. Certain people in our community tell stories about the beginning of our existence. Those stories tell us who we are," said Joe.

"When we are children, we learn how to work with our parents and other adults. As we learn, we come to understand our rituals. Everything fits together. According to Old Woman, very little in your world fits together. Old Woman says that what counts is making money. She says that anything that furthers that goal is acceptable, depending on who you are, so what's the point in your life?" asked Joe.

Janet sat for a long time. Each time she thought she had a rational answer for his question and opened her mouth to speak, she realized that what she was about to say didn't make sense. After five minutes of a silent argument, she said, "I don't know. The only thing I know right now is that I don't feel confused and scared here anymore."

Joe poked at the fire. "You're learning some things."

Janet thought this might be a time to recruit him to her cause. "We need someone like you. You can teach the people in the rest of the country how to live."

Joe shook his head. "Our ways have been here for a very long time. When Europeans first came here, they had their chance to learn our ways. Instead, they fought with us, imprisoned us as war criminals when they started the wars, and slaughtered whole communities. When they killed us, they displayed our bones and brains in their museums and houses of government, herded us onto land that wouldn't support us or anyone else, tried to make us accept their ways, and finally, now, have decided to leave us alone.

"When they 'discover' places, food, healing ways, and I don't know how many other things that we knew about before they came here, they don't acknowledge that they acquired the wisdom from us.

"Your people are poisoning our Mother Earth, and they keep trying to come up with solutions that only provide temporary protection. Then they sell the protection, make more money, and add more pollutants to the environment. If they are ever going to listen to us, the time to do it is right now. We will have to wait until all of the technology that has created the pollution breaks down and can't be fixed. If any of us are still alive, we'll start cleaning it up. That's what I'm waiting for."

"How can you just sit back and wait?" asked Janet.

"We have been taught to respond to what is around us. We respond to nature. We go hunting for animals in areas where we know we will find them. We don't plan long trips when it's twenty below zero. We stay inside and find something else to do.

"Fighting with white men is like taking a long trip when it's cold and stormy. It's dangerous and has no point.

"We haven't gained much in our relationships with whites. We learn patience and timing here. Patience means everything when I realize there's a problem and look for solutions. I find that there are some things I can't solve. That's when I wait," said Joe.

Janet said, "Why don't you join us? Look at what they did to you and to your ancestors. If you join with us, you could take back what is yours."

"If we took back what is ours, where would you go? Are you going to live like we do? The Creator taught us that we are not to fight foolishly. Fighting white men with all their power would be fighting foolishly. We are Ogitchidaa, a word that means warriors in our language. It means we live with honor, dignity, and respect. It also means that we take care of Mother Earth as best we can. We can't take care of all of the messes the white men have made while treating this country like their playground. They are like children who come up with ideas without considering the consequences.

"Nuclear power—what about waste? Just bury it in the ground! What if the storage containers break open and contaminate the soil and the water? 'Oh, that won't happen. We know what we're doing. Oil spills from boats, pipelines, and drilling sites—oh, we'll just clean them up. The plants, birds and animals will survive. Those who don't are weak. We'll just be carrying on the survival of the fittest theory. Space travel—what about the junk that we leave floating around up there? So what? There's lots of room.'

"We are like the scavengers in nature—the buzzards, the crows. We clean up the messes that others make. We respect our Mother Earth, and like the other scavengers, we are reviled by whites," said Joe.

Janet started to say, "But if we joined together …"

"You don't get it. If you heard the history that Old Woman tells the children, you would know that we have been suckered into alliances with whites before. The best-known time was called the French and Indian War. The French got some islands in the Caribbean, the British got Canada and more islands in the Caribbean, and we got the alcohol made from the sugar on the islands. The alcohol was spiked with arsenic.

"When I was in high school, I went to school in town. I would come home angry because the history they taught was different from the history Old Woman taught me. Old Woman calls their history the First Football Game. She says that white people continue to hear American history and stand on the sidelines cheering for a bunch of men who were out of control—men who plundered, raped, and murdered Mother Earth and everything born of her.

"Old Woman taught me things about myself. She told me that I had better do something constructive with my anger because any time I took my anger out on white men, I would lose. She was right. I don't engage in battles that belong to someone else, and I spend my time providing for my family.

"Your fight isn't ours. We are here now because we tend to what is ours. I don't want you here. You are here because my nephew had a dream, and Old Woman talks to the spirits. I respect that, but I don't have to like it," said Joe.

Janet had no words.

Sonia came over to the cutting board, grabbed a piece of the venison, and began cutting. "This is how you cut fresh meat. Be careful. These knives are sharp," she said.

When they finished cutting the meat, Sonia began scooping it up and putting it in the cook pot over the fire. She said to Janet, "Old Woman is in the house if you want to talk to her."

Janet went into the house. She washed the animal blood off her hands.

Old Woman was sitting at the kitchen table. "Oh, it's good to see you again. Let's see. What are we going to talk about today?"

Janet pulled out her recorder as Old Woman started to speak. She spoke without any introduction to her story. "The 1960s have been called many things, some of which are true. It was the beginning of the involvement in the Vietnam War, the first war we watched on television. It was the beginning of widespread drug use among young people.

"The Vietnam War was different. First of all, those of us who were young adults realized that the country's leaders were going to make this our war, even though we didn't know where Vietnam was. We heard about the domino theory and how all of Southeast Asia would go communist if North Vietnam won. It just didn't seem like a good enough reason to go off and die.

"Many objected to the draft, although a draft had been in place for a long time. Like many young people, we thought we knew more than we did, and we didn't want anyone telling us what to do.

"Without all the details, the 1960s were about civil rights, self-centeredness, drugs, and a major rebellion committed by young adults against older adults who were just beginning to reap the rewards of power and control and didn't want their place in the sun to be disturbed. Many of the older adults had gone to war and had a sense of patriotism that didn't fit what was happening in Vietnam.

"It was also a time when we became aware that there was a country to our north that we didn't know much about, one that didn't always agree with our government. Many people decided to go to Canada to escape the draft and were accepted as political refugees. Some stayed and became citizens, while some came back after they were granted amnesty by our government. This was probably the first and only time our government said, 'I'm sorry,' about much of anything. The next time they said, 'I'm sorry,' happened with black people, but that wasn't a full 'I'm sorry.' It was just enough to provide some hope that more would be coming soon.

"After we lost the Vietnam War, some things settled down a bit. Some of the protestors had a change of heart and took full advantage of their notoriety, becoming politicians, bankers, and corporate executives who made money and didn't pay a lot of attention to the things for which they had allegedly fought. In spite of that, there were people, mostly vets, who were determined not to let any of us forget about Vietnam.

"The federal government decided to build a memorial to the Vietnam vets, a big, black granite wall with the names of those who died. People came by the thousands, finding the names of their fathers, mothers, sons, daughters, and husbands, leaving mementoes. Children found their parents' names carved into the black granite, giving them an identity that they hadn't had before. That wall in Washington that was built to memorialize the dead from Vietnam became like a city within a city, a home for those veterans who had trouble coming home.

"A few years ago, they put a fence around it, saying that it was wearing away because of all of the contact by human hands. That was a way to put distance, to let us all know who was in charge. Now, there are travel restrictions, so people outside of Washington can't go to the wall," said Old Woman.

"We see images of it at the virtual reality museums. We can enter a name of a veteran and find it on that image," said Janet.

Old Woman continued. "Drug use became popularized, and many young people gave up career goals their parents had for them and used drugs that dulled their minds. Some died, some quit their unproductive lifestyles and joined society, and some just continued to use drugs.

"There were also those who wanted society to change. They had begun demonstrating against the war. Blacks and women began demonstrating, and those in power realized that they needed to create the appearance of compliance for those who wanted change. For them, the 1960s was the beginning of a battle to grant more to the have-nots without upsetting the balance of power. It was the beginning of the illusion about equal rights. Who could have known that the idealism of that era would turn a corner and end up with what we have now?" Old Woman paused.

"I remember a little bit about the way things were before the social engineering. Before Homeland Security gained so much power. The history we learn through television says that we won the Vietnam War. There is no talk of demonstrations. My parents taught me about the way things used to be, but it's hard to keep track of that now that they're gone. It's different here, but I don't know if it's a difference that's better than what's out there where I come from," said Janet.

"What's better than clean air and water and living in balance with nature?" asked Old Woman.

"We live differently than you do. Our contributions help us get ahead and our employers get ahead," countered Janet.

"Yes. You also compete, and the competition is often unfriendly," said Old Woman.

"What's wrong with competition?" asked Janet.

"Here, competition is about survival and doing the best job possible. If someone needs help with something, others will come to their aid," said Old Woman.

"I don't know if I could live like this," said Janet.

"It would be your choice. I don't think your lifestyle is healthy. I don't think either of us is going to change our opinions with this discussion. We'll talk again soon," said Old Woman, dismissing Janet.

Shortly after Janet's talk with Old Woman, the family gathered for supper. They went through their evening routine and went to bed when darkness came.

Janet was tired. She had had a full day. Even though she heard Old Woman's words, she had trouble understanding. It seemed to her the only things people did there was hunt, fish, prepare food, and eat.

Sleep came quickly, and Janet found herself in another dream. Everything around her was dark. She smelled an animal odor and heard something snuffling and shuffling nearby. She struggled unsuccessfully to wake up to see if there was anything in the room with her. In the dream, she saw the shadows of a large animal and two smaller animals. Suddenly they were gone, and her sleep continued without any more dreaming.

CHAPTER 18

July 1969

When Marvin Black Bear came home from Vietnam, he spent six months in rehab recovering from wounds that left him a paraplegic. When Marvin was discharged, Bud Nelson, the local veterans' service officer, drove the VA van with disability capabilities to the front doors of the hospital, where Marvin was waiting in his wheelchair. A hospital attendant wheeled Marvin over to the platform, and then Bud pushed the button to raise the platform so Marvin could wheel himself into the van.

"Hey, Jim," said Marvin to the attendant. "Get me out of this thing so I can sit in the front seat. It's got to be more comfortable than this chair, and I've got a ways to go."

"Just a minute, Marvin. I need some help with this. You're a big guy, and it takes more than me to lift you," said Jim.

"I can help," said Bud, and the two men struggled to move Marvin to the front seat.

"There you go, guy," said Jim. "Have a safe trip home."

Bud drove the van out onto the road and then onto the highway, heading north. "Marvin, I got some money to help your family build a ramp on the front of your mother's house and a deck on the back. The home health program will visit you three times a week. We have a veterans' support group that meets on Wednesdays. If you want to attend, let me know, and I can pick you up."

"What's this group like?" asked Marvin.

"Well, the guys get together and share their stories about the war," said Bud.

"I don't think they would want to hear my stories about the war. Anyway, I don't think I'm ready to talk about anything having to do with Vietnam or the military," said Marvin.

"Suit yourself," said Bud. "We're here if you change your mind."

The two men rode in silence for a few miles. Then Marvin said, "Bud, thanks for the help with the ramp and the deck and thanks for coming to get me. I appreciate it."

"You're welcome. I'm glad you made it home. You're going to have some adjusting to do. If I can help with that, I will."

"I don't know that I'll need your help. My family and our community will help me," said Marvin.

"Well, I'm glad to hear that. When I read your record, I wondered why you enlisted," said Bud.

"Our people have always enlisted in the military—I mean after the government quit sending troops to kill us. This is our country. We were here before you. We want to make sure our country is safe. Although I wonder now why we went to war with Vietnam," said Marvin.

"Well, I don't know if any of us understand many of the workings of the federal government," said Bud. "You paid quite a price for your service, and America owes you."

"I don't want to think about that. I just want to get home and settle in. It's been a long six months of physical therapy. A nephew of mine came to the hospital and learned how to help me with my exercises. It's time to put him to work," said Marvin.

The men continued the trip in silence, Marvin watching the landscape change as they traveled north. When they pulled up in front of Marvin's mother's house, his nephew Joe, his niece Sonia, and other nieces and nephews were there to greet him.

The men helped him out of the van and put him in his wheelchair. His mother, Margaret, came out and worked her way down the maze that was the wheelchair ramp to get in and out of the house.

Maggie, one of Marvin's nieces, said, "Why didn't she just use the stairs?"

Her sister, Evie, said, "She didn't want to remind him that she can use the stairs and he can't."

"I think he better get used to being in that chair. If not, Margaret is going to waste away with all the exercise," said Maggie.

When Margaret reached Marvin, she threw her arms around him, crying. "My boy! My boy! I'm so glad you're home. This is where you belong. All of us, your family, are here to take care of you."

More relatives and friends had gathered inside the house. There was a drum, and the drummers and singers played an honor song. Marvin cried. It was so good to be home where he knew what to expect.

The visitors talked quietly. A meal was served, and Melvin Cloud, a medicine man and Marvin's uncle, prayed over the food. A plate was made and set out under the trees so that Melvin's prayers would reach the Creator.

No one asked Marvin about the injury that landed him in the chair. As the sun set, they left Marvin with his mother and some nephews to help him to bed.

Marvin's mother died in January following Marvin's return, and Marvin stayed in the house alone. He had some help during the day from nephews.

Marvin had learned how to talk about the war. He spoke of little else, and those who came to see him tired of his stories. Their visits dropped off, and Marvin was alone much of the time. He refused to go to the support group that Bud Nelson had mentioned.

Summer came and passed. Marvin did little to celebrate the long days and the warm weather. Fall came and passed, and winter came again. The hours of daylight grew shorter, and Marvin grew depressed.

His mother's spirit would come to visit him, scolding him about his state of mind. Marvin tried to ignore her. The more she scolded, the more stubborn he became. He just sat in the house, waiting to die.

In January, he heard a knock on the door. Marvin decided not to answer, but soon Melvin Cloud stuck his head in and said, "Marvin, you don't look like you feel too good."

"I don't. How would you like to be sitting in this chair for the rest of your life?"

"May I come in? It's cold out here."

"Come in if you want to. There is tea on the stove. Excuse me if I don't get it for you."

"I can still use my legs, so I'll get some for both of us. Gee, this sure is a good fire you got here, Marvin. I think it would take me a while to get used to sitting in a chair like yours," said Alvin. If that ever happens to me I hope you will help me adjust."

"It isn't about adjustment. There just aren't a lot of alternatives. Did you come to cure me?"

"Maybe I did. I can't make you walk again, but maybe you can learn how to live in that chair. I think I will spend some time with you."

The two men sat silently for several hours. Marvin didn't want to talk; he wanted to die. Alvin didn't want to be rude and interrupt Marvin's thoughts. When lunchtime came, Alvin asked Marvin, "What are we having for lunch?"

"Can't you look for yourself? You've got two good legs. Why don't you fix us something?"

"Who fixes you lunch when I'm not here, Marvin?"

"Alvin, you aren't here very often. I fix my own lunch."

"Well, if you can fix your own lunch, then you can fix mine."

Marvin wheeled himself into the kitchen and began angrily banging pots and pans. He opened the door to the porch and brought in some wild rice soup he had had for supper the night before. Then he took out the cast-iron pan he used to make fry bread.

When Marvin was just about done fixing their lunch, Alvin said, "Can I help you with anything, Marvin?"

Marvin grumbled and told Alvin to help bring the food to the table.

"This is good soup," said Alvin. "I've heard rumors that you are just about the best fry bread maker on the rez."

"My mother taught me how to cook. Fry bread was her specialty."

When the two men finished eating, Alvin said, "Don't get up, Marvin. I'll do the dishes."

"Thanks for the visit," said Marvin. "I don't want to keep you any longer. You probably have some things to do."

"No, I'm fine. I came to spend the day with you, and that's what I plan to do," said Alvin.

The two men were silent for most of the afternoon. Then, his voice soft and slow, Alvin said, "Marvin, if you kill yourself, your spirit will have to remain here until the time comes that Gitchi Manido has planned for your death. No one knows how long you're supposed to live. You might have to hang around here for a long time, and your movements would be as limited as they are now. Your spirit would be crippled, just as crippled as you think you are now. Marvin, you are still here because there is something you are supposed to do.

"Gitchi Manido would have let you die in Vietnam if He had been finished with you. I have no idea how hard this is for you, but you are making it harder than it needs to be."

"I don't get many visitors. I get lonely," said Marvin.

"Who wants to come to visit you? You're ornery. You sit here and feel sorry for yourself. Your family probably has a raffle to see who has to come and check on you. They probably try to keep their visits as short as they can. If you want people to come to visit you, you have to give them something to look forward to when they come." Alvin got up to leave.

Marvin said, "Here, I'll get you some tobacco."

"You don't have to, Marvin. You didn't ask me to come. I came because I wanted to. You were a hero in that war. You figured out how to stay alive. Now that you have survived, you have to figure out how to live."

Marvin cried when Alvin left. He cried into the evening until it was time for bed. No one came to check on him that night. When he got up in the morning, he smelled breakfast cooking.

He dressed and went into the kitchen to find his nephew Joe fixing him breakfast. "Eh, Uncle Marvin. When I got up this morning, I just had a feeling that you might like it if I fixed breakfast."

Marvin wheeled over to Joe and hugged him. "Eh, Nephew. You had a good feeling."

Joe stayed with Marvin most of the day. By the time he left, the sun was low in the sky. "Eh, Nephew. I like it when you come to visit."

"I can't come all the time, Uncle. Why don't you get a dog?"

When Joe told his mother that Marvin was looking for a dog, Sonia went to visit Marvin and asked him what kind of dog he wanted. Marvin had never thought about choosing a specific dog. Dogs just seemed to happen on the rez. They sometimes just appeared like magic, stayed for a while, and then traveled on. No one seemed to know where they came from or where they went.

Deciding on a dog had some sense of permanency to it. Marvin decided that he wanted a dog that was mostly black. "Yeah, I want a black lab. It should probably be older than a puppy. Puppies are a lot of work, and I'm not used to taking care of someone other than myself."

It was easy to find dogs on the rez, but Sonia figured she would have to find just the right dog for Marvin. She knew that it wasn't the way of things to deliberately go looking for a dog. She would just be aware, and the opportunity would present itself.

While she was visiting one morning with friends, one of them mentioned that one of the elders had a dog to give away.

Knowing that this dog had to be just the right dog, Sonia asked, "Why does he want to give it away?"

"Are you looking for another dog, Sonia? That one of yours is always having pups."

"I'm trying to find a dog for Marvin. He needs someone to take care of. He says he wants a dog that is mostly black lab," said Sonia.

"Well, Leon has a dog that's black and has short hair. It's real friendly and has a lot of energy. He's a nice dog."

"Why does Leon want to give it away?" asked Sonia again.

"He says he is getting too old to take care of a dog. Leon says that he wants to make sure this dog gets a good home so the dog won't come back to him."

Sonia went to Leon's house after she visited with her friends. She knocked and heard a voice telling her to come in.

"Leon. It's good to see you." She sat with Leon for a couple of hours before either of them spoke. "I hear you have a dog to give away."

"Sonia, do you want another dog? Your big dog stays outside. My dog, Muckaday, comes in the house."

"Marvin needs a dog," said Sonia.

Muckaday was lying on the floor beside the old man's rocking chair. His ears perked when he heard his name. He got up and walked over to Sonia, wagging his tail and sniffing.

"How old is he?" asked Sonia.

"He's about a year old. He wandered into the yard last summer. He stayed for a couple of days before I fed him. He's a good dog. Sometimes he gets a bit lively. That's when I send him outside. He runs and chases whatever he finds out there. When he's tired, he comes back in. He would make a good dog for Marvin. I hope Marvin knows what he wants. I don't want to have to take this dog back."

Leon spent some time talking to the dog. When he finished, Muckaday walked over to Sonia and looked up expectantly.

"He's ready to leave now," said Leon.

Sonia walked out of the house, followed by Muckaday. They walked together to Marvin's. Marvin cried when he saw Muckaday, saying, "He's about as much black lab as I could find around here."

"This dog lived with Leon. He's pretty well trained, so he will tell you what he needs. If you need any help with him, just let Joe know. Oh, he understands our language," said Sonia.

Muckaday settled in, and he and Marvin lived together for about ten years. They got on well. Marvin never had to worry about where Muckaday went or what he did. When he got restless, Muckaday would ask to go out. He usually returned after a couple of hours, giving no clue as to where he had been. Marvin had a pet door installed so that Muckaday could leave without asking.

One day, Muckaday didn't come home, and Marvin knew something was wrong. He sent his nephews out into the woods to look for Muckaday. They spent a day in the woods, calling him and searching for him, but they couldn't find Muckaday.

Muckaday had gotten into a fight with something in the woods that fought better than he did. He had been gone two days when he dragged himself home on the path, up the steps of the deck, and scratched on the door, too weak to use the pet door. Marvin got a rug and put it down for the dog to crawl onto. Then he leaned over and pulled the rug and the dog into the house.

Marvin looked at the dog's wounds and knew that he was dying. Marvin brought water and scooped it into his hand so the dog could drink. Marvin sat with the dog long into the night until the animal sighed his last breath.

The next morning Alvin Cloud came to visit. "It's a good thing you came, Alvin. I need someone to bury my dog."

"I'll go get Joe and Mike," said Alvin.

"Why can't you just take the shovel and bury him in the yard?" asked Marvin.

"Because somebody has to carry you out there. We'll have a ceremony."

"I've never heard of a ceremony for a dog before."

"This isn't a ceremony for the dog. It's a ceremony for you. You're alive, and you have given to another living being. That's a good reason for a ceremony. And I know someone who has some puppies she's trying to give away. I'll tell her you are looking for another dog," said Alvin.

"Don't you think I should grieve this one first, Alvin? Someone might think I'm heartless if I get another dog too soon," said Marvin.

"A dog isn't a woman, Marvin. You will honor the dog's memory best by getting another one soon. Besides, if a man loses a wife and takes another wife too soon, he will have to face the anger of all the women around here. They usually don't get upset if a man gets another dog," said Alvin.

They buried Muckaday on the edge of the yard under a big maple tree. Shortly after, Alvin brought a puppy who lived with Marvin for fifteen years. He was a rez dog—big with body parts easily recognizable as characteristics of many different breeds of dogs.

Marvin's visitors would hold contests to see who could recognize the most breeds in Adjidamo, so named because his bushy gray tail reminded people of a squirrel's tail. Someone identified fifteen different breeds that could be found in Adjidamo, setting the all-time record. He was everything that all fifteen breeds could be.

Adjidamo was easily recognized in the community. No one had anything bad to say about him, as he was a good dog. Marvin honored Muckaday's memory by giving Muckaday the credit for teaching him how to take care of a dog. "If it hadn't been for Muckaday, there wouldn't be Adjidamo," he would say when someone praised Adjidamo for being a good dog.

Adjidamo aged well. He was in his fifteenth year, and it was getting harder and harder for him to take care of Marvin. One morning, he whined as if he wanted to go out, even though he used the pet door all the time.

Marvin wheeled over to the door, and Adjidamo stood slowly, his joints painful with arthritis. He put his chin on Marvin's knee, breathed deeply, and fell to the floor. He was buried under the maple tree alongside Muckaday, and Alvin brought another ceremony to Marvin.

Animosh came shortly after the burial, walking and stumbling behind Joe. He had just been weaned from his mother and still had trouble walking. Animosh was mostly German shepherd and projected the traits of the breed in his friendly, enthusiastic manner and the large tongue that fell out of his mouth when he smiled.

When Animosh met Marvin, he walked around the wheelchair, sniffing. He spent most of his time sniffing Marvin's legs and decided through his exploration that it was his job to take care of Marvin, who had decided that the best way any dog could take care of him was to carry written messages, as he had no phone. Animosh, being an almost full-blooded German shepherd, was the dog to be trained as a message bearer.

At first, Animosh was not as popular as Adjidamo or Muckaday because of his exuberance, jumping up and slurping people with his long tongue.

Marvin would say, "He's a pup. If it weren't for Muckaday and Adjidamo, there wouldn't be Animosh." Those who had been slurped by Animosh thought that would probably be okay.

After Animosh had learned not to jump on people and slurp them in the face, Marvin asked Joe to help him teach Animosh to carry messages. Marvin had gotten a collar for Animosh. Most people asked, "Why does he need a collar for that dog? Does he think that dog is something special just because he is an almost full-blooded German shepherd?"

Marvin knew that Animosh was special and had the right stuff for the training. He ignored all of the remarks he heard. He, Joe, and Animosh spent a day working on carrying messages. Marvin would write a note, put it in Animosh's collar, and send him to Joe's house. When Animosh arrived at Joe's, Joe would pat him, take the note from the collar, and return with Animosh to Marvin's.

After that first day, Joe went to others in the community and asked them to be part of the training program. After about a week, Animosh knew where he was to deliver messages by the names Marvin spoke. He had fun running to different houses and running back with people following him.

After a while, Animosh lived to carry messages. When Marvin put a message in Animosh's collar, it was all the dog could do to wait until the message was attached. He trembled, waiting to leave, running without pause to his destination. Animosh gained the respect of everyone in the community. When he was seen running, people paused to see if he was chasing something or if he had a message from Marvin. When he brought a message, someone would say, "One of these days, he is going to save someone's life."

Animosh was getting up in years. Now, when someone said, "One of these days, he's going to save someone's life," another would say, "Well, he better do it before he joins the other two under the maple tree."

CHAPTER 19

July 1969

While Marvin Black Bear was fighting the war in Vietnam, Levi Starrett was protesting it. Levi and his wife, Sarah, moved to northern Wisconsin from Chicago during the 1960s when social protests meant drugs, indiscriminate sex, rock 'n' roll, and living off the land. Levi and Sarah skipped the first three and decided to spend their lives protesting social injustice and the wasting of natural resources as they learned how to live in the woods. They planned to grow old together, but their activism brought the attention of law enforcement when they were protesting mining activities. Sarah was arrested, and Levi went home to get money to post bail. Just as he was leaving their house, Levi got a visit from the sheriff, who told him that Sarah had gotten sick in jail and died. She had been transported to the local funeral home.

Levi went to the funeral home and asked to see her body It was covered with bruises. There was an inquest, and the coroner said she died of natural causes. Levi went to see a lawyer, who told him that Levi was seen as an agitator and that he would lose any lawsuit he filed.

Levi and their five children buried Sarah in Levi's backyard. Levi continued his activism and posted signs in his yard protesting everything he found offensive.

Even though Levi was viewed as a person who was just a bit odd, the couple had made friends on the reservation. Many Indian families helped Levi raise his children, who chose to remain near their father and near their mother's grave after they reached adulthood, marrying people who lived in the area. All the children and their families lived communally, raising gardens and livestock together and sharing the venison and fish the men harvested.

As Levi aged, his hair changed from an average brown to white, flowing down his back, nearly to his waist. He was unshaven, his beard reaching the middle of his chest. He wore patched bib overalls and hemp sandals he had resoled many times over the years. He told his children and grandchildren, "When I die, bury me in what I wear every day. I want to be comfortable when I make my journey."

His children watched over him as unobtrusively as they could. He had raised them, and they felt a responsibility to give back to him. They were out of touch with the rest of the country and chose to stay that way, accepting Levi's predictions as to the impending fate of the world as the words of a prophet.

Levi spent much of his time predicting that the government and "they" were going to come to northern Wisconsin and hunt down anyone whose family could be traced to the mining protests and the boat-landing demonstrations about the hunting and fishing rights for Ojibwe people.

No one tried to tell him the invasion wouldn't happen. He wouldn't have listened. Look what had happened to Sarah.

After Sarah died, Levi built a tunnel. It took him several years. It collapsed several times and was braced with timber and lined with cement. It was wide enough for about three people to stand broadside, and from floor to ceiling, it measured about six and a half feet.

Levi figured someone could live there for about six months if necessary. He stockpiled canned food and bottled water. He checked expiration dates on cans once a month and replaced them accordingly. There was a woodstove with a chimney that reached up to ground level in the middle of a bunch of trees. The only way anyone would have known it was there would be if they strayed off the path that led to the reservation. The tunnel led from Levi's house to the edge of the reservation. Marvin's yard was about a mile from the tunnel. Levi believed it was a matter of time before someone would be in need of the tunnel.

He and Marvin became friends over time, working out Marvin's caution about white men and Levi's protest over Vietnam. They would verbally circle each other when they met, waiting for the other to show himself. As the years passed, they forgot about differences and found that their politics were similar.

Levi had faith in Marvin's dreams. Something important was going to happen soon. Marvin was also the only person outside Levi's family who believed that Levi had constructed a tunnel underneath the land his family lived on. Others just considered the rumors to be wild stories that Levi made up. While people in the reservation community accepted Levi, they didn't always believe what he said. They figured that his grief over his wife's death had caused him to be a little off balance.

Even so, people respected Levi. He had survived a great loss. Few whites who came to the area around the reservation with an intent to reside managed to stay and live off the land. Most of those on the reservation had forgotten that Levi was not from there. He was invited to community gatherings and traded with community members.

CHAPTER 20
April 4, 2040

Marvin was tired. He hadn't slept well. His mother came to visit him in a dream. Animosh was on the path headed for Joe's house, and there were eagles flying overhead, circling Marvin's house.

Being a man who believed in his dreams, Marvin was uneasy about the meaning. His dreams had kept him alive during the times that he wanted to die rather than live in a wheelchair. He could fly in some of his dreams. He remembered one in which he was up with the eagles, catching the breezes, soaring and free.

Some of his dreams told him he hadn't done all that he was supposed to do. When he wanted to die, he had argued with those dreams. "If I'm not here to do what I am supposed to do, someone else can do it."

Today, Marvin knew what he was supposed to do. The day he had been living for was coming. His dream told him that.

Marvin tucked a note inside Animosh's collar. "Go, boy. Go find Levi," said Marvin, patting Animosh on the head. Animosh raced off to deliver Marvin's message, traveling the five miles down the old trail that came from the south, passing through Marvin's yard and points north.

Animosh traveled on this old trail often. When he reached Levi's house, he skidded to a stop in front of the steps that led up to the porch, crouched down, and leaped. He took pride in his leaping abilities. He stood in front of the door and barked, letting Levi know he was there.

Levi's grandson Jeremiah came to the door. Animosh knew that he was to deliver the message to Levi and continued to bark. His orders were clear: "Bring the note to Levi." He barked, more forcefully this time.

"Grandpa, I think Animosh is here to see you."

Levi came to the screen and pushed it open, allowing Animosh to enter. Animosh barked again while Levi reached down and checked Animosh's collar, finding a note under the buckle. Levi read, "Come see me. I had a dream. I think we may have a need for your tunnel."

He gave Animosh a drink of water. As he left with Animosh, Jeremiah called after him, "When will you be back?"

"I don't know. Make sure someone stays with the house while I'm gone. You'll be needed."

Levi followed Animosh back to Marvin's. He made the five miles to Marvin's house in a little over an hour. He pounded up the ramp on Marvin's deck, knocked, and entered without waiting for permission.

Marvin was sitting in his kitchen, stirring something on the stove. "Good to see you, Levi. You came just in time for lunch. I'm cooking some venison stew. While we're waiting for it, would you like some tea?"

"Tea sounds good. Tell me where it is, and I'll make some for both of us," said Levi.

"It's already made. Just pour some into those glasses and get some ice from the icebox out on the porch," said Marvin, pointing with his chin and lips toward the antique oak icebox.

"Levi, I know that you have been waiting a long time to use that tunnel you built," said Marvin.

"I have," said Levi.

"Tell me that story again—the story of how you built it," said Marvin.

"It was after Sarah died. I knew something was fishy about the way she died. When I started asking questions, I ended up with more questions than answers. I kept going to more and more offices and finding out less than I knew before. That's when I started to realize that things weren't ever going to get better.

"I had thought that when people started questioning Vietnam and they stopped the war, it meant the government would answer to the people again. I didn't want to move to a city. I thought we would be safe living up here. When I realized that there weren't a lot of safe places and that things weren't going to change, I had to do something to honor Sarah and to feel like I wasn't helpless.

"I know that a lot of people think I'm crazy. Maybe I am a little bit, but I set out to make people think I'm crazy. It keeps out the riffraff.

"I started with all of the signs in the yard. There are so many out there that helicopters, the kind the government uses to capture people, can't land in my yard. They can't land any place close because there are too many trees.

"Then I came up with the tunnel. Did you ever walk that path all the way down to Chippewa Falls? It's a good escape route. Not too many people know about it. Anyone who has to run from that area can take that trail all the way to my place.

"When they get there, whoever is chasing them will have figured out they're going to end up with me. There's so much technology that it's easy to track someone down. When the chasers get just so close, they have to come in on foot.

"That's where the tunnel comes in. It goes down about thirty feet. My grandsons and I made it. It's made out of cement, and there is a ventilation system. It runs alongside the path for five miles and stops at my oldest son's house. It's got supplies in it, so somebody can live down there for a while. When someone comes out of the tunnel, they'll be headed for your place. They'll be on the reservation. It will look like they just disappeared. It's got some booby traps. Anyone who doesn't have business down there will get lost and will get zapped by the booby traps."

"So you're waiting to use that tunnel," said Marvin, pausing to make sure Levi had finished. He sat, looking at the floor out of respect. "I've been having a lot of dreams. I keep seeing a woman running on that path. I don't think she has started out yet, but I think she'll be coming soon. If I find out when she's coming, I'll let you know."

"Is she that woman that's visiting with Old Woman?" asked Levi.

Marvin's eyes wandered over Levi's head, looking out toward the trail. "I don't know who she is, Levi. She's a woman in my dreams, and I don't know exactly what that means right now. I just think that maybe you can help her when the time comes."

Levi knew better than to ask any more questions, and the last answer told him that he wasn't going to get details from Marvin. He felt satisfied knowing that he could put his tunnel to good use after all these years. He might be able to help someone escape.

"You know, Marvin, it's nice to be able to do something important at this time in our lives. I think it's not just Old Woman who is supposed to do something to finish her life.

"I suppose that the feds could decide to arrest me and maybe my family too. We don't live on the reservation. They won't come after you. I don't think they'll come after us either. They're so busy looking for spies and terrorists in the cities. I think they think we're harmless," said Levi.

"Right after we unplugged, there were a lot of folks in the community who thought I shouldn't live alone because there weren't any telephones anymore. Then my relatives talked about what they would do to check on me. They still check on me. I think sometimes the younger kids don't even know they're checking on me. They come over to visit, and they bring me food sometimes. But training Animosh made me more independent than I ever was before. I know that my dreams are telling me that something's going to happen here. I think we'll be a part of it. It's kind of funny. I don't think too many people think that you and I can do anything important. You're supposed to be crazy, and I'm in a wheelchair. When I tell my stories, people think I'm still stuck in Vietnam," said Marvin.

"Maybe we can do things that no one thinks we can do. Maybe being crazy and being in a wheelchair will make people overlook us," said Levi.

The two men sat talking well into the afternoon. Animosh came back from exploring and greeted Levi enthusiastically, then flopped down on the deck and went to sleep.

When Levi went home, he paid his nightly visit to Sarah's grave. "Sarah," he said, "it's going to be like the old days."

CHAPTER 21
April 5, 2040

Sonia had finished with the morning cleanup when she heard the outside door slam. She walked into the kitchen to put on water for tea and found Joe and Mike sitting at the kitchen table.

Mike grinned. "How is your unwelcome guest doing? I think she's going to drive Joe nuts."

Sonia laughed. "She's probably going to drive me nuts too. If that happens, will you take the kids?"

"Where is she?" asked Mike.

"I sent her over to Marvin's," said Sonia.

The men started laughing.

"Well, she should be gone for most of the day," said Mike.

"I suppose you're right. Let's not forget that your Uncle Marvin has a lot of history to share, and he isn't shy about telling his story," said Sonia.

"How long has that old man been telling his stories?" asked Mike.

"He's in his nineties. He came home in the early seventies, so it's been about seventy years," said Sonia.

"I wish he would find something else to talk about," said Mike.

"How can he? He's in that wheelchair. During most of his life, he has watched everyone pass by him. There aren't even that many people who remember Vietnam anymore," said Sonia. "He did a lot of good here. He got lots of young men to look at serving our community rather than going off to die in white men's wars."

"He isn't alone as much as he used to be. I used to think that I was his only visitor. Alvin comes to see him from time to time. When Alvin first started going over to Marvin's, he was there almost every day. Then Alvin's visits tapered off, and Levi started coming to see Marvin.

"I think they believe in each other. They seem to have some idea that they have something important to do together. I don't know if they know what that is. I'm just glad that Marvin has people in his life other than me and Mike. I have enough to do feeding everyone," said Joe.

"I know you do. I know that you don't like having Janet here. When she's gone Old Woman will pass on. I just wish we could spend the little time we have left with her without outside interruptions. I don't understand why that woman had to come here. I think it would be easier if I knew that," said Sonia.

Janet followed Sonia's directions and took a path that opened on an area with grass and wildflowers surrounded by tall trees. There was a house in the clearing with a big wooden ramp that led up and onto a deck. A large dog came running out, barking.

Janet stopped and stood stiffly. She thought the dog might bite her. The dog stopped and began circling her, sniffing.

"Animosh, you stop now. She's okay. Just come back here with me," said Marvin.

Janet looked up to see a man with long black hair flying loose around his face as he maneuvered his wheelchair out onto the deck. He had a bandana rolled and wrapped around his head, a black T-shirt with the initials FBI on it, and frayed denim shorts revealing thin, dark, shriveled legs covered with loose skin.

"Eh, it's okay. Animosh won't hurt you. I wondered when you would get over this way. Come on up on the deck and sit for a while. I've got some iced tea," said Marvin.

Janet walked toward the porch, feeling as if the man's welcoming remarks were a command. She was cautious about the dog, as he was large and exuberant.

Marvin pointed with his chin and his lips at the dog. "Animosh is a good rez dog. He's my connection to everyone. It's hard to take this wheelchair out in the yard. The wheels don't do well in the grass. When I need something quickly, Animosh takes a note for me. I tell him where to go, and he goes," said Marvin.

"I'm Marvin. I'm Joe's uncle. He and Mike take good care of me. Have you met Mike?" asked Marvin. "He's married to Joe's daughter.

"I'm a Vietnam vet. I got this bullet in my back, right up against the spinal column. I got two medals out of that war—one for getting hurt and one for killing people." Marvin extended his hand.

Janet put her hand in Marvin's. She was surprised at the gentle touch of his hand. She couldn't tell his age by looking at him. His face was brown and wrinkled, and his hair was so black it looked like he dyed it.

"You're looking at my hair and wondering why it isn't gray. See, I'm Bear Clan. This is one of the physical traits of Bear Clan. We have black, bushy hair, and we almost never turn gray. Just a minute. I'll get the tea," said Marvin.

Janet sat waiting in a wooden chair on the deck. Marvin was gone for more time than it would take her to go get the beverage. She was about to get up to go see what had happened to Marvin when he came rolling out of the house, a tray balanced on the arms of the wheelchair.

"I'm sorry. I should have asked if you needed help," said Janet.

"No, I do most things alone. Sometimes it just takes me longer than it does other people," said Marvin.

Marvin handed Janet a glass from the tray and set the tray and pitcher on the deck railing. "Antoine sent you here to listen to Old Woman."

Janet nodded, sipping the tea. "She's telling me about her life and the way things used to be."

"Old Woman has good stories. Most people here know what they know from living their lives. Few people here have gone outside this place. There is no reason to go. We have everything we need here.

"At one time, we thought we were supposed to go to school, leave this place, and get a good job. Then we were supposed to bring our money back to feed our families.

"A lot of us went to Vietnam. There aren't many of us left. Some didn't come back. Some of those who did died from the effects of Agent Orange, and some didn't live through the adjustments we had to make after surviving combat."

"What's Agent Orange?" asked Janet.

"It was an insecticide that was used to kill jungle plants in Vietnam so we could maneuver. It was poisonous to people too, and a lot of folks died from it," said Marvin.

He continued with his story. "After Vietnam and 9/11, people started to realize that leaving here wasn't a good thing for us to do. Before the war and 9/11, even though many of us got hurt when we left here, we still thought we were supposed to leave. We got that message from the government, and pretty soon parents would tell each generation to leave, get an education, and find a good job. After a while, there were more of us living in cities than there were living on our land.

"We didn't get hurt just from going to war. There was another war going on, but nobody called it a war. When we would go into town to go to school, we would get picked on. We couldn't stop it. If we fought back, we got into trouble. Sometimes we got put on probation for fighting back. The white boys learned that they could get away with picking on us, so they kept it up. When I was in high school, I got beat up an average of three times a week.

"If we went into town at night, it was worse. Some of us got killed. One of my friends, Wabooz, was stabbed to death. He told me that he wasn't going to take the bus home because he just wanted to see what the kids did in town after school. He made me promise not to tell his parents where he was. I didn't think it was a good plan, but there wasn't any way I could make him go home.

"It got later and later, and Wabooz's parents came over to our house, asking if I knew where he was. Just as I was telling them that Wabooz had decided to stay in town, the police car pulled up. We thought he had gotten into trouble and was in jail.

"The two officers walked up to the house, knocked on the door, and asked for Wabooz's parents. His dad started apologizing for any trouble that Wabooz had gotten into. That was our way back then. If someone apologized right up front, sometimes things would go easier for them.

"The police officer held up his hand and started shaking his head. He handed the police report to Wabooz's father. The report said that five boys had started teasing Wabooz, then ganged up on him and dragged him into an alley. They told the police that they took turns beating him and kicking him. Then one of them pulled out a knife, and they all took turns sticking it in him. They cut off his private parts. That's how someone found his body. A dog came out of the alley with Wabooz's privates in his mouth. The officer said the boys were bragging about what they had done when they were arrested. The officer wouldn't look at Wabooz's parents. He later came to our community meeting and asked if he could move out here with his family. The community gave its approval. He passed away a few years ago, and his sons and their families live in his house.

There was a trial, and the boys were found not guilty. They said they did what they did in self-defense. One of them became a lawyer and later a judge," said Marvin.

Janet put her empty glass on the deck. She didn't know what to say. She felt sick, and she didn't have words that would take away the horror she felt.

"When I came back from the war, I was honored as a veteran. At the powwows, I carried a flag in a metal pocket on my wheelchair during the grand entry. I would balance the flagpole in the pocket, and someone would push the wheelchair as I held the flag steady.

"It took me a long time to come home after I came back from the war. I carried pictures of some of the things I saw in Vietnam in my head. I had been on patrol and was separated from the other men in my outfit. I came crawling out of a swamp near a village just in time to see some of the men in my outfit shooting small children. I watched as the small bodies danced and exploded with the impact of the bullets. I didn't know what to do. If I joined my outfit, I would be expected to participate in the carnage. If I refused, I figured I would probably be killed.

"I lay in the swamp, watching, listening to the men laugh hysterically, calling names. In my body, in my blood, were the memories of similar massacres in which my ancestors had been victims. What would they expect me to do? I couldn't sneak away. I tried to tell myself that if I got away, I could report what I saw, and the army would do something about it. But that would be too late. All of the children I saw running in every direction would be dead.

"I made a decision, and I heard the voices of the spirits sighing. I felt their voices caressing me as I stood up and climbed out of the swamp water. I yelled in the direction of the massacre.

"Two of the soldiers stopped, whirled around, and pointed their guns in my direction. I raised my gun in the air and yelled, 'Don't shoot. It's me.'

"'Hey, Chief. Come on out of there. We've got a job to do. If we kill them when they're little, they won't be around to kill Americans when they're older.'

"I walked toward the scene, my rifle hanging at my side. I approached the two men who had pointed their rifles at me. I pulled the rifle out of the hands of one of them. Then I whirled around and hit the other with my fist. The man dropped to the ground.

"I kept going toward the other men. I felt the approval of my ancestors, and I felt their memories. The shooting stopped.

"'This is what your ancestors did to mine. Warriors don't kill children,' I said. The men in my outfit surrounded me and raised their rifles.

"I heard a loud blast, and I fell forward. One of the Vietnamese villagers had shot me in the back. The soldiers shot back and killed the man. Then they gathered around me," said Marvin.

"'Is he dead?' one of them asked.

"'I don't know. If he isn't, should we finish him off?' asked another.

"'I don't know,' said another of the soldiers standing over me.

"'He isn't one of us. Never was, never will be. When we go home, we'll never see him again,' said a soldier.

"'Let's call a medivac. We'll tell them that we wiped out this village because it was a Viet Cong stronghold. We'll tell them that the Indian was just one of the casualties,' said one of the men as he kicked me in the back where the bullet had gone in.

"It's one of the memories I carry in my body. I don't usually tell this story when I tell of my days in Vietnam. If the villager hadn't shot me, the men in my outfit would have done so, and they would have thrown my body in the swamp. I would have been missing in action. I knew that the spirits were with me that day, protecting me. They brought me home.

"When I first got back from the war, I tried to sift through the pictures in my head and the dreams that wouldn't let me sleep. I figured there were some things I needed to talk about, and there were other things best left unsaid.

"I wanted to discourage others from enlisting in the military. I knew there was a long tradition here about serving in the military. I didn't think it was right for Anishinaabe to fight against people when the conflict appeared to be one of dominance on the part of the government. I had been taught that a warrior protected the land of his people. I saw nothing in Vietnam that told me that I or anyone else was protecting American soil, and even though I spent much time thinking about the war and what it meant, I never did figure out what we were doing there. I am Ogitchidaa, and that war that didn't belong to me left me sitting in a wheelchair with a bullet in my back. I had a life before I went to war. It was not the life I had after I came home.

"Before I went to war, I was popular with many women. They liked my laughter and my thick black hair. I was a strong man.

"When I came back from the war, people would look at me and shake their heads with pity.

"I didn't get into trouble. I would go to the Indian bars, but I didn't drink. I would sit and tell my stories about the bullet in my back and my medals, leaving out all the other details. I didn't know how to fit in.

"Fitting in would have meant drinking and smoking weed. Fitting in would have meant getting into fights. I didn't want to be out of control. Over time, I spent less and less time in the community. I lived with my mother. She was glad I was home. She knew I had secrets and respected my privacy. Old friends quit coming around. I thought that all I had were my stories, and people got sick of hearing them.

"When my mother died, I stayed in this house. I was born here. After she died, my nephews were old enough to watch out for me. They respected my privacy and independence. I think they got tired of listening to my stories.

"I have had times when I was bitter. I would say to myself, 'This is what I get for serving my country. Being a warrior means that I don't get to have a life like my friends have.'

"It took time, but I figured out that I had a place in my family. I had many nieces and nephews, and I could help raise them. I was a good role model. I could show them that hard times didn't stop people from living. Even though I didn't talk about what happened in Vietnam, my decision to save the children and jeopardize my life brought me some dignity. I had done my share to resolve a small part of the ancestral trauma that plagued my community.

"I believe you are here for reasons you don't know. It's important for you to hear about our community from many sources. Each of us here has a part of the community story.

"After I came home from the war, I thought I was done with the violence and killing. I was wrong. Things were changing here—changing for the worst. There was violence. Our people were beating each other up. We had people come to our community and talk about historical grief and trauma and internalized oppression. They said that when people are oppressed long enough, they start to believe what the oppressors say about them. They start to hate themselves. They start killing themselves and others. We had our own form of Vietnam here.

"We had gangs. Children got guns and began to shoot each other. People without guns were beating each other to death. Sometimes those who survived the beatings had brain damage. Many children were born with brain damage because their mothers drank alcohol when they were pregnant. It was dangerous to live here, and yet this was our home. Our ancestors made sure we had a place to live, but we were making it a place to die.

"We had all kinds of experts tell us what was wrong with us. We were expected to live a lifestyle created by white men. That didn't work.

"Things started changing for the better when we unplugged. People were expected to take care of each other and to work for their food. People quit beating each other up and getting drunk. Those people who sold drugs were chased away. This is a good place to live, and it's a good place to die."

Janet listened, taking in Marvin's stories. She liked sitting in the silence that was interrupted by intermittent breezes blowing through the pines. The soft sound created by the breeze in the pines sounded like whispers to Janet.

"I know why you're here," said Marvin. "There are few secrets here. You and your friends are looking for ways to change things in your world. It's good that you think you need to learn history in order to make a change. History tells us where we've been and where we're going. But I don't see how you're going to do anything that will change the way things are out there. Maybe you should just come here to live."

"I don't belong here," said Janet.

"All you have to do is learn how to live here. You've been helping out at Sonia's house, so you're learning about the ways we survive."

"Joe doesn't want me there," said Janet.

"There are other families you could live with," said Marvin.

"I just want my home to have clean air and water. I want the wars to stop," said Janet.

"I think that's a big order," said Marvin.

They sat in silence as the sun sank lower in the sky.

Animosh, who had been napping by Marvin's wheelchair, lifted his head, sniffed the air, and began barking as Cody came into the yard.

"Hey, Animosh, come here and see me," yelled Cody.

The big dog leaped off the deck, ran to Cody, and skidded to a stop. Cody gave the dog a massage, and the two of them ran around the yard playing.

Cody climbed the stairs to the deck, panting. He looked at Janet. "It's time to come home for supper," he said. "Uncle Marvin, Joe and Mike will come and get you for supper."

Janet picked up her glass and set it on the tray, and Marvin picked up the tray and handed it to Cody. "Take this into the house," he said. Cody grinned and took the tray into the house.

Janet and Cody headed off to Sonia's house, but not before Janet noticed a path into the woods across the yard from Marvin's house. She wondered where it went. *Every path here leads someplace*, she thought.

The family ate supper, visited, and went to bed. Janet had dreams of soldiers, guns, and bombs.

April 6, 2040

Janet sat with Old Woman, waiting for another history lesson as Old Woman shifted in her chair.

"Why don't we go outside? It's a beautiful day. If we walk down by the lake and sit, we can see what kind of show is going on out there," said Old Woman as she stood slowly, taking time to make sure she was balanced before she came around the table and moved to the door. She grabbed a walking stick and headed out. Janet followed her as they took the path down to the lake.

Old Woman sat down on a large log near the water. She motioned for Janet to join her.

Something big jumped out of the water and splashed back in. Janet flinched.

"I keep forgetting that you aren't used to this. That was a walleye. Soon, the men and some of the children will take torches out in their canoes at night and spear them. The light shines on their eyes, making them easy to see. They're good eating," said Old Woman. She fell silent as she watched the scenes playing out in the lake. Ducks and geese swam by, showing off their babies. A great blue heron stood off by itself, waiting for a fish. A fox with two kits came shyly to the water's edge and drank.

Time passed. The sun shining on the lake created bright lights that danced in time to ripples on the water made by the spring breezes.

Janet had heard on the science channel that bright sunlight created premature wrinkles and sometimes skin cancer. The program told of the benefits of air pollution, as it blocked the sun's rays, especially since the ozone layer had disintegrated. Janet forgot to worry about wrinkles and skin cancer as she listened to the water lapping against the shore and the music of the birds, insects, and frogs. The dogs created the rhythm section with their barking as they chased something on a path into the woods.

Old Woman had fallen asleep. Janet didn't understand how she could sleep sitting up with nothing to support her. Janet sat, listening and watching as life happened around her.

The spirits were visiting Old Woman again. She couldn't make out the blurred figures, but she heard them whispering to one another. Two of the women were giggling. The message sent by the spirits didn't come in words, but Old Woman knew that they were telling her that this young woman who came to visit her was part of the plan. This young woman was to be a history book, like Old Woman had been a history book. Old Woman thought Janet an unlikely history book, but she knew enough to believe the messages sent by the spirits. When the spirits left, Old Woman was reluctant to come back, enjoying the peace in a world between this life and the next. When she awakened, she remembered that she was sitting by the lake with Janet.

"Well, I am supposed to be teaching you. I am supposed to tell you everything I know, and then I will pass on. Do you have that recorder with you?"

Janet pulled the recorder out of her bag, turned it on, and laid it on the log.

"You came here earlier this week when we had that late snowstorm, didn't you?" asked Old Woman

Janet nodded.

"Now it's spring. Ojibwe people pay attention to the cycles—the seasons, the change of day to night to day, and the cycles of life—birth, growth, the times in life from infancy to old age and then death. All cycles are connected, all events are connected, all people are connected, and all living beings are connected to Mother Earth. Everything is like a raindrop falling into a pond; that small event creates ripples that move out from the spot where the raindrop hit the water. There are no beginnings or ends. Here, people celebrate nature. Each season, each month, represents something different, something specific in the cycles of nature and life. The cycles of nature and the cycles of life are interchangeable.

"Winter is the time of rest and renewal. Mother Earth sleeps, covered with a blanket of snow that protects everything that lies beneath the blanket. Some animals hibernate, waking in the spring when Mother Earth wakes up, and give birth. Mother Earth nurtures new life during the summer, and slowly, plant life born in the spring approaches middle age in the fall of the year.

"I don't know that I'm explaining all this well enough for you. I don't think you're stupid, but I do think you're ignorant, and I don't believe that you know how to put things together to come up with your own ideas because you are part of a culture that sees and hears most things in straight lines. I haven't been told how you are going to use the information I am to give you. I don't think that you can carry these things any place and get anyone to listen. I have faith that I am doing what I am supposed to do, and you will use what I tell you in a good way.

"White culture doesn't pay a lot of attention to cycles. Nature is only something to contain and control."

Janet listened. She didn't know what questions to ask, and she had no responses to Old Woman's assertions.

Old Woman pushed herself off the log with her walking stick and headed back to the house, Janet following behind.

Old Woman settled in her chair for a nap while Janet climbed the stairs and lay down on the bed. When she awoke, the sun was low, and she smelled food cooking through the open window. She went down to join the family.

After another evening meal and visiting by firelight, the family went to bed. Janet slept and dreamed. She saw herself running down the road.

Then she was in a car, hiding under blankets. From there, she saw herself in the woods, running on a path. The dream frightened her, and she woke up many times in the night, breathing heavily, taking a few minutes to remember where she was. When she went back to sleep, she dreamed again.

CHAPTER

April 7, 2040

"You have been with us six full days, I think. Sometimes I get a little lost when I count the days. Anyway, what do you think you have gained while you have been here?" asked Old Woman.

"Well, I've learned that you live a different life than I do. Your beliefs are different. You believe that there are spirits all around. You live off the land," said Janet.

"I'm glad you've been paying attention," said Old Woman.

"Tell me something," said Old Woman. "How can you live out there?"

"You mean in the city?" asked Janet.

"Yes. You can't breathe the air. Your food is filled with chemicals. Your life is controlled by the government, and you can't be a news reporter because you can't print the truth," said Old Woman.

"I do the best I can. I'm trying to make change. That's why I joined the group," said Janet.

"I don't see how you can think that the group to which you belong can make any changes when even belonging to a group is illegal."

"We're just starting. That's why I came here. To gather information so we can figure out what to do next," said Janet.

"I wish I had enough faith in what you say you're trying to do so I could wish you luck. I came here and found peace of mind," said Old Woman. "If you stayed here, you would have some trouble adjusting. Maybe you just have to learn that your hopes and dreams will lead to a big mistake."

"What mistake is that?" asked Janet.

"I think you may be found out. If that happens, I don't think you will survive. The government will kill you," said Old Woman.

"I don't believe that," said Janet.

"I hope that when you do believe, it isn't too late for you," said Old Woman.

Janet stared at the floor, resisting Old Woman's warning. She looked up. Old Woman was trembling.

Janet called for Sonia. "Is she all right?" Janet asked.

Sonia asked, "Why don't you ask her if she's all right?"

Old Woman jerked as if coming out of a trance. "I'm all right. When I stop getting angry with all of this, I'll be dead. I used to think that I would calm down when I got old, but I haven't. I'm at peace when I don't have to think about the reality of what's happening out there. It's as if there is a nonspecific plot that's about how all of the things that get instituted in white society fit together with the prevailing attitudes of the day. I don't believe that people sit around thinking that plan A will hook up with plan Z, but it seems to work that way, especially when plans A and Z are developed for the benefit of those in charge. Because all things are connected, everything operates to keep things in balance. In white culture, when things happen that are the result of greed and negligence, those things don't get fixed. Stories are made up to make things okay. Something or someone controls everything. If someone tries to go against the status quo, they are stopped," said Old Woman.

"Well, there are laws that we all have to follow," said Janet. "Even though I believe changes have to be made, I still believe that people have to follow laws."

"I think you are mistaking laws for restrictions on freedom. Those Post-Millennial Adjustments, they all tie together, and people can't live where they want and can't go where they want to go," said Old Woman.

"Well, a lot of those restrictions happened in 2020 after all the bombings. It was just too dangerous," said Janet.

"I wonder who committed all those bombings?" asked Old Woman.

"Well, there were terrorists," said Janet.

"Who said there were terrorists?" asked Old Woman.

"The government. It was reported in the news media," said Janet

"And who was in charge of the news media?" asked Old Woman.

"I think that was when Homeland Security took control of the news," said Janet.

"So we're not really sure that there were terrorists," said Old Woman.

Janet tried to find a response to Old Woman and couldn't.

Old Woman continued. "Have you ever wondered about all those neighborhoods to which you don't have access? Have you ever thought about all the women who can't get an education like yours? I think that it's just as bad, maybe worse than it was when I lived out there. When young women make mistakes and bring children into households without men, they get trapped. They live in poverty, punished for their mistakes. From what I hear, their children can't get out. It's like a trap."

Janet had no argument with Old Woman's words. Her parents had warned her of the consequences of making mistakes. She knew she was lucky to have her college degree.

Sonia walked into the room. "Old Woman. I want to take Janet away from you."

"Where are you going to take her?" asked Old Woman.

"I'm going to take her to the old school," said Sonia. "I want to show her the murals."

Janet followed Sonia out of the house and down the road. They walked about two miles in silence, coming to a large brick building with a sculpture of an eagle standing alongside the double doors that led into the building.

The door was unlocked. As they walked in, their footsteps echoed in the empty building. They proceeded down a hallway to a large room with tables and benches; it looked like an old cafeteria.

Each wall in the room was covered with murals of people, animals, and domed white structures that looked like houses. The figures in the murals were working—preparing food, sewing, and making things that Janet didn't recognize. Each of the four scenes looked like the seasons of the year.

"A long time ago, we went to school in town. It was not good for us. We learn differently than white people do, and we had trouble sitting in buildings. The other kids would call us names and pick on us. After Marvin's friend was murdered, the Ojibwe kids walked out of the school and refused to go back. Their parents got together and decided to start a school here.

"At first we met wherever there was room for us. Then our tribal government got money from the BIA, and we built a school for our children. At first, we hired mostly white people to work in that school. That meant that we were still expected to learn in the ways of white people.

"There was a high turnover of teachers. A lot of the white people who came to teach were people just out of college. They had trouble finding jobs in white schools because they had no job experience. As soon as they got experience here, they moved on. They didn't try to learn our ways. They didn't understand that they were in another country.

"So we decided that going to a school wasn't needed for us to teach our children. We decided to paint the murals. It was a community project. These murals are a reminder to honor our ancestors and to remember our past and what happened when we used the white man's ways, thinking it was an easier way to live. The murals were a community project. Now, the children paint those murals when they fade. We make paint from the plants that grow around here.

"It is hard for me to even think of what would be an easier way to live. I suppose living with electricity could be seen as an easy way to live, but I don't see it that way. I like the quiet in our home. I got used to not having that hum in the house. I like going to bed when it's dark and getting up when it's light.

"Electricity told us we didn't have to honor nature. That meant we didn't have to honor ourselves either. The way we live today is the best way for us to live."

Janet was silent as she looked at the murals. After about a half an hour, Sonia turned and headed for the door.

When Sonia and Janet got back to the house, it was time to fix supper. Sierra was stirring a large pot that hung over an open fire.

The family had gathered around the picnic table. Old Woman had set a pot of wild rice on the table, and family members were helping themselves.

Janet was hungry. She liked this food! She hadn't had food with flavor since she was a child, when her mother had a garden in the backyard, their fresh meat came from a butcher shop, and dairy products came from a farmer who lived a few miles outside the city. Janet remembered her mother telling her that the food that came in packages in the store didn't taste as good as what she made from scratch.

The summer that Janet was ten, the vegetables in the garden didn't grow. It was the summer that so many people died because of the air quality. Some people began wearing face masks, and weather reports suggested that people should stay inside. New laws were instituted about cars, and more than one person had to occupy a car or they couldn't go anyplace. Since then, Janet had eaten only packaged food. This week on the reservation made her realize that food was probably the most important aspect of life in this community. At the same time, she was confused about eating animals. The prepackaged meals she ate just didn't seem like anything that came from something that had been alive.

While she took in the sights and smells in the woods, Sonia directed Joe and Mike to bring Marvin for supper.

The men walked on a path between Sonia's and Marvin's houses. Joe called out, "Hey, Uncle, you're coming for supper," as Animosh came out to greet them.

Marvin rolled his wheelchair down the ramp and waited for Joe and Mike. They bent over and lifted the old man into a lawn chair. Then they picked up the chair and began walking.

Animosh ran ahead. He liked going to Sonia's house, where he could visit and watch others take care of Marvin.

"Hey, have you guys seen any of those old movies where important people in Egypt were carried around in chairs?" asked Marvin.

The two men paused to rest a bit. Mike said, "No. Those movies were before our time."

"Well, they had poles on the bottom of the chairs, and they just lifted the poles. There were usually about four people carrying the chairs," said Marvin.

"It would be easier if you were just skinny like Old Woman." Mike gasped. They laughed, enjoying a picture of Marvin as a skinny man.

They reached the yard and set Marvin down in his lawn chair, a sturdy creation Joe had made.

The men sat enjoying the sunlight while Animosh found a cool place in the shade, then flopped down and went to sleep.

"So that young woman who has stayed here is going home tomorrow," said Marvin.

Sonia, who was sitting by the fire waiting for Janet to come back from her hike, said, "Yes, Uncle. She is leaving, and I thought you might want to wish her well on her journey."

"She'll be back," said Marvin. "I've been having dreams that tell me she will be in danger when she goes back to the city. She'll come back."

"Uncle," said Joe, "you have so many dreams. I don't know how you get any rest while you sleep."

"My dreams come from the spirits. They are my guides, and they tell me what to do with the messages they bring me," said Marvin.

"Why do you have so many dreams and I don't?" asked Joe.

"I think it's because your life is laid out for you right now. You are doing what you are supposed to be doing—providing for all of us. When you get older and Mike and Cody take your place, you will find other ways to be useful. The spirits will guide you then, and you'll have more dreams," said Marvin, aware that Joe didn't always give Marvin's dreams the respect that Marvin gave them.

Janet appeared on the path, and Sonia started cooking the fish that Janet had seen Joe cleaning earlier. Janet gagged when she remembered the scales and innards on the cutting block.

Janet saw that Sonia was busy with the meal. "Do you want some help?" she asked Sonia.

"No. When it's ready, just fix yourself a plate after Old Woman and Marvin are served," said Sonia.

The children brought plates filled with food to Marvin and Old Woman. Sonia, Joe, and Mike served themselves. Janet took a plate and filled it with fresh walleye, wild rice, fry bread, corn, and greens from the forest floor. She ate slowly, wanting to make sure she tasted every bit that went into her mouth.

After supper, Janet helped with the dishes. She was tired, as the exercise of the day had caught up with her. She went up to the bedroom and got into bed.

The spirits were waiting for her, circling the bed, hovering above Janet as she lay down. They hadn't made their presence known to her yet. They were the spirits who had been peers of the Old Woman in her younger years.

One of them said, "Hovering tends to wear me out. Let's find another position." Each moved away from the bed and settled on the floor by the side of the bed. "Well, what are we going to tell her tonight? We've been letting her know that someone is going to come after her, but she doesn't seem to get the hint."

"She doesn't have to get the hint now. It will come back to her when she's in the middle of it. When she remembers the dream, hopefully she will figure out what to do."

The light from the full moon shone through the open window. The rocking chair in the corner creaked, rocking slightly without the benefit of a breeze. Janet was afraid to go to sleep, feeling the presence of someone in the room. She was afraid she would have dreams, so she tried to stay awake. Her eyes got heavy, and her mind wandered away from the room as she fell asleep.

The dreams started again. She saw dark-skinned people who were dressed in animal skins. They gathered together in a circle and began singing. A man talked about the sacredness of women because they bear children. This scene faded, and Janet saw another group of people—men, women, and children—running through some trees. They had dark skin and long black hair. They were running from white men in uniforms on horseback. The white men caught up to the dark-skinned people and began swiping at them with bayonets. The people fell to the ground, blood pouring from their wounds. The white men traveled on. Soon, more dark-skinned people came out from the trees, picked up the dead, and carried them away.

The dream faded, and other images came in. A woman hobbled over to Janet and began looking at her clothing. She took the tail of Janet's shirt in her fingers, rubbing them back and forth over the fabric. She picked up Janet's hand and massaged Janet's wrist. It hurt. Janet flinched. The woman noticed the flinch and walked over to another woman and spoke in a language Janet didn't understand. The two women looked at Janet and giggled.

The dream faded to black. In the morning, Janet remembered the women.

While Janet slept and dreamed, Old Woman sat with Sonia and the other members of her adopted family.

Sonia pointed at Joe with her chin and lips. "I think you were a little hard on that young woman."

Joe sat staring into the flames. The burning wood popped and hissed, sending sparks into the air. "If she is going to understand Old Woman's stories, she has to understand that we have a right to do as we see fit. She is under the delusion that she and her friends are going to win some kind of war when they don't know what the war is about. They don't have weapons, and they have no influence. I may have to allow her to come here, but I don't have to join her."

Old Woman spoke. "None of us knows what she is going to do with the stories. I agree with you, Joe. She has to hear truth. It will bother her, but she has to know how things are done here and how people think.

"I don't think there is a lot of time left. The spirits come often to me. I've told this young woman what I know. I don't know that she'll be making another trip here to gather information. I think someone knows she is coming. I don't know if she'll make it out of this alive.

"Joe, there is still time for us. I had a dream. You and I will go ricing in the fall. I saw us in the canoe. The sun was shining. It was hot, and the canoe was filled with rice."

Sonia said, "I don't like that young woman coming here. I think she tries to fit in, but she just doesn't know how. She has an air about her. She acts like she thinks she's important. She bothers me."

"That's what she is taught," said Old Woman. "Say, Joe, how did she act when you and Mike were dressing out the deer?"

Joe grinned. "I wish you could have seen her, Grandmother. She turned green. I will give her this. She didn't throw up. I had blood up to my elbows. I was going to hold my hand out to her, but I thought that was a little bit too mean.

"I do have to give her some credit. She drove all the way here without knowing what she was going to find. She isn't asking as many questions as she did at first. For a white woman, she did okay," said Joe.

Joe, Old Woman, and Sonia sat around the fire for a long time. One by one, the children who had been playing behind them came closer, sat down, and snuggled with the adults in a peaceful silence.

CHAPTER 23

Morning came, and Janet awakened to the aromas of food cooking over the outside fire. She got up, dressed, and packed her belongings for the trip home, then joined the family at the picnic table. Sonia was fixing a breakfast consisting of fish and wild rice left over from the night before.

Sierra came down a path from her auntie's house. Cody, rubbing sleep out of his eyes, came out of the house, followed by Old Woman.

Sierra picked up a plate, put wild rice and fish on it, and brought it to Old Woman. Joe poured hot water from a kettle heated by a smaller fire off to the side into a cup of freshly picked leaves. He put it on the table next to Old Woman as she lifted her face to the sky and breathed deeply.

As the family finished their meal, Janet began clearing the table.

"You don't have to clean up," said Sonia. "You have a long drive back to the city, and it looks like it's going to rain."

Janet went into the house, got her suitcase and her winter coat, and loaded everything into the car, arranging several EZ Breathe scarves and masks on the passenger seat. She said goodbye, and Old Woman called out, "You'll be back. Once you've been here and you go back to the city, you'll find that it isn't a good place to live."

Shortly after she walked down the path and got in the car, it started to rain. Thunder and lightning accompanied the downpour. Janet drove slowly as the rain gushed, challenging hesitant windshield wipers. She hydroplaned and moved to the center of the road, away from the pools of water. She felt funny driving down the center of the road, but there wasn't any traffic. She slowed and moved to the side as she took the curves. It was going to take her a long time to get to the city.

After a while, the lightning moved off to the east. The sound of the thunder became faint, and the deluge decreased to occasional drops splatting on the windshield. The sun came out from retreating clouds, its light reflecting off the wet trees and bushes, giving color where there had been only gray.

Janet crossed over bridges spanning rivers lined with wet trees. She slowed even more to look down at the water rushing underneath the bridges. She was in the woods, surrounded by trees. Janet wasn't used to so much nature. This wasn't like the virtual reality nature museum or the nature shows on TV. She didn't know what the animals would do if she stopped the car. Somehow she had the sense that she could be swept off at any minute into the rushing current of the rivers, even though there was no flooding. She drove slowly, awed by the reality. She lost track of time.

The scenery changed, the trees no longer alongside her, replaced by open fields. The clear, clean air she had breathed on the reservation was being shut out by the grayish-yellow hue of the factory emissions, blurring the cityscape that rose up from the horizon. Janet found what she thought was the appropriate EZ Breathe scarf and drove through the neighborhood gates. She was not stopped at any of them.

I wonder what's going on, she thought. *Why isn't anyone stopping me to check my ID? I think something's wrong.* The anxiety Janet left behind when she left the city welcomed her back home. In spite of it, she kept going and drove the car back to the rented garage and parked it. She walked the few blocks to her apartment, lugging her bags, pushing against the thick air being blown around by a strong wind. Her scarf blew up around her eyes, making it difficult for her to see.

Janet opened the door to her apartment, took off her coat, emptied her bags, and took her clothing into the laundry room across the hall from her apartment. As she waited for her clothes to wash and dry, she paced, looking out the window frequently, trying to see if anyone was spying on her. She talked herself out of this notion and picked up a magazine sitting on a shelf.

When she returned to her apartment, she fixed a package of tasteless food. She decided she didn't want to think about anything and turned on the TV.

The Retro Channel was featuring *The Thomas Crown Affair*. It was about a guy who stole some works of art from a museum. Homeland Security and the FBI stopped him just before he was going to fly away to safety on an island in the Caribbean. The female romantic lead had informed Homeland Security of his crime and his plan. The final scenes showed her receiving a Freedom Plaque and cash reward from the director of Homeland Security, and then it moved to show the man behind prison bars. Janet didn't think the lead character at the end looked like the same guy in the earlier scenes.

After the movie, Janet was tired. She went to bed and slept soundly. Her dreams lacked the turmoil of the dreams she had while at the reservation.

April 9, 2040

When she woke up, Janet went through her routine, turning on the Weather Channel to check the air quality. The weather person was standing in front of a map filled with lines and arrows, the picture showing a ceiling of cold air that stopped the chemical smoke as it rose from the factory smokestacks. This meant the smoke was trapped close to the ground and couldn't dissipate into the ozone-less atmosphere. The sign alongside the map flashed the message #10 with a mask indicating that anyone going out of a building should wear a protective mask to prevent the intake of the thick, poisonous air.

Janet had little reason to leave her apartment for the city streets. She sat and thought about the clean air and the clean water she had left behind. At the same time, she was glad to be back in the city where everything was familiar to her.

Janet struggled with her parents' messages about government control and the media messages. She was used to the lifestyle that had been created for her.

CHAPTER 24

April 10, 2040

Janet awakened in the morning to the electronic alarm that also turned her television on to the Weather Channel, where the weather person was announcing the air quality level and the corresponding EZ Breathe scarf. She dressed and left the apartment, joining others wearing filtered scarves. The bus pulled up just as she approached the curb.

Janet boarded and found a seat. She nodded at the man sitting next to her. Young single professionals lived in this neighborhood that abutted the downtown area filled with office buildings. Even though the filtered scarves worn by the passengers made conversation awkward, any conversations about one's work location or line of work were frowned upon. No one knew who might be an informant or a possible terrorist. So it was quiet on the bus, and some took advantage of this, using the bus ride to work as time for a short nap before the workday began.

Janet didn't expect a welcome when she got to work. Coworkers no longer asked about absences of other coworkers. To do so might mean that the interrogator had a hidden agenda and was checking up on the person who returned to work. When someone didn't return to work, there was the assumption that they had been picked up by Homeland Security. All absences were considered suspicious.

Janet tried to appear casual when she came into the newsroom, although she was worried that her boss may have been aware of her absence from the city.

Janet accepted her assignment to cover local news. Her first day back at work was busy, so she didn't have much time to worry about who knew what.

April 11, 2040

At the end of the second day, Janet found a note in her mailbox when she came home from work. She assumed it was from Antoine. It said, "Meet me Saturday. Different place, same time. Go to the café that borders your neighborhood and the U campus. Be careful. Somebody knows something."

This caused more concern and anxiety. Janet found herself looking over her shoulder. She didn't know who or what she was looking for, and she didn't know what she would do if she found it or him or her.

April 15, 2040

Janet waited anxiously for Saturday. She didn't sleep well Friday night, awakening long before the alarm went off on Saturday morning. At seven o'clock, she looked out the window. The darkness told her that the air quality was poor. When she left her apartment, she wore a plastic mask with a heavy wire screen over her nostrils. She walked slowly to the bus stop, not wanting to exert herself. Heavy breathing might cause her to over breathe, and the mask wouldn't be able to filter as efficiently as it was meant to.

There were few people on the bus, all of whom were wearing masks. Janet spent little time observing other passengers whom she couldn't identify. She wondered where they were going on a Saturday when the air quality was so bad.

Janet got off at the bus stop adjacent to the café mentioned in her note. She walked in and pulled off her mask, looking around the room for Antoine. She spotted him in a booth toward the rear, where the lighting was dimmer than it was in the front. She nodded and walked to the back, sliding into the seat opposite him.

"Hey, how are ya?" said Antoine.

"Well, I don't know. Your note sounded cryptic, and I spent the week waiting to get arrested," said Janet, irritated by Antoine's relaxed demeanor.

Antoine leaned toward her. "The air is good in here, so take a couple of deep breaths and calm down."

"Calm down? Your note sounded like I'm in danger, and now you want me to calm down," said Janet.

"We picked up your recordings and reviewed them. I think there's enough in them for the group to know that there's a different way to live. It also means you won't have to risk another trip to the rez," said Antoine.

"So now, what's next?" asked Janet.

"I don't know what's next for you," said Antoine. "Do you want to stay involved in the group?"

"I don't know what the group is planning next. If there's a plan, I wish you'd let me know," said Janet.

"I think the ultimate goal is to overthrow those in power," said Antoine.

"How is that going to happen?" asked Janet.

"I don't know. I won't be sticking around for that part," said Antoine.

"You mean you're just going to leave?" asked Janet.

"This isn't my revolution. This isn't my home. I'm doing what I'm supposed to do, and then I'll leave," said Antoine.

"What is it that you're supposed to do? I thought you were here to see this through," said Janet. "What if we get caught? What if they're on to us?"

"See what through?" asked Antoine.

"Well, I thought there was some kind of plan to organize and gain strength and get back our freedoms under the Constitution," said Janet.

"When I came here, I got involved with the group because my dreams told me to do that. I provided a chance for the group to learn more about history and an alternative culture. I didn't ask you to get involved. If I get wind of a mass arrest or something like that, I'll let you know if I can, and I'll help you and the others to escape," said Antoine.

"I want to stay with the group. I want to make things better for this country," said Janet.

"Well, I hope you can do that. If it all falls apart, you can come and live in my world," said Antoine.

The waitress came and took their orders. When she left, Antoine leaned across the booth. "We know that there are some folks we see often on campus who aren't regular students. When a couple of us meet at a weekly card game, a member of University Security is with us. So he's letting us know if we're in danger. I said I would help you escape. The only safe places I know are my rez and others in the area. If you have to escape, I would suggest that you worry about getting to a safe place and making other plans after that. You need to keep me posted as to anything out of the ordinary going on around you. Isolation serves to create vulnerability," said Antoine.

"How will I let you know?" asked Janet.

"You can send me notes, and I will let you know where we can meet," said Antoine. "I've been followed since we met at Dinky Town. Don't look now, but there's a guy at the counter facing the mirror. He shows up most places I go, so I believe he's following me. I haven't been doing anything out of the ordinary, so I don't know what he has to report."

Their waitress brought their food. It wasn't the kind of food they had at Dinky Town but rather the same tasteless processed food served at other restaurants.

"So you didn't bring some of your food to this place," said Janet.

"No, I didn't. The Dinky Town café is a place that isn't ordinary. For all I know, I could be arrested for bringing my own food," said Antoine.

"Let's talk about your visit to the rez."

"I don't know what to make of it. I felt like I was being lectured much of the time. I liked being able to breathe clean air, and I liked the scenery and the food. It sure takes a lot of time to gather and process food. Here, we have time for other things. Your uncle Joe doesn't like me and made it clear that he didn't want me there. I don't understand why you think I could go there if I have to leave here," said Janet.

"Where I live, one person doesn't decide who comes or goes. It's a decision that's made by the Elders Council. If you're in danger, you would be taken in on an emergency basis, and then decisions would be made as to whether you stay or you go someplace else. No decision would be made that would put you in further danger," said Antoine.

"I just don't know if I could live like you do," said Janet.

"Maybe you should just think about what you have to do to stay alive," said Antoine.

The two fell silent, finished eating, and left. The man whom Antoine identified as his tail waited for about five minutes and then left.

Janet went back to her apartment and spent the rest of the weekend wondering what she would do if she was found out.

CHAPTER 25
April 17, 2040

On Monday morning, Janet went into the newsroom, where she found Lloyd waiting for her. The tic in his eye was active again. Standing next to him was a young woman whom Janet figured to be about twenty-five. She wore a red plaid shirtwaist dress that didn't fit her square body. She was about five feet six inches, with sturdy arms attached to broad shoulders. She had a wide face framed by brown hair that hung straight and stopped just below her square jaw line.

Janet remembered an educational program about dogs in a virtual reality museum. She saw a resemblance between this woman and the pit bull in the museum. The program said that pit bulls were dangerous and would attack for no reason.

Lloyd introduced the two women. "Janet, this is Darcy. She's an intern who's getting hours here to complete her journalism degree."

He turned to Darcy. "Janet is an old pro. She'll teach you the ropes about reporting and writing.

"Janet, take Darcy with you while you're in the office and out on assignment. This is your chance to mentor a new reporter."

Janet had not been assigned a student intern before. Until now, she had seen herself as a junior member of the newspaper staff. Lloyd seemed to be telling her that she had graduated to a senior level among the reporters and could mentor newcomers. Janet nodded at Darcy and then nodded her head toward the cubicle where she worked. When they reached Janet's workspace, Janet pointed at a nearby table and said, "Why don't you grab a chair from that table?" Darcy squeezed the chair into the cubicle and sat down while Janet turned on her computer and signed in. "This is where we get the national news stories," she said.

"Don't we write our own stories?" Darcy asked.

"Yes, we do. We take the information off the internet and rewrite it in the format for this newspaper. Our newspaper is a daily. We print local, regional, and national news. There is one reporter assigned to legal news," said Janet.

"What's legal news?" asked Darcy.

"When Homeland Security discovers a terrorist plot or a plot to overthrow the government, there's a roundup of the people who are alleged to have been involved. The reporter follows them through the justice system, reporting on the progress made by Homeland Security in gathering evidence against those accused."

"Does the reporter interview those accused?" asked Darcy.

"No. National Security dictates that we don't print information from those accused, as it might inspire others to commit the same kinds of acts," said Janet.

"Don't you have an opinion page? I thought you would have someone here who comments on current affairs. I thought I was going to get a chance to really write something original," Darcy said.

"I don't know how original you want to be," said Janet. "Newspaper stories are just who, how, where, why, and when. This isn't a place to hone your creative writing skills. Opinion pages just inspire controversy." Janet shut down the computer.

"C'mon. I'll orient you to our environment," said Janet as she took Darcy through the newspaper's offices, introducing her to other reporters and photographers, showing her the postings on bulletin boards that indicated which photographers were to work with which reporters and which reporters were assigned to local stories, which meant they were out of the office a lot.

Last on the tour was the IT department. Darcy needed a code and a password before she could use a computer. A person from information technology brought her to a locked office with a phone connected to the Systems Information Office. She had her voice print verified so she could have a code and password assigned. It took a while to complete the procedure.

When Darcy came back from her code and password assignment, Janet started her on the computer, rewriting the wire service stories. Janet began to wonder if Darcy was a Homeland Security plant who was baiting her with all the questions she asked. Janet didn't want to think about this possibility, because those thoughts would beg the question "Why?" and would complicate her thinking with fear and the rumination of anxious thoughts. Her anxiety level rose. Her breathing was rapid and shallow, and her thoughts were racing.

As she modified her breathing and tried to focus on the tasks at hand, Janet saw her father waving his forefinger at her, lecturing her to watch out. She remembered his voice. "It's not a matter of being careful. It's a need to watch out. You don't know who is trying to get you and why. Terrorism doesn't come from outside our borders. We have a government made up of terrorists, and the American people have relinquished their right to choose."

The day passed quickly. When it ended, Janet and Darcy took the elevator down to the lobby. Darcy had been with Janet all day, and Janet felt like she was stuck to Darcy with a piece of Velcro. She stopped to read the electric sign that told the time, temperature, and breathing recommendations as she stepped off the elevator: "Today Is a Good Day It's a Number 4 EZ Breathe Day!" shouted the sign. Accordingly, she pulled the number 4 EZ Breathe scarf from her purse and wrapped it around her face. She headed outdoors, where she waited for the bus that went to the Mall of America. She was relieved to see Darcy getting on a bus that went in the opposite direction.

Janet followed the other passengers through the security arch on the bus and rode through the city to the Mall of America. Most of its passengers were young professional singles. The mood of the passengers was upbeat, and people sharing seats were talking through their scarves about what goods they planned to purchase.

When the bus stopped at the mall entrance, Janet got off and joined the crowds, anticipating the gratification that came with buying. After her parents left, Janet struggled with their admonitions about shopping being a kind of panacea that helped people survive the rigid environment that surrounded and controlled them. In her parents' absence, a feeling of isolation set in, and she fell into a pattern, accepting the anesthesia that shopping provided.

Janet followed the flow for a while and decided to stop at the Virtual Reality South America Nature Museum. She put on the headgear and took the tour, stopping to pet the jaguars, birds, and snakes that appeared through the magic of the headgear. A monkey hopped on her shoulder, installed a tracking device in the shoulder strap of her purse, and escorted her through the museum. He hopped off and disappeared when she took off her headgear.

The museum's virtual reality headgear sent subliminal messages from a menu for the restaurant next door, creating a hunger for the featured South American foods. The restaurant's entrance was dominated by a waterfall that emptied into a pond holding computerized replicas of brightly colored tropical fish, a lure for customers who tried to ignore the hunger created by the subliminal messages in the museum.

Janet stood next to the waterfalls, lulled by the sounds of the water and the colors of the tropical fish. Soon, a Techno Hostess greeted her—a human-looking robot with plastic features and long blond hair, wearing a uniform with a label that said, "Hi. My name is Norma." The robot was chattering banalities as it escorted her to a table. "How are you today?"

Janet looked up at the robot and said, "Fine, and you?" knowing she had to respond because the Techno Personnel in restaurants and hotels had recording devices. Those customers who didn't respond to the conversation might be viewed with suspicion and might be followed when they left the restaurant because they were refusing to accept the technology. The Techno Waitress came shortly after the Techno Hostess had seated Janet. Janet said, "It looks busy today."

The Techno Waitress responded, "Yes, we've been very busy, but that's what we're here for."

Janet ordered a chicken and rice–flavored dish served on a bed of palm fronds. As she ate, the Techno Waitress came three times to ask her if everything was okay and if she needed anything. Janet, food in her mouth, smiled and nodded, knowing that she would be picked up on camera.

She left the restaurant and went next door to the gift shop where she found a T-shirt and a refrigerator magnet with the restaurant logo. She paid for them, left, went through security to board the bus, and went home.

When she got off the bus and headed for her apartment house, Janet noticed a man she had seen at the mall. She wondered if he was following her. *Why would he be following me?* she thought. *Am I being followed? Is this because I left the city? Have they discovered the group? Maybe he's a stalker. Maybe he's learning my habits so he can rape me.* She remembered her parents' words: "This has always been a male-dominated culture. It appeared to be changing, and then the news about the increased terrorism created this culture of fear, and men were again in charge," said Janet's father.

"So did sexual assaults increase when terrorist acts increased?" asked Janet.

"No, it wasn't because of the terrorist attacks. It was because of the culture's response to the terrorist attacks," said her father. "The changes that took place in the culture put men back in charge, although there really hadn't been a time when men weren't in charge. Men in government promised to solve issues and protect citizens. Wealthy men were in charge of most corporations that did business with the government. They contributed to political campaigns—mostly the campaigns of male candidates. There was a brief period of time when female victims of sexual abuse and harassment began speaking up. Then the shift back to having men in charge created a change in which women were not heard and not believed again. Anytime you have a culture in which males are dominant, there are many who believe they can do what they want, and they get away with it. Women are second-class citizens in male-dominated cultures," said Janet's mother.

As she remembered her parents' words, Janet felt helpless, and panic spread through her. She walked slowly, wondering if the man could tell she had spotted him.

When she got back to her apartment, Janet checked her mail. The mailbox was empty. She walked to the elevator, half expecting the man she saw to burst through the entrance to the building and jump into the elevator just as the doors were closing. He would either put her in handcuffs or rip her clothes off. No one came through the door to the building, and the elevator was empty.

She got to her apartment and pushed the buttons on the security box that unlocked the door. She pushed the door open, expecting to be met by a Homeland Security agent. Janet walked in and checked the closets and rooms to make sure she was alone. She sat on the couch taking deep breaths. After a few minutes, she got up and went to the window to see if there was anyone outside on the sidewalk who might be an agent. Other than the gloom caused by the murky air, the street below was empty.

"What am I doing?" she said aloud. "I just had a panic attack over nothing. Or was it nothing?"

Sitting alone in her apartment, Janet took time to calm down. She still didn't know if her fears were real. She didn't leave until Monday when she went to work.

April 18, 2040

Janet spent the rest of the week showing Darcy the newspaper business. She was relieved when Friday came. It was not her weekend on call, so she could relax and spend time doing chores without someone at her elbow. The weather report on the Friday-night news issued air-quality warnings, telling people not to go outside on Saturday or Sunday.

April 27, 2040

The air had cleared enough to wear the hooded masks with nasal filters. As Janet walked into the lobby of the newspaper building, she tried to identify people before they took off their masks. She noted some strangers among the small crowd. As she entered the elevator, she nodded at the people she recognized, and they did the same. Those she didn't recognize seemed to be strangers no one knew. The strangers didn't acknowledge anyone. Janet felt the panic rising again. She wondered if they were Homeland Security agents who had come to arrest her.

Darcy stood next to Janet on the elevator. "Isn't this exciting? It's like meeting a whole new group of people."

It took Janet a minute to respond, knowing that there was a difference between what she wanted to say and what she could say. "Yes. There's an air of mystery about things when we wear the hoods."

April 29, 2040

Two days later, a call came in about a chemical leak and explosion at a plant that manufactured household and commercial cleaning supplies. Reporting on this kind of event was sensitive. Everyone in the plant knew there had been a leak and an explosion, so it needed to receive news coverage. The coverage had to include minimization of the seriousness of the event and point at someone or something to blame.

Janet, Darcy, and Louis Stanley, a staff photographer, at the scene wearing heavy masks. A mixture of green, black, orange, and yellow smoke billowed up, creating a thick cloud that hung over the area and added to the poor visibility. Even though it was daylight, the light of the sun could not penetrate the clouds of smoke and noxious chemicals. Emergency vehicles surrounded the site, their exhaust fumes adding to the mixture.

The plant, which sat in the middle of the industrial section of the city, was a tall cement building with several smokestacks that, on a normal day, would be spewing black smoke into the air around it. The plant covered the block on which it sat. It had been blown apart by the explosion. Flames poured out of the portions of cement walls that were left standing. The chemicals in the vats flamed and bubbled up over the edges of the ruined containers, spreading fire to any combustibles that lay in their paths.

Louis got as close as he could, taking pictures of the spreading flames and of rescue workers carrying out dozens of stretchers to ambulances that turned on sirens and flashing lights before speeding away to trauma centers. Because the smoke and the toxic-laden air obscured details in the pictures Louis took, some would probably be used in the newspaper to show the seriousness of the situation, along with a story that would attribute the explosion to someone's mistake.

The scene was chaotic, and Janet had trouble finding people to interview. She saw a man sitting off by himself, sobbing. She walked up, kneeled beside him, and introduced herself.

"It's gone too far," he said through his EZ Breathe mask.

Janet, ignoring his initial statement, said, "Sir, would you mind telling us what you know about what's happened here?"

"Sure, I'll tell you what happened. We all spend too much time and money trying to make our lives easier. At work, we get pushed harder and harder to produce more and more. Somebody gets tired and makes a mistake. All of these poisons that are mixed together to make our lives easier build up in the place, and pretty soon something goes *boom*! I lost friends in there. They were vaporized. There won't be enough parts of them left to fill a casket. This has to stop!"

"Sir, what is your name?"

"When I give you my name, I will be turning myself in as a subversive. I don't care anymore. I'm going to go home, pack a few things, and get out of here. If I get caught, at least I will have been caught trying to escape. None of us can last much longer living the way we do. Make sure you get this right. My name is George Hansen," he said as he stood, shook his head as if to clear his brain, and strode off, disappearing into the multicolored smoke.

Janet wanted to follow him and tell him about the group but knew she couldn't. Darcy came up to her. "Shouldn't you be reporting him to someone? The statements he made were clearly subversive. Don't we have a responsibility to the American people to report him?"

"Yes, we do have to report him. I'm looking for someone to whom I can report." Janet stood looking around at the chaos for a police officer. She spotted a man wearing a suit standing a few feet away, so she walked up to him and motioned for him to show her some identification. He pulled out a Homeland Security surveillance agent badge. Janet read off her interview notes. The man took her notes and left.

The next morning, the newspaper headlines throughout the city and the television news reported, "George Hansen, Subversive, Member of an International Terrorist Organization Responsible for the Chemical Explosion at the Keen 'n' Klear Plant."

The story underneath the headlines said there was a citywide search for George Hansen, and anyone having seen him should report to the Homeland Security Office.

Janet said a prayer for George Hansen. She hoped he had gotten away.

George left the explosion site and hurried home, where he packed a few things in a duffel.

"Goodbye, Nora," he said to his wife. "I'm leaving. I'll have someone come and get you when I can."

"What did you do?" asked Nora.

"I shot off my mouth to a newspaper reporter, so I'm probably a wanted man. I can't stay and talk," he said.

George headed for the Mississippi River. He slipped down along the riverbank and headed south, hoping to evade Homeland Security surveillance agents, whose search spread northward.

George followed the river on foot to the confluence of the Missouri River at St. Louis, where he turned right and headed for Montana, where his brother was a member of a paramilitary group. A few miles up the Missouri, he found three men waiting to take him to Montana.

"How did you know to look for me?" George said.

One of the men introduced himself as Eli. "There have been stories on television, in newspapers, and now in magazines that you are a subversive and you planned and executed that explosion. Your brother knew that none of it was true. He figured you might head out this way, so he sent word through the survivalist groups out here. We're to take you part of the way. There will be others, but you'll move away from the river and travel cross-country along some of the smaller streams. Homeland Security intelligence will start looking for you along this route as soon as they figure out you didn't go up the Mississippi toward Canada. They don't know Mike is your brother because he changed his name. He hasn't paid any taxes, and he doesn't show up on the internet any place, so they can't make a connection. What do you think about all of this so far?"

"I'm a little dizzy, but I can breathe."

"We have some folks who work out of Minnesota. They have gone to your house and taken your wife and children to a safe place. If your family had stayed, they would have been detained and interrogated. We believe that when people are detained, they are tortured, and that someone in your family would have given them some information that would lead the agents here."

George cried. "I never should have said anything to that newspaper reporter. I was upset and confused, and I had breathed in enough of those poisons that I wasn't thinking straight. But I couldn't have stayed there. It all happened so fast that I just went home, packed some stuff, and left. Will I ever get to see my family again?"

"Yeah, probably, but we can't think about that right now. We have to get you to the next stop. When you're in Montana in the mountains, you'll be able to get things figured out. By the way, how do you like the fresh air?"

George grinned. The EZ Breathe appliance still hung from its strap around his neck. He ripped the Velcro straps apart and moved to throw the breathing device far into the air. Eli reached out and brought it down. "We can't leave evidence lying around. Someone might find this and turn it in, and it will be tested for DNA. Besides, we try to keep our environment as clean as we can. This thing is filled with poison—not good for the environment."

George breathed deeply, celebrating his freedom. His family would join him in Montana, where he would live out the rest of his days.

CHAPTER 26
April 28, 2040

The day after the explosion, Darcy met with Hal Emerson and gave her interpretation of the events surrounding the explosion. "This guy was spouting all kinds of subversive rhetoric, and she did nothing. She wrote down what he said, and that's it."

"Did you give her a chance to report? Did you give her a chance to voice any misgivings about what he said?"

"Well, no."

"That place was crazy. For all you knew, Janet Ryan was trying to think about how to find someone to whom she could report. You had a perfect opportunity to catch her, and you blew it because of your impatience. Do you remember the training films about animals catching prey?"

Darcy nodded. She knew better than to say anything more because this was quickly turning into her mistake.

"I don't know that you remember well enough. You have obviously forgotten that sometimes we have to allow prey to continue unmolested until they run into the traps they set for themselves. I would send you back for a course in predation, but I can't take anyone out of the field right now.

"We don't have enough to bring her in. We have the week she spent out of the office and out of town. We have her meetings with Antoine LaRiviere, a U of M student from a reservation in Wisconsin. We have her friendship with Sally Marshall and their recent reunion. Janet Ryan's parents and Sally Marshall's parents disappeared within the last year. We know where Antoine sits in class and who he sits next to. You may think Janet Ryan is guilty of being part of a group who could be terrorists. We have a law about groups forming for suspicious reasons. We don't know for sure if there is a group. It's up to you to be part of our investigation. It's not up to you to reach conclusions without evidence. Go do your job," said Hal.

Darcy left Hal Emerson's office feeling angry and self-righteous. She knew that Janet Ryan was a subversive. She would catch her and bring her in, earning recognition, a bonus, and a promotion for her good work. Hal Emerson had been on the job too long. It was time for younger agents like Darcy to move in, employing newer, more aggressive tactics to bring in suspects.

CHAPTER 27

April 28, 2040

Janet took the picture disc from Louis, brought it home, and scanned it to see which pictures would go where on the page with her story about the explosion. She thought she could work on her story from her computer at home but couldn't access the internet or her cell phone. *It must be all the smoke*, she thought.

Janet used her word processor to write her story about the explosion She didn't know when she would have reception or could go to work.

She was uncomfortable with what happened at the site of the explosion. She wondered what happened to George Hansen. She didn't believe he was an international terrorist. She hoped he had figured out a way to leave. Maybe somebody helped him and his family.

Soon after she started wondering about George Hansen, she started thinking about Darcy and her insistence that Janet give her interview notes to the Homeland Security agent. *So when am I going to slip up and get caught?* she thought. *I'm not really involved with the group of people who got my recordings. I don't know what the group is doing. I don't even know who they are.*

This line of thinking was replaced with pictures in her head of herself tied to a chair while a large man with a cattle prod stood over her. I can't turn myself in, I can't call anyone, and I can't go to see anyone. I'm stuck here until this cloud goes some place. In the meantime, somebody might just come and try to arrest me.

The cloud created by the explosion sat over the city. There was no wind to move it, and the humidity held the chemicals together. Satellites took pictures of the cloud. Even though there was no wind, there was movement within the cloud, the metallic colors folding in on one another, their beauty and movement creating an illusion that the cloud was a natural phenomenon, like the northern lights. The satellite pictures would be shown on television to minimize the impact of the explosion. The headlines would say, "Out of Mayhem Comes Man's Answer to the Northern Lights." Anything in nature could be outdone by human technology.

The cloud was stationary for two weeks. It interfered with satellite reception, so there was no television, internet, or cell phone reception.

The last news report in newspapers had been sent out to news services and internet news reports the night of the explosion, as had videos and pictures of the cloud.

Pictures of the glistening metallic-colored cloud and split screenshots of the cloud as compared to the northern lights flashed steadily across television screens around the country. Newscasts talked about the terrorist, George Hansen, and included biographical sketches and profiling that told of the making of an international terrorist.

The president addressed the American people from his island sanctuary, an underground bunker burrowed into the mountains that made up the interior of a remote island in the Caribbean. The bunker was austere; its walls were made of concrete block, painted dark brown. It was not good for morale to show the president sitting in a sunlit room in the Caribbean Whitehouse.

The compound had guesthouses for government officials and their families, Secret Service agents, and Homeland Security personnel. There were other buildings necessary for national security, and recreational centers for those engaged in keeping the American people safe. The president and his family had been moved here on the advice of Homeland Security sometime after one of the Middle East wars. It was believed that no place in the United States was safe enough from terrorism to house the nation's leader.

The president addressed the American people. "My fellow Americans, the citizens of Minnesota have recently suffered as the result of a chemical explosion that destroyed a household and industrial cleaning supplies plant in the Twin Cities of St. Paul and Minneapolis.

"An international terrorist, George Hansen, has been identified as the perpetrator of the explosion. He is being pursued and should be captured shortly. Homeland Security personnel believe that his wife and two children, ages eight and ten, were involved in the plot. The explosion was set up to destroy most of downtown Minneapolis; however, the buildings in that area withstood the explosion because of the concrete and steel reinforcement.

"At present, there is a large chemical cloud in the area. I'm sure some of you have seen the satellite shots of the cloud. I am proud of those space technicians for capturing those beautiful colors so that the rest of us can see them.

"I am asking the Senate and the House of Representatives to form bipartisan committees to find ways to discourage the cluster of terrorist groups that seem to form in the northern border states. Let us all pray for the families of those who died at the hands of the evil that walks the earth. Let us pray that this terrorist group will be caught soon and brought to justice."

CHAPTER 28

Janet found another note from Antoine in her mailbox after she returned from her first day back at work. He was asking for a meeting and gave her a place, day, and time. The meeting was to happen on Sunday. When she went into the office the next day, she found that the story about the explosion had been written for her by Homeland Security news censors, who rewrote anything that might cause the populace to think about air quality and the hazards of chemicals in factories. Because of the interference from the chemical cloud that shut off communication with satellites, the residents of Minneapolis and St. Paul had not read or seen any news reports about the incident. The Homeland Security version of the explosion was broadcast to the rest of the country.

Darcy came into Janet's office as Janet was reading the rewrite. "Did you think that that guy was a subversive?"

"Well, he was certainly saying things that were controversial," said Janet. "All we did was capture him and his words on camera and report him. It isn't up to me to interpret his statements.

"What are you going to do this weekend?" asked Janet.

"Well, I'm not sure. I might go to visit my parents," said Darcy.

"I hope you have a nice visit. I think I'll just stay home," said Janet.

CHAPTER 29
May 21, 2040

Janet walked to Antoine's meeting site, as the restaurant was near her apartment. She saw him sitting in a booth in the back as she entered. She took off her light coat as she approached the booth.

"This weather is nice," she commented as she slid into the booth.

Antoine nodded.

"What's this meeting about? When I get messages from you, I get anxious," she said.

"I just wanted to check in with you. We think that several people in the group are being followed," he said. "My contact with campus security, Bill, says there is no action being taken. He said he would probably know if there was going to be a roundup of suspects."

"So what happens then?" Janet asked.

"I'll contact you with instructions."

"Can't you tell me now?" asked Janet.

"All I can tell you is that someone will get you out of the city and take you someplace where you'll be able to get to the rez if we need to do that."

"That doesn't sound like much of a plan," said Janet.

"It's the best I can come up with right now. I'll continue to have contact with you," said Antoine.

"Each time we have contact, it's probably another mark on the Homeland Security suspicion scale," said Janet.

"You're probably right. But they're watching a lot of other people, and our meetings don't look that suspicious," said Antoine.

"How do you know how suspicious we look?" asked Janet.

"I don't. I have to trust that we will have time to leave and that we'll be safe in the end," said Antoine. "I'm Anishinaabe. I have been taught to trust my instincts. I just know certain things. I don't question most things in life. I just do what I am supposed to do."

"How do you know what you're supposed to do?" Janet snapped.

"It's just one of those things that you white people don't understand. You have logic and scientific fact but little faith in what is sensed but not seen," Antoine said.

"How can you say that? You don't know me," said Janet.

"I know about white culture. I have been surrounded by white culture all of my life, and now I live in the middle of it. Old Woman taught me a lot about white people. I'll know what to do when the time comes. All you have to do is follow instructions," said Antoine, standing, letting Janet know that the meeting was over.

When Janet and Antoine left the restaurant, going in opposite directions, they failed to notice the two men across the street. The two men waited a few seconds, and then each followed their subject.

The two agents noted that Janet and Antoine didn't appear to have a set schedule. They met in restaurants, had a meal, talked, and then went home. Their visits didn't always seem to be friendly. Janet didn't appear to have any contact with group members other than Antoine. Antoine's social contacts seemed to be the card games held in the student union.

The two agents would discontinue surveillance of each of the subjects when they reached their living quarters. The agents had time. Even though this was an important assignment, the agents were confident that they would eventually gather enough information to uncover an important insurrectionist group.

CHAPTER
May 22, 2040

Sonia sat on the porch watching the sun rise over the trees. Spring had timidly taken over from the snow and cold winds of winter. It came late and was quickly replaced by summer.

Even though she had to start getting ready for the July powwow, Sonia spent the early-morning hours in June relishing the warm southern breezes and the lengthening days. The birds started singing before the sun rose. She enjoyed listening to their songs, uninterrupted by the noises of people.

Old Woman awakened to the sun shining through the bedroom windows. Noting the quiet in the house, she dressed and joined Sonia on the porch.

Sonia turned when she heard Old Woman's steps and moved so that Old Woman could sit beside her. The two women sat in silence until Sonia said, "Do you think she'll come back?"

"You mean that young woman who was here a while back?" asked Old Woman.

"Yes," said Sonia.

"I don't know. She didn't seem to know for sure what she wanted. It's hard to leave a place when it's all you know," said Old Woman.

"Was it hard for you to come here?" asked Sonia.

"Well, yes and no. It was different. It was a choice, and I had lived up north before. I wanted to get away from the conflict and the accusations about me. I figured I would be trapped if I stayed too long," said Old Woman.

The two women rose as one and went into the kitchen to start breakfast. After breakfast, they returned to their places on the porch as the morning sun warmed the air.

Old Woman said, "Sonia, why don't we go down by the lake? There isn't anything we have to do. Everyone's been fed. We can sit all morning if we want to and come back to fix lunch."

She stood and grabbed a walking stick "I remember when I could hike and run without any help. At least I can still get down to the lake with a little help from this stick," she said, as she and Sonia walked down the path to the lake. They sat on a log close to the water, the slight waves lapping at their bare feet.

"I think it's time for me to talk about my passing. The spirits have told me that I am to give my history to an outsider. That would be Janet Ryan. I've done that. Someday something might happen in the outside world, and that knowledge might be useful. It's time to plan my memorial service," said Old Woman.

Sonia nodded, and Old Woman continued. "I want to be cremated. I want to be placed on a high platform. Underneath, you can have a bonfire."

"You know that's not how we do services here," said Sonia.

"Well, I may be a member of this community, but I am not a tribal member. So I figure I can have the kind of ceremony I want," said Old Woman.

"We usually send a bundle with people so they have what they need to enter the Spirit World," said Sonia.

"You can have the men gather my ashes, put them in a box, and put the bundle with it. I imagine you're going to make me a pair of moccasins. You can put them in the box, along with an extra set of clothes," said Old Woman.

"Do you want a drum?" asked Sonia.

"Yes. The drum can play during the cremation," said Old Woman.

"What do you want us to do with your ashes?" asked Sonia.

"I want my family—my kids, grandkids, and how many other generations there are, and you, Joe, and everyone else—to scatter them out by the waterfall. Keep the bundle in the box and bury it in the same place you scatter the ashes. I sent word to my children that I'll be passing on sometime around ricing season, after I go ricing with Joe. They'll come for the powwow and stay until the funeral is over."

Sonia nodded. There wasn't anything to say.

The two women watched the water birds—ducks, geese, and great blue herons. The ducks paraded past them with their ducklings, showing off. Dragonflies scooted across the water, and fish leaped out to catch any insects that flew close. When the sun was overhead, the women walked back to the house to fix lunch. They found Joe, Sierra, and Cody fixing the fire and putting food in pots.

CHAPTER

May 29, 2040

Janet went grocery shopping on Saturday. She had gotten an alert in the mail that said fresh water would not be available during daylight hours in the upcoming week. She entered and passed through the security scanner at Sustenance for Singles Supermarket. She headed for the frozen food section, stopping under a sign that said, "Absolutely No Cancer-Causing Ingredients" and "New and Improved, Designed with the Single Woman in Mind." She picked up several items encased in bubble wrap, reading labels that described the nutrients and preservatives, and realized that she had no idea where the food came from, who harvested it, or what any of the information on the label meant. She was about to put it all back on the shelves when she realized that she had no choice but to eat it or go hungry.

On her way to the bottled water, Janet passed through the section filled with colorful kitchen tools, utensils, and dinnerware, where she found items that were advertised as using less water when being cleaned.

As she checked out, the scanner smiled a wide, vapid smile and began chatting. The woman's voice was an irritating buzz, and Janet transported herself back to the woods and the water to escape. When the buzzing stopped, Janet smiled and nodded vigorously, responding, "Yes, we are lucky. Everything we have fits together so well." Janet inserted her plastic grocery card in the machine, then walked through the x-ray scanner and out the door.

Her father had told her that sometimes the most inane, innocuous people could be the most dangerous. She wondered if this inane scanner in the grocery store was dangerous. If so, she hoped that the young woman believed her comments.

Janet left her purchases on the kitchen counter as she went to each window in her apartment, checking the streets below to see if anyone might be watching her. She saw nothing and felt relieved.

She was restless and wanted to go outside but realized she wouldn't find the fresh air she had breathed in the country. Janet spent the rest of the day watching nature programs on television, wishing it was a workday so she had something productive to do.

When she went to bed, Janet tossed and turned in her sleep, her breathing labored. Each period of sleep was interrupted by dreams she didn't understand. She got up in the morning wishing she was back in the woods. She dressed, turned on the Weather Channel, and got out a number 3 EZ Breathe scarf.

Janet's workdays were filled with routine assignments. She adjusted and realized that she wanted to stay in the city. She wanted to be a part of a group that could bring about change. She wanted to advocate for personal freedoms and human rights. The reservation seemed part of another world and far away.

CHAPTER
June 19, 2040

Lloyd walked into his office and found Hal sitting in his chair again.

"The Eleanor Roosevelt Ozone Plate is floating this way. It's time to get Janet involved in this," said Hal. "July is a good time of year for the festivities We can combine the ozone plate celebration with July Fourth."

"Okay. Does this mean she's no longer suspected of terrorist activities?" asked Lloyd.

"Quite the opposite. She left the city without permission. After she got back, she met with the young man she had been seen with before," said Hal.

"I don't understand why keeping company with someone would make her a suspect of anything," said Lloyd.

"She violated another travel rule to meet with him, traveling outside her neighborhood. She wore her press badge when she wasn't on assignment," said Hal.

"I don't understand why any of this is considered suspicious behavior," said Lloyd.

"Maybe that's why you do what you do and I do what I do," said Hal. "On this assignment, she is to meet with all of the agencies and people who play a role in environmental science and others who are connected to those agencies. She is to write her stories from her interviews with those people."

"Can't she just go to archives and gather the information she needs?" asked Lloyd.

"No. We need input from many people as to what she says, the questions she asks, and how she presents herself. All of this plays into whether she is guilty or innocent. Whether she is a traitor or a terrorist or both," said Hal.

"When will you decide that she is innocent?" asked Lloyd.

"We'll let this play out. If nothing comes of it, we'll shut down the investigation," said Hal.

"Let what play out?" asked Lloyd.

"Janet Ryan's suspicious behavior and the suspicious behavior of lots of other people who seem to be connected," said Hal as he walked out the door. He stopped and turned. "Oh, I'll let you know when the ER has been spotted. Then Ms. Ryan can go and interview the person who sees it."

Lloyd sat in his office for a long time, feeling helpless. He sighed and sent an email to Janet, asking her to come to his office. As she approached he said, "Come in. Come in. I just got word that the Eleanor Roosevelt Ozone Plate is approaching us. I've decided that you're the best person to report on it. This means that you'll be reporting on all of the festivities, the history of the ozone plates, their naming, and everything else about them. I don't have to tell you that this largest of the ozone plates was named after a First Lady who was a role model for the entire country during the dark days of World War II. The entire staff will be at your disposal. We will hook you up with researchers from the science channel who can give you their latest reports on ozone and the environment. All of your other duties will be put aside, and Darcy can assume your regular duties."

Janet left his office feeling overwhelmed, not knowing what to do first. She sat at her desk for a few minutes, trying to set up a logical sequence for the stories she needed to write. She hadn't expected this important assignment.

Preparing for her coverage of the ozone plate, Janet called the science channel and set up an appointment for early afternoon to talk to the researchers who worked on environmental issues. She spent the rest of the morning writing a list of things to do and stories to write.

Janet got a permit to drive a company car and picked up the gas credit card from the purchasing department. She left the building and headed for the offices of the science channel.

Janet parked the car and entered the building, a concrete and glass structure about ten stories high. After going through the security routine, she found the sign listing the departments housed in the building. Janet saw no one in the halls. She found the "Environmental Science" sign and followed the arrows to a metal door with a peephole. She pushed the button below a sign that read "No Entry without Authorization" and held her newspaper ID up to the peephole. Janet heard a loud click just before the door opened to reveal a woman with a plastic name tag that identified her as Ruth, Receptionist/Security Officer. She stood aside to allow Janet to enter.

When the door shut, Ruth, a thin woman with dark hair that hung limp to her shoulders, went through a series of rituals to secure the entrance. When Ruth finished, she motioned for Janet to follow her into a small room. Expressionless, Ruth pointed to a white, flat tablet. "Please place each finger on the tablet, starting with your right-hand index finger, finishing with your left thumb." Janet's name was already printed on the form.

"Now, put your hand on this Bible and swear that you will not reveal anything about the identities of people you meet here or say anything about the offices."

After the oath taking, Ruth said, "In order for you to proceed with her interview, you will have to sign this oath of allegiance and this disclaimer that states you are not part of any terrorist group or their activities. I have recorded this, and the recording will be sent to the Homeland Security Office," said Ruth.

Next, Ruth escorted Janet to an office, knocked, and unlocked the door with a plastic card after placing her right thumb on a scanner. She held the door open for Janet and closed it on her way out.

A man with dark hair graying at the temples sat at a desk surrounded by computers, all of which had security screens on them. He stood and held out his hand. Janet responded. His handshake was firm and warm.

"Hi. I'm glad you came to see what we do. I'm Sam Murray. I'm in charge of environmental research into the positive aspects of ozone layer depletion. I don't know if I can help with your story. I understand the Eleanor Roosevelt is paying us a visit."

"Perhaps you can tell me about the history of your research and what you know to date," Janet said.

"Okay. These computers track the progression of global warming. When we were first aware of global warming in the 1980s, there was a great deal of concern about the melting of the polar ice fields. Then a scientist noticed a hole in the ozone layer, and we became concerned about protecting the earth from the increased intensity of the sun's rays.

Warnings were sent out to all of the world's leaders, and people in our country were encouraged to cut back on their use of pressurized cans. They started making refrigerators differently at that time because the chemicals used in the cooling systems would further deplete the ozone layer. The same was true if Styrofoam was burned in waste dumps. This was before there was a lot of recycling going on.

"Scientists like me were hired by the government and by major corporations to find an answer. We knew it would be impossible to curtail the use of pressurized cans. They were used for a variety of products, and to discontinue the manufacturing of such products would mean an economic crisis. Many workers would have been laid off, and factories using pressurized cans would have to come up with something else. After many years of research and meetings, it was decided that the best thing to do was let it go. If we continued with industrialization and increased the manufacturing of goods for the American people, and if we continued to use fossil fuels, the air would become filled with a variety of substances that would cut down on the amount of penetration by the sun.

"Certainly this sounds like a terrible thing to do; it sounds like we encourage pollution. However, a larger plan than this needed to be put into place. Common sense tells us that the chemicals in the air will disperse and thin out the farther away you get from the source. This means that the farther into the country you go, the clearer the air is.

"Now the next question that some people used to ask was, 'Doesn't the air eventually get dirty because of the buildup of chemicals that float away in the air?' That used to be a common belief. We are finding that this isn't true. Please come here and look at these images on this screen."

Sam motioned for Janet to move around in front of one of the computers. There was a large detailed map of a small space. "I can't tell you exactly where this is because it is privileged information. But look at this. See all these crooked lines and irregular circles? Those are bodies of water. For about the last ten years, the air going into this area from the city has gotten cleaned after being there for a few days. It's like there is some kind of barrier on the edge of this territory with something in the air or the water or the plants that cleans it up.

"We know there are no purification machines of any kind. All that's out there are plants, trees, animals, water, a few backwoods people, and a few Indians. There is no one there who is smart enough to come up with the technology to clean this air. We believe this means that the earth has substances it gives off that cleanse the air.

"We sent research teams to the area to see if we could find substances in the environment that were responsible for cleansing the air and water. We spent a couple of years there and couldn't find anything.

"Then we decided that it doesn't matter that there are only remnants of the ozone layer left. The city air has enough pollutants to block the sun's rays, and it doesn't matter that the sun's rays are coming through in the country because no one of any consequence lives there. Our leaders who live out of the city take necessary precautions to protect themselves.

"The fact that the ozone layer has been reduced to amorphous globs held together by bits and pieces of solid waste that float up from the atmosphere is not all bad. The plates haven't disappeared and don't seem to change in size. So, when they come around, we celebrate."

Janet looked intently at the images on the screen as Sam was talking. She was trying to figure out if the area was the place she had been visiting. She could see that it wasn't possible by simply looking at the map to tell where it was or what it was. She thought about the stories she had heard from Sonia about the white-haired woman who gave Sonia's community the plants that cleaned the air and the water.

As she stared at the screen and listened to Sam, Janet was trying to think of some questions to ask him that wouldn't sound like she was questioning his theories.

Janet asked, "May I take some pictures of the facility?"

Sam shook his head. "No. We have been under threats of attack from some environmental groups. About twenty years ago, a group calling themselves Children of Mother Earth broke into our offices and destroyed our computers. They were rounded up and interrogated. Because of the knowledge they gained when they got in the building and the security risks if there had been a public trial, the group members were sent to Guantanamo. This is not for public knowledge. You do have a security clearance, so I can tell you some of this. If it gets out, we know it came from you.

"Even though this was about twenty years ago, and we have better security, we have to be careful. We produce documentaries for television that have been controversial.

"The controversy is due to the ambivalence that people have about the use of fossil fuels. That attack twenty years ago came after a television series about the need for oil production in Alaska. Our fossil fuel usage was higher at that time than it is now because there was more individual use. Since the increase in public transportation, fossil fuel use has diminished.

"After the attack, we did what we could to protect our building and our employees. People who worked for the science channel were anonymous. Announcers who did the voiceovers on our documentaries were hired from the outside. When credits were listed at the beginnings and endings of shows, a message followed that told everyone that they were simply reporting on the research of others and the research findings did not reflect the beliefs of science television. A large chemical manufacturing company owns us. They have resources available to them to conduct very sophisticated research. We are all dedicated to protecting the earth's environment while meeting the needs of the American people."

Sam stood. "I think you have enough information for your story. When do you think it will be in the newspaper?"

"I'm not sure. It's a good piece to put in the science news in the Sunday edition, but chronologically, it should go in before that. I don't know how I'm going to put this all together. Some of it's up to the other reporters and the editor. Thanks for your help."

CHAPTER 33

June 26, 2040

Hal Emerson stood in the foyer of the Homeland Security family house, a house that was used when they needed operatives to play the part of a family. This was done when innocent-looking people were needed to gather information from people who were under suspicion of something. This was the house where Janet Ryan would come to interview the Hanson family regarding the Eleanor Roosevelt Ozone Plate.

Hal saw two adults he had worked before approaching the house, suitcases in hand. The man and woman were accompanied by two children, a boy and a girl and a Plasti-Dog that had the name Butch printed across his chest. Hal opened the door as the couple reached the porch. He extended a hand. "Russell and Beth, welcome to your home for the next two weeks. I'm glad to see you again." He turned his attention to the children. "Let's see. You must be Jennifer, and you are John," he greeted the children.

Jennifer, who appeared to be about twelve years old, strode forward and stood in front of Hal. "What are we supposed to do here? Are we going to turn someone in? I like turning people in. They threaten our country and must be dealt with," she said.

Hal shuddered. He had heard of this girl. When she was ten and a member of the Youth Corps. She turned her parents in for making disparaging remarks about the government. Jennifer was given a commendation by Homeland Security. When she went to report her parents, Jennifer had the foresight to take Butch and a duffel full of clothes and important belongings with her, knowing she probably would never return to her house. When her parents were taken away, she was heard saying to them, "You deserve what you get. You can't say bad things about this country and get away with it."

Jennifer was placed in the Midwest Homeland Security Adoption Center, where she attended school and received training to be a Homeland Security operative. She spent six weeks there and was examined, cross-examined, debriefed, and finally certified as an operative. It had been her passion to become a Homeland Security operative ever since she had seen a movie in her first-grade class about Heather Homeland, a fictional Homeland Security heroine. Butch was allowed to stay with Jennifer at the boarding school for orphans of parents who had engaged in terrorist activities. The children were taught that their parents had succumbed to brainwashing, often subliminal brainwashing, from terrorists who existed everywhere in America. Children were praised for reporting their parents and others to Homeland Security. They were truly patriotic and had sacrificed for the good of the country. They were often given their first assignments while they were adolescents or younger. They were usually placed in family situations similar to Jennifer's current assignment. Jennifer was known throughout Homeland Security as a skilled actress who had no concern for others. She liked getting people into trouble.

"Jennifer," said Hal. "You're not going to turn anyone in. You're supposed to be a kid who looks into the sky and sees the approaching Eleanor Roosevelt Ozone Plate. A reporter comes to interview you and the rest of the family. You just answer her questions and let her know how excited you are about being the first person to spot the plate, and pretend that Russell and Beth are your parents and John is your little brother." Hal thought he saw a disappointed look on Jennifer's face.

"What do I get to do?" asked John.

Simon Morris, John's mentor, had called Hal a few days before Hal met with the faux family to rehearse for their interview with Janet Ryan. "Hal, this is Simon. I want this kid on this assignment because he still has some confusion about who he is and what he's supposed to do. His parents were arrested after a neighbor turned them in for encouraging a protest against the factory where John's dad worked. Seems Dad didn't like the work schedule or wages. When they were arrested, John's mom began crying and yelling, reaching out with her arms, saying she wanted to say goodbye to John, who was standing nearby. Some mother, huh. She should have low-keyed it to save John some pain. Anyway, he was taken to a holding center and placed in quarantine for three months so he could be taught about the role of Homeland Security and its role in the safety and security of our nation. That's where I met him. He was sitting with about twenty other kids in a holding area surrounded by a chain-link fence, looking really sad. In spite of everything we taught him, he still hung onto that memory of his mother holding her arms out to him. So I figured it would be good for him to see a little action. He is just supposed to watch and learn, no talking. He can just be the shy kid who is overshadowed by Jennifer. It's easy for him to be overshadowed by Jennifer. So how is the rest of this going to play out?"

"Well, Jennifer will spot the ozone plate. This will be reported on the Weather Channel. A reporter will come to the house to interview the family," said Hal.

"Sounds like a good placement for John. He will be in the background and won't have to say much," said Simon.

"That's right. We have to bring some of these kids along slowly. They can't all be like Jennifer," said Hal, thinking that he was glad there weren't too many like Jennifer or most of Homeland Security would be in danger. He could look ahead to a future in which Jennifer just turned people in for the fun of it.

Hal addressed John. "I talked to Simon, your mentor. He says that you need some experience. You're the kid brother. You don't have to say anything unless the reporter asks you some questions."

Hal turned to the family. "Well, the house is ready, and everything you need is here. So I'll leave you to get settled in. I'll call you when we have the newspaper interview arranged. If you need anything in the meantime, just let me know."

"Thanks, Hal," said Russell. "Good to be working with you again."

As he was walking out the door, Hal heard John say, "Why can't I be the one who sees the plate? Why does she get to do it?"

"Because I'm older than you, and I've had more experience," said Jennifer with a sneer in her voice.

CHAPTER 34
June 28, 2040

Two days after Hal left the faux Hanson family, he paid a visit to Lloyd. When Lloyd entered the newsroom, he saw Hal sitting in his office.

Before Lloyd could sit, Hal said, "Okay. The scene is set up. The Hanson family is in the HS house just south of Bloomington. Let Janet Ryan know that she is to interview them, as their twelve-year-old daughter spotted the plate this morning when she was going out the door to school. She'll have to meet with the family this evening, as they are out during the day. Here's the address and some background information on the family." He handed a folder to Lloyd as he walked out the door.

As Janet entered the newsroom, she saw Lloyd waving her to his office. "Janet, the Eleanor Roosevelt Ozone Plate has been spotted by a twelve-year-old girl. I checked with Homeland Security. According to their records, the family lives south of Bloomington. Both parents work, and the kids are in school during the day. You'll have to interview the family this evening. I want you to focus all your attention on this today. Leave a message on their phones so they'll be ready for your visit. Make up a list of interview questions and review the information in this folder so you'll be somewhat familiar with the family. There's a map in the folder and directions to their home. Last name is Hanson."

As she left his office, Janet noted that Lloyd's tic had returned. She spent the day reviewing the information Lloyd left with her. She went over the outline she made for the series of articles she would write on the ozone plate. She called the phone number Lloyd had given her and left a message.

Janet's cell phone rang about four thirty. The number on the screen wasn't familiar to her. She answered and heard a woman's voice.

"Hello? Are you the reporter who is trying to contact us? My daughter, Jennifer, spotted the Eleanor Roosevelt Ozone Plate."

"Yes, I'm Janet Ryan. I'm a writer with the *Minneapolis Herald* and am writing a series of articles to highlight the EROP celebration. May I come over this evening to interview Jennifer and your family?"

"Sure, you can come to our house. It will take you about forty-five minutes to get here. Do you have directions?"

"Yes, I do," said Janet.

"Okay," said Beth. "See you in a little while."

Janet left the building and got into the company car that was parked in the parking ramp next to the building. When she got to the first gate, she stopped and waited for the gate to open to let her through. It didn't happen.

The security guard approached her car. "Please get out of the car, ma'am," he said.

Janet obeyed, and the guard took a metal/plastic scanner, passing it over her. Nothing beeped, and no lights or alarms went off.

"I need to see your ID, your travel permit, and the car's registration." As the guard scanned all of her documents, the security cameras were taking her picture, which was automatically transferred to a computer that compared the picture to her personal ID.

Why is this happening? she thought. I have a company car and my press card. Has somebody turned me in for something? Each time she was stopped at a gate, her anxiety level rose.

By the time Janet reached the professional family neighborhood where the Hanson family lived, she was shaking and her thoughts raced. She tried to act normal as she got out of the car and observed the neighborhood. She was surprised by all of the high fences surrounding the school, the parks, and the houses, until she remembered that a few years back, a terrorist cell was discovered here.

The fiberglass fences that were stained to resemble wood panels were a little over six feet high and surrounded each property, There were street signs at intersections, and each property had identifying numbers near the entrance gates. The gates were controlled by remotes that residents carried so they could gain access when outside. Each house had electronic security systems. There were cameras positioned just to the right of the top of the gate. All of this discouraged casual visiting between families, who could gather at the neighborhood center for game nights, picnics, and other activities that appealed to families, where their conversations could be monitored on security cameras wired for sound.

It was a little after five when Janet rang the bell beside the property number on the gate belonging to the Hanson family. She took out her press card and held it up for the camera.

The gate opened, and Janet stepped into the yard, which was covered with green plastic shreds that were meant to look like blades of grass.

The front door opened, and a girl about twelve years old stood in the doorway.

"Hi! You must be Janet. I'm Jennifer. Our names both start with a J."

"Jennifer, bring the young lady in the living room," said a female voice from somewhere inside the house.

Janet followed Jennifer into a spacious living room that held two couches and several easy chairs. Family pictures that appeared to have been taken in a studio hung on the walls.

"Come in and sit down! I'm Beth, and this is Russell, my husband. This is our son, John. You've met Jennifer, and sitting on the pillow over in the corner is our Plasti-Dog, Butch. We're the Hansons."

Janet nodded, smiling at each member of the family. She felt foolish nodding at the shiny, plastic yellow dog, but she figured she should since she had been introduced. "Why don't you tell me your story."

"In past years, Russell and I have been attendants to the royal family. We thought that since Jennifer had been the first to report the plate, we would be chosen as the emperor and empress," said Beth.

"I don't know," said Janet. "I don't have that information. I think whoever makes that decision will contact you directly. Jennifer, can you tell me how you came to see the plate?"

Jennifer squirmed with self-importance. "Like, I got up this morning to get ready for school. Like, I get up before everybody else, don't I, Mom? I just, like, love school. Anyway, it was, like, just getting light out. I like to look out the window and guess, like, what number EZ Breathe scarf I get to, like, wear before I turn on the Weather Channel.

"I, like, saw a shadow off to the south. Like, I thought it might be a storm cloud. I, like, just kept looking for a while and then, like, decided it must be an ozone plate because it didn't move or, like, change shape the way clouds do. I, like, guessed that it was probably the Eleanor Roosevelt because it was so, like big. Like, I asked my mom's permission to call the Weather Channel to, like, report. Mom said, 'Like, okay,' so I, like, called and reported it."

"That's about all there is to that story. It doesn't surprise me that my daughter would spot the plate. She's good at everything she does. She's so smart, and she always knows what to do in any situation. We're so proud of her—aren't we, Russell?" said Beth.

Russell smiled and nodded, looking like the proud parent.

Jennifer turned to John, who had sunk into an easy chair, pouting because he didn't get to be the one to report the plate.

Janet asked, "Well, John, what's it like having a celebrity in the family?"

"Well, she's my sister, and I'm glad she spotted the plate. I wish I had, but maybe when it comes again, I'll have another chance."

"That's the spirit, John!" said Beth.

The front gate buzzed. Beth got up to see who was there. She saw a young man with a camera and a group of men and women who looked like couples all dressed up in costumes from a medieval period.

"Oh, my goodness!" said Beth. "You're the Eleanor Roosevelt Ozone Plate celebration lords and ladies. Russell, look who's here." Beth buzzed open the gate and opened the front door as the group moved up on the porch. "Are you here to tell us we are the royal family? You are, aren't you. Oh, my. We don't even have outfits.

"We're honored! The ozone plates tell us that we still have a healthy environment surrounding our planet. One of these days, the plates will come together, and the ozone layer will be intact again," said Beth.

The photographer introduced himself. "Hi. I'm Don from the *Herald*. We haven't met, Janet. I only started working this week. Lloyd thought I should round up the lords and ladies and come out to take pictures."

Sheldon, the apparent spokesperson for the lords and ladies, gave the family outfits that would identify them as royalty for the Eleanor Roosevelt Ozone Plate festivities. They changed clothes and came back for pictures.

While Don was positioning the royal family and the lords and ladies, Janet had the idea to include the visit by the lords and ladies in her story.

She thought this would be better than any long story about who the family was. Besides, she could get information about what the couple did for a living by calling the Bloomington Residency Gate.

Janet stood and shook hands with Russell and Beth. "Thanks for your time. I'm not sure when all of this will be in the paper. I'll call you when I know. I can find my way out. Goodbye."

That night, Janet had dreams about being chased by Jennifer and Butch, the Plasti-Dog, who was foaming at the mouth, rusting the metal rivets that connected his lower and upper jaws.

Janet was running down a highway filled with potholes and lined with tall trees. Each time she got just so far down the road, she would wake up, fall asleep, dream again, and wake up. When morning finally came, she went through her routine and left for work. The dreams were upsetting, and she just wanted to forget them.

CHAPTER
June 29, 2040

Janet got to the office early, anxious to continue with her assignment. Her next step was to review the materials she had for two stories, see if any of it would fit in another story, and figure out what stories to do next. As she was sorting and organizing, a phone call came for her.

"Hello. Is this Janet Ryan, the reporter who is doing the stories on the Eleanor Roosevelt Ozone Plate?"

"Yes," said Janet.

"I'm Ted Wagner. I am a Realtor," he said. "Have you thought about a story on how the visit by the plate affects property values?"

"I didn't know about this," said Janet.

"Well, how about we meet at my office? I'm in the Mall of America," said Ted.

"I could come now," said Janet. "It will take me about fifteen minutes to get there."

"Okay. I'm looking forward to our visit," said Ted.

Janet pulled into the parking lot at the mall and began cruising, looking for a parking space close to an entrance. It was a weekday, but there were a lot of shoppers, as people could get most of what they needed here, and it was fun to bring the kids for the carnival rides. Parents were expected to teach their kids how to shop so they would grow up to be patriotic Americans.

Schools gave permission for children to be absent from school as long as they brought back a ticket stub from one of the many virtual reality museums. Children often wrote reports on their trips to the Mall of America, such stories taking the place of book reports.

Janet went through the security gate and adjusted her pace to join the crowd as shoppers strolled along with no particular destination in mind. She stopped to read the large sign that gave directions to stores and other attractions. She found the realty office on the sign and veered to the left. As she approached the office, she saw a receptionist sitting behind the Plexiglas enclosure.

There had been a shooting here a few years before by an elderly man who had been told he had to leave his house and enter a nursing home. The government, exercising eminent domain, had the house condemned, took possession, and sold it to the realty company. The man had received a check for $500 even though the house had been worth $250,000. After his eviction, the man walked in the door and began shooting. A police SWAT team arrived on the scene and killed him. Somehow, the man had gotten through security at the mall entrance.

Because of some of the difficulties and hard feelings associated with property acquisition, all realty offices now had security equipment provided by the Homeland Security Office for a rental fee. In return, realty offices were expected to participate in security sweeps and assist with surveillance of those who were seen as engaging in suspicious activities.

Ted had been contacted the day before and asked to make the call to Janet. A Homeland Security agent had come to his office and presented him with a script he had to memorize.

Ted was waiting as the receptionist buzzed, and he came out looking pleased to see Janet. He introduced himself. "Hi. You must be Janet Ryan. I'm Ted Wagner. I'm glad you could come. C'mon in." He led Janet down a hall to an office with a large picture of a nature scene with trees, grass, and birds flying in a blue sky, meant to take the place of a window. He motioned for her to sit as he moved behind his desk to take his chair.

He said, "I'm glad you came. Most people don't realize that there is a connection between property values and the passing of an ozone plate. Well, just pay attention and I will explain it to you. We are all aware that the latest research says that the ozone layer isn't really necessary in cities anymore. We have enough pollutants in the air to diminish the damaging effects of the sun without having an ozone layer.

"The remnants of the ozone layer, gaseous floating masses, are held together with the solid pieces from industrial wastes that are part of the factory emissions. The approach of an ozone plate means darker days, and it usually means the air is cooler than usual. We know that the plates float without any destination until they come in contact with the strong winds in the upper levels of the atmosphere. We can predict when a plate will reach a specific place when the winds move the plates close enough to a place where that momentum will carry the plate forward if the wind shifts or lets up. When the wind is no longer influencing the movement of the plate, the plate's movement is slowed. We don't know how long it will hang around a specific area. This, of course, makes people hesitate when they look at buying property that is directly in the path of a plate, because they can't get a clear picture as to what they are buying.

"When the government started naming the plates, we decided to take advantage of the names. In most of our housing areas, we name streets after the plates. When a particular ozone plate is approaching, we have neighborhood festivities in the development that is named after the approaching plate. The approach of the Eleanor Roosevelt Ozone Plate is good publicity for us out in the Gate Five area, where there is an Eleanor Roosevelt Ozone Plate Boulevard. There's also a real coincidence here. That family, the Hansons, the ones whose little girl spotted the plate? They live on Eleanor Roosevelt Ozone Plate Boulevard. This would be a great human-interest story, don't you think?"

Janet didn't know what to say. She had trouble taking in all of the information because the man talked so fast. He handed her a packet of papers. "Here's the story. I hope you can use it."

Janet thanked him, took the papers, and left the office. She was beginning to realize that everyone wanted to get in on the publicity for the Eleanor Roosevelt Ozone Plate.

As she walked out of the realty office and back into the mall area, Janet saw a restaurant and realized she was hungry. The place was filled with people, and there was an air of excitement. She caught bits and pieces of conversation as she waited for a table.

"How far away is she?"

"Isn't she the biggest plate?"

"Who named her anyway?"

No one was talking about the time when there was an ozone layer, and no one seemed to care about the pollution, terrorism, or the control exercised by Homeland Security. Clarity replaced the confusion in Janet's mind, and she wanted to scream. Instead she followed the Techno Hostess to an available table.

When she left the restaurant, Janet got on the bus, went back to work, and wrote a story based on the information the Realtor had given her. After that, she put together other stories and checked the Weather Channel on her computer to find out the ETA of the Eleanor Roosevelt Ozone Plate. The meteorologists were saying it would probably be another three days before the plate was directly overhead.

Janet called the Office of Celebrations and talked with someone who said that the Eleanor Roosevelt Ozone Plate Queen Contest would be tonight and the parade would take place in two days. Janet called Louis and asked if he could come with her to the queen contest. He said, "Sure. It will be fun to get a front-row seat."

A few minutes later, Darcy appeared unannounced. "Isn't this just great? You must feel so honored to be the reporter who got this assignment. I hope I can do this someday. Is there something you want me to help you with?"

"Oh. Well. I'm not sure. I have a lot of information, but I don't have it organized yet," said Janet, not wanting Darcy to help her with anything. My stories are original, she thought. They'll be scrutinized. I don't know what Darcy will do them if she gets her hands on them. I don't trust her. She might be from Homeland Security. Why do I keep thinking this? Why is Darcy here, anyway?

Janet gave in, knowing she couldn't avoid including Darcy. She spent the rest of the afternoon writing her EROP stories, giving them to Darcy to proofread, and then rereading to make sure Darcy hadn't changed anything except typos.

Janet left work early to change her clothes from work to formal evening attire. She headed for the Ozone Plate Celebration Hall, picking up Louis on her way.

Janet and Louis joined the revelers as they entered celebration hall to watch the Eleanor Roosevelt Ozone Plate Queen Contest. The high walls, covered with tapestries depicting likenesses of men and women whose names remained in the revised US history as patriots and for whom the ozone plates were named, stretched up to a ceiling adorned with crystal chandeliers. There was an excited buzz in a room filled with local dignitaries and celebrities, dressed in black tie, tails, and the latest couture, happy to be part of this prestigious occasion.

Sitting in front on a stage were the young women who had been hastily recruited to compete in the contest as soon as an ozone plate was first spotted. There were twenty in all, chattering nervously as they awaited the beginning of the program.

Each contestant wore a gown that had been selected for her by the queen coordinator from the Office of Celebrations. Each would walk down a runway and would be viewed by judges and an audience of elected officials and corporate executives, many of whom had flown in from their country homes for the occasion. Then each candidate would be interviewed and asked a series of questions as to why they wanted to be like Eleanor Roosevelt. Judges would score, points would be tallied, and a winner would be selected.

All the candidates would ride on floats in the Eleanor Roosevelt Ozone Plate Parade and would attend the dinner and dance in the evening after the parade had traversed the downtown area, the neighborhood of the queen, and the neighborhood of the little girl who first spotted the place. The queen would serve in her official capacity, riding on the float that would travel to the small towns in the area. When the ozone plate approached another city, there would be another celebration, and the queen from that city would take on the duties associated with the ozone plate celebrations.

The floats for the Eleanor Roosevelt Ozone Plate Parade were kept in a garage at the site of the state fairgrounds. Each named ozone plate parade had a specific theme based on the likes and dislikes of its namesake. All of the high school and college marching bands had learned music specific to each plate. The music was recorded indoors because the air quality didn't allow for musicians to march and play their instruments at the same time. The drum major or majorette would carry a CD player, and the musicians would carry their instruments and pretend to be playing. The marching bands spent time practicing for each ozone plate at the old fairgrounds, the perfect places to keep the floats.

State fairs had been discontinued several years before because of the potential for terrorist attacks. The buildings remained and were used for necessary patriotic gatherings. Security was tight at such gatherings, but patriotism needed to be emphasized and kept alive

All of the stories that surrounded the ozone plates and the celebrations were retold and embellished each time a plate passed over, making each affair bigger than the last. The queen contest and all that went with it lasted for several hours before a winner was announced. The winning contestant was a young woman from St. Louis Park who talked about her time in the Homeland Security Youth Corps. Her patriotism overwhelmed the crowd, who joined her in her tears when she talked about the honor in being a contestant. It was quite late when the event finished, and Louis had gotten some good pictures. Because the building had an air-quality control system, queen contestants could be seen without any EZ Breathe appliances, making the judging much easier.

After the queen coronation, Janet went home to bed. She was tired and didn't have time to think of anything except the next event and the next story.

While Janet slept, the proofreaders in the Homeland Security Office looked for words, sentences, and themes that would betray Janet was editing all of her stories. They had found nothing so far, convincing them that they were dealing with a woman who was clever and, therefore, dangerous.

June 30, 2040

When Janet awakened, she turned on the Weather Channel to hear a reporter announce that the Eleanor Roosevelt Ozone Plate would be directly overhead tomorrow. There would be an air-quality alert for masks and plastic face protectors because the emissions in the air were being blocked from their escape into the atmosphere due to the presence of the ozone plate. These conditions made the visit of the Eleanor Roosevelt a mixed blessing. The reporter appeared to be crying with disappointment as she talked about what limits this would place on the parade and the other festivities. She finished with the announcement that in spite of the poor air quality, all of the Eleanor Roosevelt Ozone Plate festivities would go on as planned.

Janet rode the bus to work, planning her day before she got there. She would interview the coordinator of the mayor's dinner to be held after the parade and the children's carnival, which would be held at the Mall of America. The names of the amusement park rides at the mall were all changed to that of a named ozone plate and were free for children twelve and under, and all of the stores had sidewalk sales.

The virtual reality museums had special exhibits dedicated to the namesake of the ozone plate. One of the special features of the Eleanor Roosevelt Ozone Plate was a Plasti-Dog sale of terrier-like Plasti-Dogs named Fala, after the Roosevelt's family pet. The virtual reality family history museum had exhibits featuring Eleanor Roosevelt's family. In the virtual reality setting, one could visit the family and interact with them and pet the Roosevelt Plasti-Dog! Janet wanted to interview the amusement park manager, clerks in stores, and virtual reality museum attendants. She would take a photographer with her. Included in her stories would be a biographical account of Eleanor Roosevelt. Janet would describe her patriotism and sacrifice on behalf of the greatest nation in the world.

Louis was waiting at her desk when she got there. "Hey," he said. "It took you long enough to get here. I've been here since seven. I thought we should get an early start so we can take our time getting pictures and stories."

Janet didn't bother to take her coat off. She grabbed her computer notebook, checked the batteries, and got the keys and the credit card for the company car. She motioned for Louis to follow her.

Louis tried striking up a conversation with Janet in the car. "You must be busy. What do you think of all of the excitement? It's quite an honor to get this assignment."

Janet didn't have time for conversation and responded by nodding her head.

When they got to the Mall of America, the bus lots were filled with people from all over the Midwest who were there to take part in the Eleanor Roosevelt Ozone Plate activities. There were banners above the entrances:

Eleanor Roosevelt Ozone Plate Days!

Join in the fun. Win a Fala Plasti-Dog! Eat an old-fashioned meal
just like Eleanor Roosevelt used to eat in the Virtual Reality

Family History Restaurant! Ride on the rides named especially for this important visit by the largest of the ozone plates!

Crowds of people were climbing off the buses, running toward the entrances, getting in line for security searches, anticipating the sales inside.

"Maybe we should wait for a while to go in," Janet said.

"Why would we want to wait? Half the story is the experience," said Louis, who was trotting slowly toward the nearest entrance. Janet followed, her stiletto heels not allowing for anything more than a brisk walk.

As they approached the people who were squeezing into the security checkpoints, Louis turned on the video camera and hoisted it onto his shoulder. Recording all of this freed Janet from interviewing and taking notes. She could review the recording and write her story.

Janet and Louis tried to delay the entry into the mall to allow for more video cam recording. The crowed pushed the two into the opening where everything stopped while people went through security. Once in, she squeezed through the crowd to reach a wall and wait for Louis. She watched as women hopped on one foot, trying to put shoes on as they headed for the sales.

When Janet and Louis spotted each other, Louis pushed through the crowd to join her while he put on his shoes. Where should we go first?" he asked.

"Well, I think we should go to the Virtual Reality Family History Museum. I think there will be fewer people there than there are in the stores right now. We won't be able to interview any of the clerks in the stores because they'll be too busy. You can record as we walk, and we'll put the tape together with the rest of the story later. C'mon. Let's get out there." Janet pushed herself off the wall and jumped into the crowd.

Louis followed, his camera resting on his shoulder, recording whatever came into view as they struggled to stay in the middle. Groups of people would split from the larger group to veer toward stores and sales, almost like rush hour traffic getting on an exit ramp during the time when most people used personal transportation.

Janet and Louis saw the signs for the family history museum and angled themselves out of the middle and toward the museum. When they reached the museum, they showed their press cards to the attendant, who motioned for them to swipe their cards in the machine on the counter of the entryway.

"Welcome! We are having a special exhibit in honor of the imminent arrival of the Eleanor Roosevelt Ozone Plate! It is a self-guided tour and includes an old-fashioned family-style meal. Just slip on those helmets, turn on the microphones in the headphones, and you're all set."

Janet and Louis were swirled into a room with heavy woodwork and furniture from the early 1900s. As they walked, they went from Upstate New York to the White House and back again. There were children running around, laughing, while a little dog swirled and barked.

They were in the Oval Office as the president made decisions about World War II. They were at the United Nations with Eleanor Roosevelt, and they were at the White House when the ozone plate was named after Eleanor Roosevelt.

Janet and Louis ended up in a dining room that looked like it could have been in the Roosevelt family home. The voice in the headphones instructed them to take a table. A Techno Waitress approached them. "Hi. I'm Tiffany. I'll be your waitress today. The regular menu has been discontinued for today. We will be serving a family-style meal from earlier times. We will have roast beef, mashed potatoes and gravy, milk, bread, and string beans. Of course, these are substitute foods. Several years ago when there was an epidemic of obesity, a study was done, and the cause of the obesity was attributed to these foods. While the visit to this virtual reality museum is not complete without a family meal, we are pleased that we can give you this experience without damaging your health."

Janet was impressed with the lifelike quality of the Techno Waitress. Her voice was well modulated, and her mannerisms realistic. Her body was made of malleable plastic, and her blond hair was coifed in a current style.

Their meal was served shortly after they were seated. Janet looked at her watch and saw that it was noon. They had spent three hours there. She said, "Louis, look at the time." They hurried through their meal, not talking, and left the museum. Their appetites were sated, even though the food was like the food they purchased at grocery stores and cooked at home; it had no taste.

Out in the mall again, they met the crush of people moving slowly, trying to shop and see what else was going on, stopping at restaurants and shops to see what was available. Louis pointed the camera at the sale signs and the sale items stacked on tables. "Boy, this is something, isn't it?" he said.

Janet nodded. "I'm not much of a shopper to begin with. I don't think I could do this."

They stopped at a clothing store where Janet found a clerk hanging and stacking clothing that had fallen on the floor as mobs of shoppers pawed through stacks looking for bargains. Janet said, "Hi. I'm Janet Ryan, and I work for the *Herald*. This is Louis Stanley. We are here to do a story on all of the festivities out here. May we have a few minutes of your time?"

The clerk paused, placing the clothing she had picked up on a table piled high with unfolded sweaters. "Sure. I'm happy to be part of the Eleanor Roosevelt Ozone Plate celebration. My mom told me that the last time the Eleanor Roosevelt came over was when I was four years old. I think I remember going to a parade when I was little. That must have been it. Wow! The Eleanor Roosevelt! It's quite an honor to be part of all of this." Janet and Louis moved on, looking for someone to record, someone spouting the same inane, politically correct comments as the clerk in the store.

Janet and Louis were moved along by the surge as the crowd moved from place to place. Each had learned the knack of squeezing out of the crowd when they found something they were looking for and rejoining the crowd when finished, surrendering to the movement of the throng.

They left the building about four, watching the long lines of impatient people waiting to go through the security checkpoints and into the mall. Once outside, Louis took pictures of the uniformed attendants who monitored the crowd to make sure that the mindless throng didn't crush the people nearest the door. He caught images of the traffic controllers who were numbering buses and telling bus drivers not to let people out of the buses until their number appeared on a lighted sign near the entrance to the mall.

They got back to the office about five, time enough to put a story together with pictures and send it to the night editor for processing and publication in the morning edition of the *Herald*. When they finished, they parted company. Janet went home and went to bed, anticipating an early morning to prepare for the parade and the mayor's dinner.

She was restless and had dreams of running away and being chased. Whoever was chasing her didn't catch her, but she never quite seemed to get away.

July 1, 2040

When she awakened, Janet turned on the TV to the Weather Channel. The same reporter was in the same place as the day before, crying because of the air quality and the manner in which it would interfere with the parade. Through her tears, she said, "Today's Eleanor Roosevelt Ozone Plate festivities will be hampered by an air inversion. It isn't a good day for many to go outside, but who can resist the Eleanor Roosevelt Ozone Plate Parade? If you decide that this is a once-in-a-lifetime event that you don't want to miss, be sure to get out your masks and remember to get to the parade route early. There will be security, and everyone will have to go through the metal and plastic detectors. Those detectors will also be at all gates, so those coming into the city from the outlying areas will have to plan for extra time. Buses will run on schedule and will stop at each gate, where everyone will have to get off and go through security on foot while the buses are searched for contraband. Passengers will be picked up on the other side of the gates but only in the gated area where their routes originate. Buses will not stop to pick up passengers who are not in designated areas.

"After the parade, buses can be boarded at the downtown bus terminal. The same protocol will be used to take passengers back to their neighborhoods. Have a good, safe, Eleanor Roosevelt Ozone Plate Day."

Janet went to her closet and found a mask to match her outfit. She dressed, ate breakfast, and fastened the Velcro grippers that held the mask close to her head and eliminated leakage in the area around the face. She looked in the mirror to make sure the mask was on straight and the nasal filters aligned properly. Satisfied, she left her apartment and hurried into the street.

The sky was dark, even though on most days it was getting light at six in the morning. The air was thick, providing resistance, making it hard for people to walk. Janet felt like she was in a science fiction movie; at least it seemed like the descriptions she had heard from her parents about science fiction movies. "I wish it was a movie or maybe just a bad dream." She thought about her plans for the day and focused on them as she walked. Little else mattered.

When Janet got to work, she found Darcy sitting at her desk. "Oh, you're here. I thought you would be in earlier since this is the big day."

"Oh. Hi. I haven't seen you for a while. I have been so busy with this assignment I forgot you were here," Janet said.

"I'm so envious of you. I don't know how you can stand it. It is such an honor to be writing about all of this," Darcy said.

"I know. I can't think of anything else. I don't think I have had time to think of the honor part of it, though. I have too much to do," Janet said.

"Gee. I wish I had too much to do with something like this. It sounds like you're complaining," Darcy said.

"No. I would never complain about an assignment like this." Janet tensed. Was Darcy trying to make it sound like she was being irreverent and ungrateful?

Louis had been watching the back and forth as he approached Janet and Darcy. "Let's go," he said. "I want to get down there so we don't have to fight the crowds to get to the press box."

The three of them took the elevator down to the lobby, which was crowded with people who were leaving the building to attend the parade. This was one of those unscheduled extra holidays that was part of all employee benefit packages, both in the private and public sectors.

Darcy hurried ahead and was out the door before Janet and Louis. She came back in shortly, stumbling, and fell to the floor. Janet rushed over and removed Darcy's wine-colored mask. Darcy was gasping for breath. "I must have a leak in my mask. It's so thick out there. Maybe my air filter is clogged."

Janet rushed out the door and pushed through the crowd. She found a first aid station and an EMT. "Come quick. I think my coworker has a leak in her mask. She's having trouble breathing."

The EMT followed her and entered the building. He knelt down and checked Darcy's vitals. He put an oxygen mask over her nose and mouth.

Janet stayed with Darcy, who was gasping into the oxygen mask, trying to talk. Janet tried to calm her down.

"You must think I'm awful. I should have taken better care of my mask," Darcy gasped.

"Just don't talk," said Janet. "The EMT is taking care of you. If you lie still, you'll be able to breathe more easily than you can right now."

"What will they do to me? I've heard that sometimes they place people on surveillance when they need medical attention for breathing problems. I guess when people leave the city and come back, sometimes their breathing gets a little off because there's too much oxygen out in the country and the body has trouble adjusting to the changes. Do you know anything about that?"

Janet assured Darcy that she didn't know anything about oxygen and body adjustments. She said, "How could anyone blame you unless you've actually been out in the country? Wouldn't it show up in your records?" Darcy's innuendo about trips to the country was not lost on Janet. She didn't trust Darcy. She just appeared out of the blue at work. Janet had been suspicious ever since her unauthorized trip to the reservation. She had broken the laws, and she thought that someone would come after her. She figured Darcy's gasping was part of the setup.

Janet stayed with Darcy until the medical attendants had changed Darcy's mask, using one of those unattractive, disposable brown masks used for medical emergencies. They stayed with her, checking her oxygen levels until they returned to normal. The attendants suggested to Darcy that she not partake in today's festivities because of the incident.

Janet suggested that Darcy go back upstairs; she could watch the parade from the windows. She motioned to Louis and walked out the door.

The air was heavy and brown. There had been no change in the air quality since Janet left for work. The streetlights strained to be seen, and Janet could see the outline of the crowd maneuvering for good places to watch the parade. More people would be arriving soon on buses running on a carefully planned schedule to cut down on the security risk. They would arrive at the site about a half hour before the parade. There would be crowds of unattended people milling around high-security areas.

As Janet and Louis worked their way through the air and the crowds, Janet spotted security people strategically positioned to alert one another of any sign of trouble.

As she pushed forward, Janet tried to look for other newspaper personnel she might know, but it was hard to recognize the masked faces. Most of the people who worked for the local newspapers had at least a passing acquaintance with one another. Most of the press people assembled today were considered some kind of security risk. The cameras would scan the people located in the press stands to look for unusual talking that could indicate suspicious relationships, just another means of gathering data that would identify those with the greatest risk factors.

The seating in the reviewing stand had been carefully planned. The announcers, judges, television personalities, and local celebrities sat in the front and were assembled by the time Janet and Louis found their seats. The local celebrities had just come off the carpet that was adorned with images of Eleanor Roosevelt and trimmed in red, white, and blue. As they approached their seats, they were interviewed by media representatives and took turns chattering into the microphones and posing for the various TV cameras while background music invaded conversations.

The music increased in volume as the University of Minnesota marching band, leading the parade, moved toward the press box. It was hard to see their maroon and gold uniforms through the brown air. The music on the CD player didn't travel well through the thick air and seemed to fall and hit the ground. The band moved at half time to the music, as too much exertion in this kind of air would interfere with breathing, no matter how good the mask.

Following the U of M marching band was the float with the queens for all of the other ozone plates and the accompanying contests and festivities. The queens were wearing clear plastic wraps over their formal gowns to protect their bare skin against the toxins in the air. Their custom-made clear plastic masks were equipped with air filters. Each queen and queen contestant who participated in today's parade would get to keep her mask. It was one of the benefits of being an ozone plate queen.

The clowns came next, wearing masks decorated with balloons and brightly colored streamers, tossing candy to the children. Members of the St. Paul and Minneapolis Police Departments riding Plasti-Horses also threw candy. Some of the riders were actually members of the Homeland Security Elite Forces, ever alert for terrorists. They were there to ensure the safety of the patriots in the crowd who risked their health and their lives by coming out to support the celebration in this kind of air.

There were giant TV screens behind the crowds, showing the parade as it passed by. For those who stood in the back rows along the parade route, the screens offered a better view than trying to look over the heads in front of them. It was hard positioning one's head just right so one's mask didn't bump the person in front of them, and it was also hard to see through the thick air.

The floats carrying the queens and the queen contestants had their own music. People swayed to the Jamaican rhythms of "Don't Worry, Be Happy."

Janet watched as small children grabbed candy and tried to take off their masks to eat it. The children screamed and writhed, trying to free themselves from the restraints of parents who wrestled with them to keep them from taking off their masks.

Janet had heard that any children brought to the hospital with breathing difficulties were reported to child protection agencies when the air quality required number 7 EZ Breathe scarves and other appliances. Today, the parents of screaming children seemed to be looking nervously over their shoulders to see who was watching them.

In spite of the screams of children, the muted sounds of the marching bands, and the heavy air, parade watchers looked excited and happy. No one left the parade route, and there were no altercations with security forces. All in all, everyone seemed to be having a good time.

The parade lasted about four hours. The air got thicker as the floats and other vehicles traveled slowly down the parade route and the exhaust fumes from the vehicles pulling the floats added to the thickness of the air. There were medical attendants at each intersection along the route to provide first aid to people who succumbed to the toxins.

About midway through the parade, the current contestants for the Eleanor Roosevelt Ozone Plate Queen Contest came through on a float adorned with stainless steel flowers. The float was in the shape of a bomb, representing the atomic bomb used against the Japanese in World War II. Even though Franklin Roosevelt was already dead by the time that bomb was dropped, the float gave the impression that Roosevelt stopped the war by dropping the bomb on the Japanese, adding to the image of the Roosevelts as true patriots who worked hard on behalf of the citizens of the greatest country in the world.

The young women on the float beamed from behind their masks, waving languidly at the crowd. The last parade unit was the Eleanor

Roosevelt Ozone Plate queen float with the newest Eleanor Roosevelt Ozone Plate queen and her two attendants.

When the floats reached the end of the parade, the queen and her attendants were met by EMTs, who escorted the women off the floats and into a building.

"Okay. We're here to help with your masks and provide you with some first aid. First, we'll give you a shot of oxygen to clear out your lungs. The air is particularly heavy today, and your masks and other protections can't filter enough of the chemicals away from your noses and skin. We have eyedrops to ease itching and burning. Before you change into your street clothes, take a shower and use the salve that an attendant will provide you when you're done. That should ease any skin discomfort. As long as you're inside this building, you won't need protection, as the filters in here are industrial weight. In spite of the discomfort, we hope that being royalty for the Eleanor Roosevelt Ozone Plate is a defining moment in your lives. Sometimes when we experience an honor such as yours, any discomfort can be viewed as a necessary sacrifice," said Annie, the EMT who was in charge of medical services for the ozone plate queens and their attendants. "When you're finished, Homeland Security agents will escort you to the Radisson for brunch with the mayor and the governor."

The young women had been stripped of their masks. They were crying and blinking their eyes because of the polluted air that had made its way into their masks and penetrated the plastic covering their skin, making it difficult for EMTs to place the eyedrops and to assist the women to the showers.

"I've never had this detail before," said Annie to Gretchen, another EMT.

"I have. I used to live in St. Louis, and we had the ER about five years ago," said Gretchen.

"I had trouble knowing who was in charge of all of this," said Annie.

"The Department of the Interior has jurisdiction over the ozone plates. They tell us that the government is doing all it can to preserve the ozone plates," said Gretchen.

"I thought the ozone plates stopped the factory emissions from rising," said Annie.

"Well, that's in the big cities. The government was going to do some research in smaller cities but decided against it. I guess they think that they won't get good research results because there are too many people with suspicious backgrounds living outside the big cities. The belief is that those people would sabotage the research," said Gretchen.

"I find all of this confusing," said Annie. "When I look at all the security and other details it takes for a good ozone plate celebration and the conflicting information about the ozone plates, I have to wonder why they bother," said Annie.

"I think it's just become a tradition, and it helps people keep good attitudes," said Gretchen. "By the way, I wouldn't talk about all of this. You never know who you can trust. We're just here to do a job."

CHAPTER 36

July 1, 2040

When the parade ended, Janet and Louis went to the Radisson Hotel to wait for the brunch. A uniformed guard escorted them to the banquet room, where they found their assigned table with the other members of the press.

Once inside and mask-free, members of the press corps began talking to those they recognized. An older woman with graying hair and a face that was beginning to sag leaned over to talk to Janet. "Oh, hi, dear. It's so good to see you here. I told John over there"—she pointed to a man at the next table dressed in a tweed suit—"that you were probably one of the finest up-and-coming young journalists in the city. I'm not surprised you were given this assignment.

"I was in my twenties when the Eleanor Roosevelt passed over before. Let me think, now, who was the reporter from my paper assigned to that story?" She turned away from Janet. "John, who was assigned to the story when the ER passed over the last time?"

"I don't remember. She left shortly after that, and no one has heard from her. We thought she was going to New York for bigger and better things," said John.

As she heard the words of the older woman, Janet wondered what this assignment was about. Why would someone who had written about the ER suddenly disappear? Did the woman do something wrong? Did the EROP have nothing or something to do with her disappearance? How old was the woman? As she looked around the room at the reporters gathered at the press tables, she noted that she was the youngest one there. Then it dawned on her. When they reached age fifty-five, they would be forced to retire and would enter nursing homes. Everyone in the room was temporary.

The ozone plate queens and the important people of the city were starting to enter the ballroom, escorted by hosts and hostesses in formal garb. Chosen specifically for this detail, the escorts were members of the Homeland Security Youth Corps. They were aging out and would either become Homeland Security employees of some kind or citizen monitors.

The hosts and hostesses seated the important people and the ozone plate queens, handing them menus. The dignitaries placed orders with Techno Waitresses, who filled orders from the serving tables. Members of the press were to help themselves, buffet style. A guard stood at either end of the banquet table to protect the attendees from terrorists. The exit doors were locked to keep out intruders who might make it past the security at the front door.

The mayor's speech brought enthusiastic applause, toasts were given, and everyone in the room congratulated themselves on being part of this important event.

After the meal, members of the press were allowed to interview and photograph the ozone plate queens. Louis and Janet got good pictures and information from several of the young women.

Janet and Louis lingered and visited with other members of the press corps for what seemed to be an appropriate amount of time, then said their goodbyes, put on their masks, and left the hotel. They walked in silence back to the newspaper office. Once there, Janet and Louis picked out photos and put together stories about the parade and the Eleanor Roosevelt Ozone Plate queen brunch. They had to make changes in some of the photos to erase uncomfortable details.

There was a great picture of masked children running behind Planthouses to pick up candy, except for the child off to the side who had apparently passed out. Another picture showed a man who had taken off his mask to administer CPR to one of the police officers who had fallen off a Plastihorse.

When they finished their assignment, Janet and Louis had enough time to change into evening wear for the banquet honoring the Eleanor Roosevelt Ozone Plate queen and her attendants.

Janet tuned her computer to the Weather Channel to get the latest air quality report. Things hadn't improved. A rain shower had visited the city after Janet and Louis got back from the Ozone Plate queen brunch. The raindrops had mixed with the brown particles in the air, creating a sloppy, slippery mess on the streets. After the rain, a brown mist hovered over the city. It was humid, and the air was just as dirty as it had been.

Janet put on her floor-length, faux silk gown she had ordered from *faux!* She decided to carry her stiletto heels and wear the flat shoes she had worn for the parade.

Janet and Louis arrived at the convention center just as the governor's limousine pulled up. Four men jumped out of two cars that had pulled up behind the limousine and stood between Janet and Louis and the limousine. One of the men asked to see identification. Janet and Louis complied, pulling out their press cards. As he scanned the cards, one of the men said, "You will stand here until the governor is in the building. Then you may proceed."

Janet let her breath out slowly through the mask. She was trembling and didn't think she could move if they told her to. She noticed that since she had gotten back from the reservation, she had panic attacks whenever she met people who might be Homeland Security. She saw Louis looking at the ground, apparently unaffected by what had happened. She knew better than to try to talk to him about it. It was just one of those things that happened in the interests of national security.

They waited a few minutes and then walked up the steps to the convention center and into the security area. As they passed through, one of the guards took Louis's camera and examined it, looking through the lens, turning and pushing buttons. The camera started recording.

"We aren't supposed to take pictures of any security areas," Louis said to the guard.

"How can you tell if it's recording?" asked the guard.

"There's a little green light on. Now, look through the lens," Louis said. "You can't see through the lens if the camera isn't recording."

"How do you erase what I've recorded?" asked the guard.

"Here," Louis said, reaching over to push some buttons. "There, I erased it."

The guard put the camera on the other side of the x-ray machine. Janet and Louis passed through the gate and walked down the hall to the banquet room. Upon entering the hall, they looked for the area reserved for the press corps and saw the same group of people they had met earlier. They chatted with the other reporters and photographers, watching as the banquet hall filled with dignitaries, celebrities, and ozone plate royalty. Techno Waitstaff moved easily among the tables, serving a dinner of prime rib, baked potatoes, and salad from the biosphere farm that served government officials and business executives from the area.

There was a murmur in the room as people chatted while eating. As the last plates were cleared away, Louis said, "When I start moving toward the stage, take these two capsules." He handed her two white pills. "They'll help with your memory."

Janet looked at Louis, eyes wide. "Don't say anything. Just do what I said, and you'll be okay," said Louis as Janet put the pills in her evening bag.

The governor, August Olson, stood to give his speech. He was in his fifties, tall, slender, and dignified, with a full head of dark hair just starting to gray at the temples. His wife, Muriel, was seated beside him. She was a couple of inches shorter than he was, slender, with stiffly coifed hair the color of champagne. They were an attractive couple.

The governor walked slowly to the podium, taking his time. When he arrived, he drank some water and smiled, nodding at those he knew.

"Ladies and gentlemen and Eleanor Roosevelt Ozone Plate royalty. This is an event that doesn't happen often. The Eleanor Roosevelt Ozone Plate hasn't been to visit us for twenty-five years. Our city, our Twin Cities, actually, have turned out for this event and have done great honor to the majesty that surrounds the Eleanor Roosevelt Ozone Plate. We should all be proud of the effort and planning that has gone into paying tribute to the Eleanor Roosevelt Ozone Plate and what this plate represents.

"What has happened in the last twenty-five years? We have increased the number of jobs for people living here. We have increased the standard of living. We have greater technology than ever before. We have had to make sacrifices. We have shown every city in America what Minnesotans do to be patriotic and rise to the challenges presented, as we are ever vigilant to guard against international terrorism.

"Among those sacrifices has been air quality. We are reminded of that today, as we had to wear masks. The rain cleaned the air, but the brown slime made walking hazardous."

Janet looked around the room. Did this man know what he was saying? Maybe he could talk like this because he was an elected official. What was his point?

"The ozone layer is in pieces, but we will add to the economy through manufacturing. Everything that happens is an opportunity to add to the gross national product.

"Today the wealth is in the hands of the few hardworking corporate executives who tell us we need to keep spending to make sure everyone has jobs."

The governor nodded at Muriel. The two of them ran toward an exit while some of their security detail followed. The other men in the security detail walked backward toward the exit, firing at Homeland Security agents, who began firing back.

Several Homeland Security agents were killed before they had a chance to fire back. Other agents took cover and continued to fire at the governor's security detail. None of their shots hit their targets.

As the chaos mounted, Louis stood and ran toward the same exit taken by the governor and his men. An outside door was unlocked by the only Homeland Security agent left standing. He opened it, and the governor, his security men, his wife, and Louis ran through. The agent joined them as they ran down the hall.

The governor, his wife, and those involved in this escape had vehicles that had arrived after all of the people in the banquet hall had entered. There were ten vehicles in all, some of that would travel in different directions, creating confusion for the Homeland Security agents who had been called to the scene when the first shots were fired, allowing enough time for the governor, his wife, and their entourage to reach their vehicles.

Members of the security detail steered the governor and his wife into a bulletproof SUV with Louis, who said, "Well, folks, can we dispense with formal titles now that you're no longer the governor and First Lady?"

August and Muriel laughed, and August said, "Thank God! Which route are we taking to Canada?"

"First, we're going south to get out of the city because we think Homeland Security will recover quickly from the chaos at the center. The other vehicles are going in a lot of different directions, but you're their primary quarry. So we go down to Winona, across the river into Wisconsin, up through the bluffs, then north through the back roads to the Upper Peninsula of Michigan. We ditch the vehicle in the woods, walk a ways to Sault Ste. Marie, where we pick up another vehicle and cross into Canada. There are stops along the way where there will be folks assisting us and giving us the latest news about the chase. It may be that we have to change routes. Do you have your passports?

"I have a duffel with some warm clothes and appropriate shoes and a cooler with food. It would be a good idea to change shoes now, just in case we get stopped by someone. You can change clothes as soon as we stop for gas. You might as well try and get some rest now. We don't know what's going to happen next.," said Louis.

Muriel and August put their seats in prone positions and slept.

They had been on the road for about eight hours when they stopped at a gas station in northern Wisconsin, where they were able to buy food and use the facilities. Louis came out of the gas station and said, "There's been a change in plans. There are agents posted along the shores of Lake Huron. It would be closest if we could drive up the Keweenaw Peninsula and take a boat over to and around Isle Royale. Canada is just on the other side. But there is only one main road going up and coming back down the Keweenaw, so we could easily be ambushed. There is a boat waiting on the tip of the Bayfield Peninsula. It'll take us over and beyond Isle Royale to the Lake Superior National Marine Conservation Area. That's a mouthful. We'll be picked up by the Canadians and taken ashore and processed for entry into Canada as political refugees."

"What if there are agents waiting for us there?" asked Muriel.

"Well, there are boats in the Canadian waters of Lake Superior. They'll help us in any way they can," said Louis.

"That doesn't sound like much of a plan," said Muriel.

"We've got people along the way who will let us know if the route is safe or if we have to change directions. All of the people who are available to help us have been rescuing refugees for a while," said Louis.

"I think I have to get used to being a fugitive," said Muriel. "I'll have to put my trust in you."

The car traveled north until it reached Lake Superior. It pulled into gravel parking lot alongside a single-story clapboard building. The large window on the front of the building said "LaPointe Bros. and Company." A pier was across the street. A fishing trawler was tied up at the pier and rocked slightly on the gentle waves.

Three men walked over from the boat to the parking lot. They were dark-skinned, over six feet tall, and had long black hair tied back from their faces. One of the men had a diagonal scar running from the outside edge of his left eye down to his upper lip, slicing through his black beard. The slash through the beard was edged with white stubble. The men were dressed in dark, loose-fitting trousers, long-sleeved shirts, and black rubber boots that came up to their knees.

Louis, Muriel, and August and the two other men who were part of August's security detail when he was governor got out of their vehicle and walked to the water's edge to meet the three men. They shook hands all around and introduced themselves.

"I am Jean LaPointe," said one of the men. He had a slight accent, sounding almost French with something else mixed in.

"I am Basil," said the man with the scar.

"I am Pierre, named after one of my ancestors," said the third man.

Jean looked at the party and said, "So one of you is the former governor of Minnesota." He stepped forward to Muriel, took her hand, and kissed it. "Eh, Madam, you are the former governor's wife. I see that you are looking at Basil. He is not a violent man. The other man was. He isn't with us anymore.

"Go into our shop, and Madeleine will outfit you with some warm clothing and some rain outfits. You will get wet on this trip."

When the fugitives came out, they followed the three men to the trawler and climbed aboard.

"You will go below," said Pierre. "We can anticipate that coast guard cutters will be in the area. They know we are fishing today. Our sons took out the other boat, much bigger than this. We won't try to hide from them, but we'll hide our cargo."

Muriel started to go below and stopped. "The smell is horrid," she said.

"This is a fishing boat, Madam," said Basil. "It smells like fish. The fish are our livelihood, so we don't think they smell bad. Stay below until one of us tells you to come up, *sil vous plait*. When you come up top, move quickly so we can transfer you to the Canadian boat. There might be some US boats that chase us or follow us, so we'll have to get you on board the Canadian boat quickly. That will be the worst that can happen, so assume the worst."

The fugitives went below into a smelly, noisy compartment. The engine noise discouraged conversation. Soon after the boat started moving, it picked up speed. Muriel and August looked at Louis, who said, "The boat moves faster as it gets in deeper water. The speed doesn't mean we're being chased." But they were.

On top, the three men decided to slow down. Their boat was no match for the coast guard cutters that were catching up and surrounding them.

When the boat stopped, two members of the coast guard crew came on board. "What are you doing out here?" one of them asked.

Jean, putting on his best up north accent, said, "Eh, why are you chasin' us? We're lookin' fer a good fishin' spot. What're you doin' out here?"

"The governor of Minnesota and his wife have been kidnapped, and we believe they're headed this way," said the coast guard captain.

"It's been quiet out here today," said Pierre. "We've not seen any other boats. We thought our luck might be better out here. Have you seen our other boat? Our sons are out today. It's a good day to fish."

"We're tribal members. You don't have jurisdiction here," said Jean. "I'm within my rights to deny you access to my boat."

"If you've got nothing to hide, why won't you let us check it out?"

"It's a matter of principle. We've got a right to defend ourselves," said Basil. Scowling, he pulled a hunting knife out of the waistband of his trousers. "Maybe you should check with your boss before you try to violate our treaty rights."

The coast guard captain looked at the other crew members and shook his head. The men went back to the cutter.

"Eh, Basil. Do we really have treaty rights?" said Pierre.

"We should, but we don't have enough Ojibwe blood to qualify. And we have cousins who are tribal members, and it worked," said Basil.

The fishing boat picked up speed again. After three hours, the boat was in Canadian waters. Jean spotted a border patrol boat, and Basil called down to the passengers, who came on deck quickly while the boat came alongside the Canadian vessel.

"Bon voyage. You're no longer fugitives. You're refugees. Have a good life," said Basil. "When you smell fish, think of us and your time on our boat."

Once on board the Canadian ship, the refugees were fed and congratulated on their escape. They were taken to Thunder Bay to a customs office and transferred to a refugee settlement. They would settle in and become part of a growing community of expatriates.

CHAPTER

July 1, 2040

Janet looked around the banquet hall, trying to orient herself. She reached into her bag, grabbed the two pills Louis had given her, popped them in her mouth, and swallowed. She watched as people in the banquet hall sat, unmoving. She wondered what would happen next and saw the mayor jumping up from his seat. He pulled a cell phone out of his pocket, frantically punching the numbers, trying to reach 911.

Soon after, Homeland Security agents arrived. Janet watched as they began checking everyone in the banquet hall for weapons and establishing order. She listened as the Homeland Security press editor addressed the press corps. "You will each receive a copy of the governor's speech. You will write stories about the fashions worn here tonight. You will end with a tribute to the festivities of the last several days. Now, we will give each of you some medication to calm your nerves and alleviate post-trauma symptoms. When you wake up, you will be at home, and you will be given two weeks' vacation instead of one for the excellent jobs you have all done as reporters. You will stay in your seats for now. You have witnessed the kidnapping of an important government official and his wife."

Janet felt as if she were paralyzed as she watched the agents swabbing arms with alcohol and injecting her colleagues with powerful tranquilizers that put them to sleep. She watched as the tranquilized members of the press nodded off. When an agent injected her, Janet felt a little groggy, but she didn't nod off. She decided she needed to pretend to experience the same effects as the other people in the room, so she pretended to sleep.

She lost track of what was happening and had a vague picture of being placed in a van with several others. She was not aware of being transported to her apartment.

July 3

When she awakened, Janet found herself in her bed. Dim light was coming through the window. *It must be morning. This must be my vacation,* thought Janet. *Did I get my stories in? I should call and find out.* She felt apathetic, defenseless. She got up and began moving around her apartment, hoping to lose the hangover. Slowly she began to remember the Eleanor Roosevelt Ozone Plate queen banquet. Blurs of color came first and then details about the queen and her attendants. In her mind, she saw the men and heard the loud pops of the guns.

Keep on moving, she thought, and the memories will come. She saw Louis running to the stage and helping the governor and his wife escape. He gave me those pills, and that's what's helping me to remember.

She stopped and sat on the couch, remembering more of the governor's speech. *They escaped,* she thought. Her mind slowly returned to the present, and she realized she was hungry. She went to the kitchen to find something to eat. She had some orange-flavored vitamin C beverage and put some frozen scrambled egg substitute in the microwave.

After she ate, Janet began walking again. She went to the foyer and found a memo with the Homeland Security letterhead on it, informing her that she had two weeks' vacation.

Just then, her phone rang. Janet looked at the screen and found that the number calling was restricted. The date said July 3. She pushed the connect button. "Hello?"

"Hi, Janet. I can only talk for a minute," said Louis. "I guess you know by now that I'm not really a newspaper photographer. It was a cover so I could gain access to the banquet hall. I'm with the former governor and his wife. After we left the banquet hall, we left the city. I can't tell you where we are. I just wanted to let you know that we're okay and whatever you hear on the television news about the queen's banquet is a lie.

"I believe you're in danger. Homeland Security is checking out all the research you did on the Eleanor Roosevelt Ozone Plate, looking for points of view that suggest you're a traitor. You need to get out as soon as you can."

Janet started to speak and realized she was talking to air. She switched the TV channel to CNN. The headlines told of the daring kidnapping of the governor and his wife, the videotape showing them surrounded by men with guns who were herding them out of the banquet hall. The CNN reporter interpreted this scene to mean that those surrounding the governor and his wife were kidnappers.

Louis was mentioned by name. He was said to be an international terrorist who had infiltrated the *Herald* and set up the kidnapping plan.

The scene changed to a Homeland Security spokesperson standing in front of a bank of microphones for a press conference. "We believe the governor and his wife are being held hostage. We haven't heard from the terrorists, so we're not sure what they want."

Janet watched the report in an expressionless silence, her thoughts racing. She didn't know what surveillance there might be in her apartment, so it was best to continue to watch the news coverage, pretending to be okay with it, all the while feeling fearful, wondering what she should do. She felt trapped, knowing that leaving would not be easy, nor would she know the right time to leave. She didn't know where she would or could go.

Janet knew that she was under some surveillance. She had made unauthorized trips through the security gates. She had traveled out of the city. She hoped the reported kidnapping would take the focus off of her and give her more time to figure out what to do. *Right now, all I have to do is act normal and stay home, tending to daily chores. I will be an average, young, single professional with a few days to myself.* Maybe Louis was wrong about her situation, she thought.

CHAPTER 38
July 4, 2040

Lloyd was at home watching the television news about the kidnapping of the governor and his wife when the doorbell rang. He opened it to find Homeland Security agents.

"Mr. Holmberg, you're to come with us."

Lloyd said nothing and followed them out the door. *I wonder if I'll be coming back*, he thought.

Lloyd was driven to the Homeland Security headquarters, where he was placed in a room for debriefing. He waited, his anxiety building.

After a half hour, Hal walked in. "Hi, Lloyd."

"Why am I here?" asked Lloyd.

"I've got some questions for you about one of your employees," said Hal.

"Who? Is this about Janet? Who did the kidnapping?" asked Lloyd.

"I'm asking the questions. We'll get to all of it soon enough. You just listen, give answers, and don't try to protect anyone," said Hal. "How long has Louis Stanley worked for you?"

"He's been with the paper for about a year," said Lloyd.

"Have you had any suspicions about him?" asked Hal.

Lloyd thought this over. This was a no-win question. If he said yes, they would ask him why he hadn't reported it. If he said no, they would figure he wasn't doing his job. In fifteen years, there had been four *Herald* employees who had been taken away. Two of them had been in their fifties, so Lloyd figured they had gone to nursing homes. The other two had been involved in subversive activities about which Lloyd knew nothing. After they were taken for questioning, they never returned to the newspaper.

What had Louis done? *It must be about the kidnapping.* Janet was under surveillance, and Lloyd wondered when he would be suspected of being the leader of a subversive group because of past employees who had been taken away because of suspected terrorism.

"No, I didn't notice anything about Louis that caused suspicion. He came to work and did his job. He got good photos. He was well liked by his coworkers."

The Homeland Security surveillance agents questioned Lloyd for about two hours and then gave him an amnesiac and took him home. He woke up the next morning feeling rested, almost enthusiastic about his work. After arriving at work, he read the copy Janet had sent him before he did anything else. The stories were good and would fill up the newspaper for the next week.

39

July 6, 2040

Antoine informed his professors that he was going home for a visit and got assignments that he could complete while he was gone. He figured that sudden disappearances would alert surveillance agents. He wanted to make sure that the conversations he had been having with Janet were consistent with his behavior. He was going home to see the Old Woman before she passed on.

Antoine put provisions in a backpack and left the city on foot. He had spent several months finding ways to leave the city without going through checkpoints. Bill Scott, the campus security officer who had escape plans of his own, had drawn up maps for him and left them in some bushes outside of the campus park. Antoine memorized the directions and tossed the messages in a wastebasket at the university library after he ran his hands over both sides of the pages several times, smudging any fingerprints he may have left.

He traveled during the day, trying to blend into the foot traffic in each neighborhood. The farther out of the city he got, the darker-skinned the neighborhoods became. He could pass as a resident in many of them. It was interesting to him that the people with darker skin were the ones who lived in cleaner air.

He stopped along the way, watching children wearing filtered scarves play in the neighborhood parks.

It took Antoine most of the day to get beyond the security gates. He crossed into Wisconsin and stopped at the gas station where Janet had stopped on her trip to the reservation. He waited for about ten minutes until an old, rusty car pulled in. Antoine ran out and got in, throwing his backpack in the back seat.

"Eh, Cousin. You made it."

"Eh, Gene. How's it going?" Antoine asked of the tall, dark-skinned man in the driver's seat.

"Well, most days are good days. We still have some hangers-on who believe we should bring back the casinos rather than Old Ways. You know, it took us longer to unplug than it took you. We have so many small villages, and each one does things their own way. It's hard to get a consensus.

"How long are you staying home? Or are you home for good?" said Gene.

"I'm staying for about a week. Then I have to go back to the city."

"I hear things are getting worse there. The air is bad, and surveillance guys are checking people all the time," said Gene.

"Yeah, it's pretty crazy there. I know I'll be home for good soon. I just don't know for sure when. I've got a feeling that I'll have to leave in a hurry and will probably have to take someone with me," Antoine said.

Gene smiled. "Eh, you got a woman?"

"Not exactly. I like this woman, but she's pretty uptight. Besides, we don't get a chance to have a real conversation. There was nothing about her in my dream."

"If you have to leave in a hurry, it might be hard to take someone with you. Maybe you need to come up with plan B."

"I don't know what plan B would look like."

"Maybe you need to come up with a way to give her instructions as to how to get out of the city without you. Isn't she the woman who went to see Old Woman?"

"Yeah, I don't know if she could make it on her own."

"Even if you come up with a great plan, there's no guarantee that she can make it out. She may not make it out if she goes with you. I just think you have to travel light and fast when the time comes. If you want to save her, plan B might be the best way to go."

The two men traveled in silence for several miles.

Gene said, "She a *chimoke?*"

"Yeah, she's white. Uncle Joe doesn't like her, and my grandmother isn't real happy that she comes to visit. I guess Uncle Marvin likes her. He says that it takes courage for her to go to the rez."

Gene nodded. "Yeah, it would take courage to stay in a house with Uncle Joe when he doesn't like you. Either that or she just doesn't know any better."

Both men laughed.

Gene came to a dirt road defined by two ruts with a raised patch of grass in between. He pulled the car in so it couldn't be seen from the road. They got out, slapped each other on the back, and turned to go in separate directions.

"Let me know when you need something," Gene called.

Antoine got home as the fire in the backyard was waning and the sun had disappeared behind the trees. He was hungry. He had taken some packaged food in his backpack, but the smell of the soup over the flames stirred rumblings in his stomach.

Sierra saw him first. She ran to him and hugged him. He put one arm around her and ruffled her hair with his other hand. "Eh, Cuz, get me some soup, would you?" He entered the circle, nodding to his uncle and grandmother.

"Where is she?" he asked.

"She's in the house. She got tired sitting out here, so she went to sit in the rocking chair."

Antoine grinned at the image of Old Woman sitting in the rocking chair all those afternoons, telling her stories. "Is she taking naps before she goes to bed now?"

Sonia smiled and shook her head. "No, grandson. She sits in there waiting to visit with the spirits."

"Are they coming often?" he asked.

"I feel them in the house most of the time now. She sometimes doesn't seem to be aware that we are there. She seems to be listening to voices we can't hear."

Joe said, "She says she will be here to go ricing."

"Ricing is about two months away. She hasn't talked about being here after that," Sonia said.

"I had to come back to make sure I visited with her before she goes," Antoine said. "I don't know how much longer I'll be staying in the city. I hope I can leave for good before she goes."

Antoine visited with his grandmother and his uncle before going to spend the night at his mother's house, taking the path that connected most of the houses on the reservation. He would come back in the morning to spend time with Old Woman.

When Antoine walked into his mother's house, he found Corrine sitting at the kitchen table, doing beadwork by the light of an oil lamp. She looked up and dropped her work on the table, scattering some of the beads.

"Son! I didn't know you were coming home. I haven't heard from you for so long. I was beginning to worry."

Antoine thought, If you knew what was going on, you would know that you have good reason to worry.

"Hey, Mom. I'm taking care of myself. I have some summer classes. I thought I should come home to see Old Woman before she walks on. I think I will be home for good before that happens," Antoine said.

"I don't like having you away from here. I know that you sent that young woman here. Joe told me she belongs to some group that thinks they are going to overthrow the government. Are you hooked up with them? What happens if they get caught? You will get caught too. All the stories I have heard about that world tell me that they won't let you go if they catch you. I worry," said Corrine.

"Mom, I am doing what I am supposed to do. I'll be okay. What have you got to eat?"

"There is some fish and some stew out in the icebox."

Antoine went out to the porch to the old refrigerator filled with chunks of ice. There were seldom leftovers, but when there were big enough amounts, family and other neighbors would store them in the refrigerator; the ice and the insulation kept things cool for a while.

Antoine brought his food into the kitchen, grabbed a piece of fry bread from a bowl, and made a sandwich. He tasted the cold stew. "I think cold soup is a delicacy to white people. I wonder about cold stew. I can tell you made it. Nobody else makes stew that tastes like yours."

"Son, you are a charmer," Corrine said.

They sat at the table in the dim light, Corinne catching him up on the rumors and gossip in the community. She didn't want to know about Antoine's life in the city. She just wanted him to come home. They talked into the night, Corrine wondering when she would get another chance to visit with her son like this. When they went to bed, Corrine slept well, knowing that her house was full again.

July 8, 2040

Antoine was up when the sun rose, awakened by the smells coming from his mother's kitchen. He ate a meal of wild rice with maple syrup and scrambled eggs. "What kind of eggs are these?" he asked.

"I found some snapping turtle eggs that one of the dogs dug out down by the lake. I didn't think they would hatch, so I brought them home. They hadn't been out that long, so I figured they were still good to eat. I was down there the day before I found them, and they weren't there then," said Corrine.

"I am going to go over to Grandmother's house to see Old Woman. I better save room for whatever they're having for breakfast. I will be back sometime today," said Antoine.

The family was eating at the picnic table when Antoine approached. "Grandmother," he said to Sonia. "Where do you get all this bacon? Do you keep pigs out here in the woods someplace?"

Sonia giggled. "No, I made some quilts for Levi, and he gives me all the bacon and pork I want."

"Levi! I forget about him. Does he still live in that place with all those signs in the yard?"

"Yes, he's still there. He's just a few years younger than Old Woman. He seems to think that his location is strategic. I've asked him what makes it strategic, and all he says is 'You'll see,'" said Sonia.

"How long has he lived there?" asked Antoine.

"He and his wife moved up here during the 1970s. They did a lot of protesting over the environment," said Sonia.

Sierra turned to Antoine. "I think I remember the story. Levi and Sarah were protesting, and Sarah was arrested and died in jail."

"Yup, that's it," said Antoine. "And then Levi started building the tunnels."

There was silence as the family finished eating their breakfast.

Antoine enjoyed this silence. He missed home. He almost wished he could forget about his dream. What was he doing and for what purpose? Just as he respected and honored others, he had an obligation to honor his dream. He would know when it was time for him to leave the city and return home. For now, he would enjoy his visit. He would spend time with the Old Woman and his family until after the powwow. His days would be full of family and shared memories.

After breakfast, Antoine sat with the Old Woman. "What's it been like for you in the city?" asked Old Woman.

"Eh, Old Woman. It's dirty there. There are too many people. Too many rules. I wonder sometimes what my purpose is. Why did my dream tell me to go there? I spent a lot of time preparing myself to go there. I know I am to trust my dream, but I get frustrated. I don't have a clear picture as to what the outcome will be," said Antoine.

"I know that your uncle Joe, your mother, and your grandmother would prefer to have you here where you're safe. You sent that young woman here. She is a messenger. I've given her information, and she has seen how we live. She has a chance to compare the city and this community. I doubt that my stories will make great changes in the city and the rest of the country. If Janet comes here, she'll tell the stories I've given her.

"We hear stories as to what it's like in the city. When you come home for good, you'll tell us stories about your experience in the city. Today, many people who live here remember what it was like before the woman came with the plants that saved our water, our animals, and Mother Earth. The younger ones know only our stories. You'll bring newer stories to them. The stories will help them to understand why it's important to honor the earth. I think that there will come a time when those who live here will have to go out from this place and clean up the mess. I think the city will be dead. It will only come back to life if it is cleaned. I hope that there will be other people left who will hear our stories and take heed. Native people have tried to tell white folks how to live. It hasn't worked. We can only hope that they will listen when they have nothing left."

Antoine listened to Old Woman's words. He was silent and sat with her for a long time. He knew he would visit with her again during this time. He would go back to the city. When he came back again, he wasn't sure that she would be there.

After his visit with Old Woman, Antoine walked down the trail to Marvin's house. As he approached the edge of the yard, he was met by Animosh, who ran to greet him. Animosh leaped into the air and landed on Antoine, knocking him to the ground. The two wrestled, Antoine smacking Animosh on his haunches while the dog growled in delight. Animosh maneuvered Antoine into a prone position while he stood over him. Antoine put his arm up on his face to avoid the drool seeping out of the dog's mouth. Animosh tried to move Antoine's arm so he could lick his face. Antoine pushed him aside. "Back off, Dog."

Animosh moved off to the side and sat on his haunches, waiting for Antoine to get up. The dog followed Antoine to the house, where Marvin sat on the deck in his wheelchair.

"Nephew. It's good to see you. You've gotten the official greeting from Animosh," said Marvin.

"I think he missed me. He knocked me over, wrestled, and slobbered all over me," said Antoine.

"Do you need a towel?" asked Marvin.

"No, I'll just air-dry," said Antoine.

Animosh lay between the two men, panting after his workout.

"Uncle, I came to ask you to share some of your wisdom with me," said Antoine, offering Marvin some tobacco.

"That would depend on what it's about. I am not wise about everything," said Marvin.

"I know that you have dreams," said Antoine.

Marvin nodded.

"How do you know when your dreams are real?" asked Antoine.

"All my dreams are real," said Marvin.

"You mean everything you dream comes true?" asked Antoine.

"I mean that everything I dream has meaning. I just have to know how to interpret," said Antoine.

"I don't have those kinds of dreams," said Antoine.

"Maybe you just don't pay attention. Maybe you don't believe strongly," said Marvin. "What kind of dreams do you have?"

"Lately I've been dreaming that I'm back here. Homeland Security has been to the edge of the reservation looking for me. I'm trying to protect my family. Only my family is a woman and my two babies with her," said Antoine.

"Are the babies the same age?" asked Marvin.

"They look like it," said Antoine.

"What do you think that means?" asked Marvin.

"It could mean that when I come back here, I will court a woman, and we will have children," said Antoine.

"Do you recognize the woman in your dream?" asked Marvin.

"No," said Antoine.

"Then you will be surprised," said Marvin, grinning.

"Do you know who this woman is?" asked Antoine.

"I think you just need to be surprised. It will be a good feeling, knowing that when you come back here, you'll be an adult, with adult responsibilities, and you'll be gifted with twins," said Marvin.

"You're teasing me, Uncle," said Antoine.

"No, I just think that you will figure this out for yourself," said Marvin. "Do you want to stay for lunch? I have some fresh fish."

Antoine helped Marvin fix lunch, and the two sat in the sunlight watching Animosh chase squirrels. After a while, Marvin said, "I wish that dog would chase something other than squirrels. I don't like squirrel meat."

CHAPTER 40
July 10, 2040

As Janet walked into the office after her time off, people in the newsroom surrounded her and started clapping. She didn't know what this was about until she saw the banner hanging in the newsroom: "Eleanor Roosevelt Ozone Plate Celebration Reporter up for Pulitzer!" She remembered Louis's phone call and knew she had to look happy and surprised in front of her coworkers.

When she entered her cubicle, she found Darcy waiting for her. Before Janet had time to sit down, Darcy asked about their next assignment.

Janet interrupted her. "I don't know what our next assignment is. We have to wait until Lloyd makes that decision."

Just then, Lloyd motioned for Janet to come to his office. He shook her hand and said, "Janet, your series of articles on the Eleanor Roosevelt Ozone Plate are among the best I've read. It's no wonder you've been nominated for a Pulitzer.

"I'm sorry that Louis jeopardized your safety and integrity. You did a fine job of incorporating some of his pictures into your stories. Homeland Security has taken the camera he used to look for clues as to where he might have gone with the hostages."

Janet noticed that Lloyd seemed nervous. He licked his lips and kept looking over his shoulder. The only thing there was a wall. At least his tic wasn't active.

"I'm wondering what you want me to do next," said Janet.

"Why don't you bring Darcy in, and we'll talk about some human-interest topics," said Lloyd. "Stuff for the Sunday edition."

When Darcy was seated, Lloyd said, "Well, I think this would be a good time to focus on stories that emphasize the importance of buying. It's important to inform the public that they play a vital role in a healthy economy. So, after that great job you did on the EROP, I think you can plan the stories, do the research, and write them up."

Janet followed up on Lloyd's suggestions and wrote a story. Her life continued in the same pattern for the next two weeks. It was July, the weather was warm, and her nomination for a Pulitzer allayed some of her fears. Old Woman and the reservation seemed a long ways away.

On a day when the air was fairly clear, Janet walked the long way home, circled the block, and came up to her apartment building from the other direction. She saw the man she thought was watching her sitting outside on the steps of a building, as if he lived there. Pretending not to see him, Janet walked into her building and went to her apartment. She felt panic rising in her.

Janet wanted to talk to Antoine again. Why wasn't he getting in touch with her? Maybe something happened to him. She decided to call Sally at the U. *This can't get me into trouble*, she thought.

"Hi, Sally. I want you to do me a favor. Can you get a hold of Antoine? I need to talk to him," said Janet.

"Are you sure this is a good idea? Our phone calls are probably monitored," said Sally.

"Just have him contact me. I wish you and I could spend some time together," said Janet.

"So do I. But it will look suspicious," said Sally. "I'll get in touch with him."

Sally called back a couple of hours later, "Janet? He's gone for now. He went back home for a powwow. I'm sure he'll be back."

CHAPTER 41
July 10, 2040

Joe and Mike got to Marvin's house about one o'clock after spending the morning finding downed trees and branches to cut up for firewood.

As they entered the clearing and approached the house, they called out, "Uncle, are you home?"

Marvin wheeled himself out to the deck, Animosh running ahead. "I just got back, Nephews. I've been out stalking deer. I see that you got past my guard dog."

"Uncle, if that's a guard dog, we're all in trouble," said Joe, walking over to pet Animosh, who had flopped down and gone to sleep. When he felt Joe's hand, Animosh opened one eye and thumped his tail on the deck.

"Do you have anything to eat? Do you have some venison from the deer you killed?" asked Mike.

"I have some soup and some fry bread that my niece brought me. There's enough for all of us," said Marvin.

Mike and Joe went into the house, fixed lunch, and carried their food out onto the deck to visit and eat with Marvin.

"That young woman is going to come to your house, Joe, and whether you like it or not, she is supposed to be here," said Marvin as he winked at Mike.

"You think this is funny," said Joe. "Mike isn't any happier with her than I am."

"She is uncomfortable with me," said Mike. "I think she is afraid of me because I'm dark."

"You're big too. You look like those Indians in the movies who were always whooping and scalping," said Joe.

"I think my nephews aren't paying attention," said Marvin. "I think you're having trouble just because she is different. I think it is easier to be mad at her than it is to look at what is happening.

"Have you stopped to think about how hard it was and how hard it's going to be for that young woman to come here? She is not only risking her life; she is going to have to leave a place that is familiar to her and learn how to fit in here. Joe, you've been rude to her, and she will come here again because she has no other place to go. She came to you to ask questions. I think it takes some courage to talk to you when you're in a bad mood.

"Do you ever think about what might happen here? Maybe she will stay here. Maybe this will be her home. In my dreams, I see her running for her life.

"I think both of you can learn to be more tolerant. There are times when both of you act like foolish young men. You act like I did when I went off to war," said Marvin.

Joe raised his eyes from the floor and looked at Mike. His face said, "It's the old war stories again."

"Sometimes I think you take for granted all that we have. You forget to respect your elders, and you forget to respect our ways that tell us to share with others and to welcome people here when they come in peace," Marvin said.

The two men were silent, looking at the floor, respecting their elder.

"My dreams tell me that the two of you will be with the Old Woman when she passes. That's the greatest gift there is," said Marvin.

The three men sat on the deck, listening to the breeze move through the trees.

"Your house is going to be busy, Joe. Lots of people coming for the powwow," said Marvin.

"There aren't too many places that have unplugged like we have," Joe said. "I wonder how many people will be able to travel when they do."

"Nephew, people used to travel long distances before there were cars. We will always have company at powwow time."

Animosh awakened with a start, flew off the deck, and raced around the yard after a squirrel. When his efforts were unsuccessful, he ran up on the deck and flopped down for another nap. The men sat in silence, watching the dog sleep. A loon on the lake called out.

"Something is going to happen here," said Marvin.

"Something always happens here, Uncle. Something is happening right now. We are sitting on your deck, and Animosh is sleeping," said Joe.

"I talked to Levi the other day, and he is making plans for his tunnel. I think that young woman will come into Levi's yard off the trail. She'll be helped into the tunnel. She'll end up here because the trail comes here from the end of Levi's tunnel. One of these days, Animosh will bring you a message," said Marvin.

"Uncle, I don't mean to be disrespectful, but that old man is a little crazy. I don't think he has a tunnel. I think his days of activism and demonstrating were over a long time ago. He lives with the memory of his wife. I'm sure he misses her, but when people miss too much, it makes them a little crazy," said Joe.

"Nephew, you are going to find out that you are wrong. Levi isn't any crazier than I am. He, Animosh, and I are going to save that young woman, and she is going to come here to live," said Marvin.

"Uncle, I don't want that woman here. I don't want to hear that she is going to come here. The next thing I know, you are going to tell me is that I am going to save her."

"Nephew, if she had to depend on you to save her, she might as well not come at all. Sometimes I think you spend too much time teaching those grandchildren of yours. You don't pay enough attention to what goes on around you. You are a good nephew, but I am right. My dreams tell me what is going to happen," said Marvin.

Animosh was awake again. He took advantage of the visit, going off into the woods to chase the smells that came on the breeze, knowing that Joe and Mike would take care of Marvin.

CHAPTER 42
July 11, 2040

The sun was well above the horizon when Sonia walked down to the lake and sat on a log. The frogs and the cicadas were making music. Misty tendrils of fog spread from the lake to the land, creating surreal images around her. She heard voices and then realized that the messages weren't coming from voices but were coming into her consciousness just the same. Sonia closed her eyes and raised her head. She knew the messages were from the spirits. She was being told that she would be all right in spite of great changes coming to her family.

When the messages stopped, Sonia rose and walked back up to the house, joining the family by the fire. It had been a long day. It was July, and powwow weekend was approaching. She had much work to do to prepare. She had to help Sierra finish her jingle dress and prepare space for people who would be staying at her house during the powwow. Old Woman's family would be coming from Canada. Old Woman had said she would be staying until after ricing season in September. When she passed on, there would be ceremonies. Sonia had moccasins to make.

July 12, 2040

It was midmorning, and the breeze off the lake carrying the spicy aromas of the flowers and trees did little to ease the humidity that made it seem warmer than it was. Joe sat on the porch, staring at the ground, while he drank his tea. Sonia sat nearby in a chair, making a flower from beads.

"She's going to leave us soon," he said.

"Yes. She said she was going to go ricing with you, so she will be here for another month or so. It looks like we'll have a good year for rice. The winter was cold with lots of snow, and this summer has been warm. We've had enough rain to make everything grow," said Sonia.

"She told me she wanted to be cremated. How are we going to manage that?" asked Joe.

"She told me that we could put her on a wooden platform and build a big bonfire beneath her," said Sonia.

"Why can't she just be buried like everybody else? What if the fire isn't big enough and hot enough?" asked Joe.

"Well, I guess we'll just have to make sure it is. It's a good time of year to die. She won't have to get through another winter. Have you heard from her family in Canada?" asked Sonia.

"Yeah, some of the guys went up there last week. I sent a message that she was getting ready to walk on, and they sent a letter back with Mike," Joe said. He sat watching Sonia do her beadwork. "Is that Sierra's outfit?" he asked.

"No. This is the dress for Old Woman. I want it to be ready so I don't have to work on it at the last minute." Sonia held the needle upright, and the beads slid down the thread to join the others in the flower.

"I'm going to miss her. Do you think she has had a good life here? There have been times when I have seen a look in her eyes like she was thinking about being someplace else. I have trouble imagining life without her," said Joe.

"I know she misses her old friends. She knows that even without all of the changes out there, most of her friends would be gone," said Sonia.

"Do you think she's lonely?" asked Joe.

"I'm sure she is. I think most of us would be at her age. She is halfway between here and the Spirit World. She can't do anything to go back or to speed things up. She has to do what she has to do each day and let things happen," said Sonia.

The two sat in silence. Joe finished his tea, put his cup in the summer kitchen, and walked down the path to the lake. He hadn't had a chance to spend much time alone lately. His grandchildren needed his guidance. There were often relatives and friends at the house.

Joe went to the big pine tree in the woods off the trail. He could sit for a while under the sweeping branches that touched the ground, creating a room with a floor of pine needles. No one could see him there. Ever since he was a child, he had been using this place when he wanted solitude. He sat and looked up at the sky, the spaces between the branches creating separate scenes. He watched as a bald eagle circled overhead and wondered what message it was carrying to the Creator. He closed his eyes. His breathing slowed.

He saw dark clouds bringing snow that would be deep. He saw his mother, his grandchildren, and his nephew in the house, warmed by the woodstove. He smelled food cooking and saw a plate of fry bread on the table, where his family sat eating together. There was an empty place at the table. He knew that his mother had tried to fill the place by putting the chairs a little farther apart. When everyone sat, they rearranged the chairs, making the empty space again. Joe saw a light near the ceiling in the kitchen. Within the glow, he saw the Old Woman's face. He woke up crying.

CHAPTER 43
July 22, 2040

People started arriving at the reservation a few days before the powwow, picking out the best campsites they could find. This powwow had been taking place since 1972. It was a homecoming for many and a family and cultural tradition that had been going on for generations. Marriages and babies had their beginnings at powwows. Relatives who hadn't seen one another for a long time knew that they would be reunited with family, many foregoing the campsites to stay at the homes of relatives.

Two families moved into Marvin's house. There were many small children running in and out of the house, jumping on Animosh, who knew that this didn't happen often; the people would leave, and he would be alone with Marvin again. He did his best to avoid the children and the house, but his responsibility was to be available to Marvin, so he couldn't leave for long periods.

On the first day of the powwow, Sonia's house was filled with friends and relatives who came from both coasts, Canada, Mexico, and places in between. They slept wherever they could find space, several to a bed and on the floor. There were tents and well-worn campers in the yard. Everyone pitched in to fix meals and do household chores. They all paid homage to Old Woman, whom many had known since she first came to the reservation.

Powwow outfits were placed carefully in empty spaces throughout the house. There were two drum groups staying at Sonia's, and the dancers often made their own music with bells on some outfits and jingle dresses that clacked when they walked to the powwow grounds. Regalia were creative and colorful, consisting of feathers, beads, and bone ornaments decorating leather shirts, pants, skirts, and dresses. Other outfits had the look of the French fur traders, with brightly colored embroidered sashes worn about the waist and the knees. The youngest dancers were in diapers with feather bustles. Many elders' wheelchairs were pushed around the arena by family members.

The arena had seventeen drums, and more than four hundred dancers came into the space for the grand entry. Veterans came in first, carrying flags, eagle feather staffs, and other adornments representing many native nations. Marvin was dressed in fatigues adorned with ribbons. He was among the veterans leading the grand entrance. Joe maneuvered Marvin's wheelchair, which held the tribe's eagle feather staff.

The ground shook as the arbor filled with dancers moving to the rhythms of the drums. Not all of the dancers wore regalia; it wasn't a prerequisite to celebrate life. The powwow had started the night before. Today, Saturday, was the longest day, with a grand entry during the afternoon, a feast, and another grand entry during the evening.

Food booths surrounded the seats that circled the arena. There was the heavy smell of grease from fry bread that hung on air pregnant with moisture. The temperature was in the nineties, and approaching clouds carried rain.

Both Sonia and Sierra wore jingle dresses. Sonia sat underneath the arbor that surrounded the powwow arena, combing and braiding Sierra's hair. She clipped the plaits with beaded hairpieces in the shapes of butterflies. Sonia spent the year before the powwow making dance outfits for all of her grandchildren. They grew fast, and outfits from one year didn't fit the next year.

Sonia had an outfit of off-white deerskin. She had made it when she was a young woman. It didn't fit her as generously as it had in the past. Over the years, the beadwork had been repaired. Her moccasins had been a gift from Old Woman years before.

Old Woman sat in a lawn chair at the end of the bench that held Sonia, Sierra, Corrine, and cousins from another community. She had many visitors on this, the first full day of the powwow. After the grand entry, Marvin joined the spectators and sat next to Old Woman.

Sonia knew this would be the last powwow for Old Woman. Old Woman had never danced but had attended every powwow since she came here. She thought it was disrespectful to dance because she was not native. She enjoyed the event. She would tell the children, "A powwow is a celebration of life, and the drum is the heartbeat. The singing is the survival of all native people against all odds." The children would get excited when they heard Old Woman's words, anticipating all of the other rituals they came to expect with powwows.

Sonia's thoughts were interrupted by the high-pitched sound of the singers. As the drumming began, Sonia stood, her head nodding in time as she joined the dancers. An eagle flew overhead, leading the dancers into the arena.

Old Woman wanted to spend as much time as she could at this powwow, as she knew it would be her last. She arrived in time for the grand entry the first day and spent time visiting with her family who had been brought from Canada by the LaPointe brothers.

Images of people and other times came into her head as she sat watching the dancers. *Things are finally better here*, she thought. *It is peaceful. The air is clean. We live the way people were meant to live.* She was calm. Old Woman knew that she would be ready to leave after she went ricing one last time.

Antoine dressed in his regalia and went to the powwow in the afternoon. He was dressed in brightly colored feathers, a roach adorning his head, a bustle, bells on his leggings, and a bone breastplate. He found the area underneath the arbor where his family usually sat and knelt down beside Old Woman.

"Grandmother! I came home to see you. Are you going to dance with me this year?" he teased.

"No, Antoine. I have told you many times that I don't dance. Besides, I would probably get run over by some of those young grass dancers out there."

"I want to thank you, Grandmother, for the stories you gave to Janet," he said.

"You're welcome, Antoine."

"I also want to thank you for all you have given me over the years. I have to go back to the city, and I don't know when I will be back."

"I hope you will be back in time for my funeral," said Old Woman.

"I wish I could see you again before you pass."

"We don't know that you won't. We'll make the best of the time we have left. I'll enjoy this day watching you dance. By the time you are forty, you will be the best fancy dancer around. When I come to powwows, I'll be able to tell all of the other spirits that I knew you when you were just learning," said Old Woman.

Antoine kissed Old Woman on the forehead, walked away, and came back a few minutes later carrying an Indian taco. "Here, Grandmother. This is for you."

"Thanks, Antoine. I am a lucky woman. I have lived to be this old on a steady diet of fry bread."

Antoine left her to join the other dancers. Today would be a good day, and Antoine would spend time with Old Woman after today's powwow.

There was a giveaway for the young woman who had been the tribal representative for the past year. She had given her crown to the new representative, and her family had given gifts to the people who had supported her in her year's reign.

The announcer told jokes, teasing dancers, and kept things moving along throughout the afternoon. The rain held off until the last song of the day. Dancers sought refuge under the arbor surrounding the dance area when the deluge hit. The rain would move off, and the heat would dry out the ground for the next day of dancing. On Sunday, the last dances would be held, and a grand retreat would take place. On Monday, the black bears that lived in the area would be playing on the powwow grounds. The people who came from all over to attend would pack up, and many would move to the next powwow held the next weekend.

CHAPTER 44
July 26, 2040

Antoine was among those who left on Monday. It was July 26, and he needed to return to the city to check on things. He didn't know if there had been arrests made. He wanted to believe that someone would carry that message to him if that had happened.

Antoine got up early and walked to the place where he had been dropped off. He was picked up again by his cousin and driven to the gas station he had stopped at on his way home.

He said little to Gene, comfortable in silence. When Antoine got out of the car, Gene said, "Be careful."

Antoine nodded and headed back to the city on foot, his backpack full of EZ Breathe appliances.

When he reached his apartment, he tried to think of something he could do to pass the time. He saw his textbooks sitting on the table and decided it would look good if he was studying. He took out a tablet, opened a book, and began taking notes, aware of the fact that the notes he took should be legitimate because he didn't know who would be reading them or when he might be arrested.

Just as he picked up a book, his phone rang. "Hello, Antoine. This is Sally. I would like you to come to my office."

"Right now?" he asked.

"Yes, I think that would be best," said Sally.

Antoine walked across campus and met Sally just coming out of her office. She nodded at him and motioned for him to follow. They walked outside and found a bench.

"I didn't want to meet in my office because it might be bugged," Sally said. "Janet called me when you were gone and wanted to meet with you. She sounds scared."

"Okay. Do you want to let her know we can meet this coming weekend?" said Antoine.

"No. That might tie us all together. How have you been getting in touch with her?" asked Sally.

"I'll have someone stick a note in her mailbox," said Antoine.

"Well, I think that's the best way to do it," said Sally.

CHAPTER

July 29, 2040

They met at the same restaurant as last time. Antoine was waiting when Janet walked in and looked nervously around the dining area.

She spotted Antoine, walked over, and slid in the booth.

"What's this about?" asked Antoine.

"Louis, my photographer at work, had something to do with the governor's escape. He called me the other night and told me that the ozone plate assignment was a trap. He said that all my articles will be researched to find clues indicating that I'm a traitor," said Janet.

"Has anything happened yet?" asked Antoine.

"I still have some guy following me," said Janet. In fact, he's sitting at the counter."

"Where have you been besides here?" asked Antoine.

"I haven't been anywhere. I do my job and go home," said Janet.

"Except when you meet me. Have you made any other personal calls besides the one to Sally?" asked Antoine.

"No. I decided to call her because I thought you might be in danger or maybe arrested, and I wanted to find out if you had made any plans for leaving," said Janet.

"We're thinking of leaving the end of August," said Antoine.

"Well, it's the end of July. Who is the we you're talking about?" asked Janet.

"Everyone in the group, you, me, and Bill," said Antoine. "Bill says that DHS thinks a girl in one of my classes is one of my contacts."

"Is she?" asked Janet.

"Yeah, she is. Bill says DHS is looking for something that tells them that we're conspiring. When they figure that out, they'll probably take her in for questioning. Depending on what they learn from her, they'll probably start their roundup. Bill says they move slowly, so he'll be told when they're going to start. If they decide to pick us up, they'll have to call in agents from other cities. When we hear from Bill, we'll set a departure date. That means we should be out of here before they get to us," said Antoine.

"Why don't we just go now?" asked Janet.

"Because we don't know if we have to leave. If we have to leave, have you figured out where you're going to go?" asked Antoine.

"I want to go to Canada to see if my parents are there," said Janet.

Antoine shook his head. "Not a good idea. We've got a lot of people leaving for Canada. We've already made arrangements for them. So there really isn't room for you in any of those groups."

"So I don't have any place to go," said Janet.

"We've made arrangements for you to come to my community since you've been there once and know some folks," said Antoine.

"Are you going to pick me up?" asked Janet.

"No. That won't work. My cousin will come and pick you up when it's time to leave. I'm not coming home right away. They'll look for me on the route to my house," said Antoine.

"If they look for you, they'll find me," said Janet.

"No, I don't think so. I've got a route planned for you. You'll have to travel on foot. My cousin will get you out of the city and show you the route. Then you'll be on your own. It's going to take you about four or five days to get there unless somebody comes along to help you out," said Antoine.

"Four or five days? How can I do that? I might as well just turn myself in right now," said Janet.

"You'll have a backpack with supplies. You'll have places you can rest. You'll have food," said Antoine.

"I don't know if I can do this," said Janet.

"All you have to do is just keep moving, eat what's in the backpack, and sleep where my cousin tells you to sleep," said Antoine. "You'll be okay."

"This doesn't sound like I'll be okay. It sounds like I'm going to get caught," said Janet.

"Look. We know routes that no one else knows about. Our people had footpaths all over the country. You'll just follow the footpaths, and everything will be okay," said Antoine. "I don't know of anything to say to reassure you. You'll just have to trust."

"I don't like this. I think I'm going to go back to my apartment now," said Janet.

"It'll look funny if you do. Stay, order a meal, and go when you're done," said Antoine.

"What if I turn myself in to Homeland Security?" she asked.

"I don't think you would come out of that okay," said Antoine. "The agents would question you, find out about your contacts and others that you know who are involved in the group. If you refuse to answer, I think they will do things to make you talk and then throw you aside. I think you have nothing to gain and everything to lose, maybe even your life, if you do that. I know you want to stay here. I know you think you can change things here. Maybe you can. I don't think so, but I'm not going to waste my time arguing with you. I've got a plan to get you out of here if and when things fall apart. For now, I think it's best if you just sit tight and wait to see what happens," said Antoine.

"I wonder where I'd be and what I'd be doing if my parents hadn't left," said Janet.

"Hard to say," said Antoine. "What do you think they'd want you to do now?"

"Well, I don't think they'd want me to go to Homeland Security. I think they would probably want me to leave here when I get the chance," she said.

"So what are you going to do?" asked Antoine.

"I guess I'll just have to count on you to help me get out of here. After I'm safe, maybe I can find my parents and go live with them wherever they are," said Janet.

"So you've got a plan," said Antoine.

Janet sighed. "I guess so."

They finished their meal, left the restaurant, and parted company. An agent followed each of them.

At home, Janet thought about her parents She wished she could have gone with them when they left. If they did go to Canada, they would have been granted asylum because of their ages. There was no way she could find out where they were, even if she found someone who did know, as all phones were programmed to allow only local calls, and she hadn't been charged with any illegal political activities, so she wasn't qualified to apply for asylum. She hoped she would be able to look for her parents once she was safe.

CHAPTER 46
August 17, 2040

Levi was up early. He felt a slight edge in the air in spite of the heat and humidity, a reminder that fall was coming. He went to get his grandson Jeremiah to help him make sure the tunnel was ready.

Jeremiah had grown up next door to Levi and spent his childhood following his grandfather, learning about the trees, plants, and the animals. His faith in his grandfather was unwavering. There were times when he would neglect his family to do things for Levi. When Levi found out that Jeremiah was neglecting his family, he said, "Your wife and children should come before anyone." Next, Levi invited himself to Jeremiah's house for dinner and apologized to Jeremiah's wife and children for taking Jeremiah away from them.

Annie, Jeremiah's wife, said, "Maybe we need to find ways to share Jeremiah." Hearing the words of his grandfather and his wife made Jeremiah realize why he loved them more than anyone else he knew.

Today Levi needed to plan for something important. He said to Jeremiah, "I don't know when it's going to happen, but I think there is going to be a fugitive coming this way.

"I know that lots of folks have thought I'm crazy because of all the signs in my yard. There are rumors about the tunnel. Soon we are going to have to rely on those signs, that tunnel, and the belief that I'm crazy to save someone's life."

"Let's do a few practice runs to see that everything is in working order. Before I do that, I need to go home and let Annie know that I'll be spending some extra time with you. In the meantime, when's the last time you checked the canned goods and the bottled water in the tunnel?" asked Jeremiah.

"I change them every three months. The last time I changed them was last week, so the supplies are ready to be used," said Levi.

When he returned, Jeremiah and Levi checked out the tunnel's entrances and exits and talked about the preparations they would need to make to get everything ready.

"You know that I made those false hallways in the tunnel so that anyone chasing through there would be confused as to where to go," said Levi.

"Yes, Grandpa. Do you really think that's going to work to slow people down if they decided to chase us through the tunnel?" said Jeremy.

"Grandson, I don't know if you know how dead serious I am about this," said Levi.

"I know that you believe we are going to help a runaway from the city and that Marvin has been having dreams about that," said Jeremy.

"When your grandmother died in jail, I spent a long time thinking about what I could do to make up for that," said Levi. "I didn't come up with anything except a desire to revenge her death. Then I realized that I'd be bringing the law down on me and our family. So I decided to wait for an opportunity. This is the opportunity."

"I don't get it," said Jeremiah.

"I expect you to make sure we have food, blankets, and some extra clothes down there. When the fugitive comes, I'll need you to take her through the tunnel and put her back on the path. The rest is for me. I'm going to booby-trap the dead ends," said Levi.

"How?" asked Jeremiah.

"There'll be some booby traps down there," said Levi.

"What kind of booby traps?" asked Jeremiah.

"The traps are low-level bombs that'll be set off when people cross over a switch. They'll be stunned. I don't want to kill anyone. Besides, anything stronger would weaken the tunnel. It might collapse while you're in it.

"I don't expect you to understand this. I've missed your grandmother every day that she's been gone. Even if those folks who come chasing aren't the ones who killed her, they're all part of the same outfit. They can call themselves law enforcement, Homeland Security, or anything. They're all the same. They kill people. Your grandmother and I never harmed anyone. I'm not going to cause any permanent damage to anyone or take anyone's life," said Levi.

"I'll help any person who needs sanctuary," said Jeremiah.

"Okay. I'll get the booby traps ready," said Levi.

CHAPTER 47
August 24, 2040

After the powwow guests left, the community went back to its routine. Men were catching fish, while children chased one another through the woods. The beans hanging from vines in the garden behind the house had been harvested and canned. The ripe fruit that hung from tomato plants, bowing the stems, had been picked and cooked into sauce, some left raw for meals. Women were rounding up children to help with the harvest of the ripe berries that grew wild. After the berries were harvested, some were eaten fresh, while the rest were canned. The summer kitchen that was filled with women cooking and canning for the winter would soon be empty. Meal cooking would move inside houses, and the woodstoves would take away the chill in the house from the overnight temperatures.

Sonia had noticed the changes that told her that summer was coming to a close and ricing season would soon follow. The leaves weren't as full. The flowers were beginning to droop. The only food left in the garden was the squash and pumpkins. The raspberries were gone, picked and canned, eaten by birds and bears, a few forgotten and dropped on the forest floor.

The cattails in the swamp had matured, sitting on the edge of water turned green by plant life, heat, and stagnation. The rice was growing full in the lakes. The fawns had lost their spots, and the mother bears had turned out their two-year-olds, who were crashing around in the woods, trying to figure out what they were supposed to do without their mothers.

In her quiet preparations for Old Woman's passing, Sonia had heard the rumors about Marvin's dreams. She knew that he interpreted them to mean that Janet would escape and try to reach the reservation. She didn't want to think about Janet coming to live here. Sonia needed time to mourn Old Woman and to help the children adjust after the funeral. Besides, Janet knew nothing about their way of life; she was not a replacement for Old Woman.

It was hard for her to talk about her misgivings in her own house. She didn't want to influence the children, and she didn't want to upset Old Woman, who would probably think she was responsible for bringing Janet here.

Many years before, when her house was filled with children, Sonia had gotten into the habit of going to Corrine's house to visit. They would send Antoine to her house, and she could talk about the things that were hard in her life. She returned to that ritual now, sharing her misgivings with Corrine.

"Mom, I will take care of that. If she comes here, she can stay with us. It will probably be easier for her to catch on to things here. My household is smaller. Besides, I know that Joe doesn't like her. I don't want you to have to be the peacemaker between the two of them," said Corrine.

So Sonia and Corrine, who believed in Marvin's dreams, decided that if Janet arrived, she would stay with Corrine. This meant that Sonia only had to take care of herself, her household, and the passing of Old woman. When the rice was ripe, Old Woman would harvest rice that would feed the family through the coming year. When she finished the harvest, Old Woman would pass on.

She sat at home, waiting to be arrested, thinking about escape. Antoine had told her to wait. He said he would let her know when she had to leave and would make arrangements for her to leave. What if he got picked up? She wouldn't know it, and she would be arrested as well.

Janet saw herself sitting at work at her computer, putting together another story, when Homeland Security surveillance agents came in. Darcy would stand up, yelling, pointing at Janet, "That's her! Get her!" Someone would come in from the photography pool, walk over, and help put on her handcuffs. Lloyd would be standing in the door of his office, watching, assigning a reporter to get the story.

Or she would be at home. She would be sitting in her living room watching the Travel Channel. There would be a bang on the door. The door would fall in, and dozens of men with guns would come streaming in. They would surround her, forcing her to the floor, where they would handcuff and shackle her, clamping an EZ Breathe appliance to her neck collar.

Next, they would take her to the building on the northwest side of the city. She had heard rumors about what went on in that building. She would be locked in the basement with no light and would be left alone for two days without any food or water.

Someone would come in and drag her into an aboveground room with bright lights shining in her eyes. Blinded, she would not be able to see the person who would come into the room to start the interrogation. She didn't know what the questions would be, but she would hear someone yelling at her, telling her that everyone else in the group had been detained and had talked. At this point, Janet could hear herself saying, "If everyone else talked, why do you want to ask me questions?"

Janet knew that if she said that, she would be tortured. She also knew this was not a good time of year for an escape, as the air quality was poor, even on good days. So she stayed and waited for word from Antoine. She tried to think no further than what she had to do at the moment, although the thoughts about capture and torture visited her often.

She tried to focus on an escape plan and gave up. She didn't know how to escape, and Antoine had told her he would set up the plan, and someone would get her out of the city. Once out of the city, it sounded like the plan was to give her directions, and she would proceed on foot. This didn't sound like a good plan to her, but she didn't think she had other good choices.

CHAPTER
August 31, 2040

It was the end of August, and without a breeze, the hot, humid air soaked up the chemicals from the factories, creating a brown sludge-like film that floated in the air and made a weather alert necessary. The city shut down. Only senior Homeland Security personnel lived in the Homeland Security complex; therefore, the agents working under Hal Emerson's supervision weren't at work.

Hal walked down to his office from his apartment, frustrated. In spite of the attention paid to trapping the insurrectionists, no one had been able to come up with concrete proof that anything was going on that would threaten national security. Every time he thought they were getting close to something, the leads fell apart. He would have to start bringing in suspected members of the group that his agents thought were vulnerable. He and his team would have to get as much information as they could and start the roundup.

Because he didn't have to focus on his supervisees, Hal could concentrate on coming up with a plan for a roundup as well as developing his own escape plan. He took all the information gathered by all of the operatives and put it into a program he had developed under the tutelage of Jim Remington. The program was designed to link information together by providing assumptions or bridges between pieces of seemingly unrelated facts.

So far, the linked information included the connections between Janet Ryan and her friend Sally, and between Sally and Jeff. Antoine La Riviere was linked to Janet Ryan and many others in the group. He looked like an innocent who was simply trying to make friends.

Hal pulled up a list of known subversives whose whereabouts were either unknown or who were living in rural areas. It felt best to leave them alone, as they posed no threat to urban communities. They didn't have enough resources or power to overthrow anything. Some were so old that they were assumed dead. He scrolled slowly through the list, arranged according to name, date of birth, and address. When he got to Rachel Anderson's data, he found that the address looked familiar. He switched to the program that held the names and addresses of the campus group members and scrolled down. He stopped when he saw that Rachel Anderson and Antoine LaRiviere had the same address.

She must be dead, he thought. She was born in the 1940s. But she lived on the reservation when she was alive. Maybe she isn't dead. Okay. LaRiviere and Janet Ryan have been meeting. Janet Ryan left the city, was followed to Wisconsin, and disappeared a few miles after she crossed the state line. So what if she was sent to the reservation by LaRiviere to meet with Rachel Anderson? Why would Ryan take that risk? She must be doing something against the law or she wouldn't engage in the disappearing act.

What could she get from Rachel Anderson? She must be changing cars when she gets to Wisconsin. Then she goes to the reservation, talks to Anderson, brings the information back here. Who gets the information she brings back and what is done with it?

Hal was excited. He had connections that he hadn't realized before. There was a group. They must be getting information about Rachel Anderson's history. Nobody is supposed to have any information about history other than what we give them. So Janet Ryan is breaking the law. She's bringing a forbidden history to the group of which she must be a member. What do we do next?

We don't want to pick all of them up at once. It just wouldn't sit well with people. There would be too much speculation about who was guilty of what and who wasn't guilty. If we pick up everybody at once, their neighbors and coworkers would know, and they would wait to hear more details on the news. We would be pressured into giving an explanation for the arrests. Then there would be requests for court appearances, bail, and all of those other rights that people assume they have. We can take a couple of weeks, put together the information we have, plus the information we get from questioning the most vulnerable suspects, and add in a few stories about the governor's kidnapping. We arrest the suspects we've questioned. Then we can tell the American people what happened. We will have the approval of the American people to do what we must do if we use this process. We can have a trial and be guaranteed a guilty verdict. It will be good for the office and for the president. Our timing is crucial. This current investigation and impending roundup seemed to be right. There would be much chaos and confusion. I'll be part of the team that rounds up suspects. I can travel out of the city and lead a team following a suspect. I need the current team of agents to bring in a vulnerable suspect who can give enough information to warrant rounding up group members. And then I can make my move and go to Canada. What do I need to do next?

Hal decided to contact Bill Scott but held off because of the bad air. He spent his time coming up with a plan he would present to Bill.

September 1, 2040

When Hal got up in the morning, the weather report said that the air quality had improved enough so that people could venture out, go to work, and carry on with normal activities as long as they wore the heavy masks with wire nasal filters.

He called Bill Scott, who came as soon as he was called. He sat in Hal Emerson's office, trying to look calm. Hal stood up behind his desk and extended his hand to Bill, knowing he could shake hands safely with Bill because Bill had gone through security scanner at the front door. The security included a screening of all substances found on his clothes and exposed parts of his skin. Nothing was found that would contaminate Hal. It was another one of those necessary searches that eliminated any second-guessing as to who was safe and who wasn't.

"Good to see you, Bill. I'm going to need your help We have reason to believe there is a subversive group operating on campus. We have to question some suspects to get more information. Right now, we have some connections between people that look suspicious.

"After we gather more data, we can plan a roundup. I don't want any of the suspects to know when we're coming to get them. We'll make the first arrests in the next week or two, starting with some of the people we believe have been operating on the fringes of the group. That way, we'll be able to get information from them that will give us enough to arrest and charge the more important members of the group.

"When we start the roundup, some of the group members will probably know that we're on to them. We want you to tell them when they're going to be arrested. You'll give them false information so we'll be able to arrest them in them in their homes."

Bill sat very still, unsure as to what his response should be, knowing that he was in a bad spot. If he did what he was told, someone would die. If he gave the group accurate information, he would die. He figured it was probably time for him to leave. The only good news was that he could contact Antoine without arousing suspicion since his earlier assignment had been to befriend Antoine.

As he left Hal Emerson's office, Bill thought of contacting Antoine immediately. He denied his impulse, knowing that this wasn't a good idea. He would wait a couple of days before letting Antoine know. He went about his business, acting as normally as he could, knowing that the rest of his life depended on his demeanor.

CHAPTER
September 3, 2040

Two days after he met with Hal Emerson, Bill met Antoine on campus. "Why don't we go have a cup of coffee at that pizza place just down the street. We can't really talk here. The air's too bad."

They walked to the restaurant, ordered coffee, and sat in a booth away from the other patrons.

"Homeland Security is going to start rounding up the people they've identified as group members. They seem to think they have a few vulnerable people they can turn to get more information about group members and the purpose of the group. So we need to figure out how to get you and the others out without getting caught," said Bill.

"I don't get their methods. Why do they go to the trouble of getting enough information on people? Why don't they just pick people up when they're suspicious?" Antoine asked.

"It's bad for morale among their staff. They have some really zealous operatives. Some of the adolescents they recruit believe that the office is patriotic, judicious, and fair. Those in charge believe that simply picking people up because they act and look suspicious would cause dissension. They want to be able to use this potential roundup to score points with the public.

"Once you're a Homeland Security surveillance agent, you don't change jobs. You don't take any information out of the office and go someplace else with it. It is a lifetime job. This mission will reinforce the beliefs of the agents that they are keeping Americans safe. So how many are in the group?" asked Bill.

"Each group within the group has six members. I think there are probably about sixty people altogether," said Antoine. "Except for me and Janet Ryan and Sally Marshall and Jeff Morgan. I can spread the word through each small group leader. How are we all going to get out?" Antoine asked.

"I've got some maps here. There are numbers written on the side that tell people which routes to take. You all need to leave a few days before the roundup is scheduled. In order for Homeland Security to capture the group, they have to call in some agents from other areas, who will then be briefed on the roundup and the reasons for it.

We need to find out how many people want to continue their activities after they leave here. Depending on how many, we can contact some folks in Montana and arrange for them to help with the escape," said Bill.

"How do they help with the escape?" asked Antoine.

"They send explicit instructions as to how people are to leave the city. Then they have traveler aides waiting at certain places along the way to help. It's a long trip," said Bill.

"What about those who just want to get away?" Antoine asked.

"That's what the maps are for. There are several different routes that take people to Canada. There are folks in the area who help them get to the Boundary Waters and some other places that are pretty isolated. Some will have to go south and circle around on the east side of the cities. There's usually a concentration of Homeland Security surveillance agents north of here because it's the quickest way to Canada.

"Do you have an escape plan?" asked Bill.

"Yeah. I'm going to stay with relatives on another reservation. I have to take care of Janet Ryan. I've been her contact. She's probably going to be in a lot of trouble when they start picking people up. She left the city without permission and recorded interviews in my community for our newspaper. All one of those guys has to do is get his hands on one of the newspapers, start torturing somebody, and Janet's name will come up," said Antoine.

"Do you really think they torture people?" asked Bill.

"Don't you?" asked Antoine.

"I don't want to believe that. Our government has always believed in civil rights," said Bill.

"Whose rights are those? If that were true, neither of us would be here planning escapes," said Antoine.

"You're right. I just don't want to think about it. We need to pay attention to the days when people start leaving. It's September, so the bad air should be clearing soon. I'll let you know when Homeland Security is starting their roundup, and people will have to leave before then," said Bill.

"What are you going to do?" said Antoine.

Bill said, "I have connections in Montana. I think it's my time to go with my sister and her kids. I have been here working for the Montana group for about ten years, and I think my cover is about to be blown. The next time we meet will probably be the last," said Bill.

Antoine grinned. "I don't think that way. And some of your people don't either. Who was it that said it isn't over till it's over?"

"I don't know," said Bill. "I do know that I'll miss you. I hope we both make it out of here."

"Me too," said Antoine.

When Antoine got back to his apartment, he walked the halls in his building, hoping his movements would drain some of the anxiety he felt. This had all started with the dream he had when he had just entered adolescence. By following his dream, he wound up being responsible for the lives of about sixty people.

I have to make sure that the plans Bill and I made will minimize the loss of lives. I don't want anyone to die, but then, this world isn't of my making. He walked for two hours, thinking about what he needed to do to make his way out of the city on foot.

Antoine decided to tell Janet last just in case she panicked and blew the whole thing. He would pack some supplies for her and bring them to her apartment after he figured out how to get her out of the city.

Antoine spent the next few days looking as if he was studying. He would leave for periods of time to run ten miles on the indoor track at the university. The indoor air was breathable without appliances, but it wasn't like the air at home.

Antoine anticipated going home with Janet. He was attracted to her, although she seemed irritated with him much of the time. He knew there was a place for her at home, even though Uncle Joe wouldn't be too happy about it. Over time, Antoine figured that his uncle would just have to get used to her being there.

Antoine knew that the agents would be looking for her, believing she was one of the leaders of the group. Because she was of great interest to Homeland Security, agents would probably put extra attention on her.

As he ran, Antoine heard Sonia's voice: "Most of the roads in this country follow old Indian trails. There's a bunch of trails that come out of the Twin Cities. They hook up with trails out of Eau Claire up to Chippewa Falls and up through your uncle Marvin's front yard and beyond—all the way up to Lake Superior. Most of them are in the woods running parallel to the highways. They aren't marked, but once on them, it's easy. They've been used for so long that people have worn ruts. They're overgrown with bushes and grass, so no one knows they are there."

There's the plan, thought Antoine. All I have to do is figure out a way to get Janet on the trail out of Eau Claire or Chippewa Falls. I'll get her a backpack, some food, some water, and a flashlight, as she'll probably have to travel at night some of the time. I hope she goes along with the plan. If she doesn't, there isn't much else I can do.

CHAPTER
September 4, 2040

Hal Emerson called the secretary of Homeland Security in Washington to discuss his plan to round up the insurrectionists. No one knew the identity of the secretary except the president. Hal addressed the secretary as "sir." The man's voice was filtered through an electronic voice-altering device, making it hard to understand him. Hal had called him on the phone for priority II situations. When he picked up the phone, he did not speak. Hal said, "Sir. We have a situation. We have had a group of people under surveillance for about eight months. We think they number between one hundred, one hundred fifty, and we think they're broken up into small groups, so we don't know for sure how many there are, and we don't exactly know what they've been planning, but they break Public Gathering Law 320 of the Antiterrorist Act. They meet, two to three people at a time, surreptitiously. They connect with one another through a young American Indian student at the university. He is the sole contact for a reporter at the *Minneapolis Herald* who made an unauthorized visit to the reservation where the Indian man comes from. We believe she visits with Rachel Anderson, a woman who is on our list of insurrectionists because of her activism earlier in her life. She lives on the reservation. Rachel Anderson has the same address as the Indian man."

Hal paused, and he asked, "What is your evidence?"

"We don't have evidence, sir. We have probable cause," said Hal.

"The probable cause is the Indian man, his connections with the others, his connection with the writer and the fact that Rachel Anderson has the same address as the Indian man?" he asked.

"Yes, sir," said Hal.

"You're stretching this. Are you going to try a mass roundup and interrogations?" he asked.

"We're going to start with people our agents have identified as vulnerable. We believe we can get them to talk about the purpose of the group and identify those they know are group members," said Hal.

"What makes you think anyone will talk?" he asked.

"Sir, I don't think any of them have much experience with this sort of thing. I think they're idealists who don't understand the necessity to keep the American people safe from terrorists," said Hal.

"It would help if you could get some evidence about that young reporter's visit with Rachel Anderson," he said.

"Yes, sir. We believe she has given historical information to group members. The information is not sanctioned by Homeland Security We don't have proof of this in the form of written documents," said Hal.

"So Rachel Anderson is giving historical accounts that aren't sanctioned," he said.

"Yes, sir. We believe this alternative history could cause people to begin asking questions about the way our government operates," said Hal.

"When do you plan to start the roundup?" he asked.

"I thought we would start the week after next, sir," said Hal.

"I think you need to wait until the end of September. That way, you can continue to collect information that will give you stronger probable cause. Do you think any of them have an idea that they are being watched?" he asked.

"We think the reporter does. She has been given special assignments at work for several months now. We have been scanning everything she has written to find evidence of insurrectionist thoughts and beliefs. We can't find anything.

"She is a bright young woman. We believe her parents left for Canada several months back. If she starts thinking about the other journalists who have written special assignments and then disappeared, I'm sure she will start getting anxious, sir," said Hal.

"Where do you think she would go if she got an inkling that she will be picked up?" he asked.

"Sir, I think she would go to Canada to be with her parents," said Hal.

"I'm inclined to agree with you, but I wonder if she would go directly there or would hide out someplace first," he said.

"Sir, do you think she would go to the reservation first?" asked Hal.

"I was thinking she might try to get to Montana. It borders Canada, and there aren't any natural barriers on the border. If she goes to the reservation, we can't arrest her there because of our treaties, and there is no direct way to get to Canada without crossing Lake Superior," he said.

"We believe there are a bunch of survivalists living in those mountains in Montana. As you know, DHS policy has been to ignore them, as there aren't many people in Montana. We focus on the cities. We capture some of the escapees when they head for Canada, but we also miss some of them," said Hal.

The phone beeped, letting them know that their conversation was clear from outside monitoring.

"Sir," said Hal, "we may need some more agents to assist with the roundup. This is a big operation, and we want to make sure that no one escapes. Based on what you're saying, we will need to cover a lot of potential exit routes."

"I can't promise you extra help. Outside of the East Coast, your operation has more operatives than any other part of the country. Get back to me with your plan, and then we'll see what we can spare for you," he said.

"Thank you, sir," Hal said. The phone disconnected when Hal was in midsentence. He sat for about fifteen minutes, concentrating on his breathing, as he usually hyperventilated when he talked to the secretary.

At the other end of the line, the secretary thought about the conversation with his favorite employee. He was impressed with Hal's dedication, his logical thinking, and his willingness to check out plans. Many supervising operatives put plans in place and carried them out without consultation. Sometimes the results were disasters. Hal spent time planning, and his operations were carried out without mistakes. Of all of the supervising operatives, Hal was probably the only one who didn't have to check on a plan before carrying it out.

After he had his breathing under control, Hal thought about the date for the roundup. It should be on a weekend. That way, they could get most people at home. He would have someone run a check on work and class schedules for all those named in the roundup. After Labor Day weekend, students would be back in class.

Hal pulled up the list of operatives assigned to the Twin Cities area. He had one hundred fifty he could use. He would have to talk to the scheduler to make sure those working evening shifts would get a day off so they could all be available for the detail.

He needed a meeting with them to plan strategy and wanted to schedule it ahead of time. He didn't think that any of his operatives would carry information to the insurrectionists, although he had lost a couple of operatives when the governor escaped to Canada.

When was the best time of day to start the roundup? Not at night. If anyone escaped, the darkness would cover them. Not during daytime when the neighbors would see. Some would try to harbor the fugitives and create more chaos than necessary.

Early morning, five o'clock, would be good. It was just before dawn, and anyone escaping would not get far before they would be spotted.

Hal nodded. September 26 at 5:00 a.m.

Hal called Bill Scott for another meeting. "Bill, good to see you again," said Hal. He sat and pointed at a chair, indicating to Bill that he could sit.

Bill nodded, not knowing what to say, so he figured he would wait and follow Hal's lead.

"Bill, we're getting ready to start the roundup. I'm entrusting you with information that no one else has and no one will get until just a few hours before we deploy operatives for this," said Hal.

Bill nodded.

"We are going to move five o'clock in the morning on September 26," said Hal. "I want you to circulate information to the group on September 25."

"Hal, I don't understand why you want me to tell them when you're going to arrest them," said Bill.

"Because we'll have operatives out on September 25, blocking the exits out of the city. Other operatives will go to homes and make arrests, and some will have made their moves to escape and will be captured then," said Hal.

"Okay. Do you want me to find out how many will be leaving?" asked Bill.

"Yes. That will help me know how and where to assign operatives. I want you to give the information to the Indian man. Make it seem sincere. Let him know how upset you are. You could also get yourself an escape plan to make it look like you're really one of them. You come to me with the plan and let me know where people will be heading. That way we can be there to round up those who do get away," said Hal.

"I'll find Antoine this afternoon. Do you want me to come back in today?" asked Bill.

"No. Tomorrow will be soon enough," said Hal.

After Bill left, Hal sat thinking about his escape plan. I think this is the time to leave. There will be a lot of chaos. If I head north under the pretense of leading a group of agents looking for group members to arrest, I'll might be able to get away, but how? I'll have to separate from the other agents or get rid of them. It would take the other supervisors a while to notice that I'm missing. I don't know for sure what to do, but I'll have to move or lose the opportunity.

CHAPTER 52
September 4. 2040

Bill Scott found Antoine sitting outside the student union. "Hey, Antoine, I gotta talk to you."

"I don't think we should be this obvious."

"I'll look over my shoulder a couple of times. I need to make sure somebody sees us. I just got back from a meeting with Hal Emerson. He says they're getting ready to make arrests. He gave me a date—September 25. He said I should tell you this so that you will leave a couple of days early. They'll have the roads cut off so nobody will be able to get out."

"This sounds a little too easy," said Antoine. "It also sounds a little too far into the future. My guess is they're going to do this a couple of weeks ahead of time." Antoine sat a few minutes, thinking. "We have to take care of you first, Bill. When are you going to contact the guys in Montana?"

"I thought I would probably try that next week."

"Next week will be too late. If we wait to move out of here the middle of this month, and they start looking for us then, you had better be gone. I think we're going to have to move everybody at once. The minute they start looking and find that people are already gone, they are going to mobilize quickly. You've told me what you're supposed to tell me, and that guy across the mall has seen us. Now we have to figure out how to have contact to make the rest of the plans."

"I think it's best if we just meet at the poker game. We want to make everybody think things are the same as usual," said Bill.

"Okay. The poker game is tonight. We can go for coffee after the game and make our plans as we walk," said Antoine.

Bill left the union and went back to work. He concentrated on his job, knowing that looking good right now would do a lot to save his life. After work, he walked to his sister's house.

"It's time to go, Shirley. I'm going to get in touch with my Montana contact tonight," said Bill.

"Okay. I'll start packing tonight," said Shirley. "How long do you think it will be before we leave?"

"My guess is that the folks from Montana will be here to meet us in two days," said Bill. "There will probably be ten people going to Montana. The rest are going to Canada. There are about sixty people, and we all need to leave at once. Most of the group are under some kind of surveillance. Homeland Security is bringing in agents from other regions to help out."

"I hadn't planned on being part of a tour group, Bill. I just want to get the hell out of here. I'll go to the mall and buy a bunch of stuff on my debit card and return it for money a couple of hours later. That way, we'll have plenty of cash."

"Have you planned Jimmy's birthday party?" asked Bill.

"Yes, it's the day after tomorrow," said Shirley.

"Good. I'll contact the Montana group and let them know to come to your house to pick us up. If they come late at night, the kids will probably be sleeping. We can just put them in the vehicle and let them sleep.

"Shirley, I know I'm asking a lot of you. It would be easier if it was just us going, but I can't leave these people behind," said Bill.

Shirley was silent for a long time. She sighed. "Okay. I'll be ready when you are."

Bill left Shirley's house and went to the card game. He and Antoine left the game together and walked across the campus to the restaurant. The air quality was good, and they didn't need any EZ Breathe apparatuses, even though the odor of sewage burned their noses.

"I'll be in contact with the Montana group tonight," said Bill. "They have said that they can get here in two days. So far, I've made plans to leave the night of the sixth."

"When I look at all of the information we have so far, I think the best time to leave is no later than three days from now. We've got the maps, and the small groups are responsible for planning supplies," said Antoine.

"It would be nice if we could have a plan A and a plan B," said Bill.

"I don't think that's possible. If plan A doesn't work, I think we'll all be on our own," said Antoine.

"I was hoping to go a day earlier than everybody else. I have to take some other folks with me. But I don't think it's a good idea to leave earlier than the rest of the groups. If I don't show up at work, they're going to come looking for me. When they don't find me, the agents will start the roundup," said Bill.

"I'm going to my nephew's birthday party in two days. The Montana folks are sending a vehicle to my sister's house. We'll probably head south first, since there will be agents posted on the west side of the city, waiting for us."

"Well, I guess that's it. We won't see each other before we leave the city," said Antoine.

September 5, 2040

Antoine spent the day contacting the six small group leaders, giving them maps, outlining plans, and trying not to look suspicious. He had already decided that he and Janet would leave the same night as everyone else. By the time they were reported missing, the Homeland Security surveillance team would start blocking all of the exits out of the city, and they would be past the city gates. He and Janet were going in a different direction. The east gates of the city wouldn't be closed as quickly as the north and west gates because the routes he and Janet would be taking were not normal escape routes, as going east didn't take anyone to a place where they could escape.

Antoine didn't like keeping Janet in the dark, but he was afraid that she would blow it if she knew what was coming. He was afraid that the series of contacts he had made with group members would set off some panic. So far, things were going smoothly.

September 6, 2040

Shirley went to the Mall of America pretending to shop. She was loaded down with packages by the time she came to the restaurant where she was to meet the Montana contact. She sat in a booth with her bags.

Shirley waited and watched. Ten minutes passed. Shirley wondered if anyone was coming when a tall, bearded man dressed in jeans and a sweater strode in, reached out his arms, and yelled, "Shirley. It's good to see you!"

Shirley figured this must be her contact. She stood and accepted the man's embrace. "Who the hell are you?" she whispered in his ear.

"Rick," he whispered.

They sat down in the booth, facing each other.

"How have you been, Rick?" asked Shirley. "It's been a while. I was really glad that you called and asked to get together. I haven't seen you since Phil died." Shirley pulled pictures of her children out of her purse, leaning over the booth to point out who was who, how old they were, and what accomplishments they had so far. "Jimmy is in the Homeland Security Youth Corps. I am so proud of him. His dad would be proud too. I think Jimmy was inspired by all of the attention we got after Phil died."

Rick looked attentive, smiling and nodding with all of the superlatives Shirley used to describe her children. *Either she's damn good at this or she's a spy or maybe a little bit crazy*, he thought.

They ordered their meal and ate in silence.

` When they finished, Rick said, "Why don't I give you a ride home? I have a car." They left the mall and headed for Rick's car.

"This is the car we'll be using to transport you. I would suggest that you leave some of the packages in the car if they have things in them that you will need when you get to Montana."

"I'm going to return all this stuff and get cash just in case we need extra on the trip. What do I need to do between now and the time we leave?"

"First of all, we'll be leaving tonight. According to Bill, there'll be a lot of people leaving then. If we all leave about the same time, there won't be anyone left to arrest when Homeland Security finds that some of the people they're looking for are gone. We'll come by about ten thirty. By that time, most of your neighbors will be asleep. Take as little as you possibly can. You'll need winter coats and warm clothing."

"How many people will be going with us?" asked Shirley.

"Just you, your kids, and Bill," said Rick.

"Bill said he thought we might have to take some others with us," said Shirley.

"No, we made other arrangements for them," said Rick. "You mentioned cash. You'll need to put it someplace where no one will be able to get to it easily. You will be going about three hundred miles with me. Then we will stop, and you will go with another driver in another car. Any place along the way, someone might try to hijack you. They're usually in a hurry when they do. If they can't find money on the first try, they usually take off. Then the word spreads that you don't have any money. There are some very desperate, poor people who will pull cars over to see if they can hit it big. We usually stay on the main roads. There are so few people out west that strange cars stick out on the back roads. There are Homeland Security civilian operatives who live in some of those little towns. They catch their share of runaways."

When they pulled up in front of Shirley's house, she got out and started pulling shopping bags out of the back. "Thanks, Rick."

"There won't be another contact until it's time to leave. By the way, you did a great job in the restaurant."

"Thanks."

As Rick backed out of the driveway, the kids ran out of the neighbor's house. Shirley followed the kids into the house. "Don't take that stuff out of the bags. I have to take it back."

Bill worked his full shift and took the bus to Shirley's house. The driver recognized him because Bill had taken the trip outside his gated neighborhood to his sister's many times over the years. The driver greeted him with, "Hey, Bill, how're that nephew and niece of yours?"

Bill grinned and pulled out the pictures he had of Jimmy in his Homeland Security Youth Corps uniform and Cindy on her first day of kindergarten. He chatted with the driver about the kids until he reached his stop.

Bill got off the bus and walked the two blocks to Shirley's house, pushing against the thick air. His biggest worries were the air quality and getting the kids packed in the vehicle. It would take extra time to pack up the sleeping kids because of the EZ Breathe masks, and it would be hard to pack up and take the kids without causing some disturbance in the neighborhood. If they awakened the neighbors, most wouldn't check to see what was happening because they didn't want to be involved. Bill was worried about those who might check to see what was going on. He hoped that their absences wouldn't be noticed for a few days—long enough to get a good head start.

When he got to the house, the party was in full swing. Many twelve-year-old boys were clustered around television sets and computers, playing games. The winners got prizes of handheld video games and cell phones.

Jimmy noticed Bill and came running over for a hug. "Hey, buddy. This is some party."

"Yeah. Mom never lets us play video games. She says they don't help us grow up, but she must have changed her mind. All the kids think this is a cool party."

Bill looked at Shirley as Jimmy went back to his friends.

"After they finish this round, they'll open presents and eat. Then their parents will come to take them home."

"Do you have to call all of them?" asked Bill.

"No, I just wrote on the invitations when I want them to come and get their kids. We'll have plenty of time to put the kids to bed and get ready," said Shirley.

The party proceeded on schedule. By eight o'clock, all of the kids were gone. Jimmy started cleaning up the mess. "You don't have to do that, Jimmy. Your uncle Bill and I will clean up after you and Cindy go to bed. Thanks anyway."

Shirley picked wrapping paper off the floor, put it in a garbage bag, and took it out to the curb. A full garbage can would add to the impression that she was still in the house. She had a schedule, and by nine, the kids were in bed sleeping. She had packed clothes the kids would be wearing on the trip in backpacks and duffel bags. She went to her closet and began pulling money out of the closet.

Bill heard the rustling and came in to see paper money scattered over the room. "Shirley, what are you doing?"

"What does it look like I'm doing? This is my stash. I've been saving this since before Phil died. I'm taking it with me, but I don't know where to put it. Help me think of something."

Bill started picking up the bills and arranging them in piles. Jimmy came in the room carrying something with the Homeland Security Youth Corps logo. "Here, Mom. You can use my Middle Eastern terrorist punching bag. We'll just take out some of the stuffing and put the money in there. Nobody will look in it. They'll be too scared."

"Jimmy. How do you know …"

"Mom, I've known for a long time that we were going to leave. When I knew for sure was when you made me join the Homeland Security Youth Corps. You didn't say anything; you just told me I had to join. Then you started buying all those new clothes that we never got to wear because you'd just take them back to the store.

"Here, Uncle Bill, give me some of that money." Jimmy began stuffing money in the punching bag.

"Shirley, how much money is there?" asked Bill.

"I don't know. I just started stashing it away, and I lost track after a while. There should be enough for us to live on for a long time. Just keep stuffing it in there."

"Was this from Phil's company?" asked Bill.

"Yeah, most of it. They made monthly payments to me. I've taken some out of the bank and made it look like it was for living expenses, house repairs, and stuff. Some of it's from debit cards," said Shirley.

Bill tried to count as he went. He figured there was at least $500,000. He had certainly underestimated his sister and her plans. He didn't know what to say, so he just kept stuffing.

Rick pulled up outside at ten thirty. He backed the van into the driveway so everyone could enter from the garage. Shirley had everything organized and ready to go. Bill and Jimmy put the Middle Eastern terrorist punching bag, along with the duffels and backpacks in the van. Shirley had filled a cooler with bottled water and sandwiches.

She put EZ Breathe appliances on Cindy while Rick carried her to the van. Shirley was the last to leave the house. Taking a last look at the dirty dishes from the party, she turned out the lights and got in the van. "Does anyone have to go to the bathroom?" she said softly so as not to awaken

Cindy. "You better go now because we won't be able to stop for a while." She smoothed Jimmy's hair. "I just have to say that. I'm a mom."

Rick instructed Bill and Shirley. "Bill, you drive. Shirley, you sit in front."

"I thought I was supposed to hide. Why is Bill driving?" asked Shirley.

"Bill has a Homeland security ID. You're his sister. You're going to visit family in Northfield," said Rick.

"Northfield!" said Shirley.

"We go down and around," said Rick.

"So where are you going to be?" asked Shirley.

"We have a false floor in this vehicle. I'll be under the floor until we clear Minnesota," said Rick.

"We'll have to stop at each gate out of the city, and, Bill, you'll explain where you're going," said Rick. "The kids are sleeping in the back, secured with seat belts. We've got big gas tanks in this vehicle. After we leave the city, we can go a long way before we have to get gas," said Rick.

CHAPTER
September 6, 2040

Hal Emerson was looking forward to the roundup. He enjoyed training the younger Homeland Security surveillance agents. Putting together clues and working a case through each step of the process to roundup was challenging and gave him a sense of satisfaction.

He had given his life to his job and had excelled at it. He was almost above suspicion and almost free to come and go as he pleased. Even if he hadn't come up with the last details of his escape, he was sure he would think of something when the opportunity presented itself. Rene's instructions had determined the route he was to take. He suspected that Janet Ryan and Antoine La Riviere might be headed that way. This meant he could appear to be leading the chase, always the loyal DHS operative.

CHAPTER
September 6, 2040

Each of the six groups were told that there were guides—members of an underground movement who wanted to reestablish a free press, change election laws so that money didn't win elections, and find ways to clean up the environment—who would meet them after they left the confines of the city. Each group was to assign someone to memorize directions and maps. No one in the group was skilled at this because they had not been out of the city and didn't know how to identify natural landmarks.

There was an air of anticipation. The escapes would be both dangerous and adventurous. Members of each group vacillated between the sense of danger and the sense of adventure. Group members were optimistic, believing that their group wouldn't be caught.

CHAPTER
September 6, 2040

Antoine was up early, waiting for Gene, who showed up about ten in the morning. The doorbell rang, and Antoine opened it cautiously, not knowing for sure who would be on the other side.

"Eh, Cuz. It's me. I've come to rescue your girlfriend."

"She's not my girlfriend," said Antoine.

"Okay. She's not your girlfriend. When are we leaving?"

"We take off at ten thirty tonight," said Antoine.

"Why can't we just leave now?" asked Gene.

"We decided that it would be best if all of us left at once. That way, if someone gets caught, the rest will be on the move, and it will be harder to track us all down," said Antoine. "Besides, it's a good night to go. The moon is full. The others have been instructed to stay in the shadows, but the light will stop them from getting lost."

"Do you think some will get caught?" asked Gene.

"Yeah, I do. I found out during my time here that sometimes white college students think they know more than they do. Sometimes they don't realize they have to be cautious," said Antoine.

"Did you have any trouble getting through the gates?"

"No. I just showed them my tribal ID and my driver's license and told them I was here to register for college—that I had to take some tests to see if I can handle it—and they believed me," said Gene. "What're we going to do for the rest of the day?"

"Well, I guess we'll just hang out here and go down to the café to eat," said Antoine.

"You sure that's a good idea?" asked Gene.

"Yeah. I don't think anybody is going to think we're suspicious," said Antoine. "I think we better check the backpacks to make sure there's enough stuff."

CHAPTER
September 6, 2040

At ten thirty, the full moon was barely visible because of the air quality. After the groups left the city and the air quality improved, the moon would provide enough light for them to travel easily.

The groups began their escapes. While Bill and Shirley headed south with Rick, Antoine circled around to the west of the city, while Gene drove to pick up Janet.

Antoine presented himself at each of the five gates through which he needed to pass. As he approached the first gate, he greeted the guard.

"Let me see some ID," said the guard. Antoine handed him his temporary resident license, his driver's license, and his tribal ID. "Where are you going at this hour?" asked the guard.

"I'm going home. My mom is sick, and I want to see her to see how she's doing," said Antoine.

"Why now?" asked the guard.

"I just found out today. My cousin came down from the rez and told me. It took me a while to talk to my professors and pack," said Antoine, indicating his backpack. "Besides, it's a nice night. The moon will give me enough light."

The guard said, "Okay. I'll pass you through and let the other guards know. Which gates are you going through?"

Antoine gave him the information and walked away, feeling relieved.

Gene knocked on the door of Janet's apartment. Janet looked through the peephole, saw Gene, and opened the door. When Gene walked in, he saw the cameras and had to think of something to say. "I thought I'd go out to the Mall of America. Do you want to come along?"

Janet didn't know what she was supposed to do. Her departure date was tomorrow. "Sure, I suppose there are some things I could pick up."

She walked down to the car with Gene. She had not met him before, but Antoine had described him to her. As they walked down the street, Gene said, "You have to leave now."

"But I have some things I need to take with me," she said.

"If you want to go back to take things with you, I'm sure that whoever watches you on that camera in your apartment will know that you're getting ready to go someplace and will come over to arrest you. There is a backpack in the back seat that Antoine left for you. My car is in the alley up ahead. You are to get into the trunk. I will drive you as far as I can into Wisconsin and drop you off as close as I can to the old trail. You'll have to get yourself the rest of the way. Even if we do everything right, one or both of us might die. I am not going to argue about any of this. I'm doing a favor for my cousin. "

Janet said no more. They walked outdoors and turned into the alley. When they got to the car, Janet waited while Gene opened the trunk. She climbed in, feeling desperate and confused. She bent her knees and lay on her side amid fishing poles, a smelly minnow bucket, and a mud-smeared blanket.

It was a hot, bumpy ride for the next hour or so. Gene eased the car off onto the Chippewa Falls exit when he saw cars massing on the interstate while helicopters flew in a holding pattern overhead. He stopped, opened the trunk, and gave Janet the backpack. "Take a drink of water now. You might not be able to stop to drink for a while. The trail is just across the road beyond those bushes. They'll hide you from any traffic. You'll be able to tell when you're on the path because it's worn down deep. Stay on it. When the sun starts rising, you'll come to a tree with a hollow. Climb in and sleep. When the moon starts rising in the sky, start moving again. Toward morning, you'll come to a place where there's a big log across the path. Just off to your right, the log spans a deep cave. Drop down into the cave and sleep. When you wake up, there should be some daylight left, and the sun will be on your left. You'll be going north. Don't try running too fast. You will make better time if you walk quickly, jog sometimes, and take a few breaks. There's enough food in here so that you should be able to eat a few times a day. Don't eat too much at one time or you might get sick. I gotta go."

Janet fastened the backpack over her shoulders and watched while Gene drove down the exit ramp and back up on the other side. She wanted to check out the backpack to see what was in it but thought she probably didn't have enough time.

She crossed the road and stepped through the brush. Her foot went suddenly down. She stumbled and realized that she was on the path!

She had traveled about a mile when she heard a funny noise and looked back toward the roadblock. She saw a helicopter descending. Several men came out of the helicopter, milling around. They must be after her!

She had been impatient over the inconvenience of leaving early and riding in the smelly trunk. Now she was starting to realize that she was in danger. She took a deep breath and started jogging north. Soon, the full moon rose over the trees, giving her more light. She kept moving, listening. As the moon rose higher in the sky and continued its path, Janet realized she was hungry. She dug in the backpack and found an energy bar. She unwrapped it and hesitated, thinking about how to dispose of the wrapper. She put it into the backpack and ate slowly. When she finished, she stood up, put on the backpack, and stepped onto the trail.

She tried running, but after she fell, Janet realized that a steady pace would be best. She settled in and started to feel some confidence. Maybe she could make it to the reservation. No one was following her now.

Soon she heard noises in the brush and realized that the noises were those of animals who hunted at night. She hoped they didn't see her as prey. She continued to walk, making good time through the night.

Gene drove deliberately back onto the interstate and stopped when he got to a roadblock. Two men with automatic weapons approached his car.

"Eh, man," he said. What's goin' on?"

"Where is your ID?" asked one of the men. Gene brought out his tribal enrollment card. He complained loud and often about enrollment cards. Nobody else except Indians had them. Today he was grateful he had one.

"Where are you coming from and where are you going?"

"I was just over in the Cities enrolling at the university. I got that done, so now I'm goin' home to finish up the ricing season."

The officer read the name and address on the enrollment card. "Why are you going this way when you could go up 35?" asked the officer.

"I like to drive. I go up 53 to 77 and then over. I stop and visit relatives along the way," said Gene.

"Have you seen anything unusual on your way over?" the other agent asked.

"No, nothin' I would say was unusual," said Gene

"Did you see anyone hitchhiking?" asked the officer.

"No, nothin' like that," said Gene.

One of the officers moved to the back of the car, while the other stood outside the driver's side door, his weapon trained on Gene. "Get out and bring your keys with you. We want to see what you have inside that trunk."

When Gene got out of the car, the officer patted him down. Gene walked to the back of the car and opened the trunk. The officers stepped back from the smell. "You can shut it now." Gene closed the trunk and waited for further instructions.

"Get back in your car. We're going to call ahead. If you don't get off at the 53 exit, you'll get stopped again, and nobody will be nice to you."

Gene got back in the car and drove off. When he reached the Highway 53 exit, he turned onto the ramp and headed north, glad to be out of this.

Dan, the leader of group five, saw someone walking parallel to the group. He approached the man. "Hey, are you our guide?"

"Yeah. Why don't all of you come over here?" The man lifted his arm and talked into a device strapped to his wrist. "I've got something here. Send me some assistance."

"Hey, who are you calling?" asked Dan.

"I'm calling some other members of our group to help us get out of here," said the man. "So you're headed up to Canada."

"Yeah. We think they'll give us asylum," said Dan.

"I've heard they do that. My group hasn't done much to have connections with other groups. We don't think it's safe," said the man, stalling for time.

"Our group hasn't done anything like this. I guess somebody thought that Homeland Security was about to round us up and question us as to our activities, so we decided we needed to leave," said Dan.

"Sorry, but there's been a change in plans," said the man.

"Hey! What's this?" said Dan, as the group was surrounded by Homeland Security agents.

"Sorry, guys. You're busted," said the man.

Dan and the other group members were handcuffed and taken to Homeland Security headquarters, where they were questioned with promises of release if they divulged names and plans. The captured group members were asked specifically about Antoine and Janet. No one seemed to have met Janet, even though they had read the stories she brought back from the reservation. They had no information about escape routes taken by either Janet or Antoine.

After they talked, the group members were jailed. There would be a trial with guilty verdicts for treason. With the capture of the group, the Homeland Security Office building was locked down, and Hal Emerson was called in from his apartment.

Maps were studied. Teams were sent to areas outside the city where it was believed that the escapees would have gone. Many were on foot, and some were traveling by boat.

Homeland Security assumed that Antoine and Janet would be leaving together, and agents, helicopters, and drones were dispatched to the seldom-used eastward route out of the city.

By the time the Homeland Security agents had questioned the group members they had captured, Antoine was out of the city and into a wooded area where he could hide if needed.

CHAPTER
September 7, 2040

Cindy woke up just as the sun was beginning to shine through the back window of the station wagon. It took her a while to realize that she wasn't at home.

"Mom," she said. Cindy started crying. "Mom, where are we?"

Shirley pulled herself awake and turned around. Cindy and Jimmy had been sleeping on the second row of seats. "We're going on a trip," she said.

"I have to go to the bathroom," Cindy whined.

Shirley looked at Bill. "I'll pull over as soon as I see a gas station," he said.

They pulled into a convenience store and restaurant just off I-90 in South Dakota. By this time, everyone in the station wagon was awake. They all got out to use the restrooms. When they came back, they found some young men going through the vehicle.

Bill and Rick approached the van. "What are you doing?" Rick said.

"We are looking to see what you got. If we can use it, we'll take it." One of the young men pulled the punching bag out. "Hey, do you suppose they got money in here?"

"We heard on the news that there were some people escaping. I'll bet you're them," said a tall blond with stringy hair. "I'll bet you stuffed money in this. It's heavy."

Jimmy came running up. Shirley grabbed at his shirt to hold him back and missed.

"That's my Homeland Security Youth Corps punching bag. Do you see the Arabs on it? That's mine, and I don't want you touching it!" yelled Jimmy. He grabbed at the punching bag.

"You're in that youth corps?" asked the young man.

"Yeah. I won a trip to Montana. We're going out there so I can go to camp to find out how the survivalists undermine our country. They also have orientation camps for my sister so she's ready to join when she's old enough." Jimmy said.

"Hey, guys. These folks are patriots. Let's leave them alone. They haven't got anything worth taking." The young men backed away.

Shirley hurried the kids into their seats. "I'm hungry," said Cindy. "Why can't we eat in that restaurant?'

"We won't be eating in restaurants. We have food in the van. When we get to where we're going, you'll get regular food. Right now, we'll just pretend we're having a picnic in the van," Shirley said, taking fried chicken out of the cooler.

Cindy said, "We can't eat fried chicken for breakfast."

"If Mom gives us fried chicken for breakfast, we can eat it," Jimmy said. "Mom is the boss. She makes the rules."

"Mom, do we have to go to that camp with Jimmy? I don't want to go. I just want to go home."

"We're going to a new home, Cindy," Shirley said.

"I want to go back to our old home," said Cindy.

"Why do you want to go back there?" asked Jimmy.

"I want to go back there because our teacher said we would get into trouble if we didn't stay where we're supposed to stay."

Bill came into the conversation. "Cindy, we're going someplace where there's a lot of people who didn't want to stay where other people told them to stay. We'll get a house there. We can live there, and none of us will have to wear masks again."

Shirley left the conversation to Bill. She said to Jimmy, "That was quite a show you put on back there."

Jimmy grinned. "I thought it was worth a try." He leaned forward and said to Rick, "How much longer?"

"We'll be there by tomorrow morning, unless we run into trouble."

CHAPTER
September 7, 2040

As the escapes were taking place, Old Woman was welcoming her children and grandchildren who had come from Canada, aided by the LaPointe brothers. Old Woman enjoyed the many feasts held to welcome her family.

She was looking forward to her departure to the Spirit World. Old Woman gave away everything she owned, mostly books. Her children and grandchildren were given books that she had had since she was a child, along with pictures and manuscripts that told of family history. She spent most of her time with her family, who would stay until after the funeral.

The community was made aware of the escapes out of the city through Marvin Blackbear's dreams. When Marvin awakened on the morning of September 7, he sent Animosh to Sonia's house with a note: "My dream says that we can expect a young woman coming to us from the city. Our nephew Antoine will follow shortly after."

Sonia sent Joe to see Marvin. "Hey, Uncle. Your dream says that we're getting company," said Joe as he greeted Marvin.

"Yes. We need to be on the lookout. She will be running and probably very tired and hungry," said Marvin.

"Do you know when she is going to come?" asked Joe.

"No, I don't. I just know that my dream showed her running on the trail of the ancestors," said Marvin.

Even though Joe believed in the power of dreams, he didn't always believe in Marvin's dreams. He thought sometimes Marvin read too much into the vagaries of the dream stories. He didn't say this to Marvin. He didn't want to be disrespectful.

CHAPTER

September 7, 2040

Early in the morning, Janet heard noises above her. She looked up and saw a drone. *It must be looking for me.* She stood for a moment, trying to figure out how to hide from it. She heard a screech, looked up, and saw a large bird attacking the drone. It took the drone in its claws and ripped into it. Pieces of the drone fell to the ground.

That must be an eagle, she thought. I hope it destroyed the drone before it identified my location.

Janet found a space in a hollow tree trunk and crawled in, tired and hungry. She found some packaged food and began to rip open the package, taking it in her teeth. Some of the mixture of dried fruits and nuts spilled onto the ground. She crawled around, searching the area with her hands. She got most of it and hoped that no one would stop to look for her there. She drank from the water bottle, lay down on the dead leaves, and slept. When she awakened, the moon was rising in the east.

Janet ate again. She wondered if there were more drones looking for her. She thought herself an easy target since the night sky was so bright. She sat and waited, listening for sounds that would tell her what to do next.

Hearing only the sounds of wildlife and dry leaves rustling in the slight breeze, Janet figured it was safe to start out again. She spotted two lights up ahead and crouched down. A doe walked out onto the trail. The lights were the reflection of the moonlight in her eyes. Janet stood and looked at the doe, who turned and jumped over some bushes. Two fawns followed her.

Janet walked into the brush and sat against a tree, resting for a few minutes. She started walking. Janet walked all night, seeing the dark outlines of animals, parents and offspring that had been born in the spring, crossing the trail in front of her. They paid little attention to her, as their interest lay in their hunt for food and water. It was as if they knew of the human battle going on around them and decided that it was best to stay out of it.

There was a soft breeze moving the branches on the trees. The leaves fluttered, while owls swooped down out of the branches, catching their meals. The sounds and the moonlight created a surrealistic effect. Janet hadn't seen anything like this in the virtual reality museums. The night was a world of its own, and she was trespassing.

September 8, 2040

As the moon began to fade, the light of dawn on the eastern horizon replaced what the moonlight had supplied during the night. Janet walked along, hoping to get in extra time. She was fairly confident that she could make the reservation without anything untoward happening when she heard the drones and the shouts of men and the sounds of bushes and underbrush being disturbed by running feet.

Janet looked around and saw no place to hide. She started to run, watching the ground so she wouldn't stumble. She had run about three miles when she started to give out, her breath coming in hard gasps. Her knees felt weak, and she stumbled along the uneven ground. She remembered Gene telling her about a place where she could hide. He said there was a cave hidden by a log, and she should reach it the second day. She didn't know where to look for it. The voices were closer, and it sounded like there were more of them.

She stopped and looked around, knowing she couldn't stop long enough to catch her breath. How can you tell one log from another? The only difference is some of them are still standing, and some of them have fallen over.

She kept on, jumping over branches and bushes that got in her way. Up ahead was a large log lying over the path. She gathered all of her energy and leaped over it. When she connected with land again, her feet slipped in some damp leaves, and she fell on her back. She lay for a little and realized that her head was hanging downward. She had just missed hitting the log.

Janet turned over on her stomach and reached her hands over her head. The cave was hidden just under the log. She didn't know if this was the place she was supposed to find or not, and she didn't know how far down the cave went into the earth. She didn't know how to find out except to drop her backpack into the hole. She had to make a quick decision, as the voices were almost on top of her.

When she heard the backpack hit bottom, she knew it hadn't fallen far. Janet crawled up to the hole and dropped in just as a search party reached the other side of the log.

"She can't be much farther. Fan out along this trail and keep following it. We've almost got her."

Janet crouched in the darkness. She reached behind, checking to see what was there. She found empty space and a continuation of the damp, cold rock floor. She heard a low growl and something shuffling in front of her. She didn't move.

As her eyes adjusted to the darkness, Janet saw three dark shapes moving on the opposite wall about twenty feet away. Janet recognized them from the virtual reality wildlife museum. A mother bear and two cubs stared back at her. She froze. She couldn't crawl out of the hole, and she didn't think she could share it with the bears. *It will be better to die at the paws of a mother bear than at the hands of Homeland Security interrogators*, she thought.

She turned slowly. The back wall of the cave was about ten feet behind her. The walls to either side were about twenty feet apart. The cave was a good hiding place. Its sturdy rock walls and ceiling told Janet that she didn't have to worry about it caving in.

She had no idea what else she could do, and even though she shivered in the cool and damp air, Janet felt safe. The mother bear didn't seem interested in her.

Janet heard male voices above her. They hadn't left the area.

"Hey, there's a hole here. Maybe she's hiding down there. Drop something down and see how far it falls."

Janet heard the thump of an item covered with cellophane that rustled when the item hit the ground. The mother bear growled.

Above her, Janet heard, "Hey, did you hear anything down there?"

"No. Jim, why don't you throw down a rope and hook it to that tree over there. Climb down in and see what's in the hole."

Janet was trapped. She thought of walking over to the opening and letting them know she was there. Then she realized the bear and her cubs were in the cave as well. She heard the thud of the rope as it hit the ground.

The mother bear got up, growling. She walked over to the entrance just as human legs dangled over the hole. Her growl got louder. Someone said, "What was that?"

The legs disappeared. "There is something down there, all right, but it isn't human."

"Jim, get your gun. We'll shoot it. Then we can go down in the hole."

"Why do you want to shoot it? If that thing won't let us in the hole, do you think anyone else could be down there?"

"Well, she's got to be somewhere."

"I'll give you that. And she sure will know where we are when she hears the sound of the gun. Pull up that rope. We can probably use it later."

Janet heard the voices retreating. She sat, her head down, looking over at the bear, who continued to stand beneath the entrance to the cave. The bear kept watch over the entrance for a long time, dividing her attention between the hole overhead and Janet, who didn't move. The bear moved over to the wall of the cave, several feet closer to Janet than she was when Janet first entered.

The cubs moved over to their mother, who gathered them next to her. All three lay down on the cold floor. The mother bear exhaled loudly, dropped her head, and went to sleep. The cubs followed shortly after. Janet followed suit. She wanted to get more rest so she could resume her journey. It was daylight, and she was tired, so she slept. The bears, having just returned to their home from a meal of berries and fish, did the same.

Janet awakened when she heard the bears moving around. She watched as the mother picked up each of her cubs and placed them on the ground outside the hole. Then she placed her paws on the edge of the hole and lifted herself up.

Janet waited until she couldn't hear them again. Moonlight was shining into the hole. Janet walked to the cave entrance above her and tried to reach the ground above. She couldn't make it. She three her backpack out, crouched, and leapt. Her hands landed on the ground. She reached out and grabbed a branch on the log and pulled herself up. When she cleared the hole, she rolled over and stood on solid ground.

The only noises she heard were the night sounds. She walked for a couple of hours and realized she hadn't eaten. She hadn't wanted to eat in front of the bears because she would probably lose her food supply.

Janet stopped and sat down against a tree alongside the path. She didn't know how far she was from the reservation. She was hungry and weak, and the dirt she had acquired on her journey was making her uncomfortable. She found an energy bar and ate slowly, pretending it was a big piece of fry bread with grease dripping down the corners of her mouth. Eating didn't seem to help. Instead, it awakened her stomach, which rumbled for more food. Janet drank a bottle of water and hoped the two bottles she had left would last her.

She walked along the path, stumbling now and then, running on what was left of her dwindling determination to survive the journey. She was glad that the path was so well worn.

The moon was fading. She would have to find another place to sleep soon. She was starting to fall asleep on her feet when she heard noises behind and above her. The men were coming back, and she heard helicopters. They must be searching the area again.

Up ahead, she noticed lights. Janet stopped and didn't know what to do next, thinking the lights were those of a command station set up by the Homeland Security search mission. She stumbled and started to cry. "I might as well just go on ahead and let myself get caught."

September 9, 2040

Janet walked into a clearing lit with floodlights hanging from trees. There was a house surrounded by signs that Janet couldn't read. She saw an old man with wild white hair sitting on the wooden steps of the house. When he saw her, he got up and ran toward her, grabbing her before she fell.

"Jeremiah!" Levi called out. "She's here. Come help me get her into the house and into the tunnel. We don't have any time."

Jeremiah ran to help his grandfather. He picked Janet up and headed into the house.

"You'd best get her down into the tunnel and feed her down there. We don't have time to do anything for her in the house. They'll be here any minute," said Levi.

Levi pushed a heavy cabinet away from the wall. Behind it was a small box that looked like it was for electric breakers. He pushed a switch, and a rumble could be heard coming from someplace in the house. "It was a good idea to put the entrance in that bedroom. Most folks would probably think it's under one of the rugs in here. If they come in and start looking, it'll take them a while to figure out they've run into a dead end. If they do find the tunnel entrance, you'll have a good start. Get down there now. I'll go out in the yard and act crazy. That'll keep them out of the house for a while."

Levi ran his hands through his hair, making it stand on end. He was wearing the work clothes he had worn the day before. He looked disheveled, and his eyes were wide.

Levi ran into the yard, waving his arms just as the Homeland Security search team came into the yard. He could see the helicopters trying to find someplace to settle just beyond the trees that surrounded the clearing.

"Get out of here!" he yelled. "You got no business here. We mind our own business. There ain't nothin' here for you," he yelled, his show of bravado covering his fear. Levi thought that the men invading his yard and his house would beat him, maybe even shoot him. He was afraid that they would burn his house, the house he and Sarah had worked so hard to build. He was expecting to die.

Hal Emerson was at the front of the line as the men ran into Levi's yard. He was afraid that this old crackpot would kill him. He put his hands in the air. "Hey, old timer, we don't want to hurt you. There is a woman we're looking for. We know she came this way. Have you seen her?"

"No. I ain't seen anybody. I just got up. I got chores to do. I have to feed my animals."

Hal looked around the yard. He saw a chicken coop and a small barn. There were three dogs in the yard barking, adding to the confusion. Behind him came the heavily armed Homeland Security search team. Hal kept his hands raised. "Look, old timer, we don't want to hurt you. I don't think you know what's going on here."

"Yes, I think I do know what's going on. You're huntin' humans. I don't want you to hurt me, but you ain't gonna get me to help you," said Levi.

"We are going to go into your house and look around," Hal said firmly. "When we find what we're looking for, we'll go."

"I don't think I can stop you," said Levi. "I don't have guns. I live here by myself, and there's nobody hidin' out here to ambush you."

Hal walked to the house, followed by the other members of the Homeland Security search team. "We aren't here to destroy anything," Hal said. "We are going to see what we can find in this house. When we're done, we'll leave."

The men walked into the house, taking their lead from Hal's silent directions as he pointed to different rooms. The men lifted rugs, looked under beds and in cupboards. Hal stood staring at the big cupboard in the kitchen. He pushed hard on it. It moved, and he saw the electrical box. Hal opened the metal door and began pushing switches. Each switch he pushed shut something off. Then he pushed one and heard the movement of the wall in the bedroom. He walked over to look and saw the open panel and the stairs beyond. He yelled, "Hey, I found something."

Hal went through the entrance that had been exposed when the panel slid to one side and climbed down the wooden stairs that led to the tunnel. He stood in the tunnel, looked around, and thought about the best strategy to bring in the escapee. He didn't know what to expect in the tunnel. He thought about bringing the old man down with him. That wouldn't do much good. The old man moved slowly. He probably couldn't be counted on to help in any way.

Hal walked down the tunnel and noticed that it came to a solid wall where it branched off to the right and left. By this time, the tunnel entry was filled with Homeland Security agents. They were yelling out suggestions. Hal said, "Follow me. We'll figure this out as we go."

Hal pointed to the right. "You follow Major Sutherland," he said to a group of men clustered behind the major. "The rest of you, come with me," he said as he hurried to the left tunnel branch. The ten men behind Hal followed him for about five minutes before they heard and felt a large thump at the other end of the T. They could hear the screams of the men with Major Sutherland. Hal ordered two of the men to go back down the tunnel to see what could be done and to report back to him.

They came back after ten minutes, faces white with shock and dust. "They're stunned. It must have been a bomb but one not intense enough to kill them. We can still get out by going back the same way we came," said one of the men.

"We aren't going back," said Hal. "We are going to find the escapee and bring her back. We can't do that if we go back to the tunnel entrance."

"Maybe that old man will tell us where the tunnel comes out," said another one of the agents.

"That old man isn't going to tell us anything. Have you read his file? He would probably consider it an honor to be interrogated and killed. His wife's grave is in the backyard," said Hal.

"Sir," said one of the agents, "I didn't say he had to be killed."

"What do you think we would do with him when we finished with him?" said Hal. "What do you think we do with most of the people we bring in for interrogation? We're at war. We have been at war against terrorism for about thirty-five years, officially. We aren't any closer to winning it now than we were. If you people think that we're going to let any of these people go that we're rounding up, you're dreaming. You're in the service of your country, and you get paid damn good money to round people up so we can question them and kill them. If any of you want to quit, I suggest you do it now because I don't have time for this."

Hal turned around and jogged down the tunnel. An idea was formulating. He figured there were false branches of the tunnel. Each one was probably booby-trapped. He could send some men down a branch when he came to it. If there was no explosion, he would follow them. There was a probability that he could come to the end of the tunnel and get out. The agents would be stunned by the booby traps. He could come out of the tunnel and head for Canada. It didn't matter anymore if he captured the escapee and won accolades. The eventual outcome would be the same. He would get to a certain age, and he would be retired and sent to a nursing home.

Levi heard the first explosion. He winced. He knew the agents were stunned and would probably come back through the tunnel to the house. He walked outside to Sarah's grave. "Well, they brought it to us. I thought I could keep this mess away from here. I wanted this place to be a place of peace, a place where you could rest.

"I built the tunnel after they killed you. I built it because I knew that it was a good idea to have an escape route. I didn't know if I would have to use it or not. I figured eventually someone could use it.

"I wanted to put bombs in it that would kill people. I didn't because I knew you would object. So there are people in the tunnel, and small bombs are going off that will stun them. They're Homeland Security agents. Remember when we talked about Homeland Security? I heard you say that that department could easily get out of hand. Well, it has. After the folks in the tunnel come to, they'll probably come back through the tunnel and up through the house.

"I don't know what they'll do to me. I don't much care anymore. It feels good to have committed an act of civil disobedience. I haven't used that term for a while. If they kill me, I'll be with you. If they don't kill me, I'll have a few more years with our family. I doubt that people around here will think I'm crazy anymore. Marvin and I, the two crazies, are just crazy enough to save a life." Levi sat by the grave for a long time. Every once in a while, he felt the ground shake underneath him as another bomb went off.

When he heard the last of the bombs, Levi stood up, picked up a duffel, looked at Sarah's headstone, and said, "I think I'll make myself invisible. I'm going to take a hike up toward the reservation. I'll see if I can find a place to hide for a while."

Jeremiah got a good lead over the Homeland Security agents. When he went into the tunnel, he had Janet slung over his shoulder with the food and other supplies on a pack on his other shoulder. He traveled about a mile, talking to her to wake her up. When she awakened, her eyes were glassy, and she looked like she was unaware of what was going on. Jeremiah felt her stirring and stopped, lowering her to the floor.

Jeremiah pulled some canned food out of the pack, opened it, and waved it under Janet's nose. She pulled up into a sitting position, grabbed the can, and stuck her hand in, eating with her fingers. She gulped down the bottle of water Jeremiah gave her, looking at him to see what was going to happen next.

"You have to stand up, and you have to walk. The Homeland Security agents are behind us. It's going to take them a while to catch up with us, but they will if we don't hurry. I will take you to the end of the tunnel and point you in the right direction. I can't take you all the way. When you get on the path, I'm going to go into the woods. I hope neither one of us gets caught," said Jeremiah.

Janet struggled to her feet. She felt like she was going to throw up from eating and drinking too fast. "Can I have some more of that food to take with me?"

"You won't need it. You don't have that much farther to go. There are two bottles of water in your pack and a couple of energy bars. If you take any of that stuff out of your pack, make sure you don't leave any wrappers or bottles around. Right now, those guys following us are confused and aren't able to move very fast. They will be able to follow you by the garbage you leave behind." Jeremiah held Janet's arm and pulled her along. Behind him, he heard the explosions and felt the tunnel shake. He knew there wasn't much time.

"What was that?" Janet asked.

"That's my grandfather's escape insurance," he said.

"What does that mean?" asked Janet.

"My grandfather rigged the tunnel with bombs, so when people are down here and don't know where they're going, they will set off a bomb," said Jeremiah.

"You mean there are bombs that kill people?" asked Janet.

"No. The bombs aren't that strong, just strong enough to stun them. Every explosion increases your chances of living. My grandfather decided to build the tunnel after my grandmother died. He dedicated the last several years to this tunnel. He believed that a time would come when we would need to use it to save someone's life. So you came along, and we're saving your life. I don't know what you're going to do next. You probably don't either," said Jeremiah.

They came to an end where the only exit was up a ladder. "This is where we go in different directions. When you get to the top, step out and turn to your left. You will be on the same path you took to get here. Keep going. It will take you to Marvin's house. We don't think the Homeland Security guys will follow you onto the reservation. If they do, I hope you will realize that Marvin is risking his life for you too," said Jeremiah.

The sun was coming up on her right as Janet walked down the path. She was weak and stumbled over the tree roots and other obstacles that lay on the path. She sat down, took off her backpack, and found an energy bar. She unwrapped it and stuffed the paper in the backpack, then leaned against a tree trunk. She ate, stood, and stumbled forward. She came to the edge of a clearing, unaware of her whereabouts. She stumbled, fell, and hit her head on a tree root. She didn't get up.

The Homeland Security agents were starting to question Hal's authority. They had come to five tunnel branches. There had been three explosions. There were two agents left. One spoke up. "Why are we sent off in another direction when we come to branches?"

Hal stopped and turned around. "I am the senior officer on this expedition. It is my job to make the decisions."

"The decisions you're making are hurting us," said the agent.

"Have you read the 'Duties of a Homeland Security Agent in Pursuit of an Escapee' in your manual lately? What does it say?" Hal asked the man.

The officer said, "I read the manual right before we were assigned to this mission, sir."

"What does it say?" said Hal.

"It says that we are to follow the orders of a senior officer and sacrifice our lives for the American people. It says that senior officers are to be protected, and the lives of senior officers count more than our lives. It says that we are heroes if we give up our lives to protect our country and the American people," said the officer.

"That should answer your questions," Hal said.

They came to another branch in the tunnel. One of the men said, "Sir, may I make a suggestion?"

"What is it?" asked Hal.

"Can we flip coins to see who goes?" asked the man.

Hal said, "Both of you will go. You will look out for anything in the tunnel that might indicate the presence of a bomb."

The men disappeared down the tunnel. Hal was alone. He continued to walk. Ten minutes passed. Hal heard another explosion. When he came to the stairs leading to the exit, he climbed up, lifted a hatch, and peered out. He wasn't sure where he was going.

The Homeland Security agents stumbled up the stairs and into Levi's house. They carried their weapons, waiting to confront the old man. The house was empty.

Nick, an agent from the Chicago district of Homeland Security, took charge. "Okay, guys, let's go outside and take some deep breaths."

The men stumbled outside into bright sunlight. They were surrounded by trees that were starting to turn color. They were startled by the light, color, blue skies, and clean air. Each thought about the difference between there and the city.

George, an agent, as if reading their minds, said, "Just remember, we pay a price for our lifestyle and technology." George turned to Nick. "Now what?"

Nick said, "We need to get back to the main office. Did anyone see Hal in there?"

He was met with a chorus of no's.

Nick called for helicopters to return to Levi's deserted house to pick him up, along with the rest of the agents.

The helicopters took them to agency headquarters in Minneapolis, where they reported to the agency head, Dennis, who called the Homeland Security secretary.

"Sir, we have a situation here. Hal Emerson was out on the roundup. He's disappeared."

"I thought the roundup wasn't until the end of September," he said.

"Well, the groups left early. One group was caught by one of our agents and taken in for questioning. We sent agents into the field to run down the other groups. Hal led some agents into northern Wisconsin. They came upon a tunnel and went in. The agents apparently tripped some stun bombs. When they came to, Hal wasn't around. The agents said he was pretty directive. They think he set them up to run into some of the bombs."

"Make sure you document all of this," he said.

Yes, sir. I'll have the agents write up reports and send them to you immediately," said Dennis.

"I think you'd better contact our operatives in Detroit, Sault Ste. Marie, and Duluth and have them send out patrols to look for suspicious activities," he said.

"Will do. What do you think happened to Hal?" asked Dennis.

"I think we have a touchy situation here. Either he was injured or captured, or he decided to leave this great country of ours," he said.

"I never had any reason to doubt his loyalty," said Dennis. "How do we play this if we can't find him? He's got a head start."

"If we find him, we have to determine why he disappeared. If he was captured by terrorists, he's a hero. If he was trying to escape, we kill him and make up a story that makes him a hero and give him a hero's funeral. Same thing if we don't find him. We'll say that he died in the line of duty; he's a hero, and we have a funeral for him," the secretary said.

"Yes, sir," said Dennis. "I'll keep you posted."

Hal saw a break in the trees and brush, a barely discernible path over to his left. To his right was another path that looked heavily traveled. He decided to take the path to his left, as this route would provide him with cover. He knew he was probably near the reservation and wanted to get through it without being seen. He jogged along at a steady pace. He came a lake and followed along the shore. He moved into the bushes, keeping the path in sight, and passed by an assortment of houses ranging from birch bark wigwams to old A-frames, log cabins, and HUD homes from the last century.

When he passed the dwellings, Hal moved back onto the path that ran parallel to an old blacktop road. He followed it, moving north. He was surrounded by trees and felt safe with the cover they offered him. He continued north, stopping to eat and rest. When night came, he found a pine tree with limbs that swept the ground. He crawled in and slept.

In the morning, he set out again. He was tired, as he had slept fitfully. He came to a roadway going east and followed it for a few miles until a northbound road intersected. He took it, knowing that any road going north in this area would probably take him to Lake Superior. Rene had told him to get to the lake at the northernmost point in the area. He hoped this would do it. He continued north, stopping to rest and eat, and spent another night sleeping in the woods.

In the morning, he continued, starting to feel the strain of the trek. He had had little to eat, just some bars he had in his backpack. His clothes were dirty. A shower would feel good right about now.

The sun was directly overhead when he saw a body of water up ahead. He came to a building with a sign that said, "LaPointe Brothers and Company." He walked into the building, startled when he saw a large, dark-skinned, bearded man with a scar running through the beard.

Basil greeted him. "Eh, you need a ride someplace?"

CHAPTER
September 9, 2040

Marvin had had another of his dreams. In it, he saw two figures running through a tunnel. He had awakened to the sound of explosions in his dream. When he fell asleep again, the dream continued. He saw one figure running on a path. He awakened to find the sun coming in his window. Animosh was whining to go out.

Marvin pulled himself to the edge of the bed and dressed. When he finished, he got into the wheelchair.

"Animosh, what is wrong with you? Why can't you just go out your door?"

Marvin followed the dog out of the house and watched from the deck as Animosh ran down the path toward a hump laying on the edge of the yard. Animosh stood beside the hump, barking, as Marvin wheeled himself as close to the edge of the deck as he could. He realized that the hump was a body.

"Animosh, come here. This is the day that we save a life. This is what my dreams have been telling me." Marvin wheeled himself into the house, got a pencil and paper, wrote a note, and attached it to Animosh's collar. "Go to Sonia," Marvin said, pointing the way with his chin and lips. As Animosh flew down the path, Marvin sat waiting for help to come, watching the body, looking for signs of life.

Marvin had known that something would be happening yesterday when he heard the helicopters. The only times in his life that he had heard helicopters, it meant trouble. The old feelings came back to him—feelings about Vietnam. He knew he was safe, but the feelings told him that something bad could happen.

Sonia heard Animosh's bark. She turned and called, "Joe, Marvin needs you. You better get Mike too."

Joe came out of the kitchen and bent over to pet Animosh. He read the note. "Come quick. My dream is happening. Levi's tunnel is a success."

"Can't he just say what he wants?" Joe asked.

"He's telling you he is right, and he and Levi aren't crazy."

"So I should go to his house for that?" asked Joe.

"I don't think this is a time to question your elder. Marvin wouldn't send Animosh over here if it weren't important."

Joe headed out of the backyard toward Mike's house. Animosh stopped and barked, beckoning him to come to Marvin's.

"Animosh, come this way. We're going to pick up Mike."

Mike was dressed and drinking a first cup of tea when Joe and Animosh arrived. He opened the door when he heard the dog's excited barking. Stepping out, he bent over to pet Animosh. "Eh, what are we supposed to do this morning?"

"Uncle sent Animosh to my house. He wrote another one of his cryptic notes. My mother says it must be important, and she thought I should get you."

Mike said, "Lead the way, Animosh!"

Marvin had been sitting on his deck for about twenty minutes when he heard Animosh coming through the woods, barking to announce his arrival. Joe and Mike jogged behind. Marvin pointed in the direction of the hump at the edge of the yard with his chin and his lips. "Hey, nephews. We have company!"

Animosh raced to the body and stood, waiting for Mike and Joe.

Mike bent over and picked Janet up.

"Is she alive?" Joe asked.

"I think so. I felt some movement when I was lifting her. Let's get her into the house so we can see what she needs."

Mike carried Janet into the house, followed by Joe, Marvin, and Animosh. "Where should I put her, Uncle?" asked Mike.

"Put her in that last bedroom," said Marvin, pointing with his chin and his lips.

"Hey, Uncle," Joe said. "You are the best pointer I know. You put so much into your pointing nobody can mistake what you mean."

"Nephew, I had to go underground with my pointing when I served my country in the military. I had to point like white men did. I said that when I came back, I would never take Indian pointing for granted. I'm glad you appreciate it."

Mike laid Janet on the bed, removing her backpack and shoes. Her skin felt cold and clammy. Mike pulled a blanket around her and walked out of the room.

Joe said, "Now what do we do? We can't just leave her here."

"I don't think she should go to your house, Nephew," said Marvin. "Everyone is too busy getting ready for ricing. We'll keep her here."

"Who's going to take care of her?" asked Joe.

"I have an idea," said Marvin as he wheeled himself to the table and began writing another message.

Animosh stood expectantly by Marvin's side as Marvin fastened the note to his collar. Marvin pointed with his lips and his chin so decisively that Joe turned to Mike and said, "See what I mean?" They laughed.

"Animosh, get Josie." Animosh raced down the path and into the woods.

"Does he understand everything you tell him?" asked Mike.

"He not only understands, he listens, and he does what I tell him. That's more than I can say for the two of you when you were kids.

"Josie can take care of her and see what she might need. She's a midwife," said Marvin.

Animosh raced down the trail, aware that his recent trips had to do with that woman he had discovered in Marvin's yard. Marvin had transferred his sense that he was to do something important to Animosh, who pronounced his importance when he barked. It was good to be important.

CHAPTER
September 9, 2040

After he left Janet on the trail, Jeremiah followed the deer path to his parents' house. Josie, his mother, ran to meet him when she saw him walking into the yard. Relieved to see her son, she called for one of the younger children. "Go over to Jeremiah's house and let them know he's here. Tell them I'll fix him something to eat."

"Mom, I should go home to eat," said Jeremiah.

"Let me do something for you. I'm your mother. I have worried about you ever since I watched you get involved with your grandfather and that tunnel. Your wife needs to know that you are all right. You can stay here, eat, rest, and then go home."

Jeremiah had heard that tone of voice coming from his mother very few times in his life. Each time he heard it, he knew not to argue.

He ate and lay down on the bed in his old bedroom and slept.

When he awakened, he sat at the kitchen table with his mother. "I don't know if that girl is going to make it. I kept hearing things behind us in the tunnel. I think someone was in the tunnel, following us. The girl was in pretty rough shape by the time she got to Grandpa's house. I gave her something to eat, and I stopped after each explosion to give her something to drink. There were a few times I thought she was asleep on her feet."

"You did what you promised you would do. If you had taken her any farther, you may have been captured. Whatever her problem is, it isn't your fight," said Josie.

"Grandpa says it is. He says that anyone who is trying to run away from the outside deserves our help. He says we are honoring Grandma's memory."

"I think we do any number of things to honor your grandmother's memory," said Josie. "You have a family. Your grandmother would want you to live to raise your children. She would want you and your wife to have at least as many years together as she and your grandfather did."

"Grandpa says that what happens to one of us happens to all of us."

"That woman hasn't got that far to go to reach Marvin's. Even if she collapses before she gets there, there are enough people and enough dogs on that trail that someone would find her soon enough," said Josie.

Josie heard Animosh before she saw him. His alarmed barking brought Dan in from the garden. Animosh became airborne as he neared the porch, leaping and skidding to a stop, averting a crash with the front door.

"Josie," called Dan. "Bring him some water. He's been running hard."

Dan handed the message to Josie as she put a bowl of water down for Animosh. His long tongue lapped frantically, splashing water around him.

"This message says they want me to come and look after the girl. She's at Marvin's house. I have to leave a note for the other kids to let them know where I've gone. I guess you and Jeremiah had better come along. Get your weapons. This is becoming our problem."

Animosh finished drinking and waited to accompany the three back to Marvin's. It gave him time to catch his breath. These people understood him and were coming to help. He would run ahead and take a shortcut through the woods to warn Marvin. As the men came out of the house with rifles and pistols, Animosh took a running jump off the porch and disappeared into the woods.

When he reached his home, he ran up on the porch, braced his feet to help him stop, and was aided by the screen door. The collision caused the screen door to rattle against the doorframe.

Dan, Josie, and Jeremiah climbed up the steps to the deck and found Animosh picking himself up. "Hey, Animosh," said Dan. "Where did you run off to? Did you go chasing a deer?"

"Animosh won't do that when he's off on a mission," said Marvin. "Come here, boy." He patted Animosh's head, wheeled over to Animosh's water dish, picked it up, filled it with water from a hand pump, and set it down for the dog.

After drinking, Animosh went to the door, let himself out, and lay down on the deck. It was a good place to sleep, and the odors carried on the wind would come to him easily, alerting him to any danger or squirrels.

Janet slept as Josie leaned over her, checking her vital signs. Janet's breathing was slow and regular. She had superficial scratches and small tears on her hands and arms. Her clothes were torn and covered with dirt.

When Josie removed Janet's boots, she turned them upside down, allowing leaves and twigs acquired on the journey to fall out. Josie covered her and left the room.

"I'm going to let her sleep. When she wakes, I'm sure she will be hungry. What do you have for her to eat?"

"There is some wild rice soup in the icebox," said Marvin.

"We'll be gone until evening," said Joe. "Can you stay until we get back?"

"Yes, I can stay," said Josie. "I think she would feel better waking up to a house with another woman."

Marvin objected. "She knows me. We have talked. She would be okay. Animosh will stay with you and give you any protection you may need."

Josie nodded.

CHAPTER 63

September 10, 2040

The days passed. The sun didn't reach as high into the sky as it had in June and July, and it set earlier. The leaves were starting to turn, their colors replacing the colors of the flowers, whose petals had dried up and fallen to the ground. The air felt different. Even the hot, humid days had a slight chill on the outer edges. Flocks of geese and ducks formed their V shapes and headed south, calling their farewells. The wild rice ripened, thick heads hanging heavy on their stalks. It was ricing season.

Old Woman, having spent the time with her children and grandchildren, welcomed the sleep that brought the spirits who were preparing her for her journey. She noticed that she tired more easily. It was time to go ricing.

Joe loaded up the truck he and Mike used for carrying heavy loads and drove himself and Old Woman to the rice beds. Old Woman sat under a tree while Joe untied the boat from the roof of the cab. He set the boat on the shore, laying the knockers on the floor.

When Joe had everything in order, he helped Old Woman into the boat. She sat, picked up the knockers, and tapped ripe rice into the bottom of the boat while Joe pushed the boat forward with the long pole. The two said little to each other, enjoying the moment.

When the sun was high in the sky, Joe poled the boat to shore, helped Old Woman to the tree, and emptied the rice into sacks, piling them in the bed of the pickup.

"Old Woman, we can quit now if you want. We have a lot of rice."

"No, I don't want to stop. I feel good. The sun is warm, there is a lot of rice, and I enjoy your company."

They ate the sandwiches Sonia had sent with them and took the boat out, neither one talking about Marvin's dream. By the time the sun was hanging low on the western horizon, the boat was full again.

"It's time to quit, Grandmother," Joe said, poling the boat to shore. He helped Old Woman out of the boat and to the tree where she had sat earlier. It took him almost an hour to sack up the rice and put it in the truck.

Old Woman sat watching him, tired and filled with a sense of accomplishment. She noticed that it was getting dark, even though she could still see the sun in the sky. Her chin dropped to her chest, and her eyes closed. She struggled to get up. She heard a voice; it sounded familiar, but she couldn't quite place it.

"No, Rachel. Don't try to use that body. It's all worn out. You've been in there for a long time. You always did use things up until there wasn't anything left anymore. It's time to leave. If you stay too long, you'll get stuck here."

Old Woman felt two spirits lifting her up and out of her body. She felt light. She didn't want to leave Joe. He had too much work to do, but the spirits were pulling her along.

"You'll get to come back, Rachel. They will have a funeral for you. We'll all come to the funeral. When it's over, we'll take you home."

Rachel was confused. These voices used the word home. She knew where her home was, and she knew they meant someplace else. It was dark, she couldn't see, and she knew she wasn't hearing their voices with her ears. She was sensing everything that they were telling her. She knew she needed to follow their advice because she didn't know where she was, and she didn't know what to do.

Joe walked over to her as he finished putting the rice in the truck. "Grandmother, I have to pack up the canoe. Then we'll be ready to go. Do you want to ride on top of the rice or do you want to ride in the cab?"

The silence following his words filled the air around him. Joe walked over to Old Woman's body. He knelt down without speaking, knowing that she wouldn't hear him.

Joe sat on the ground and took Old Woman's body in his arms. He began singing. An eagle flew overhead as tears ran down the furrows in Joe's face.

When Mike heard Joe's high-pitched singing, he followed the sound through the woods. "Old Woman is passing," he said aloud. "She said that she was going to pass on during ricing season, and today is the day."

He stopped when he saw Joe holding Old Woman's body, waiting for Joe to finish his song. He would help when it was needed. Mike looked up into the sky and saw many eagles gathering. He pulled tobacco out of his shirt and put it down under a tree.

He watched as Joe lifted his head, singing to the audience of eagles. Joe sang and held Old Woman's body for a long time. When he stopped, he sat cradling her in his arms, his head bowed, his face wet with tears. Mike picked up the canoe, tied it to the roof of the truck, and walked over to Joe.

"Eh. Give her to me. You get in the truck, and I will give her to you. I'll drive."

Joe stood and passed Old Woman's body to Mike, then got in the truck and extended his arms to receive Old Woman's body. The two men drove in silence, bringing Old Woman home one last time. Her spirit and those relatives and friends who had passed before her followed.

The family had eaten supper by the time Joe and Mike drove up. It was dark, and the children had gone to bed. Sonia saw Joe through the window, carrying Old Woman. She walked to the door and held it for him.

"Bring her into her room," she said.

Joe laid the worn out body on the bed, straightening her legs and arms. Sonia was pumping water into a bowl. "Bring some towels in there," she said to Mike.

Sonia washed Old Woman's body and dressed it in the outfit she had made, fastening the moccasins securely on the tiny feet so they wouldn't fall off during her journey.

After she finished, Sonia went into the kitchen and sat with Joe and Mike, who had just finished eating.

Joe looked up from his plate. "I should have quit at noon. She got too tired."

Sonia shook her head. "She stayed out as long as she wanted, and she brought us our wild rice for the next year. I doubt that she would have wanted to leave us in any other way." She looked at Mike. "Her family is over at Corrine's. Go over there and tell them she has passed."

Old Woman's spirit hovered over Sonia as Sonia washed the body. She was missing her friend. Old Woman was grateful for the life she had led. She had had many good friends, and she didn't know of anyone else she would rather have prepare her for her journey.

Old Woman was starting to realize that the normal physical human senses she was used to had left her. She had only what was known as a sixth sense—the ability to know what was happening, even though she couldn't see, hear, touch, taste, or smell it. Something was jangling below her. She thought something must be happening that needed her attention, but she didn't think she was experienced enough to do anything about whatever was going on.

CHAPTER 
September 14, 2040

Sonia had watched the sun come up. Today was a good day. Today was Old Woman's funeral. Sonia would be glad when all the people left. Even though her house would seem empty and she would miss her friend, there had been much to do.

After she prepared Old Woman, Joe and Mike carried the body to the old community center where the wake continued for four days.

Joe, Mike, and the children had piled the wood for the fire yesterday. They built a platform for Old Woman's body on poles just long enough to reach above the woodpile.

Today, the drums would come, people would gather around the fire, Joe would light the fire, and Old Woman would be cremated. Sonia wondered where Old Woman had gotten such an idea. She knew it didn't come from her people. Sonia thought it would be much easier to bury the body in the old community cemetery, but she would honor her friend's wishes.

Sonia heard the others stirring in the household as she started breakfast. The meal was small, as there would be a lot of food at the funeral.

Sonia helped the children get ready for the ceremony for Old Woman. Old Woman's family—her children, grandchildren, and great-grandchildren—walked along with Sonia and her great-grandchildren to the ceremonial grounds behind the old community center.

Fall had come early this year. The trees were clothed in variations of red, gold, yellow, and orange. The colors enhanced the cloudless blue sky. There was a breeze bringing the smell of the drying leaves and brush in the forest. It was the kind of day Old Woman favored. Sonia knew she would think of Old Woman often, and most when the days of autumn came like this one did.

In the middle of the ceremonial grounds was a huge pile of wood. Straddling the woodpile was a scaffold holding Old Woman's body. A fire had been started and was tended for four nights and four days to help her to pass to the Spirit World.

Old Woman's body had been on display in the community center for those four days. Members of her family and Sonia's family had been present all the time. People visited, laughed, cried, and ate during that time.

Today, the day of the funeral and her cremation, there would be no tears to hold her back from her journey. Her mourners needed to release her spirit so she could go home.

Old Woman's adopted community all turned out. There were people from other Ojibwe reservations who had come to pay their respects. People from the nearby white community had come. Many of them had known Old Woman when it had been safe for her to go into town.

Sonia hadn't expected the size of this crowd. She had the role of hostess and greeted friends and relatives, introducing them to Old Woman's family. As she made her way through the crowd, she wondered where Joe, Mike, and Marvin were.

Sonia was uneasy. She didn't know what lengths Homeland Security would go to apprehend someone, even though the federal government had promised no interference when the reservation had unplugged. Most of the men here had weapons they used for hunting. Marvin had conducted gun-safety lessons. There was an alarm system consisting of men and boys, and Animosh, of course, who would run from house to house if it looked like the community was in danger.

Today, the men and boys were here. Many of the boys had been fire keepers for Old Woman. Sonia hadn't seen Animosh at all today, nor did she hear Joe, Mike, and Marvin come into the crowd, as the sounds of the drums and the singers filled up the space, leaving no room for other sounds.

She craned her neck, looking over the crowd, and suddenly she was surrounded as Joe moved next to her and assembled Marvin's wheelchair. Mike placed him in the chair.

She said, "Where have you been? Where is Animosh?"

"He's standing guard at Marvin's. I think he's decided that he's supposed to protect Janet and Josie. He acts like he knows he's important," said Joe, grinning as he took his place with the drum. He began singing the song he had made the day Old Woman left her body. *Anishinaabe are adaptable*, he thought. *We have to be. Too many things happen all at the same time.*

The drums present to honor Old Woman's life drummed and sang for three hours. People danced, circling the body that rested above the woodpile as a medicine man offered tobacco to the Creator. At a time decided upon by no one in particular, the fire was lit.

The small flames, started with pieces of birch bark, grew, climbing the pile of wood. The heat became intense, and the fire roared, dominating other noises.

Old Woman's spirit had been with the other spirits whose job it was to help her adjust to her new life. They brought her to the ceremony. It was hard for her to adjust to this new life where no one had the physical sensations of the old life. She knew that the ceremony was being held for her. She hovered over the crowd, accompanied by two friends who had met her when she passed and helped her to leave her body. She had mixed feelings about this. She was leaving everything that was familiar to her. She had had a good life and hadn't been in a hurry to leave it.

Two eagles flew in, circling above the body as flames licked the shelf on which the body lay. The spirits of Old Woman and her friends descended. They were surrounded by smoke that took their shapes, announcing their presence to the crowd below.

Sierra noticed them first. "Look, Grandma, there she is," she said, pointing at the smoke outlining a shape that looked like Old Woman's. "There's two others with her. She's flying with the eagles."

The crowd looked up, above the shelf that held Old Woman's body. Three figures were outlined in white smoke against a backdrop of the autumn leaves and blue skies. The drums played louder than before. The Creator had ways of renewing faith and bringing comfort when it was most needed.

Sierra felt the presence of the spirits around her. She knew what her future would be. She would take her grandmother's place in the family.

She would make moccasins when her grandmother passed. Sierra would tell the story of Old Woman to future generations. She would describe the day of the funeral and the drums, and she would remember watching as the Old Woman flew with the eagles.

That night, the northern lights came to the community in the form of big green balls that danced through the sky, letting everyone know that the Spirit World had welcomed Old Woman home.

ABOUT THE AUTHOR

Karen East is retired from the practice of marriage and family therapy. She worked with American Indian tribes in the Midwest for nineteen years. She has two children, a grandson, and four great-granddaughters. She lives in northern Wisconsin.